Heart
of the
Hustle

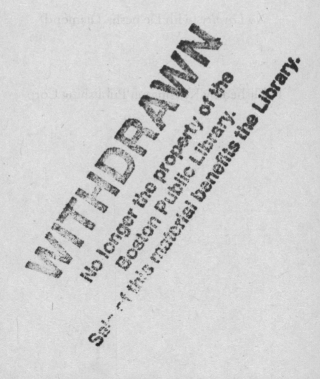

Also by A'zayler

Passion of the Streets

Heart of the Hustle

In Love with My Enemy

No Loyalty (with De'nesha Diamond)

Published by Kensington Publishing Corp.

Heart
of the
Hustle

A'ZAYLER

Dafina
Books

KENSINGTON PUBLISHING CORP.
www.kensingtonbooks.com

DAFINA BOOKS are published by

Kensington Publishing Corp.
119 West 40th Street
New York, NY 10018

All Kensington Titles, Imprints, and Distributed Lines are available at special quantity discounts for bulk purchases for sales promotions, premiums, fund-raising, and educational or institutional use. Special book excerpts or customized printings can also be created to fit specific needs. For details, write or phone the office of the Kensington special sales manager: Kensington Publishing Corp., 119 West 40th Street, New York, NY 10018, attn: Special Sales Department, Phone: 1-800-221-2647.

Dafina and the Dafina logo Reg. U.S. Pat. & TM Off.

ISBN-13: 978-1-4967-1810-5
ISBN-10: 1-4967-1810-0
First Kensington Trade Edition: February 2019
First Kensington Mass Market Edition: February 2020

ISBN-13: 978-1-4967-1813-6 (ebook)
ISBN-10: 1-4967-1813-5 (ebook)

10 9 8 7 6 5 4 3 2 1

Printed in the United States of America

Chapter One

You can do what you want

The sound of the bullets being released from the gun rang through Emelia's ears even though she wore earplugs.

"Aim higher, Emelia." Her father, Mack East, walked behind her and stopped. "You're doing good, but always aim for the chest and up. Death shots, darling."

Emelia nodded and squinted her left eye before pulling the trigger again, this time sending a bullet straight through the head of the black silhouette printed on the paper. She had been at the gun range with her father for the past two hours—since she'd gotten out of school— and would probably be there for another few hours if she didn't get it right. Her father was a perfectionist, so she had to be perfect.

Emelia took two more shots.

"Much better, darling. Do it again," Mack instructed.

Emelia aimed her gun a little higher and fired three more times. When the paper she had been shooting at flew backward, she smiled.

"Happy now?" she asked as she spun around in her brand-new olive-green sneakers.

Mack was standing there in his cream-colored linen suit with his arms folded across his chest. "Very happy." He let a half smile spread his lips.

Eighteen-year-old Emelia jumped up and down, clapping her hands with a broad smile on her face. "So, does that mean I can go?"

Her father's eyes glistened with happiness as his mouth formed a full smile. "Yes, you may, but be home before midnight."

"Thank you, Daddy!" Emelia jumped onto her father, hugging his neck.

His hearty laughter resonated throughout the gun range before he lowered her to her feet. Emelia kissed his cheek before scrambling to gather her things. Once she had her backpack and keys, she took off running toward the exit.

"Where you running to?" Angel's voice stopped her in her tracks just as she got outside.

Emelia turned around to find her closest friend, and the only person she spent most of her time with, standing behind her. Angel DeLuca was the son of her parents' best friends. Emelia's mother and father had been in business with his parents for ages, and because of that, she and Angel instantly became comrades as well. He was the only boy that her father didn't get on her nerves about, and for that she was grateful.

The red gym shorts and black tank top he was wearing hugged his body, while his wavy dark hair blew in the subtle summer breeze. His dark, piercing eyes were squinted as he held the basketball in the crook of his arm. Angel's smooth, brown skin shined beneath the sun as a light sheen of perspiration covered his forehead.

She'd been crushing on Angel since their senior year of high school started and had been doing everything in her power to hide it. Their families were too close, and she didn't want to make things awkward by exposing her true feelings for him.

Emelia gave him the once-over as she hoisted her backpack over her shoulder. "To get dressed. My daddy said I could go to Juanita's party tonight."

Angel frowned. "What you trying to take your ass over there for? You know what people be saying about her."

"So? What does that have to do with me?"

"You want people to talk about you like that too?"

Emelia frowned, because Angel was about to ruin her mood. He was killing her excitement, and she hated it. Juanita did, in fact, have the worst reputation in the school for sleeping around with all the boys, and although Emelia was nothing like that, she still wanted to go to the party. She had been hearing everyone talk about it at school for the past week, and it sounded like fun.

"They're not going to talk about me just because I'm at the party. If I don't do what rumors say Juanita does, then they have no reason to talk about me. Right?"

"But they will. That's just how boys are. Every girl that's going to be there is just like her. If you go, you'll be just like them."

Emelia rolled her eyes and placed her hand on her

hip. "No, I won't either. People know me, and people know who my father is. They'll never believe, or even fix their lips, to say some mess like that about me."

Angel shrugged and began bouncing his basketball. "If you say so."

"How would you know anyway? You don't ever go anywhere."

Angel was one of the only boys in school who never hung out socially. He spent all of his time studying and playing basketball. If he wasn't with her doing things for their families' drug cartel, then he was at home with his parents and older brother. Emelia didn't mind being with her family, but she was young and still liked to hang out sometimes.

Angel was one of the most popular boys at school, but he still turned down every outside activity that was offered to him. The only person who could get him out of the house was his older brother, D'Angelo, and even that was rare. Though when it came to D'Angelo, Emelia could understand why Angel steered clear of him. All D'Angelo did was get into messy situations, and that was most definitely out of character for Angel.

"I don't have to go anywhere to have ears. I hear everything." He looked at her with a smug look. "But you can do what you want. I was just trying to help you out."

"I don't need your help," Emelia sassed with attitude.

Angel nodded. "Cool. Have fun." He turned to walk away, and Emelia immediately felt bad.

The attitude she'd gotten with him just then wasn't necessary. He really was merely trying to help. She just hadn't wanted to hear it because it was the truth. It had been the same thing she'd been thinking about Juanita all day, but she'd done her best to ignore it so that she could talk herself into going to the party. It was Friday night, and she'd been training and doing homework all week. She needed a break.

"Angel!" She shouted his name.

He turned around and looked at her with his eyebrows knitted together.

"You'll have to hang out with me if I don't go."

He shrugged. "I can. What do you want to do?"

"Something fun."

"Well, I got a new video game." He smiled. "We can go to my house and play that if you want, or we can watch some movies."

Emelia frowned, because that didn't sound like much fun, but she agreed anyway. If that was what it took to get things back right with Angel, then so be it. Besides, being at his house with him was enough for her.

Her teenage hormones were raging, and spending so much time with Angel while they were being trained only made things worse. Although she was almost certain he didn't feel the same way about her, she couldn't control herself long enough to simmer down the feelings she felt growing for him.

"Okay. What time you want me to come over?"

"You can come now if you want. It doesn't matter to me." His nonchalant attitude drove her crazy . . . in a good way.

Emelia nodded. "Okay, well, you can ride with me if you want to."

Angel looked toward Emelia's car before walking down the sidewalk to the passenger side and getting in. Emelia turned her music all the way up before backing out of her parking spot and cruising down the street. She was in heaven right then. She always was when Angel was around. Though he never really said too much, she enjoyed his company.

"You know Esmerelda is going to the party, right?" Emelia quickly looked at him out of the side of her eye.

Esmerelda was Angel's girlfriend, whom Emelia did not care for whatsoever, but she would never tell him that. There was no reason to. He didn't need to know that she visualized punching his girlfriend in the face every time she saw them together.

Angel shrugged and moved his basketball from his lap to the floor in front of him. "I don't care what she does."

Emelia leaned over in her seat with a large smile on her face. "Since when? You're normally all extra possessive, and now suddenly you don't care what she does?"

"I told her to come chill with me tonight instead of going to the party, and she said no, so I broke up with her."

Emelia's mouth fell open at his admission, while her insides leaped with excitement.

"Oh, dang," she said with fake sympathy. "You okay?"

Angel looked out of the window and nodded. "Yeah. I'm good. I don't want to be with a girl that doesn't listen to me anyway."

"Angel, just because you're someone's boyfriend doesn't mean they have to listen to you." Emelia chuckled.

Angel looked at her with his eyebrows scrunched up. "My mother does whatever my father tells her to do, and so does your mom with your father." He looked at her momentarily before looking back out the window. "It's not like they're being bossy or anything, they're just looking out for them. If a man is trying to take care of you, you should listen, and let him."

Emelia's heart was melting inside her chest. Angel

was right. Both of their fathers were the dominants in their marriages, but in a good way. Neither her mother nor Mrs. Empress looked like they minded being told what to do. They actually looked to enjoy being led by their man. Emelia considered that she would be like them one day. Not *that* day, but one day.

"I guess," she told him as they pulled into the driveway of his house. "Where your mama them at?" She looked around the driveway for their cars.

"Business meeting. They're going to be gone until later, and D'Angelo is out of town with his girlfriend for the weekend," he told her nonchalantly and got out of the car, with her following.

Together, they walked into his house and down the stairs to his room. It was quiet and dark until Angel moved around the lower level of his home, turning on lights and lighting candles. The basement level of their mini mansion had been decorated completely for Angel, while the attic was given to D'Angelo. The basement was immaculate. It was almost as if he had his own apartment; there was a kitchen, bathroom, sitting room, and his bedroom.

It was nice and private. Too private for Emelia right then, but that was probably her own fault. She'd been in Angel's house a million times, and not one time had she felt like she was feeling right then. She wasn't sure if it was because of the growing desire she'd formed for him over the past few months or because his parents weren't home.

"Why you sitting there like that?"

Emelia looked up and Angel was staring at her. He'd removed his shoes and leaned against the dresser. She paused for a moment, just taking in his appearance before shrugging.

"Like what?" she questioned, genuinely confused.

"Like you're scared to be with me or something."

Emelia swooned. His wording had her heart shivering. She was most definitely not afraid to be with him, but she was sure that wasn't what he'd meant.

"I'm not scared, it's just your parents are normally here when I'm here."

Angel waved her off before putting his game into the game system and taking a seat next to her. "I know you're not worried about them tripping about you being here." He looked at her as he scooted back onto the bed some, making their thighs touch.

Emelia's body warmed a little from the delicate contact. "Nah, I'm just . . ." She looked off and ran her hand though her hair before kicking off her shoes. "I don't know. It just feels weird."

Angel looked over his shoulder at her, his handsome face calm. The way his eyes scanned over her face had her feeling uncomfortable, but it had nothing on the way he made her feel when his eyes lowered.

She wasn't exactly sure what he was looking at, but she was more than positive that it was her breasts. The shirt she was wearing fit snugly and showed them provocatively. Judging from the way he'd just begun biting the inside of his cheek, he appreciated what he saw.

"Why you feel weird today, Emelia?" He sat up some so that they were face-to-face.

She shrugged.

"You want me to cut on some music?"

When she nodded, he got up and hit the switch to the large stereo system near his TV. When he turned around, he stopped and raised his eyebrows at her. "Better?"

Emelia smiled and nodded. "Yeah, now let's play the game."

"Cool." Angel walked back to the bed, but instead of sitting on it, this time he sat on the floor in front of it and pressed his back against his mattress.

Emelia grabbed the game controller he was extending toward her, and they began playing. Though it had been unwanted at first, the game became a much-needed distraction for her. She was no longer as nervous or scared to be around him. Back was the playful and silly demeanor she always had when they were together. She'd gotten so caught up playing the game that she thought nothing of the simple kiss she placed on his forehead after beating him for the sixth time.

"Better luck next time, boo," she screamed before tossing her controller down onto the bed and dancing around his room to the music.

"Man, I let you win." Angel twisted one side of his lips up.

Emelia frowned. "Boy, please. You ain't let me do nothing. I beat your ass fair and square," she told him before dancing playfully in front of him.

Angel was still seated on the floor, so when she danced, the lower half of her body was in his face. She was so busy gloating in her consecutive wins that she didn't even see him get up from the floor until he was right on her. With the front of his body pressed against the back of hers, he grabbed her around her waist.

Everything in Emelia stilled in that moment. Since she wasn't sure what to say, she said nothing, but she didn't have to, because Angel did.

"Is this how you were going to dance at the party?" His voice was just as low and calm as it always was.

"I don't know, probably." Emelia turned her head to the side and looked up so that she could see some of his face.

"You was gon' dance on them other dudes?"

Her breathing picked up a notch when she felt his breath on her neck. "If they wanted me to."

"So, you do whatever people want you to do?"

A deep breath left her body as she began to get nervous again. Never in all of the years they'd been friends had they been as close as they were then, not intimately anyway. They'd hugged a few times, but never anything like the way they were right then.

"Yeah, but only if I want to do it too."

Angel took a step closer to her, further pressing his body into hers. When she felt his hardening erection on her butt, her breath got caught in her chest. She didn't know whether to move or to continue standing still, allowing him to control the situation. When he bent down some so that his lips were close to her ear, she jumped subtly.

"So, if I want you to dance on me like you were going to do the boys at the party, would you do it?"

Emelia nodded quickly. She didn't even have to think about that. That was most definitely something she already knew.

Angel circled her waist with his other hand before pressing his hips forward so that she could really feel him straining through his gym shorts.

"Well, dance for me, then," he told her calmly.

"Okay," Emelia whispered before bending over and rolling her bottom slowly into him as the slow song played in the background.

Emelia danced the best she could after that. Her nerves were getting the best of her, but she refused to embarrass herself. In her mind, she had a point to prove. Angel wasn't just some random boy at a party, he was her friend. She had to see him every day.

"I can't believe you were going to dance with other

boys like this," he said from behind her. "I would be mad as shit."

Emelia smiled to herself at his possessiveness. Obviously, she was doing a good job. She had already had somewhat of an idea that she was when he'd grunted and whispered some stuff she couldn't make out, but him voicing it out loud confirmed it.

Before answering him, she stood up so that her back was to his chest. She continued grinding her body into his.

"I wasn't." She looked back at him over her shoulder. "I'm just dancing like this for you."

He winked at her and smiled. "I know." He slid his hands from her stomach up to her breasts. "You want to do something else for me?" His voice came out a little huskier that time.

Emelia nodded slowly, and he released her before grabbing her hand and pulling her toward his bed. When they were in front of it, he grabbed her neck and looked into her eyes.

"You okay?"

"You bring a lot of girls down here, don't you?" she asked before she could stop herself.

"Nah." He smiled, and Emelia knew then that he was lying.

Angel was too fine, and too popular, not to have a plethora of women, even if he did have a girlfriend. Emelia was young, but she was no fool. She knew how boys their age got around, and he was probably no different. Well, almost no different. The difference between them and him was that she felt things for him that she didn't feel for them. They could have sex with as many girls as they wanted, but Angel . . . she wanted him for herself.

"Don't worry about that." He rubbed his hand through her hair. "Worry about us."

Emelia nodded, and that was all it took. His lips were on hers immediately afterward, while his hands roamed all over her body. On the inside she was screaming, but on the outside she remained cool. Emelia was a virgin and had never even been close to having sex with a boy, until then. Though she was anxious, she was happy it was Angel she was with.

He was being so nice and gentle with her. He removed all of her clothes, minus her undergarments, before freeing himself of his own. Emelia did her best to shield her body from his eyes, so the moment she was in his bed, she pulled the covers up to her neck. To calm herself down, she tried to focus on something else. When she could find nothing, she breathed in deeply and relaxed.

Chapter Two

I'll love him forever

The smell of cinnamon apples permeated the air as she lay perfectly still on her back. The gray cotton sheets beneath her skin were cool. The room was dark while the slow music continuously played softly in the background. The light blue lights from his surround sound speaker system illuminated only a small space of the room, mellowing out the atmosphere. Emelia's eyes squinted at the Clemson University posters posted around Angel's walls.

Though she wasn't very interested in them or anything else, for that matter, they were advertising, and a very welcome distraction. The same bright orange posters had held her attention plenty of times before while she sat leisurely in his room, but this time was different. Very different.

Going into it unknowingly but too far to turn back,

the two of them would use that night to take their relationship to another level. Being that she already knew what was brewing deep down inside her, when Angel suggested sex, she obliged willingly. Now she was lying in his bed in nothing but her panties and bra, waiting for him to find the condom he'd so desperately been looking for since they'd undressed.

"I'm sorry, Emelia. Just give me a minute," he said as he rummaged through drawers.

"It's cool," she replied.

His tall, lean frame towered over his dresser as he sifted through the top drawer of it. For a twelfth-grade boy, Angel was fairly tall. At six one, he was taller than most guys their age.

Aside from his loving personality and impeccably unique talent of making Emelia laugh, he was so handsome, and so fun. His skin was lighter than hers, and he had the cutest pink lips and slanted eyes. Everything about him was perfect to Emelia, which was why she'd secretly chosen him to be her *one*.

Losing her virginity to him wasn't something they'd talked about, but it was about to happen, and surprisingly, she was ready. Unbeknownst to Angel, she'd replayed it over and over in her mind for months. Hopefully she wouldn't regret it.

"I found it," he whispered to her as he pulled the blue covers on his bed back.

They had been shielding her body before, but now that he'd moved them so that he could join her, she was on full display. The light breeze from his ceiling fan cooled her skin, bringing about a light sheen of goose bumps across her arms and legs.

She shivered as he stared down at her. She fidgeted nervously as his eyes moved from the pink bra covering her full breasts to the pink and white panties adorning her small hips. With both hands at her sides, Emelia waited patiently. She wasn't sure what was next, but she was ready.

Angel finally slid into the bed and hovered awkwardly above her. "You okay?"

Emelia looked up at him briefly and nodded.

"You sure you want to do this?"

Again, she nodded.

After that, he said nothing else. Instead, he leaned down and covered her mouth with his. Emelia entangled their tongues together as her thighs fell open enough for him to situate himself comfortably between them. They kissed for a few minutes until they were both a little more comfortable with the situation.

Angel moved first, sitting up on his knees and pulling at the hem of Emelia's panties. She lifted her butt from the bed just enough to aid in his efforts. He eyed her private area as he slid her panties down her legs. Unable to watch him, too afraid of what he might be thinking, Emelia closed her eyes.

"Why are you closing your eyes?" he asked.

Emelia opened them again and looked at him. He was smiling at her in that calming way that he always did as she shrugged.

"I know you ain't scared already. We ain't even did nothing yet."

"I'm not scared," she lied.

"Well, keep your eyes open, then," Angel told her as he used one of his long fingers to touch her *there*.

Instinctively, Emelia's legs closed, but he opened them right back up before scooting down a little more on his bed. Her breathing stilled as she watched him move until his head was between her thighs. She could feel her heart beating faster and faster as she anticipated what was about to come.

She'd heard people in school talk about oral sex all the time, but being that she'd never even had regular sex, she didn't know what to expect, and she most definitely didn't think Angel was going to do it to her. After all, he was always so quiet and laid back. Even the few times they'd talked about sex with other people, he hadn't mentioned doing it.

"Emelia, what we do is between us. Don't go around school telling our business. Okay?"

"Okay." Emelia's voice came out a little hoarse, so she cleared her throat and spoke again. "I won't."

Even though she wanted to know how it felt, and why so many girls liked it, she was nervous. She was clean, and she knew she didn't smell, but what if he thought she did? What if it didn't taste right or something? All kinds of negative things went through her mind as she waited for him to get started.

"Emelia?" Angel paused for a minute. "If I'm bad at this, it's because I've never done it before. Okay? I mean. I'ma try it because you're my girl and we're close, but I don't really know how to do it."

His girl. Her heart smiled.

"It's okay." Emelia's insides grew warm and tingly as she bubbled over with passion for him.

The room fell quiet again as the two of them allowed their current situation to take over. When she least expected it, Emelia felt Angel's tongue. It was so thick and warm as it slid over the most sensitive part of her. Emelia gasped loudly and clenched the sheets.

"You good?" Angel looked up at her with alarm spread across his face.

Emelia opened her eyes and looked down between her legs at him. He was so handsome and innocent looking, not to mention seeing him with his face that close to her private parts made her feel all kinds of wonderful. That was enough by itself to set her off. Her entire body got hotter as she said the only thing that she could think of in that moment.

"I love you."

He looked just as caught off guard hearing it as she was saying it. For a minute, she almost wanted to take it back, but it was true. She did love him, and she wanted him to love her too.

"Did I do something wrong?" he asked, blatantly ignoring her last statement.

Emelia shook her head. "No. It, um . . . it felt good."

He nodded before scooting down again and going back to the task at hand. Emelia lay in the center of his bed with her eyes squeezed tightly closed, enjoying the feeling of her best friend's tongue on her body. He had been licking really slow at first, but the more she moaned and moved, the more he sped up.

Emelia wasn't sure how long it had been before he stopped, but she was almost disappointed that he had. It had been feeling so good, and now it was over. He was back on his knees maneuvering his body so that he could pull his boxers off.

When he'd done so, he tossed them to the floor and grabbed the condom from the nightstand next to his bed. Emelia tried her hardest not to stare as he rolled the condom on, but she couldn't help it. His male parts were like something she'd never seen before.

Sure, she'd watched porn a few times, and even had a few boys send her pictures of theirs, but she'd never seen one in person. When he finished, he looked up at her again before wiping his mouth and leaning over her.

"Did you like it?" he asked.

Emelia's eyes darted to the side in embarrassment as she nodded. When she finally looked back at him, he was smiling.

"I knew you did, because you kept moving and making noises." His goofy grin brought along one of her own. "That's our secret, though, okay? Nobody needs to know but us."

"I know."

"You want to take your bra off?"

Emelia looked down at her bra, totally forgetting that it was there. "No. I'll keep it on." Her breasts weren't the biggest, and she wanted to shield them for now.

Angel nodded and moved around so that he was back between her thighs. When he was comfortable and ready, he reached between them and grabbed his penis in his hand. She watched him as he looked down and guided himself to her opening.

When she felt the tip of it poking her, she almost changed her mind, because it was already hurting, but she didn't. She wanted to do this, and she wanted to do it with him. Her body tensed even more the farther in he pushed.

Emelia squirmed and squeezed his arms tighter as he tried to push himself in. "It hurts."

"I'm sorry, but I can't really get it in." He pushed a little harder, and harder, and even harder, until Emelia finally screamed.

Her scream wasn't too loud, but it was loud enough for it to be heard throughout his room. "Angel, ow!"

He chuckled lightly as he looked down at her. "Sorry, Emelia. I'm in now."

His eyes closed, and his mouth fell open as he moved in and out of her. Emelia wanted to push him right back out and put all of her clothes back on, but she couldn't.

He looked to be enjoying it and she didn't want to be the one to quit, but it was hurting so bad. It even burned a little bit.

Once Angel got himself together and found a rhythm of his own, he was moving inside her. Had Emelia not been in so much pain, she actually might have enjoyed it; however, that was not the case.

"I'm sorry it hurts. It'll feel better next time."

"I know . . . I'm okay," she whispered.

For the next few minutes, Emelia lay beneath him as music played in the background. Her mind was all over the place as the pain subsided a little. She was nowhere near enjoying it, but it wasn't as bad as it had been in the beginning.

The low grunts that Angel was making made her feel a little better, because that meant he was enjoying it. She knew for sure he was a few moments later.

"I love you, Emelia." He lips brushed against her ear when he spoke. "More than a friend . . . fuck Esmerelda, you're my girl."

Emelia's legs instinctively wrapped around his waist, as did her arms. She held him tight as he moved. His breathing picked up with each move he made. To hear him say that he loved her too made her feel that much better. Because he loved her, and she loved him, she did her best to take the pain.

When it was finally over, she almost hated it. She liked the feeling of being beneath him. It had come and gone all too quickly for her liking, but she just shrugged it off. Maybe that was how it was supposed to go the first time. When he slid away from her and rolled the condom from him, she noticed that it was coated with something red.

Alarm spread through her body when she realized it was on his legs as well. For a second she lay still, par-

A'zayler

alyzed from embarrassment. Little did she know it was only about to get worse.

"You bled on my bed." He looked at the spot she was lying on.

Emelia sat up and looked at the dark circle of blood in the center of his bed. Mortification encompassed her entire being as she tried to think of what to say.

"Oh no," she whispered.

Angel touched her arm, and when she looked at him, he was smiling. "Why you look so scared? It's supposed to be like that."

Emelia squinted a little as she replayed the many conversations she'd had with her mother about sex, while reaching for her panties.

"I'll just wash my sheets before my mama comes home later."

Emelia nodded as she proceeded to get dressed. How and when he cleaned was nothing of her concern at the moment. All she wanted to do right then was get dressed and go home. When she had her panties on, she shifted so that she could stand up and put her jeans back on.

Pain shot from her center, immediately slowing her movements. Why on earth did her body hurt like he was still in it? Emelia tried her best to get dressed without being too obvious that she was in a ridiculous amount of pain but failed miserably and had to lean on the dresser to pull her pants up.

"You're hurting?" Angel stood up and walked over to her. Still naked.

"Yeah," she admitted, wincing just slightly.

He kissed the side of her face. "Just take a warm bath when you get home." He kissed her again. "You'll feel better after that."

"Okay," she said lowly, not really fond of his response.

Emelia hated that he was so knowledgeable when it came to sex. All it made her think about was how many other women he'd been with. That thought alone made her stomach hurt. When she pushed the thought out of her mind, she continued getting dressed.

The two of them moved around each other, making sure his room and their clothes were back in place before he walked her outside to her car. They leaned on the side of it and hugged before he leaned down and kissed her mouth again. This time he added a little bit of tongue. When he pulled away, he was smiling.

"I love you, Emelia."

She smiled and hugged him again. "I love you too."

Something totally unplanned had been the best night of her life. Never in a million years would Emelia have thought sex with Angel would have that type of effect on her, but it had. She didn't know what the future held for them, but the one thing she did know was that she'd love him forever. Little did she know, time had a way of changing things.

Chapter Three

Young, handsome, and rich

Ten years later

The loud revving from the engine roared as Angel sped down the interstate toward nothing in particular. Just a fly young hustler on the rise, enjoying life. With it being only two hours from his twenty-eighth birthday, he'd decided to take his early birthday present out for a spin.

The black Bugatti Veyron with the red bottom had been customized just for him by his mother, and it was quickly becoming his new favorite thing. The shiny black wheels spun in circles faster than any eye could see as he pushed one hundred and twenty miles per hour on the speedway.

The surge from the boost of gas in his engine had

him feeling like he was at the peak of his favorite roller coaster, headed down. The energy and rush of adrenaline had his body shaking with excitement.

With his old-school Tupac blasting throughout the small sports car, Angel switched lanes and pressed his foot harder on the gas. Instantly, the car sprang out even faster, which to the normal cars around him seemed to be impossible.

After the front end of the car lifted a tad from the road, the car zoomed in and out of lanes. Angel shifted gears, swooping between cars, barely missing some and cutting off others. Driving the car gave him a feeling of being free. Almost like he was flying. Just floating through the air enjoying the breeze.

There was nothing like this. Being young, handsome, and rich had its perks, and getting anything and everything he wanted had to be the best. He'd handpicked his car, and one week later, his mother had made it happen.

Being the only responsible child to the largest male-and-female narcotics connect duo out of California was another perk. Angel DeLuca, the heir to the entire DeLuca dynasty, was well on his way to the top with little to no effort. His mother and father had been running it since long before he was born and had no reason to require his help now. Even if his older brother was too reckless to handle that type of responsibility, that didn't mean they would just toss it in Angel's lap.

A medical student at the University of South Carolina School of Medicine in Columbia, South Carolina, and a year away from graduation, Angel had plans of his own. He'd been in medical school since the fall after he graduated with his master's. Unlike any of the other men in his family, Angel aspired to be more than just the common thug.

Growing up in a cartel full of killers and dealers,

Angel hadn't had it very easy when he refused to take
any part in the drug business. However, that was something he wouldn't worry himself with. He had enough
on his plate with his classes and schoolwork.

Oftentimes, busier than everyone in his entire family, he never really had time to just get out and enjoy
himself, but this weekend was different. He'd taken his
last final for the year, his birthday was a few hours
away, and he was planning to celebrate both with as
much fun as he could handle.

The wind blew through the driver side window,
through his hair, and into his face as he sped up a little
more. The smell of fresh air brought a small spurt of
tears from the corners of his eyes, while the potent
smell of weed and chili cheese fries filled his nostrils.

After finishing off the rest of his neatly rolled blunt,
he'd stopped by Jack in the Box and grabbed one of his
favorite foods. Every time the wind wafted the smell
of the greasy calorie-packed potatoes up his nose, he
pressed the gas a little harder in an effort to make it
home a little quicker so that he could demolish them.

This was the life. Nothing but success was on the
rise, with legal and legit money in his pocket. Angel
DeLuca screamed at the top of his lungs in excitement.
Life couldn't get any better than it was at the moment.
He was happy, and that was all there was to it. Too bad
good things didn't last forever. The blue lights flashing
in his rearview were evidence of that.

Angel rolled his eyes and released an exasperated
breath as he pulled his car over to the side of the road.
Annoyed and ready to be on his way, Angel checked
his rearview mirror once again to see the officer who
had pulled him over. He was short and chunky with a
crooked hat. Angel was tempted to hit the gas and drive

off on his ass while he was fixing his pants, but figured that would be more trouble than what it was worth.

The closer he got, the more annoyed Angel got. By the time the officer had gotten to his window, his irritation had maxed out. He hit the button to turn his music down and eyed the officer with disdain.

"In a rush, sir?" the officer asked.

"Kinda," Angel replied.

"Where you headed?"

"Why?"

The officer's bushy brown mustache curved upward as he frowned. "Don't question me, DeLuca."

Angel's head whipped around quickly once the officer called him by his name. His face held a frown just as deep as the officer's. They stared at one another for a minute until the officer's frown was replaced with a smile.

"Wondering how I know you, huh?" A boisterous laugh resonated throughout the darkness as cars continued whipping along the highway past him. "You dumb fuck. Who doesn't know the DeLuca boys?"

Angel's body grew hotter and hotter as he sat listening to the officer. Still a bit dumbfounded but angrier than he'd been seconds prior, Angel shifted his car back into gear.

"Oh, you're going to drive off now, huh?" The officer hit the roof of Angel's car before leaning down closer to his face. "You're not above the law, even if your father has you thinking you are."

"Fuck you. You don't know my father."

He laughed again, this time harder than the last. "You know"—he tapped his chin—"I know your father quite well . . . we all do." He touched his police badge for emphasis.

Without another word or thought, Angel shifted gears and drove off. The speedometer flipped from one end to the other rapidly as Angel surged the gas. He was so riled up, he ended up staying on the highway a lot longer than he should have.

He spent the time trying to calm himself down. His mind was everywhere. Never in all of his years had he or his family had a run-in with the law, and when they did, it was on simple shit. Never anything that insinuated that the cartel was on the radar because half of the cops were on the DeLucas' payroll anyway. When Angel could no longer take the rapid thoughts, he called the only person who would know what to say.

"Son," Vinny answered.

"Daddy, I just got pulled over for speeding," Angel said into the phone.

Vinny laughed. "I told Empress not to get your ass that car."

"The police was talking slick shit about knowing us, and thinking we're above the law and shit."

The phone went quiet before he heard Vinny clearing his throat. "No worries, son. I'll take care of it."

"You think it's some fight behind his bark?"

More laughter from Vinny. "Hell no. It never is. Don't worry, and don't tell your mother."

Angel chuckled. "I won't."

"See you in a minute." Vinny ended the call.

Like always, after talking to Vinny, Angel was able to calm down. He'd slowed down, making the ride to his parents' house longer. The time was spent ridding his mind of the negative, and focusing back on the positive. His life was too good for him to stress over something that small. He had everything that he could possibly want, from his family to his personal life.

Even with school stressing him completely out, it was all worth it. He had his girl, Genesis, whom he loved with every fiber of his being. And unlike some of the guys he went to school with, he didn't have any kids . . . neither did his girl. The two of them spent most of their free time partying and hanging out. They shopped in the highest-end stores, balling out at clubs, toasting with the stars, and just having fun. A young, get money couple with no worries, doing their best to enjoy life while doing their own thing.

With his music blasting and his head back bobbing to the beat, Angel slowed his car down and took the exit to his parents' estate. He had an hour before he had to pick Genesis up from class, so he would use it to chill with his family.

Being that they were the only part of the DeLuca Cartel that was in South Carolina, they were pretty much all each other had. The DeLuca Cartel was mostly run in his home state, California. They ran dope through the West Coast—California, Mexico, Nevada—and a few southeast states, Georgia, Alabama, Florida, and recently, South Carolina.

He hadn't been at all happy about his father deciding to push dope through the city of Columbia, South Carolina, but what say did he really have? That was the way they ate and the reason he had gone to school with not one student loan since graduating from high school. He'd made it very clear that he wanted to live a life outside the cartel, which was why he'd moved to a state that they didn't serve, but they'd changed all of that with hardly any effort.

With not much argument from him since it all started, Angel accepted the fact that his parents were going to do what they wanted, so he had to do the same. He did his best to move around the product and plans his father had for their newest city without any involvement, and so far, he'd done a pretty good job.

Hopefully he would be allowed to continue, but judging by the unnecessary traffic stop just then, he wasn't so sure anymore. He'd bent over backward to keep his name from being tied to anything dealing with the cartel, but clearly that was inevitable.

When he turned into his family's estate, passed the guards, and headed through the entryway of trees, he parked behind his mother's cranberry-colored Rolls-Royce and cut his car off. He hit the locks on his doors, grabbed his food, and hopped out of the small car. Before moving, he stretched his long legs and arms. Once he'd worn off the tightness from his limbs, he began walking down the winding sidewalk to the front door.

Angel was busy digging in his pocket for his keys when the front door opened. He raised his head to find his mother standing there. She was cloaked in a white and gold dress with an array of colorful jewels decorating her neck and wrists.

Her dark skin sparkled beneath the fluorescent lights on their porch, and her smile brightened the darkness of the night. His beautiful black queen. Empress DeLuca was pure royalty, and the key to his heart. Everything about her represented the essence of what a woman should be. She was loyal and nurturing, and the most important person in his world.

The connection that he shared with his mother was out of the world, and she loved him just as much as he loved her. Empress loved Angel, her youngest child and third protector, like no other, and he knew it. Even if she hadn't said it to him enough to last three lifetimes, the smile on her face every time he came around expressed it for her.

She loved his older brother just the same, but the bond she shared with Angel was different. He was sure it was because he was a good man who made her proud. Even with him wanting nothing to do with their family business, he was still her favorite. He was a stand-up guy who never indulged in unnecessary shit that caused problems for the family like D'Angelo did. D'Angelo was the oldest but acted as if he was the youngest.

"You must have been sitting in the window waiting on me?" Angel asked her with a smile as large as hers on his face.

"Actually, I saw you on the cameras."

Angel stretched his arm out and circled her shoulders with it when he was close enough to her. "Ma, who do you think you're fooling? You were probably sitting in the window waiting for me to get here. I know how you are."

Empress tittered and pushed at his side playfully. "Boy, please, I wasn't thinking about you."

Angel and Empress walked farther into the massive great room, immaculately decorated in gold and black. Their sitting space was larger than some people's entire house put together, and that was the way Vinny liked it. Vinny DeLuca was Angel's father and one of the flashiest men Angel had ever known.

For as far back as Angel could remember, every home they'd ever had had been over the top. Vinny had money and loved to show it. His ostentatious attitude, with Empress's expert eye for interior design, made their homes look more like castles than ordinary houses. Pictures, plants, statues, and a host of other things occupied the walls and floors of their three-story home.

"Lies, I tell you." Vinny's subtle laughter tainted every word he spoke.

Angel found his father seated in the La-Z-Boy large enough to fit four people. That was his favorite chair, and where you would probably find him 90 percent of the time. Angel smiled as he studied his father's sandy-brown skin with the reddish-brown hue to it and the jet-black hair surrounding his head, lips, and eyes.

"She's been there since you called an hour ago." Vinny shook his head without moving his eyes from the enormous flat screen TV mounted on the wall in front of him. "I tell her over and over, you're not a boy anymore." Vinny threw his hands up in defeat. "She won't listen, so I'm just going to keep my mouth shut. If she wants to sit in the window like a puppy until you get here, I'll let her."

Angel and Empress both laughed as they took their seats on the plush, white furniture; he on the love seat by himself, she on the couch, at the end closest to his father. Her feet were tucked comfortably beneath her, while she rested her elbow on the fluffy arm cushion.

Though she was seated fully on the sofa, the top part of her body was leaned over toward Vinny. It was obvious that she wanted to be near him, and Angel wasn't the least bit surprised. The love his mother and father shared was unlike any other.

Outside the fact that Empress was a passionate woman, she loved Vinny DeLuca. They had been married going on forty years but still acted as if they'd just begun dating, from the way they hugged every time they parted ways, to the small comforting kisses and soft touching they did throughout the day.

Like right then, Vinny's hand had just found its way to the top of Empress's leg, while the hand she wasn't leaning on rested on top of his. Angel craved a love like that. One that was so magnetic that he and his lover couldn't fight the desire to touch one another. He'd once had a love that felt like it would last forever, but that had been a lifetime ago, and things changed.

"How'd you do on your test?" Empress asked her son.

Angel was busy removing his fries from the brown bag when he answered her. "I think I passed."

"You think?" Vinny finally made eye contact as the sternness in his voice subtly corrected Angel's uncertainty.

"I know."

"That's more like it." He nodded before looking back at his television.

Ever since he'd been a child, Vinny had accepted nothing less than Angel's best, no matter what it was. Nothing was too small or too big for either of his sons to master.

I don't care if you boys are emptying trash for a living, as long as you're emptying the most trash. Vinny's voice echoed in Angel's head. Angel had been hearing that line his entire life and hadn't understood it one bit until he'd grown old enough to demand the most from himself as well.

"Was it hard?" His mother's tone was much softer than his father's had been.

Angel shrugged and stuffed a fork full of chili and cheese in his mouth. "It was hard, but I'm smart and I've been studying nonstop for weeks now. I did fine."

"Well then, we should celebrate!" Empress beamed at him. "I could invite some people over for a small party tomorrow."

Angel rubbed the back of his neck in anticipation of what was to come next. "I kind of already made plans for tomorrow."

Empress's neck snapped toward him, while Vinny's large stomach shook lightly from laughter. Clearly Vinny knew just like Angel did that Empress was about to show out.

"Plans? With who?" she asked.

"Genesis." Angel spoke lower than he had been.

The loud noise coming from his mother sucking her teeth had Angel clearing his throat in discomfort. He had known before he even said his girlfriend's name that his mother wasn't going to like it.

"How are you just going to make plans with that little trick without even considering the fact that we might have wanted to celebrate with you? After raising you for twenty-eight years, I would think we could at least get that courtesy."

"Ma, it ain't like that. She suggested it after we finished studying last night."

"I just bet she did." Empress mumbled something a little lower, and Angel had to strain to hear what she'd said, because there was no way she'd said what he thought he'd heard.

"Say what, Ma?"

"Leave me alone, Angel."

Angel sat up so that he was on the edge of the love seat. "Nah, tell me what you said. I ain't hear you."

Empress rolled her eyes at him but said nothing.

"She said Genesis probably suggested it after she finished sucking your dick last night." Vinny serenaded the room with a robust chuckle.

Angel looked from his mother to his father before they both burst out laughing. That was what he'd thought he'd heard, but he hadn't been sure. Empress was known to get a little catty when it came to Genesis and had even said similar things like that in the past, but it still came as a shock to Angel every time.

His mother was one of the sweetest people he'd ever met but could say and do some things that made a person feel like only a black woman could.

"Ma, I can't believe you would say something like that." Angel was still laughing. "Daddy, you need to get onto her. That mouth is ridiculous."

Vinny's laughter became more boisterous as he looked over at Empress. "Sorry, son. There's nothing I can do for you. My darling has been this way for years. I think it's too late to try implementing any type of change now."

Empress stood from the sofa. "You're damn right it is. I am who I am." She looked to her son. "Angel, if you don't like it, all you have to do is get you another girlfriend. Nobody told you to fall in love with that little gold digger anyway."

With that, Empress stormed from the living room, but not before leaning over and slapping Angel upside the back of his head. He and his father both watched her walk out of the living room before falling into a fit of laughter. Empress hated Genesis, and it always made for a good laugh for him and his father.

Much like any other mother would, Empress did nothing to hide the way she felt about Genesis, which left the door open for all types of nasty comments and attitude-filled moments. Angel did his best to keep the two of them away from each other, but sometimes it was inevitable, and one of them would end up mad with him.

"She'll be all right," Vinny said. "She's just mad right now. She hates that girl you like."

"I know." Angel wiped his mouth and stuck his trash back into his bag. "I don't know why, though. Genesis is cool."

Vinny's head turned in Angel's direction. His face was serious, void of the humor that had just adorned it.

"Your mother doesn't dislike people for no reason, so if she hates Genesis like that, that should tell you something." Vinny rubbed his chin. "We can't tell you who to date, but we raised you to be a lot smarter and more observant than you are."

Angel frowned. "Ah hell, Ma done brainwashed you too?"

"You know me better than that," Vinny told him without blinking. "I'm not brainwashed, but I value my wife's feelings and opinions. Like I said, if she doesn't like that girl, then she apparently sees something she doesn't agree with. I'm sure you will too in due time."

Versus arguing with his father, or saying anything in an effort to disagree with him, Angel sat back on the love seat and pulled his phone from his pocket. Arguing with his parents wasn't something he liked to do because he always ended up feeling slighted in the end.

The three of them were practically best friends, so of course he took the things they said to heart. Even when he didn't want to hear what they were saying, he heard them. Which was why he was so troubled when it came to Genesis. He was in love with her, and yet his parents couldn't stand her. That was pure turmoil.

Angel had just scooted farther down into the cushions when his phone began to vibrate. When he saw that it was Genesis calling him, he stood and answered it. "Yo."

"Hey, bae. I'm ready."

"Okay, I'm on the way." He grabbed his trash from the table. "Let me call you when I get in the car."

"Why? Where you at?"

"My house."

Genesis sucked her teeth before hanging up in his face. Angel hated when she did that. It was so disrespectful, and he was going to make sure she knew it once he got into his car, but right then he let it slide. The last thing he needed to do was draw attention to her defiance in front of his father. Vinny may have been sitting there watching TV, but Angel was more than positive that he was listening to and watching Angel as well.

"I'm out, Pops. I'll slide back through a little later or in the morning."

"Be safe, son, and don't forget what I said. The cop thing," Vinny used his pointer finger to motion between him and Angel, "is between me and you."

"Got you." Angel nodded, and left the house.

He hadn't wanted to leave without telling his mother he'd see her later, but he was more than positive she was still mad, so he'd just call her later. When he got into his car, he picked his phone up to call Genesis back and tell her about herself, but instead of doing that, he flipped his music on and bobbed his head to the beat.

Music was a calming mechanism for him, and exactly what he needed right then. Empress and Genesis were going to have to get it together soon, Genesis more than Empress. Genesis called herself no longer liking Empress either after finding out she didn't like her. Angel thought that was the most immature thing ever, but it was what it was.

Empress was his queen, but Genesis gave him pussy, so more times than not, he let Genesis off the hook quicker than he probably should have, and he hated it. Angel sometimes found himself falling too weak for Genesis, and it was so annoying. He'd been soft with his women for as long as he could remember, but with Genesis it was worse.

It didn't matter how hype he was with her, the moment she smiled or kissed him, his attitude would dissipate against his will. Much like right then. He'd been angry with her pretty much the entire ride to their school, but now that he'd laid eyes on her, he was good.

Gone was the anger he'd been harboring on his drive over. It didn't even bother him that she was talking to her little friend, Emmanuel. He was a dude in one of their classes that they studied with from time to time. Definitely not a nigga Angel would see as a threat.

After Angel pulled his car to a stop along the curb and hopped out, all eyes were on the shiny luxury vehicle as he rounded the hood and headed toward where Genesis stood. A few people waved and called out to him. He responded coolly but kept his focus on the love of his life.

"Hey there, pretty girl." Angel's smooth voice brought a smile to her face. "What's good, Emmanuel?" He nodded.

Emmanuel dapped him up with a smile and told them he'd see them later, while Genesis had to be her usually dramatic self.

"Don't be trying to run game on me." Genesis turned toward Angel and crossed her arms over her chest.

Angel could tell she was trying to keep her little attitude, but he wasn't having that. He walked right up to her and grabbed both sides of her waist, pulling her to him. Being that he was a little over six feet tall and Genesis was barely five feet two, he towered over her easily.

He looked down at her before pecking the top of her head. "Let that li'l shit go." He pecked her head again. "You ain't even got no reason to be tripping." Angel rubbed his hand through her hair.

"Why I don't?" she asked while looking toward the voice that had just called his name.

Angel followed her eyes and observed the group of women that had just walked past. They were staring at him, while one of them waved.

Angel gave a light smile and nodded. "What's going on, ladies?"

They offered an array of greetings, but he was no longer focused on them. Genesis had his full attention, even if she didn't think so.

"What you doing?" Angel frowned when she pulled away from him.

"Go talk to them. Clearly they're important enough for you to ignore the fact that I'm standing here."

"You can't be serious right now." Angel looked at her as if she'd just grown two heads. "All I did was say hello. I know you ain't tripping about that when you were just standing here talking to another nigga."

"Why you even had to do all that? You didn't even have to look over there. They were only speaking because they saw you standing here with me," she sassed. "And Emmanuel ain't nobody and you know it, so don't even try it."

Angel chuckled because she was right. Emmanuel wasn't shit, just a smokescreen for him right then.

She rolled her eyes. "Yeah, you know I'm right. Trying to throw that nigga up to cover up your mess."

"Man, stop that, Genesis. The girl that called my name is in my study group."

Genesis rolled her eyes and waved him off. "Sure, she is. Just like Emmanuel is in mine, right? You wouldn't like it if I did you like that."

"Don't even play with me like that."

Genesis shook her head from side to side and rolled her eyes. "You make me so sick sometimes."

Angel stood stuck for a minute, because he couldn't believe the full-blown attitude she'd just developed all because he'd spoken to another woman. Had he known it was going to cause all of that, he would have just nodded and kept everything else to himself.

"You ready?" she asked him with her eyebrows raised.

Angel looked at her for a little while longer before stepping close to her again. "I ain't leaving until you tell me you're not mad at me anymore."

With his arms now circling her waist, Genesis rested comfortably in his embrace. She was looking everywhere but at him, trying her best to hold on to her little attitude. When she didn't answer him, he began placing kisses all over her face. It didn't take long before she was falling into his chest, laughing and smiling.

"I don't know when you're going to realize you're my baby and stop cutting up."

"When you realize I'm the only girl in your life that matters." Genesis locked eyes with him and stared.

In the back of his mind, Angel could tell that was also a shot at Empress, but he would disregard it for now. He knew no one came before Empress, and that was all that mattered. If he had to lie and pretend for Genesis to believe she was number one, then so be it. Whatever made her happy. That was a stupid argument that he was tired of having with her.

"I know that already. It's you that obviously keeps forgetting." He grabbed her hand and pulled her toward his car. "Another woman should never make you feel inferior when it comes to me."

Genesis smacked her lips. "Other bitches don't make me feel inferior, threatened, or none of that other shit. That be you."

Angel was glad his back was to her when he closed his eyes and sighed deeply. "Just get in the car, Genesis."

"I'm getting in the car. I'm just reminding you."

"You don't have to remind me about anything I already know."

Angel hit the locks before opening the door for her and standing to the side so that she could get in. She looked at him the entire time she got into the car. She wanted a fight, he could tell, but she was going to have to let that go. He wasn't in the mood to entertain her foolishness right then.

"I love you." He winked and closed the door.

He peeked through the windshield as he rounded the car. When he saw her smiling, his chest eased a little. Maybe she would calm her rowdy ass down long enough for them to enjoy their night. He'd just rid himself of a boatload of stress by taking his final. He wouldn't allow her to pile it right back on.

Chapter Four

He's just not the one

"Oh damn," Angel groaned out. "Your pussy is hot as fuck." His eyes fluttered. "And greedy. You must wanted some dick bad this morning."

His eyes were closed as he allowed his head to fall back. In the small bathroom of Genesis's apartment, with her on the counter in front of him, Angel held her legs in the crooks of his arms as he slid in and out of her body slowly. The grip that her pussy had on him was damn near handicapping, and Genesis knew he loved it.

As bad as he wanted to move his legs and change positions, he couldn't. She'd watched him try and fail too many times already. The feeling that she was giving him right then wouldn't allow him to do anything more than he was already doing. His knees were buckling and his abs were getting tight as he tried to brace himself for the orgasm that would be coming soon.

"Genny," Angel moaned out to her as he opened his eyes. "Squeeze me like that again."

Genesis was lying back, looking straight at him. His slim yet muscular body was bare, giving way to all his manly glory. The veins in his arms pulsed with every stroke he delivered, and it made her shiver every time.

Angel was so fucking sexy it was unreal. The sandy-brown skin he'd inherited from his father held a darker brown tint as well from his mother. She was a lot darker than he and his father, and Angel's skin showed it.

His jet-black hair was thick with continuous waves, and if his face didn't make you fall in love, that hair surely would. He was a unique mix of pure sexiness, and Genesis couldn't get enough of him. He had the perfect bad-boy look, but a heart of gold. The way he loved her was unlike anything she'd ever experienced before.

A young, black girl from the suburbs, she'd had her share of men, but none of them had ever made her feel like Angel had in the few short years they'd been dating. Relationships hadn't always been her strong point because of her insecurities, but he handled them well enough for the both of them, and she appreciated him for it.

"I love you so much." The smooth bass in Angel's voice took over his words.

Genesis looked at his handsome face and smiled. "I love you too."

"Marry me, then."

Genesis's heart began to speed up as she lay there looking at him. She did her best to maintain eye contact, but when she couldn't anymore, she turned her head. Why did he have to do that? Their night had been exceptional, and their morning had been even better. Why couldn't he leave things how they were?

"Angel." Her tone was desperate and filled with sorrow. "Don't do this."

He frowned. "Don't do what, Genesis? Don't ask you to be my wife? To spend the rest of your life with me? Let me love on you forever? Which one? Don't do what?" he bellowed.

Genesis closed her eyes, because she already knew when he asked that his question was about to ruin their moment. It always did. She could understand his frustration, but that didn't deter her feelings. She didn't want to marry him, that was it.

"Calm down, Angel." She tried to soothe him, but he said nothing.

Instead, he pulled her from the countertop and turned her around. When she was bent over the sink, he plunged back inside her. Genesis yelped upon contact but got back with the flow easily. Her body was familiar with Angel's dick. It had been a part of her for years now, so it didn't take long for her to find their rhythm again.

He was pounding her body roughly when she looked up at him through the mirror. He frowned as he looked down to where he was connecting them. Genesis watched his facial expression change over and over before he looked up at her. When they finally made eye contact, she could tell that he was angry, but she couldn't help that right then.

For the rest of the time they made love, Angel said nothing to her. When he reached his peak, he snatched out and released himself in his hand before turning to flip the shower on. With no words uttered to her, he stepped in and washed himself clean. Genesis remained in her spot near the counter for a little while be-fore opening the shower door and stepping behind him.

He was facing her with his hands up rubbing shampoo into his hair. He opened only one eye when he felt the cool breeze from the door. He didn't look at her long before turning his back and rinsing the soap from his hair.

"Baby, don't be like that," Genesis whispered solemnly.

He was silent as he continued to wash away the soap from his head and body. Genesis felt bad as she took another step toward him and wrapped her arms around his waist. She pecked his back.

"I don't want you to be mad at me."

"I'm not." His nonchalant attitude was easily detected.

"Yes, you are."

"If I said I'm not, then I'm not."

Genesis heard what he was saying, but he was lying.

"Well, stay mad, then." She sucked her teeth and snatched her washcloth and body wash from the holder in the corner.

Angel stepped out of her way so that she couldn't touch him. Genesis wanted to slap him, but she knew better than to put her hands on him. It was so irritating how mad he got about the same thing every time. He'd asked her to marry him two other times in the past, and every time she'd said no. He should have been used to it by now. If she wasn't ready, he couldn't make her.

A few more minutes passed before he opened the shower door and stepped out. When he didn't bother to close the door, Genesis rolled her eyes.

"Why are you being like that, Angel? Damn! It's not

." Genesis walked under the showerhead so that seri water was cascading down on her.

that h, i ain't that serious?" His returned presence rtled her. She'd just watched him walk out of the bathroom. "I guess that's why you keep saying no, huh?" Ie leaned down so that his face was only inches from hers.

Genesis wasn't exactly sure what to say, because that wasn't what she had meant. She hadn't intended to dumb down his proposal so blatantly.

When she didn't say anything, he looked her up and down and stepped away from her. "Glad to know how you feel."

She watched him walk away again before closing the shower door. Genesis closed her eyes and did her best to gather her thoughts as she showered. A little over an hour later, she was seated on the sofa in her living room when she heard him coming down the hallway.

When he walked in, he was fully dressed and looking too sexy for her to still be clad in her pajamas. Genesis watched him walk toward the door like he was about to leave without her.

"Damn, no invite?" she asked.

He stopped and looked over at her. "You put that shit on like you was in the house for the day, so I ain't know you was trying to make moves," he told her nonchalantly while eyeing her pajamas.

Genesis hated that he was looking so sexy. If he had looked a mess, her copping an attitude right back would have been much easier. The flannel pajama pants and two-sizes-too-big shirt she was sporting made her look like somebody's old auntie, so she would hold her attitude down for a minute. At least long enough for her to comb her hair.

"You didn't bother to ask me if I was," she said.

Angel looked at her with a look of impatience. "Genesis, you're a grown-ass woman. I shouldn't have to hold your hand through everything. If you're riding, go put on some clothes. If you're not, that's cool too, but I'm about to slide."

Genesis rolled her eyes and tossed the remote onto the sofa next to her. She stomped past him and walked toward her room. Being that he was already ready and waiting on her, she didn't take as long as she normally would have to get dressed.

With the attitude he had right then, he would probably leave her if she took too long anyway, so she moved as quickly as she could. When she was completely dressed, she stopped in front of the mirror. Her honey-colored skin was blemish free, while her short hair rested stylishly on her head.

Her hazel irises meshed well with the yellow dress hugging her body and with the camel-colored wedge sandals. Genesis turned her small nose up a little before rubbing a little more blush on her high cheekbones. When she felt she was ready, she sprayed on her perfume and grabbed her purse.

She padded down the hallway and into the living room. Without stopping, she walked right over to where Angel was leaned against the wall texting on his phone. When he looked up at her, he paused for a second, obviously taken aback by her beauty, as always, before going back to his phone.

"You ready?" His tone still held an underlying hostility that she didn't appreciate.

"Don't it look like it?"

Angel looked at her with furrowed brows. "You can leave that smart-ass mouth here." He looked her up and down again before letting himself out her front door.

Genesis watched the way his body moved as he dapped down the sidewalk toward his car. Even with him being one of the sexiest and coolest niggas she'd ever met, she still wasn't ready to commit her life to him. His money, and the stability he provided for her, was a bonus that she had no intention of letting go, but she was still young. Being tied down to one man wasn't on her agenda for another few years.

When Angel got into the car without opening the door for her, Genesis wasn't surprised. "You ain't have to open my door for me," she sassed as she got into the car and snapped her seat belt on.

Angel's new car silently came alive. "I know. You don't like nice shit, so why even bother? Right?" He looked at her quickly before backing out of the driveway and out of her complex, headed for the interstate.

"What's that supposed to mean?" Genesis rolled her neck with much attitude.

"It means you don't like nice shit. Exactly what I said." He drove with one hand on the steering wheel, the other resting behind the headrest of her seat.

"Why would you even say something like that? I love nice things."

Angel chuckled. "Yeah, as long as it doesn't involve commitment, huh? You can love the way I pay your bills, buy you all those expensive clothes and shoes, keep your hair and nails done, and ball out in the fucking clubs with you." The angrier Angel got, the faster his car went. "You love that kind of shit, huh? As long as I do it all while being your boyfriend." He huffed. "I'm out here buying you new cars, house shopping, and all this other shit that husbands do for their wives, and you're in love with it as long as you don't have to be my wife to get it." Angel cut his eyes at her and surged down the highway.

Genesis looked from him to the highway in front of them. She wanted to say something, but the speed of the car had her scared to talk.

"Oh, you quiet now? But you like nice things?" He turned his nose up toward her. "You don't like shit."

"Angel, I'm sorry, baby. I'm just not ready."

"Yeah." He chuckled. "I know. You show me that every time you say no." After that he flipped his music up and kept his mouth shut the entire time they rode.

Genesis didn't know where they were going until she noticed the route toward his house. Well, his parents' house. In her opinion, Angel was too old to still be living with his mama and daddy, which was why she pushed so hard for them to get their own house. Well, her a new house that he could live in with her.

He hadn't been too open to the idea at first, until she ran game on him about having a family. She knew Angel was the family type, so as soon as she mentioned something about having room for kids and a dog, he began contacting Realtors. True enough, it was wrong to play those kind of mind games. Genesis wanted what she wanted, and she'd do what she had to do to get it. She had a lot ahead of her, and she wanted to be ready for it.

"Why are we here?" Genesis looked around at all the cars in the driveway of his parents' home.

"To celebrate," he answered sharply.

"Celebrate what?" She rolled her eyes.

For the first time that day, Angel wasn't frowning when he looked at her. Though his mad face was horrible, this one was worse. It was something along the lines of sadness, maybe disappointment even.

"My birthday."

Damn. Genesis's mouth fell open and she hurried to cover it with her open palm. She had been so busy cutting the fool all morning, she'd totally forgotten it was his birthday.

"It's cool. My birthday probably ain't that serious either." He threw her words back at her.

Genesis instantly felt like the worst person on earth. How had she been so focused on herself that she'd forgotten it was his day? She scolded herself because she should have known. If only she'd paid more attention to what was going on with him, she would have known it had to be something special about that day for him to propose again.

The other two times he'd proposed to her had been special as well. Once was on Christmas last year, and again on her birthday. She'd declined each time, giving them a bad memory for each of those days.

"Don't sweat it. If it mattered to you, you would have remembered." He gave a weak smile. "Get out. My mama threw me a party."

Angel let himself out of the car and waited for her. Genesis felt so bad, she couldn't even make eye contact with him as they headed up the walkway. She'd been so caught up in herself that she hadn't even thought to get him a present. It wasn't like she hadn't known it was coming. As if things between them weren't going bad enough, before they could even get to the front door, his mother had opened it.

The royal blue dress flowed around Empress's body, and a thin scarf, the same color as the dress, wrapped around her head and hung down her back beneath her long tresses. The jewelry she wore lit up the block as she smiled and waved at Angel.

"My baby, happy birthday!" she screamed and rushed to him with open arms. "Look at you! You look just like today is your birthday." She grabbed the bottom of his face and smiled. "Standing here looking all handsome and stuff."

Genesis wanted to roll her eyes at Empress but controlled herself only because she was telling the truth and because of how close to her she was. Angel was decked out in all black with labels dripping from head to toe. His dark hair was freshly cut and shining beneath the sun. Today he wore a little more jewelry than usual, and his cologne was smelling up the air around them. Genesis cowered inwardly from her carelessness and lack of concern for him.

"Stop, Ma." Angel laughed like a little boy, and again, Genesis found herself barely able to stop her eyes from rolling. "It ain't that serious. I'm almost thirty."

Empress stepped away from him and placed her hands on her hips. "What do you mean it ain't that serious? Why wouldn't the day you came into this world be a big deal to the people that love you?" Empress sucked her teeth. "Boy, you must be crazy. This is one of the best days of my life. I'm going to celebrate it even if you don't."

Angel was smiling so hard, Genesis could see the subtle shaking of his cheeks. "See, this is why you're my girl." He kissed her cheek and she smiled.

As if on one cue, both of them turned toward Genesis. She was sure Angel had his own reason for looking at her, while it was written all over Empress's face why she was looking at her.

"Hi." Empress spoke dryly.

"Good afternoon, Mrs. Empress. How are you today?" Genesis faked excitement.

Empress looked from Genesis's feet to her hair before going back to her face and stopping. "Fine." She looked from her to Angel, then back to Genesis. "I'm surprised I even get to see him today. I assumed you would have taken him on some expensive trip like he did for you for your birthday." The disdain for Genesis was laced all through Empress's words. "You know how y'all do. Spend money, spend money, spend money. As long as it's Angel's."

"Ma, stop that." Angel grabbed her hand and gave it a light squeeze.

"Yeah, Ma, stop that." Genesis couldn't help herself.

Empress's entire face changed in annoyance. "Little girl, don't try to be funny. I already don't like your ass."

Genesis heard something similar to a groan come from Angel's throat as he leaned his head slightly to the side.

"Y'all cut it out. Let's just party and enjoy the day." Angel looked from his mother back to Genesis. "I can't have fun with my two favorite girls at each other's throats."

"Don't ever equate me with her." Empress rolled her eyes and walked away. As she was still holding Angel's hand, she pulled him along with her.

Genesis stood in the same spot, giving herself a pep talk before following them into the house. Angel knew his mother hated her, with Genesis's feelings toward his mother just as hostile. She had no idea why he continued to bring them around each other.

"Just ignore her ass, Genny. Ignore her or slap her. One of the two will make her old ass act right," Genesis told herself over and over as she entered the already crowded house.

She searched the room for Angel, who was standing near the window talking to his father. Genesis could already tell this was about to be a long day.

Chapter Five

All grown up

"**I** don't even know why he brought the little tramp." Empress's voice carried over Angel's shoulder as he stood with his back to his mother and godmother, Zulema.

"It's his birthday, Empress, and that's his girlfriend. Give my baby a break," Zulema told her best friend.

Empress and Zulema had been best friends since the third grade and had remained loyal to one another since. They'd been through everything together: marriage, childbirth, and drugs. Just like Vinny and Empress, Zulema and Mack had been in the drug game for years.

With Mack being Vinny's right-hand man, the majority of the things they'd done in the streets had been with each other. Like the riders that they were, Empress and Zulema went with the flow. From California to the Southern states, they ran drugs alongside their men. Though Angel didn't like it, he had no other choice but to respect it. His mother and Zulema were some of the most thorough women he'd ever seen do it. Black queens who had proven plenty of times that they were down to ride with their men no matter what.

They'd dealt with fiends and cocaine bosses with smiles on their faces, never flinching in the face of danger, nor folding when times got hard. Angel had been given an unwanted front seat to it all, and he had nothing but the utmost respect for both women, which was why he was trying his hardest to ignore the way they were speaking on Genesis.

"Come on now, Zulema. You know just like I know, all that trick wants is my baby's money. If Angel went broke today, she'd be gone."

"I know, but that's up to him to see, not us."

Empress sucked her teeth. "You make me sick. You're always taking up for him."

The women's laughter flowed to Angel's ears and he smiled.

"That's my baby. He means well. He can't help that he doesn't have good taste in women," Empress said.

Their laughter brought about his own this time. Angel spun around and looked at them both. "Y'all do know I can' hear y'all, right?"

Zulema smiled while Empress shrugged.

"I don't care if you hear us," Empress said. "You ain't gon' do nothing about it. You gon' keep right on being with that little troll like you've been doing."

Angel wasn't the least bit deterred by his mother's smart mouth. It was what she was famous for. Vinny had her spoiled, but she was still a black woman with a mouth that could get down with the best of them.

"I keep trying to tell your mama that you'll learn your lesson once you go broke." Zulema high-fived Empress as they both fell out in laughter again.

"Let me get away from y'all two." Angel chuckled and headed to find Genesis.

She'd walked away from him the moment his mother and Zulema had stood behind them, and he hadn't seen her since. He scanned the room for her and stopped when he spotted her in the corner on her phone. She was pecking away so intently that it almost made him want to check her and see who she was talking to, but he'd never been that dude.

"Go 'head on over there, you know you want to." A sultry voice came from beside him.

A smile a mile wide spread across Angel's face when he turned to the side and saw *her*. Angel grabbed the center of his chest when he felt it tightening. Damn, she was beautiful. Emelia, the secret love of his young life, standing there. Her chocolate-colored face and big beautiful smile were a sight for sore eyes. The loose curls in her shiny black hair cascaded around her face and rested on her shoulders every time she moved.

The brightness from her big round eyes seemed to glow as her skin glistened sexily. Her lips were painted a dark burgundy color, with a small mole denting her cheek just above the dimple on the left side. Angel's eyes roamed over her face before venturing down over her full breasts, small waist, and wide hips.

Her curvaceous body had him captivated, and it was like no matter how hard he tried to push them away, sinful thoughts of her womanly essence continuously circulated through his mind. Before he could stop himself, Angel spoke without thinking.

"Damn, Emelia, when you get thick like this?" he asked with a lust-filled smile on his face.

She looked down at herself before pushing his chest lightly and giggling. "Boy, hush."

Angel grabbed her hand and leaned his head to the side, trying to observe the back of her. "I'm for real. Last time I saw you, you were skin and bones."

"Well, I'm eating good these days, unlike somebody I know." She side-eyed him and rested her other small hand on her hip.

After releasing her hand, Angel looked off and ran his hand over his face quickly. He already knew what she was talking about. Emelia, affectionately named Snow by the streets, was the queen to see these days. Being that she had been placed in a front seat to drugs right next to him, it was no surprise to him that she dove into it headfirst. Totally different from Angel, Snow had been working with the cartel since they'd graduated from high school.

Unlike Angel, Snow was Mack's only child, and the only person to take over all of his hard work. She'd paid attention and learned everything she could about the drug game. She was in so deep now, she practically owned Mack's share of it all. Being the daughter of one of the originators of their cartel, her respect came without question, not to mention the work she'd put in to be the boss.

Pretty, but cold. That was Snow. And though Angel hated to love it, he did. It was something about the roughness of her that turned him on differently from the girls he normally encountered. Not to mention the old feelings he could feel stirring in the pit of his stomach.

"Man, go ahead with that." Angel smiled and waved her off.

"I'm for real. Mrs. Empress told me you ain't trying to have no part in the good life."

"If that's what you want to call it."

"I do." Snow's voice grew serious. "How could you say no to something like this?" She raised her arms and then allowed them to fall to her side. "This is our life."

Angel looked at her. "Nah, that's *their* life. It doesn't have to be ours." He gave her the once-over. How could something so gorgeous be so tainted? "I don't even see how you live in that shit."

"I don't see how you don't," she snapped at him with attitude.

"What I don't understand is why everybody continues to try and force it on me. Why not train D'Angelo's ass?" Angel fumed.

Snow's face soured, and she rolled her eyes. "You know damn well D'Angelo would fuck shit up." She scoffed. "I wouldn't trust that nigga to take my dog out for a piss, let alone run an entire drug empire . . . his stupid ass, and you're stupid for suggesting it."

Although Angel wasn't too fond of her snappy response and wanted to correct her for it, she was right. D'Angelo may have been old enough to take over, but he still wasn't ready. An immature and irresponsible delinquent who kept shit started was D'Angelo.

He'd been in and out of jail pretty much their entire life, which justified Snow's opinion of him. However, as right as she was about him, right then wasn't the time or the place to discuss it. It was Angel's birthday, and he had no interest in ruining it by entering a debate that would never meet in agreement. To lighten the mood, he gave Snow his full attention.

"I see why they call you Snow." He grabbed her in a hug. "Calm your li'l mean ass down. You can't beat my ass, so you'd might as well chill out."

Snow's laughter showed her acceptance of his peacemaking. "You know I don't fucking play."

"I heard. I ain't seen your ass in so long, though, I had to see for myself." He touched her hair and looked into her eyes, remembering the old days when she stepped closer to him. "How long you gon' be here?" he whispered as he surveyed her face.

Snow lived in Southern California and rarely ever came to South Carolina. She spent so much time out there working and running the streets that it was rare she got free time to vacation. From what Vinny and Empress had told him about her, she was the truth. She didn't render any free passes.

Niggas and bitches were getting dealt with on the regular if shit wasn't adding up right. Her numbers and suppliers had increased in the past few months, and to say she was making boss moves would have been an understatement.

She was doing so good, there was talk about handing her the control in Georgia as well. Snow wasn't fucking around. Just like he wasn't when it came to his mother and Zulema. Angel may not have agreed with her lifestyle, but he respected it. She was handling shit, and he wouldn't hate on her for it.

"A few days, why? You trying to go back with me?" She raised her eyebrow in question.

Angel's laughter meshed with hers as he shook his head. "Nah, I'm staying my ass right here until I finish school."

"Oh, that's right. This is your last year, ain't it?"

Angel nodded.

"I don't know why you trip so hard on me. We'll both be pushing drugs." Her smile was infectious, and so damn pretty.

Angel found himself smiling again. "Well, the kind of drugs I push help people and won't have me either dead or in jail."

"It's life." Her tone was back cold.

The tone of her voice did things to Angel that he couldn't explain. It was like the seriousness made him feel disloyal, or something frowned upon like that. To hear how seriously she took their families' choice of business made him feel small. Almost fake. It was weird, and he didn't like it. He knew Snow and had been tight with her since they'd been born, so he knew she wasn't judging him, but it didn't stop him from feeling like she was.

"You have to make time to come kick it with your boy more often. I be missing you."

She blushed before her smile reappeared. "What you call this?" She looked around the room. "You think I came all this way to hang out with myself?"

It wasn't until then that Angel realized she was there for his birthday. His chest swelled in happiness, as he grabbed her into his arms. He held on to her tightly and allowed her smell to suffocate him. She was soft and smelled better than anything he'd smelled all day. Her scent was strong, yet faint and so intoxicating.

"Damn, I ain't even think about that."

"Clearly." She snickered into his chest.

She too was a shorty. Not as short as Genesis, but shorter than him, so he towered over her pretty much the same. Her arms were around his waist as her fingers tapped his back lightly.

"I couldn't let my first love's birthday pass me by. I had to come see how much you've grown." She laughed again as she allowed her hand to slide down the center of his chest. The air between them grew thick for only a moment before she lightened it back up. "For real, though, I'm proud of you, Angel. You're doing big things, baby boy."

For reasons no one would ever understand, her approval meant the world to him. To have someone as powerful, feared, and respected as Snow express her gratitude for him made his day. Her respect wasn't given lightly, so he was honored. He may have known her since she was just a kid, but she was no longer that. She was a queenpin, and her admiration wasn't to be taken casually.

"Thank you, sweetheart. I'm glad I make you proud."

She covered her mouth as she giggled girlishly.

"Shut up." She pushed him away as the buzz from the crowd around them drowned out the silence. "So, we're hanging out or what?"

"I think not." Genesis's voice stilled everything in Angel.

He turned to her quickly, trying to defuse a dangerous situation she was blindly putting herself into.

"Genny, this is Emelia. She's the one I told you I grew up with."

"Snow," she corrected him.

"Snow?" Genesis asked with her face frowned up.

"Yes, Snow. Only the people that I love call me Emelia." Snow looked Genesis up and down with a murderous glare. "And I don't even like you, so it's Snow, bitch." She gave Genesis the once-over again before looking at Angel. "I'm about to go check on our mamas. When you get rid of your ho, come holla at me."

Angel died slowly on the inside for Genesis, because it was obvious that Empress had gotten to Snow. He wanted to smile at her because her nickname was perfect for her. She hadn't let up since he'd been talking to her, and she had placed her foot on Genesis's neck the moment she walked up. Her loyalty was obviously unquestionable. She'd never met Genesis a day in her life, but all she needed to know was that Empress hated her. Now she did as well.

"I'm so tired of your family." Genesis sucked her teeth. "They're so disrespectful, and you just let them say anything to me."

"No, I don't." Angel sounded exhausted.

"Yes, the fuck you do."

Angel stared at her through piercing eyes, and she simmered down. She might have been mad, but she'd better remember who she was talking to.

"You do." She spoke a little softer that time.

"Genesis, just let it go. Let's grab some food." Angel grabbed her hand, but she pulled it away.

"Nah, I'm good. I'm ready to go."

Angel looked at her like she was crazy. She couldn't possibly think he was about to leave a house full of people who had jumped through hoops to celebrate his life for one who hadn't even remembered the significance of his day.

"Genesis, I'm not about to leave. We ain't even been here that long."

"Well, I'm ready now."

"I can't leave my own party, Genny."

"Well, you can stay without me." She rested all of her weight on one of her legs and crossed both of her arms over her chest.

Angel could tell that she was serious about her little

ultimatum, but what she didn't know was that he was just as serious as she was. He wasn't leaving his own party. That was just flat-out ungrateful, and he had been raised better than that.

"How you getting home? You rode with me."

"I'll call me an Uber."

Angel sighed and ran his hand over his face. "A'ight. Fine." A small smile curved her lips but was short lived. "I'll have my dad's car service take you home. Give me a minute." Angel walked off, leaving her standing there.

He heard her scoff as he walked away, but he didn't have time for Genesis's drama right then. All day she'd been acting like a child, and he was annoyed with her. If she wanted to continue throwing a tantrum, she'd do it alone. She wouldn't ruin his birthday.

"Ay, li'l bruh, you good?" D'Angelo walked up to Angel with an open bottle of champagne in his hand.

D'Angelo's tall frame was similar to Angel's, but he was a lot thicker. All of the time he'd spent in jail had paid off in a good way. He was ripped with muscles, with a face that carried years of stress and street smarts. Before going in, he and Angel had looked so much alike that they could have passed for twins, but now that he'd gained at least another hundred pounds and had cut his hair, they looked their ages.

"Yeah, I'm good. Genesis's spoiled ass is just getting on my nerves, as always."

D'Angelo looked toward Genesis before looking back at Angel, laughing. "That's your fault. You're the one got her spoiled like that."

Angel wanted to pretend that wasn't the truth, but he couldn't. D'Angelo was right, and so was his mom. He did go out of his way more than he should when it came to Genesis, which was why she carried on the way she did.

"I'm regretting that shit now." Angel took the bottle of champagne from D'Angelo and took a long gulp of it. "I should make her ass stand over there with an attitude all night. Shouldn't even take her home."

D'Angelo and Angel were cracking up at Genesis's expense when she walked over to them with much attitude.

"If you're done being childish, can you take me home now?"

Angel stopped laughing, while D'Angelo stood next to him barely able to catch his breath from the comedy unfolding in front of him.

"Nope. My dad's car will take you."

"Fuck no. I don't know that damn man. He could do anything to me." She spoke dramatically.

Angel groaned inwardly. "Well, stay here, then, because I'm not leaving my party."

Angel watched Genesis's face form deeper into her scowl. Her bright skin was flushing red from obvious anger, but he didn't give a fuck. She was doing that to herself. All she had to do was act like she had some sense and chill with him there. If she wanted to go out of her way to be a nuisance, he'd treat her like one.

"You make me so fucking sick, Angel."

Angel was about to tell her just how tired he was of her as well, until D'Angelo intervened. "Look, li'l bruh, go enjoy your party and I'll take her home."

Genesis gave D'Angelo the same frown she'd given Angel, while shaking her head. Angel, on the other hand, didn't give a damn.

"Cool. Call me when you get home so I'll know you made it."

"Fuck you, Angel. If you wanted to make sure I was

safe, you would take me yourself instead of staying at this stupid party with these people."

Angel couldn't believe how selfish Genesis sounded right then. Yeah, it was definitely time for her to go home. She was making him think things about her that weren't right.

"You mean at this stupid party with these stupid people that loved me enough to even host a party in my honor?" He chuckled in disbelief. "I don't know why I'm staying either. Take your ass home," he told her before turning and walking away.

As soon as he walked back into the foyer of the house, his eyes fell on Snow. She was walking up to him dancing smoothly to the music. He watched the way she rolled her body sexily to the beat before she grabbed his hands.

"Come on, birthday boy. Don't let that little bitch ruin your day." Snow danced closer to him as she pulled him toward the dance floor.

The music was loud as she sashayed around in front of him. People moved out of their way with every step they took. Angel had never really been a dancer, but he needed a serious pickup right then, so he fell in stride with her.

The soulful Southern jazz played throughout the house as the sway in Snow's hips captured his attention and kept it. Angel could feel himself getting lost in her curves. He'd diverted his eyes a few times, but they invariably traveled right back to her. Her entire aura was too hypnotizing to ignore.

"Stop looking at my ass, Angel. It doesn't belong to you."

When he looked back at her face, she was smiling playfully. He couldn't even deny the fact that he was busted.

"You're twirling it around for me to see, don't get shy now." He grabbed her and pulled her to him so that her back was to his chest.

"Shy is what I'm not," she told him over her shoulder as they stood in the middle of the floor dancing.

The feeling of her hips moving against his growing erection put Angel in such a place of peace that he wouldn't have been able to describe it if he tried. The closest thing he could compare it to would be coming home from a long day's work and falling face first into bed. Her body next to his felt as good as coming home. That was a feeling he hadn't felt in a long time, but one he could most definitely get accustomed to.

"You're rubbing your ass all over me like you know what to do with it," Angel whispered in Snow's ear, while at the same time his right hand palmed her abs.

"You're holding on to me like you know how to handle it," she tossed back at him. "I know you remember what happened the last time I danced for you."

Angel's body flushed warm from the thoughts of their very first sexual encounter with each other. Even with it having been so many years ago, just the thought of being inside Snow's warm body had his mind freefalling into the gutter. He looked down at the way she was grinding all over him. What he would give to be buried deep inside her like that again.

"I figured that would hush you up," she boasted.

Angel leaned down and pecked her ear swiftly. "It did, because I remember . . . and I want it again."

Snow moved slower and laid her head back onto his shoulder. "Angel," she moaned with her eyes closed. "Don't do that."

He could hear the uncertainty in her voice, so he toned it down a little. "My apologies, beautiful."

When Snow spun around and wrapped her arms around his shoulders, she smiled up at him. "Apology accepted. Now, let me help you enjoy your birthday." She beamed at him and he smiled back.

Angel was in heaven. Now, that was how a man celebrated his birthday.

When Snow was around the younger Depakins
met this attitude, she could care less; an insignia
assumed Smith for anything that grew...

Chapter Six

Respect goes both ways

The smoke from D'Angelo's blunt floated from his mouth and over toward Genesis. He could see her fanning the smoke away but continued to exhale the potency of his neatly rolled weed. She was in his car, so she would have to deal with it until she got out. Had she been acting like she had some sense, she wouldn't be with him anyway.

"Can you please put that out?" she sassed.

D'Angelo looked at her out of the side of his eye. "Nah."

Genesis sucked her teeth. "You're just like your brother. Empress didn't raise y'all worth shit."

Had D'Angelo not already been aware of how spoiled she was, he probably would have taken offense to her talking about his family, but he didn't. Angel had Genesis's head so far up her own ass that she would probably talk down on her own family if the situation was to arise.

"Your mama must not have been shit either. You're a horribly ungrateful little ho that doesn't know how to talk to people."

"Muthafucka, don't be calling me names. You don't even know me like that."

D'Angelo shrugged and pulled into her driveway. "I know enough."

He could feel her looking at him as he kept his gaze straight ahead, but he ignored her. It was past time for somebody to bring her back down to reality, and he was the perfect person to do it. D'Angelo and Angel were complete opposites when it came to women. Angel made women believe the world revolved around them, while he made them question whether they were even in his world at all.

"You're welcome," he tossed at her as she was getting out.

"Nigga, fuck you." Genesis slammed his door and headed up the sidewalk.

D'Angelo's whole body got hot as he hopped out of his car and followed her to her door. That tantrum shit might have worked with Angel, but he wasn't the one. She was going to respect him or get her ass beat; one of the two. When it came to his respect, he had no problem putting his hands on anybody who needed it. Whether it be a woman or a man.

"Bitch, you done lost your muthafucking mind slamming my door and talking to me like that."

Genesis spun around with just as much attitude as she'd had all night. "I haven't lost shit. I said what I said." She gave him the once-over before turning her back on him and unlocking her door.

D'Angelo stood behind her trying to mask his anger

long enough for her to get in her house and away from him. He'd almost made it, until she walked through the door and turned back around to face him.

"Get your ass off my porch before I call the police."

The police?

This ho had him fucked all the way up. Before she could even see what was happening, D'Angelo had Genesis by the front of her neck. He pinned her against the wall in her living room, kicking the door closed behind him.

"Why you like to fuck with me?" he grumbled in her ear. "You like when I'm rough with you, don't you?"

Genesis nodded feverishly while snatching her dress up so that it was around her waist. As soon as her feminine parts were exposed, D'Angelo dropped to his knees in front of her and pushed his face between her thighs.

Genesis's head fell back as she held on to the back of his head for balance. He was feasting on her goodies and taking away her breath at the same time.

"Fuck, D'Angelo," she squealed.

"Open your legs some more," he growled without bothering to move his mouth from her sex.

Genesis did as she was told, and he went full throttle. D'Angelo had a face full of Genesis's pussy, and that was how he liked it. He'd been hungry for her from the moment he tasted her. As much as he tried to think of her as Angel's girlfriend, he couldn't. She belonged to him. Fuck Angel.

Angel may have been his brother, but that didn't change how D'Angelo looked at him. He was weak for women and allowed them to run all over him. D'Angelo, on the other hand, dicked bitches down and gave them his ass to kiss if they had a problem with that.

"Give me the dick, D'Angelo," Genesis demanded.

D'Angelo took one last long slurp of her juices before standing and picking her up. Genesis's legs wrapped around his waist instantly. Not even bothering to go all the way to her room, D'Angelo laid her on the sofa in her living room and commenced to taking his pants off.

Once his dick was free and he'd shielded himself with a condom, he was back between her legs and entering her center. Genesis's mouth fell open as her body welcomed him.

"Damn, it's been too long. You've been letting my brother up in my shit?"

Genesis's head shook, but D'Angelo knew she was lying. Angel lived and breathed for Genesis. There was no way he wasn't hitting it, especially as good as it was. Hell, that was probably why Angel was as gone off the pussy as he was. The gushy, wet drug Genesis had between her legs was enough to make a nigga cry, so Angel would have been a fool to not be hitting it.

"I don't give a fuck if you do, he ain't doing you like I do, is he?"

"No, baby," she moaned in his ear.

D'Angelo was pushing deeper and deeper into her, making sure to touch bottom. When her legs shot straight up on both sides of him and she screamed, he knew she was near an orgasm. It never took her long to bust, which was another reason he loved fucking her. He didn't have to go all night without climaxing early like he had to do with most women. Once she was done, he could be done.

"Ohhhh, D'Angelooooo." Her breathing was ragged as she tried to catch her breath.

D'Angelo continued pounding her down until he felt himself on the verge of an orgasm as well. The moment the tip of his dick began to tingle, he pushed deeper and released into the condom. They were both breathing hard as Genesis moved from the sofa to get him something to clean up with and to flush his condom down the toilet. When she returned, D'Angelo cleaned up and got dressed.

"Lock up, li'l mama. I'll see you later."

"Hope it's not too far away."

D'Angelo gave her a lazy grin before kissing her mouth. "That all depends on you. You're the one in a relationship." He winked at her and exited her house.

Once he was back in his car, D'Angelo checked his face to make sure he was good and then pulled off. He was more than positive the party was still in full swing, and he needed to make his rounds. He'd spotted some serious eye candy up in there before he'd left, and he needed to make sure she saw him as well. It had been a long time since he'd enjoyed the beauty of the chocolate Snow. D'Angelo chuckled to himself. This was about to be fun.

"So, you never miss California?" Angel asked Snow as they stood in front of the waterfall in the backyard of his parents' house.

She shrugged her shoulders before tossing the flower she'd been picking the petals from onto the ground in front of her.

"It's nothing to miss for real. My life is in California. Has been for years. There's nothing for me here to miss here except Empress and Vinny."

"Damn, just leave me out, then," Angel said sarcastically.

She looked at him with a small smile on her face. "I will, because you don't matter. I never even think about you anymore."

Angel turned so that he was facing her. "You for real?"

He didn't want to be bothered by it, but he couldn't help it. The serious way she'd said it let him know that she wasn't joking one bit; that was seriously how she felt.

"Yeah, I'm for real, nigga. You don't think about me, so I don't think about your ass either."

"How do you know what I do? You don't know if I think about you or not."

She waved her hand toward him dismissively. "The fact that I never hear from you says enough for me. If you thought about me you would call, email, hit me up on social media, any damn thing that you never find time to do." She rolled her eyes at him and posted up with her hand on her hip. "Now, say I'm lying so I can slap you."

Angel rubbed the back of his neck and looked away. He thought about lying but couldn't think of anything fast enough that she might believe.

"Exactly. So, like I said, there's nobody here for me except your parents. I talk to at least one of them, if not both, every day. Empress calls me every morning, sometimes on three-way with my mama, and sometimes just me and her. Vinny calls me every night to see how my day went." She walked closer to him and took a seat on the small bench he was sitting on. "I don't know where they got you from. You ain't nothing like us."

"Sure as hell ain't."

"You say that like you're proud of it or something." She frowned.

Angel turned his head so that he was looking at her. Snow was seated sideways on the bench so that she was facing him. She had one of her legs tucked beneath her body, with the other one dangling over it. Her arm was propped up on the back of the bench, holding her head up.

She was so chocolatey and tasty looking. She wasn't doing anything in that moment, but all he kept thinking about was sniffing her neck and kissing her mouth. The ache in the pit of his stomach was actually starting to annoy him, because it had been a long time since he'd felt it, and it was refusing to go away. Angel was calm around women, so he was maintaining his cool, but she wasn't making it easy. The part that was irritating him the most was that she wasn't even doing anything. No suggestive gestures or words; just chilling.

"I actually am proud of it. Not in the way that you probably think I mean, but I am proud of myself. I'm a few months away from being a doctor, debt free, kid free, just living life. It's a lot more than most black men that are my age. So when I say I'm proud that I'm nothing like y'all, I mean it."

Snow watched him intently but didn't say anything. Her eyes darted from his face, up to his head of silky dark hair, then back to his face.

"You see what I'm saying?" She began rubbing her hand across the waves in his head. "What black boy you know with hair like this? None of the niggas I know have hair that's softer than the women they be fucking. All the men I know either got nappy-ass heads or a semi-decent texture with no waves."

"Man, your ass be saying anything."

"So, your hair ain't softer than Genesis's?"

Angel thought about the cute little short cut Genesis sported, and a smile crossed his face again. "That's not fair, though. Empress has some good-ass hair, so I ain't have no other choice but to have some too." Angel looked away from the comical smirk on Snow's face. "Genny's is cool, though. I keep telling her to grow it out for me, but she won't."

Snow sucked her teeth and moved her hand from his head. "That's because she's disobedient. I don't know why you're so stuck up her butt anyways."

"I'm not stuck up her butt. I just love her."

"That ain't enough. Love don't mean shit."

Angel's head spun in her direction because he couldn't believe she'd said that. She'd said it with so much feeling that he'd felt it in his chest.

"You sure you came from Zulema and Mack? Outside of my parents, those two are the most in love people I've ever met in my life. You're talking about me, but apparently you're not much like your parents either."

Snow looked away and shook her head. "They don't count. Love was real back then when they met. These days, love ain't shit. Ain't nobody out here loving people right no more. Especially not men. Y'all don't do nothing but use us for what we can give y'all, then be on to the next." She turned so that she was looking at him again. "Love is for weak bitches. Hos like Genesis."

Angel wanted to laugh at the little jab she'd taken at his girlfriend, but he didn't. Instead, he squinted his eyes at her. There was clearly something she needed to get off her chest.

"What nigga done broke your heart? Because you're sounding like a woman scorned over there."

"There ain't a nigga alive that I would ever give the opportunity to have me down that bad, so don't even try my gangsta like that. I've just seen it happen too many times before, so I'm steering clear of that shit."

"Nah, I don't want to hear that, Emelia." Angel

reached out and ran his hand through her hair before stopping to massage her scalp. "You don't have to be Snow with me. Tell me what's up. We've always been open with each other. Don't stop now because you done grew some hips and ass, and it got you thinking you're grown."

Snow covered her mouth as she giggled in that girly way that women did. "You're so fucking ridiculous, Angel. What do my ass and hips have to do with this?"

"I guess they got you feeling yourself now or something. They obviously got you thinking you're either too grown or too cool to be real with me."

"Oh, whatever. You're the one feeling it. You're the only one that keeps bringing attention to my ass. I don't care about it. It's been this size for years."

Angel smiled bashfully. "I'm an ass man. I can't help myself."

The two of them shared another laugh before the air between them grew still again. Angel watched her lean into his hand and close her eyes as he massaged her head.

"Is this one of your moves?" She smirked, but her eyes remained closed. "I bet you rub these hos' head and they get to telling you all of their business, don't they?"

Angel was cracking up immediately. He even stopped rubbing her head for a minute. Snow was hilarious. The same jokester she'd been their entire life. She was probably worse as an adult, because she was grown and said anything that came to mind, whether it was appropriate or not.

"Your mouth is filthy, Emelia."

"It has to be."

"Why?"

She opened her eyes and looked at him. "I deal with

niggas all day and every day. They curse worse than me, and I'm their boss. I have to stay ahead. I can't be out here looking and sounding all soft."

Angel nodded, because he could understand that. Though cursing didn't make her who she was—her heart did that. It did provide her with somewhat of a rougher image.

"If you weren't in that line of work, you wouldn't have to be someone you're not."

Snow's face grew serious as her eyebrows knitted across her forehead. "This is me."

The two of them participated in a staring match for a little while longer before he nodded once, letting her know that he understood. When she looked away, so did he. He was lost in his thoughts when her voice interrupted him.

"I don't value love because love has fucked me over one too many times already."

Angel looked in her direction, but she didn't look at him.

"The main one being with men. My last man slept with my best friend, and I couldn't handle it."

The tone of her voice made Angel want to hold her, but he wasn't sure if that was appropriate for the type of relationship they had at the moment. It was obvious she was still hurt over the situation, because he could hear the pain in her voice and see the anguish on her face, even though she was trying to hide it.

"What did you do?"

She twisted her mouth to the side momentarily before looking at him. "Killed her."

Angel frowned slightly before allowing his face to relax again. "And him?"

She bit her bottom lip. "Nothing."

Angel stopped rubbing her head and stood up so

that he could look at her. "Hold on, so you mean to tell me your friend had to die, but you ain't do nothing to your nigga? What kind of shit is that? He was the one that was at fault. He should have respected you more than that."

"It wasn't that simple, or I would have killed his ass too." Snow ran her hand through her hair absentmindedly. "She was my best friend. I trusted her. She should have never done that. You don't hurt people that trust you."

"And he deserved a second chance?" Angel asked incredulously.

"I said it wasn't that simple for him. You're not listening."

"Well, stop mumbling and tell me what's up," Angel told her.

He was tired of her being evasive. She needed to get to the meat of the story, because he wasn't understanding. From his viewpoint, if anybody had to lose their life, it should have been that nigga.

"I'm not mumbling, nigga," she yelled at him defensively.

"Watch how you talk to me." Angel's eyes darkened as he scolded her forcefully. "All that yelling ain't necessary."

She squinted her eyes and stood up so that she was facing him. With not an ounce of fear in her heart or eyes, Snow got into his face with the speed of lightning. Her eyes were just as hard as his, if not harder, as she glared at him.

"First of all, you watch how the fuck you talk to me. I'm not one of these little country bitches that bows to a man. When you talk to me, you better speak to me as your fucking equal, or don't say shit at all." The underlying coldness took over full throttle as she spoke to him through clenched teeth. "We're family, but I don't tolerate disrespect from anyone."

Her eyes were squinted so tight from anger that Angel could barely see how pretty they were anymore. Angel's frown got tighter as well, because one thing he didn't do was allow a person to openly disrespect him. He was the man for a reason, and in his mind, a woman was to respect his position. He could deal with a little attitude, even a little smartness every so often, but the way Snow was trying to handle him was way out of line.

"Emelia, you're the boss in California. I get that, but when you're in my presence, it'll do you justice to remember who the fuck I am. Just like you're not one of my country bitches, I'm not one of your little drug-pushing workers. Next time you open your mouth to correct me, you better do that shit in a respectful manner." Angel stepped closer to her so that his mouth was to her ear, and grabbed her chin. Her hand went to his immediately, trying to push it off her, but he held her tighter. "I don't fuck with the cartel because I don't want to, not because I can't handle it." He shoved her away from him hard enough for her to stumble. "Now get the fuck out of my face and stay in a woman's place."

Snow's chest was rising and falling rapidly as she stood in front of him, frowning and breathing hard. Her eyes were dark slits as her plump lips formed a small pout. With one of her hands at her side and the other resting behind her back, Snow took a step backward.

"Snow, don't!" Vinny's voice came from the distance.

Neither Snow nor Angel looked in his direction. They stayed in the same combative stances they'd been in before Vinny had ever said anything.

"Don't tell her nothing, Daddy. She knows better than that shit." Angel's voice was just as calm as it always was, but a tad bit harder than normal.

Angel's eyes bored into Snow's as her hand remained behind her back. He wasn't at all afraid of her or the fact that she probably had her hand on the gun he'd seen tucked into the back of her pants earlier. The moment he'd noticed her ass had gotten bigger, he'd acknowledged that so had the gun she'd been taught to carry. It had been secured snugly in her waistband, casually rubbing against the buckle of his belt as they danced.

"Snow, just relax, sweetheart." Vinny finally walked close enough for both of them to see him.

He was limping slightly as he stepped between the two of them. He looked at Snow first before looking to Angel.

"What the hell is this madness?" he yelled at them both. "Stop this bullshit, right now!"

Angel and Snow both visibly took heed to his warning, but neither of them moved from where they were standing.

"She started it. Just like women always do," Angel taunted sarcastically.

Snow's gun was out and pointed at him immediately after that. She still hadn't said anything, but she didn't have to. Angel knew how serious she was, he just wasn't afraid. He'd been brought up just as rigorously as she had. Just because he didn't actively involve himself in confrontation didn't mean he couldn't handle himself.

"Stop it, I say!" Vinny spoke again before turning completely toward Snow. "Put that shit away."

She looked at Angel for a moment longer before looking over at Vinny and stuffing her gun back into the band of her jeans.

"Oh, thank God." Empress's voice sounded in the distance. "Zulema, go get that damn girl."

Angel smirked at his mother's comment. He hadn't looked to see where she was yet, but he was more than positive she was on the deck connected to their back porch. It was the only exit into their backyard and overlooked the large courtyard Vinny and Snow were standing in. Being that she was always somewhere lurking, she'd probably seen the entire exchange and sent Vinny to simmer it down.

"Girl, Snow wasn't going to kill Angel, or he would already be dead." Zulema's voice was heard next, followed by a collection of nervous feminine laughter.

"Sorry, Vinny," Snow finally said.

"Family trumps it all, got dammit," he yelled before looking from her to Angel. "Don't provoke ill will, Angel. You were taught better than that shit!" he fumed.

Angel nodded. "Yes, sir."

Vinny hardly ever raised his voice, but when he did, Angel knew to listen. Vinny was getting older, but he was still the king of all the shit Angel was running from. He was the only person on the face of the earth that Angel would allow to handle him.

"You two are no longer kids. Bickering and nonsense stops here. Got it?" He looked between the two of them before they both expressed their understanding in their own way.

He looked at them for a moment longer before throwing his hands up in defeat and shaking his head. "How can I leave things like this?" was the only thing he said loud enough for them to hear before walking off and mumbling to himself in anger.

Angel watched his father slowly take the stairs to their house before looking back over at Snow. She was no longer looking at him but at the water fountain in front of them. Her face was stoic as she held her arms crossed over her chest. She said nothing, so neither did he.

They stood together in silence until Angel took his seat again. "Y'all women are too difficult. I've been dealing with bullshit since I woke up this morning." He sighed. "All I wanted was to enjoy my birthday, and I've gone from one woman not even knowing what today was to another one trying to kill me." Angel leaned over and held his chin in his hand. "I guess love really ain't shit. Huh?"

Snow was quiet for a long time before turning to face Angel. "I told you it wasn't." She looked at him for a long time before taking the same path his father had just taken and going back into the house, leaving Angel to his thoughts.

Chapter Seven

The biggest mistake
of my life

The cool porcelain felt so good to the side of Genesis's face as she lay with her head pressed against the top of her toilet seat. As unwelcome as her resting place was in that moment, it was the only place that made her feel even halfway alive. Everywhere else she'd tried to lie after eating a small meal for lunch and the many lunches prior made her question whether she was living or dying.

The pillowtop mattress she'd been so in love with ever since she'd moved into her apartment felt more like her deathbed than her self-proclaimed happy place. It had been weeks, and it seemed as if every day got worse than the last, and Genesis didn't feel like she could handle any more.

She had been doing all she could to make herself

feel better, and nothing worked, other than starving herself to death. Anything outside of that put her right back into the position she was in right then. Head spinning, body weak and racked with shivers, while she puked out whatever nourishment she'd attempted to take in.

"Why me, Lord?" She sniffed hard as her tears began to flow again.

Genesis's tears rolled out of her eyes and over her nose as she lay with her head practically inside her toilet bowl.

"Just take me, God. I didn't even ask for this."

Genesis prayed out loud, a tad bit ungrateful for the life growing inside her. She'd found out a little over two months ago that she would be expecting a child in a few short months, and she'd been devastated ever since. Though she'd always wanted kids, she hadn't wanted them that young, and most definitely not like that.

For years she and Angel had discussed their life plan, and kids were always a part of it, but Genesis had made it very clear: It would be when she was ready. She'd factored in all the things that she thought might arise before then, and not one time had she considered that Angel wouldn't be the father.

More tears fell. Every time she thought about it, she got sick all over again. How was she supposed to tell him that she was pregnant, but not by him? A low wail left her lips as she circled her abdomen protectively with her arm. She may not have been ready for a baby, but she'd never abort it. It had been four months already, and she was feeling more and more attached to her unborn child every day.

Between the stress from school and the drama with Angel, her pregnancy had gotten pretty far past her. So when the doctor told her she was well into her second trimester, she wasn't surprised. She'd noticed that her bottom had widened a little, but that had been the only change. It was crazy, though, because the doctor spoke it out loud to her body, and she had been sick ever since.

Eating food and getting full were a thing of the past. Nothing stayed down long enough for her to even digest it, and she spent more time vomiting than eating, so oftentimes she declined food altogether. Angel had been asking questions here and there, but for the most part, he had no idea she was pregnant, and with good reason.

The sick feeling she felt every time she thought about how hurt he was going to be when he found out came over her as she grabbed her cellphone from the floor. It rang a few times before *he* picked up. Since she was home alone and had no energy to even hold the phone to her ear, she put it on speaker.

"Emmanuel," she said.

"What's going on?" he asked nonchalantly.

"I don't feel well."

He sighed. "What do you expect, Genesis? You're pregnant." The annoyance he felt for her was so obvious that she could hear it through the phone.

"You could at least act like you care."

"I'm at work, Genesis. What can I do from here?"

Genesis sucked her teeth. "I don't even know why I call you."

"Because that's my baby, that's why."

She cried even harder. To hear another man claim what should have been her and Angel's baby made her stomach turn. Though she was glad that it wasn't D'Angelo's, she was still upset about it being Emmanuel's. Had she and D'Angelo not used condoms every time they had sex, and Angel not been out of town with his parents the month the doctor had confirmed conception, she wouldn't even know it was Emmanuel's. Sadly, he'd been the only one she'd been freely having sex with around the time she'd gotten pregnant, so unfortunately, it was his.

"I wish it wasn't."

He chuckled. "Me too."

"Well, it doesn't have to be."

"Good. Keep it that way." He laughed again before hanging up in her face.

Genesis clicked her phone off and continued to cry. Much like her body had the moment she heard she was pregnant, Emmanuel had been sick as well. He was so mean and rude all the time, and she couldn't understand it one bit. Before, he and she had been really good friends. Never anything more, because she had Angel. But Emmanuel was fun.

He was always there to make her laugh and smile without asking too much from her. Never pressuring her to give more than she was ready to, like Angel did constantly. Emmanuel had been a fun and welcome break that, on the night of her birthday, turned into more.

Just like every other time Angel had proposed and she'd said no, Angel had gotten an attitude with her and left her house. Genesis hadn't been in the mood to spend her day lonely, so she hit D'Angelo up. He told her that he was busy with one of his other women and couldn't come, so she called Emmanuel. He'd come over with cake and gifts. The two of them drank and laughed the entire night. One thing led to the next and they'd been sleeping together off and on ever since.

Being that Emmanuel hadn't wanted more than friendship from her from the beginning, he hadn't been a problem with her and Angel, until now. His baby was the biggest problem he could have ever caused. He had been so awful to her since finding out about her pregnancy that she almost wished it was D'Angelo's, which was completely foolish. Had he and she not used a condom every single time they had sex, she would have even pinned it on him just to get away from Emmanuel, but that wasn't happening. D'Angelo made sure to strap up every time they were intimate.

"Oh, God," she cried to herself.

Hours passed before Genesis was able to pull herself from the floor and get herself together. After a shower and a little makeup, she looked the old her.

"If he doesn't want me and my baby, he doesn't have to have us." She spoke to herself as she dabbed the lipstick on her lips. "We're better off without his dusty ass anyway."

Genesis pepped herself up the entire time she got dressed to leave. When she was finally dressed and ready to go, she grabbed her purse and left the house. It had been almost a week since Angel's birthday, and she had a lot of making up to do. She'd acted like such a brat that day and the days following.

Between ignoring his calls and not allowing him to come home, she was sure he was angry with her. At first, she had planned to use that as her out with him, so she could be with Emmanuel, but that was clearly a no go. She hadn't even entertained the thought of being with D'Angelo, because that would most definitely never happen. What they did was cool, but that's all it was. She was no fool to think he seriously cared. They were just two foul people doing foul shit, but Emmanuel was different. She'd actually allowed herself to fall for him for some reason, and now he was getting harder to shake.

With D'Angelo being an unavailable option, and Emmanuel acting like a jackass, she was better off staying with Angel. If you can't be with the one you love, might as well love the one you're with, right? Genesis hoped like hell that she could stick to that motto until she grew to feel the same way for Angel that he felt for her.

When she got outside to the brand-new red Lexus truck that Angel had gotten her a few months prior, she smiled. How could she not want a man who gave her a new car as a "just because" gift? Maybe spending her life with Angel wouldn't be too bad, especially since she didn't deserve him. If he was that good to her, she could only imagine how he would be with her baby.

Her stomach flipped again as she got into her truck and pulled off. "This baby isn't going to look anything like this boy," she said to herself.

Emmanuel and Angel were total opposites. Emmanuel was extra dark with hair that was nowhere near as good as Angel's. When Genesis felt the urge to close her eyes while she was driving, she knew it was time to think about something else, so she thought of baby names until she pulled up to his house.

She groaned inwardly when she noticed Empress's car in the driveway next to Angel's. Empress was one bitch who needed to get a life. Genesis hated her and would have beat her ass a long time ago had she not been Angel's mother.

"Here goes nothing," Genesis said to herself as she got out of the car.

She pulled the long. red dress down so that it was no longer bunched up. It dropped to the buckle of her sandals and flowed around the top of her feet. Before closing her door, she grabbed her purse out of her passenger seat and threw it over her arm.

Her hands shook in nervousness as she padded up the walkway. She was sure nosy-ass Empress was watching her approach, but she wouldn't give that enough thought to make herself angry. She had enough on her mind right then. When she finally got to the door, she rang the doorbell and waited. A few minutes passed before she rang the doorbell again.

Empress snatched the door open with a frown on her face. "Little girl, please don't ring my bell like that."

"Is Angel here?" Genesis purposely ignored Empress's attitude.

"Didn't you just walk past his car in the driveway?"

Genesis blinked her eyes slowly to refrain from rolling them. "Can I speak with him, please?"

"You haven't wanted to talk to him in the past week. What changed today?" Empress placed her hands on her hips. "You must have run out of money."

Genesis rolled her neck and placed her hand on her hip. "Listen here, Empress," she started.

"I'm listening, ho." She cut Genesis off before she could complete her sentence.

This old bitch.

Genesis's nose flared just as Vinny walked past the door. He doubled back for a second before walking to the door behind Empress.

"Darling, leave this girl alone," Vinny said to his wife, then opened the door wider while simultaneously grabbing Empress's arm and pulling her. "You know the way to his room, sweetheart. Go ahead."

"Yeah, go ahead before I put my hands on your trifling ass," Empress said.

Genesis spun around like she was about to say something but stopped when Vinny shooed her away.

She huffed and turned back around, taking the stairs to Angel's room. When she finally got there, she didn't even bother knocking, she just walked right in.

Angel was sitting on the corner of his bed with a textbook in his lap and a notebook on the bed next to him. He was shirtless in a pair of gym shorts.

When he looked up, his eyes were dark, but they lightened when he noticed it was her. He stood from the bed immediately and set his book down, along with the pen he'd been holding, before going to her. His body was pressed against hers when his lips found the side of her neck.

"You can't be staying away this long." He inhaled before squeezing her closer to him.

Genesis closed her eyes and wrapped her arms around him. "I'm sorry," she whispered.

"I'm sorry too. I shouldn't have let you leave."

"I shouldn't have left."

Angel didn't say anything after that, he simply held her in his arms until he was finally ready to let her go. Even then, it wasn't fully, because he was still holding her hand when he pulled her onto his lap. When they were comfortable on his bed, he ran his hand up and down her back.

"I missed you." His sexy, calming voice was low and making her center ache wildly.

She'd been wanting sex for days but refused to talk to him long enough to get it. But today was a new day. Genesis leaned over to pull her dress up some before turning so that she was straddling his lap. Her arms went around his neck at the same time his went to her waist.

Angel wasted no time getting in the groove of things with her. His touches were just as greedy as hers as they sat wrapped up in each other.

"Angel," she moaned into his ear. "Hurry up."

"I got you," he mumbled as he sat up enough off the bed to push his shorts down.

Luckily, he hadn't gotten a chance to get them down, because his bedroom door swung open. Both of their heads whipped in that direction. When Genesis saw Empress, she rolled her eyes so hard they should have fallen out of her head. She was tired of that bitch. If she wanted to keep disrespecting her, then Genesis would disrespect her ass right back.

"Oh, no, ma'am. You can get your li'l fast ass right on up off his lap. You won't make no baby over here and drain us dry." Empress walked all the way in the room. "Take that shit back to your house."

"Maaaaaa!" Angel's word dragged as he let his head fall into Genesis's breasts. "Get out, please."

"When she gets off your lap, I will," Empress said, not bothering to even attempt to exit his bedroom.

Genesis slid back and freed Angel's lap of her ass. "I'll get off him, but that won't stop me from getting a baby." She smiled at Empress. "It's a little too late for that, boo." Genesis snatched her purse off the bed and pulled the sonograms out for Empress to see. "Angel, meet your son, baby."

Empress shrieked. "Angel, you got this trick pregnant?"

Angel sat on the bed looking dumbfounded. "I guess so," he mumbled as he looked over the black-and-white pictures of the baby growing in Genesis's womb. "Damn."

"You little gold-digging bitch. You may have Angel fooled, but you won't get shit from him or us until we get a blood test."

"Tell her, mama," D'Angelo chimed in. He'd just walked up eating a piece of chicken.

Genesis's stomach flipped at the sight of him, but she held it together. "Fine with me."

Empress and Genesis stood staring at each other until Empress got mad enough to storm out of the room, with D'Angelo following behind her laughing. She even had the nerve to go back and slam the door behind them.

Genesis stood in the same place and looked at a laughing Angel. "What's funny?"

"My mama hates your ass, and I don't think my brother is too far behind her."

Genesis was quiet before she too began laughing. If only Angel knew just how much D'Angelo hated her. She snickered to herself again.

"Well, that makes two of us." She sat down next to him. "I don't give a fuck about D'Angelo's no-life-having ass. But Empress, she'd better get a better attitude, or my baby won't be coming over here. He will not be around somebody that doesn't like me. Empress won't be over here pinching my baby."

Angel stopped laughing. "My mama wouldn't do no shit like that."

She could tell he didn't appreciate the way she spoke about his mother, but she didn't care. She was tired of Empress.

"If you say so, but I'm serious. I can't be around no mess like that. Your mama be stressing me out."

When Angel scooted closer to her, she knew then that she had him. "Don't worry about my mama. I'll handle her." He touched her stomach. "Just worry about our boy, and I got the rest."

Genesis basked in the joy of Angel being excited about her child. That was how Emmanuel should have been, but it was what it was. No need to cry over spilled milk. If Angel wanted to be there, then that's who would be there.

"You happy?" she asked him.

He smiled brightly. "Hell, yeah, I'm happy! All you have to do is marry me now, and we can be one big, happy family."

Genesis swallowed the lump in her throat as tears of sorrow filled her eyes. "I will."

Angel scooted to the floor in front of her quickly with a look of surprise covering his face. "You for real?"

When Genesis couldn't force herself to say it again. She nodded. Thankfully, he hugged her immediately afterward, so he couldn't see the look on her face. It probably would have broken his heart. She sniffed hard because she would bear the burden for them this time. There was no need to have two broken hearts in one relationship. Her shattered one was enough for the both of them. Maybe her son would mend them, maybe not. Only time would tell.

Chapter Eight

When it all falls down

"*Angel, I'm ashamed of you, son.*" *Vinny's words cut deep as Angel sat in the living room on the sofa across from his parents.*

"*I'm sorry you feel that way, Daddy. My intentions were never to hurt either of you.*"

"*You didn't think changing your last name would hurt us?*" *his mother asked in disbelief. "You're a damn DeLuca. I don't care how much you want to pretend you're not.*"

"*I'm not pretending anything, Ma. I just don't want people to associate Dr. DeLuca with the DeLuca Cartel. Our name is ringing in the streets and has been for a few months now. If I'm going to practice medicine here, Ma, I have to make sure I'm legit.*"

"*And you couldn't do that with the name*

DeLuca? Fuck these people, Angel!" his father fired off at him. "You are who you are."

"I know that, Daddy. I'm just going to be myself with Mom's last name instead."

Empress's head fell forward for a minute. "The cartel is more than just a name, Angel. It's a legacy. You've seen all we've had to do in order to make ourselves, and this is what you do?"

Angel sat silently as he watched his mother's eyes start to water.

"Ma, please don't cry. I'm just trying to do what's best for my family and me. It's not y'all. I promise."

"Your promises are no good here." Vinny pointed at Angel before hugging Empress to him in comfort. "Just get your ass out of here. No son of mine would pull the stunt you just pulled. From this moment on, D'Angelo is the only son deserving of my respect. He may not be the best, but at least he's loyal."

Angel sat wounded by his parents' words. He hadn't known changing his name would make such a large impact on them. He'd been thinking of his and his son's future when he'd made the decision. If only he could get his parents to understand his reasoning, he would be okay.

"Ma," Angel started.

"Just leave, Angel. Go home to your family." The word family *rolled off her tongue as if it was the nastiest thing she'd ever tasted. "I know that little bitch was behind this."*

"Genesis had nothing to do with this, Ma. It was my decision."

"Sure, it was. Your family is all you talk about since finding out about that baby. The DeLucas

*are your fucking family, boy!" Empress stood up
and walked toward the door. "You're making all
of these stupid changes when you don't even
know if that fucking baby is yours." With that she
left the room.*

*Vinny stood and looked at Angel over his
shoulder. "Let yourself out, and don't come back
until you're ready to be yourself." He shuffled toward the door. "Don't sit idle too long, I don't
have time to waste."*

*Angel watched his father walk to the door and
his chest got tight. This was not what he wanted.
He needed his family; they were all he had. Why
couldn't they just accept him for who he was?
Why was that so hard?*

*"I pray to God when you do come back, it's
not too late. I love you, son." Vinny's voice resonated in Angel's head over and over for the rest
of that night and the many nights that followed.*

The falling-out with his parents had been almost
five months ago, and he hadn't spoken to them since.
He'd talked to D'Angelo off and on, but not even he
had much to say to Angel. It had been the hardest, most
grueling time of Angel's life, but his parents had made
it very clear that he wasn't wanted there. All the locks
had been changed, his fingerprint entrance to their estate gate had been erased, and every call he'd placed
had gone unanswered.

Although he had Genesis and would have their son
at any moment, he needed his parents and brother.
He'd always known the relationship they had was un-
touchable and unlike anything he'd ever experience
with anyone else, but what he hadn't known was how

empty he would feel without it. His nights had been long and his days had been dark without them.

He'd give almost anything just to talk to them, but he'd made a decision, and he'd stick with it. It may have been hard at the moment, but hopefully it would all work out in the end. He needed to think about the bigger picture for Genesis and his son. They were the most important thing in his life, and he'd do whatever he had to do to ensure their safety.

The only reason he knew his parents were still okay was because of Zulema. She was the only person in the entire DeLuca Cartel who still talked to him. The changing of his name had been disloyal in all of their eyes, and they'd made sure to show him their truest feelings about it.

"Angel, you didn't hear me?" Genesis asked as she wobbled into the room.

He looked up. "Huh? What you say, baby?"

"I said, my water just broke."

Angel's eyes got big as saucers when he noticed the water running down her legs. He stumbled to his feet so fast that he almost fell over the boxes in front of him. They had been in their new house for almost a month and still hadn't finished unpacking. Genesis was always too tired, and school was wearing Angel out. She'd taken a semester off due to being so sick, so he'd been finishing alone.

"Where's your bag?" He rushed to her and grabbed her hands just as she doubled over in pain. "Genny!"

She squeezed his hand so hard it felt like she was about to break it. No words left her mouth until she stood back upright.

"In the closet. Get it, please, and hurry." She winced

in pain. "I need to get to the hospital. That contraction hurt like hell."

Angel nodded nervously before walking away in a hurry to gather her things. He moved around the house as quick as he could, getting everything they would need before helping her to her truck and speeding them to the highway.

When they got there, everything happened so fast that it passed Angel by in a blur. One minute, Genesis was on the bed screaming at the top of her lungs, nearly shattering every bone in his head. The next minute they were in a hospital room alone while Genesis slept and Angel held his sleeping son on his chest.

Angel was lying back on the small sofa rubbing up and down his son's back, and scrolling through his social media stories. When he'd read them all, he pulled the phone away from him and recorded a small video of his boy. He was lying peacefully asleep with his little fists balled up. His skin was a little darker than most newborns, but it made Angel happy, because he'd surely inherited that from Empress.

The thought of his mother pained his chest deeply, so he focused back on his phone. Once he'd uploaded the video to his social media account and sent the same video to Zulema, he immediately began getting messages about how cute his baby boy was, or how sweet he looked. Angel was busy responding to people when his son began to cry. He dropped his phone immediately.

"What's wrong, little man?" Angel sat up quickly and turned him over on his back so that he could see his face. He was sucking on his fist feverishly. "I know your little ass ain't hungry. Your mama just fed you."

The baby continued to suck on his tiny fist, so Angel stood to walk to the counter where the bottle Genesis had been giving him earlier was. He was stopped in his tracks when his phone beeped with a text message alert. Since the baby had stopped crying, he turned and went back to his phone. It was Zulema.

Mama Z: He's so precious . . . and dark. Let me see his hair.

Angel: I know, like my mama. Hold on, let me take his hat off and take it.

Angel sat back down on the sofa and removed his son's hat. His hair was jet black like Angel's, and full of tight curls. They were so tight on his head, you could see his scalp. Angel chuckled when the baby squirmed and frowned as he positioned him to get a good picture. Once he snapped the picture, he sent it to Zulema. His phone was beeping immediately afterward.

Mama Z: Looks nappy. Y'all got that blood test yet?

Angel sucked his teeth and sighed inwardly. He was the happiest he'd been in months, and he really didn't want to argue with Genesis right then. She'd been complaining about feeling disrespected pretty much her entire pregnancy. How getting a blood test was disrespectful, he had no idea, but let Genesis tell it, it was the worst thing in the world.

Mama Z: I know you're probably over there wanting to play house, but test that baby.

Mama Z: Your hair too good for that baby's hair to be that nappy. That shit should be straight.

He stared at her message before looking back at his son. He stared at him for a minute, searching for any similarities between the two of them, but he hadn't found any yet. He looked a lot like Genesis, which helped ease his mind, but that was it. A few seconds passed before his phone beeped again with another

message from Zulema, this time with a picture. When
he opened it, he noticed it was a baby picture of him.

**Mama Z: That ain't your baby, Angel. Get that
damn test before I come up there and swab his little
ass myself.**

Angel: Yes, ma'am.

**Mama Z: I love you, and I'll let your mama know
the baby is here. She's been waiting.**

Angel smiled.

Angel: Love you too. Tell her I love her.

**Mama Z: She's not going to say it back, but she
does. Ttyl, Angel baby**

The truth hurts was a true statement, because Zulema
was right. Empress was most definitely not going to pass
her love along. Angel had sent his too many times with
no return, so he didn't even look for it anymore.

"Why are you looking at him like that?" Genesis's
voice got his attention.

"No reason. Just thinking about my mama."

Unlike she'd been doing every other time he mentioned his mother, Genesis nodded. She had been grip-
ing and complaining at the slightest mention of his
mother's name for months, so he was surprised.

"What about her?"

"Nothing, I just miss her. I wish she could be here
today."

"If she wanted to be here, she would be here." Genesis sounded a little irritated.

Now, that sounded more like her. Angel sat still not
saying anything at first, just trying to build up the
nerve to ask her for a blood test, but was cut short
when the door to her room opened. He frowned momentarily when he saw Emmanuel, but he was her
friend, so it wasn't surprising he'd want to show his
support by coming to the hospital to see that baby.

"What's good, Angel?" Emmanuel walked into the room casually.

Angel looked him up and down because for some reason, his demeanor was off. He seemed a little cockier than he normally did as he sat down on the small chair on the other side of Genesis's bed.

"Ain't shit. What up?" Angel spoke nonchalantly as he watched Emmanuel pick up Genesis's cup of water and drink out of it.

Angel's nose turned up because that nigga had lost his mind drinking out of his fiancée's shit. They may have been friends, but wasn't no nigga that damn close to her but him.

"Ay, my nigga, you good?" Angel asked with his brows knitted.

Emmanuel smiled mischievously, and for the first time in Angel's life, his murderous instincts kicked in. For some unknown reason, he felt like he was being disrespected. Emmanuel had never presented a threat before, but right then Angel felt like he was trying him.

"I'm good as I can be. You?" He grinned at Angel again before looking down at the baby. "Got your new li'l baby over there and shit. Fatherhood feeling any different?"

"Nigga, don't ever speak in riddles when talking to me. I said what's good?" Angel scooted to the edge of his seat while wrapping the baby securely in his blanket.

"Angel, calm down, baby," Genesis said.

He had totally forgotten she was in there, she'd been so quiet. He glared at Emmanuel for a second before standing and preparing to place the baby in his bassinet.

"Can I hold him before you lay him down?" Emmanuel asked.

Angel looked at Emmanuel out of the corner of his eyes. "Nah, he's asleep."

Until Angel figured out what the hell was up with that nigga, he wouldn't lay one finger on his son. He didn't trust shifty niggas, and right then, Emmanuel was looking shifty as fuck.

"Genesis, I can't hold the baby?" He tossed his question to her like Angel hadn't just said no.

If that didn't confirm that nigga was on some other shit, then Angel was blind as a damn bat.

"Emmanuel, you better get your ass on up out of here. I can see you on some bullshit that's gon' make me handle your ass." Angel stretched his neck while rubbing his bottom lip with the pad of his thumb.

Emmanuel chuckled lowly, and Genesis looked at him with a distressed look on her face.

"You need to leave. I don't even know why you're here." Genesis's voice sounded a little unsteady, but Angel tried to ignore it.

"You don't know why I'm here?" He laughed. "That's how you feel?" He raised his eyebrows at her.

Angel looked between the two of them and his entire body got hot. He could feel his temper flaring, and though he really didn't want to cause a scene at the hospital, Emmanuel was about to get his issue, because clearly that's what he wanted.

"Genesis." Angel called her name coolly. "Put your friend out."

"Emmanuel, leave!" she practically yelled.

"Nah," Emmanuel stood, shaking his head. "I got just as much reason as this nigga to be here, if not more." He shot Angel a sadistic smirk before looking down at the baby. "Judging by the color of his little skin, I'm thinking more."

Everything in Angel's life went red after that statement. He lunged his entire body over the hospital bed and landed on top of Emmanuel. As soon as he laid hands on that nigga, all rationality went out of the window. Angel's fists pounded Emmanuel's face relentlessly. He was so angry that every blow he landed hit harder than the last. He could literally feel the bones in Emmanuel's face begin to break.

Blood from Emmanuel's mouth and nose was everywhere as Emmanuel did his best to gain some sort of leverage on Angel but failed miserably. Angel was angrier; there was no way Emmanuel would be able to stop him or even get a fair fight right then.

"Stop! Angel, please!" Genesis's voice could be heard in the background.

Angel could hear her, but all he saw was Emmanuel. She had played him in the worst way. Fucking off with a nigga beneath him wasn't just disrespectful, it was soul crushing. He'd given up everything for her, and the more he thought about it, the angrier he got.

His hands were moving so fast that every single punch felt like two. His mother's crying face, his father's disappointing words, the cartel turning their backs on him, everything that had been paining him for months came out in his rage. He couldn't be stopped. Nothing would stop him. He'd lost it all, he had nothing else to lose. Fuck being a doctor, what would that mean with no one to share life with?

"Argghhhh!" Angel yelled as he snatched Emmanuel's badly beaten body from the floor and slammed him into the wall. "I'ma fucking kill y'all!" he growled out as he slammed Emmanuel's head into the wall as hard as he could. "You wanna play with me, bitch?" He spun around and pointed at Genesis while still holding Emmanuel in his grip. "I was a fucking fool for you, huh?" He gritted his teeth at her before throwing Emmanuel's body toward the bed where she was.

Emmanuel stumbled some and fell over the side, bumping the baby's bassinet en route to the floor. Angel wanted to care, but he couldn't. That was Emmanuel's fucking baby who would get hurt if his weak ass knocked over the bassinet. Angel was breathing hard as he watched Genesis leap from the bed toward the baby. That one action angered him again. He'd been taking care of that bitch for months, playing her fool.

Angel was furious as he thought about how dumb he must have looked. "I'm the wrong muthafucka to play with." He hit his chest before marching toward where Emmanuel was trying to pull himself from the floor.

A swift kick to the chest halted all of that. Angel was about to hit him again but was stopped. "Angel! Stop it, baby. Come here."

His entire world stopped when he heard his mother's voice. Angel spun around quickly with a look of a lost child on his face. When he spotted her at the door, he went right to her. With open arms, she welcomed him to her. The tears Angel had been holding in for months finally rolled down his face.

"Ma," he sobbed. "They played me. They fucking played me." His voice broke toward the end of his sentence.

Empress was much shorter and smaller than her son, but that meant nothing when he was in need. She held on to him with all of her might, allowing him to vent his feelings to her.

"It's okay, baby. You don't need them." She rubbed his back as he hugged her.

Angel nodded but said nothing as he tried to get a hold of himself. It took a little while and a few more people to help usher him and Emmanuel out of Genesis's room, but after a few minutes, it was all over. He and Empress were seated outside in the waiting room while he relayed to her what had happened.

"How'd you get here so fast?" He looked at her, and she smiled weakly.

"I knew that damn baby wasn't yours, so when Zulema sent me the video of him, I drove straight up here. You're a sweetheart, Angel, but a fool you are not. I knew once you noticed that baby wasn't yours you were going to go apeshit." She covered her face and sighed dramatically. "I'm just glad you beat on that man and not that girl." Empress shook her head. "I don't like her at all, and she does need her ass beat, but I didn't raise you to put your hands on women."

Angel looked at Empress before laughing lowly. "I missed you."

"I missed you too, baby. You came back to your senses yet?"

Angel nodded slowly as he took in the stress lines and dark circles near her eyes. Her smile was still as beautiful as it had always been, only it didn't touch her eyes like it normally did.

"You look tired, you okay?"

She nodded. "I'm fine." Her mouth was saying one thing, but the sullen look on her face was saying another.

"You sure?" He turned in his seat so that he could look at her. "You haven't been worried about me, have you?"

Empress patted the top of his hand. "You're my baby, Angel. Of course I was worried about you." She cleared her throat. "But you needed to learn your lesson."

"I learned it," he told her exasperatedly.

"Good. Come on, there's some stuff you need to know."

Angel pulled her arm and stopped her from getting up from her chair. Her tone was too serious for his liking.

"Like what?"

"I'll tell you at home. Come on, before these people change their mind about locking your ass up."

Angel nodded and rose to his feet. He bypassed the officers, nodding at them subtly before stopping at the door to Genesis's room.

"Hold on, Ma. Let me holla at her really quick."

Empress rolled her eyes. "Angel, your father's grace can only go so far. These cops have let you off the hook once on his behalf, they're not going to do it again."

"I'm good, I promise."

Empress waved her hand toward the door, sending him on his way but making sure to follow right behind. When they got into the room, Genesis was holding the baby with tears on her face. When she saw Angel, the tears began to fall faster. Angel watched her for a minute before touching his chin.

"You were prepared to just let me think that baby was mine, huh?"

Genesis said nothing, just continued to cry.

"I can't believe I was that big a fool. It's cool, though. You ousted you and your baby out of the best life y'all could have ever had. I loved your dog ass from my soul, and you stomped all over me for a nigga that wasn't worth the ground I walk on."

"I'm sorry, Angel," Genesis finally choked out.

"No need, it's your loss. Take care of yourself." He walked to the bed and placed a kiss on her forehead.

Genesis's body began to rock with sobs as her reality overtook her. Angel lingered in her presence a little longer before pulling away and kissing the baby as well.

"Sorry about all of this, little man. You deserved better."

When Angel stood up, Genesis sat helplessly, obviously realizing there was nothing she could say to talk her way out of the mess she'd made.

"Angel," she called out to him as he walked toward the door.

"Save it, Genny. It's over. Don't contact me ever again. Keep all the shit I've gotten for you and little man. Y'all need it more than I do."

With that, Angel walked out of the room and out of Genesis's life . . . forever.

Chapter Nine

You've been gone too long

The atmosphere in their living room was calm and rich, as it always was when Angel walked in. It had been so long since he'd been there that he'd almost forgotten how peaceful he felt whenever he was in his parents' home.

Everything was exactly the same, minus the new locks on the doors and a few other safety precautions that hadn't been there before. Angel bypassed everything and went straight to his room for a shower. He'd been asking his mother over and over on their ride home what was it that she needed to tell him, but she continued brushing him off. Being that he was already tired, Angel simply nodded and left her alone.

"It's about time you came to your senses." Snow's voice startled him.

Angel had just walked out of the bathroom and was securing his towel around his waist when he heard her. She was seated on the bed in a dark gray jogging suit with her hair in a bun at the top of her head. She was just as beautiful as she had been the last time he'd seen her.

"What are you doing here?" He frowned.

"Don't worry about me." She rolled her eyes quickly. "Empress sent me up here to check on your traitorous ass." She stood to her feet and switched toward the door.

Of course, Angel's eyes went directly to her bottom. It was huge and looked even bigger in the thin material of her sweat suit.

"Emelia, get your ass out of my room."

"Gladly, traitor."

His body grew warm, but not warm enough to make him want to say anything else to her. Not that she left him the option. She'd walked out and slammed the door behind her with no hesitation. Angel didn't know who she thought he was, but he could see he was going to have to get her ass together sooner rather than later.

It took him a little over ten minutes to get himself together and get down the stairs. It was quiet, minus the sounds of the television coming from the living room. When he walked in, Empress was seated in her usual spot next to Vinny's La-Z-Boy recliner, while Snow sat across from them on the love seat, and D'Angelo in the corner on the floor. Vinny was watching the large TV as usual and still hadn't looked Angel's way.

Angel wasn't surprised in the least. He had known his father was going to be harder to win over than Empress was going to be. The baby not being his probably hadn't moved Vinny not one bit, because he didn't care about that kind of thing. If he felt that Angel had been disloyal, it was going to take a lot more than a hospital fight and a DNA test to make things right between them.

"What's going on, Daddy?" Angel sat on the stone bench next to the fireplace so that he could be closer to his father.

Vinny's head slowly turned in Angel's direction. He stared at him for a long time with his face frowned in confusion. Angel instantly began to get nervous in anticipation of what was to come next. Whatever it was, he was ready, because he deserved it.

"Angel, what are you doing out of bed this time of night?" Vinny looked down at the watch on his wrist. "Get back to bed right now. You have to be at the schoolhouse in a few hours."

Angel wore a confused expression as Vinny waved him toward the door.

"Did you hear me, boy? Get to bed."

"Daddy." Angel raised his eyebrows. "I don't have school tomorrow. What are you talking about?"

Vinny sat up in his recliner. "Are you calling me a liar, Angel?"

"No, sir. I just don't have school tomorrow." Angel was genuinely confused.

He and his father never talked about his schooling, and he most definitely never spoke to him in that tone. Vinny's voice sounded a little softer than normal, as if speaking to a child. Angel's confusion only heightened when Vinny looked at him and his expression went from distress to flat-out anger. He'd even begun to turn red as he looked over Angel's face.

"Empress, get him away from me. What is he doing here? He chose that damn girl over his own family." He looked back at Angel. "Get out of here right now! You're no son of mine," he fumed.

"Vinny, calm down, baby. Angel's home. He apologized. He misses us." Empress rubbed one of Vinny's hands with both of hers. "Aren't you happy to see him?"

Angel watched as Vinny looked between him and Empress a few more times before nodding slowly. The entire ordeal was throwing Angel for a serious loop, because Vinny had been fine the last time he'd seen him.

"Ma, what's going on?"

Empress gave Angel a sympathetic look as she continued to rub Vinny's hand. "Come help me in the kitchen for a second," she told him before trying to stand.

Vinny's sudden grip on her wrist stopped her. "Don't leave me again, Empress. Stay here please. I won't get angry like that anymore. I'm sorry," he pleaded as water gathered in her eyes.

Angel's heart was breaking as his confusion slowly began to turn into realization. He was almost a doctor—he knew what this was, even if he didn't want to believe it.

"Okay, baby. I'll stay with you." Empress lowered herself back to her sitting position on the sofa and looked at Angel with wet eyes. "Go with Snow, baby. She'll tell you."

Angel looked at his parents for a minute, trying to calm the rapid beating of his heart. This wasn't right, and he could feel it in his gut that whenever his observations were confirmed, he probably wouldn't be able to handle it. He looked between the two people he loved the most in the world, then over to D'Angelo, but his face was just as sad as Angel's. Angel was completely lost until Snow stood to her feet and left the room. Figuring it was better to follow her before he broke down, he rose to his full height and left the living room.

When he walked into the kitchen, Snow was leaning against the large island with her arms folded across her chest. Her face was still as hard as it always was as she watched him walk in and stand in front of her. Angel leaned on the counter with his head slightly bowed. He wanted so badly to confirm what was going on, but he didn't want to ask.

In the back of his mind, he entertained the thought of not listening to anything Snow said. Maybe then whatever it was would go away. All Snow had to do was keep her mouth shut, and he could ignore the inevitable and his life could go back to the way it used to be, with happy and healthy parents.

"Vinny has dementia," Snow said.

Angel's knees buckled, and he felt himself get weak. He hurried to steady himself by placing both of his hands on the counter behind him. His head was starting to spin, and it almost felt too hard to breathe. Snow's one sentence had him on the verge of passing out.

Though she hadn't told him how bad it was, or any of the specifics, he didn't need her to. Angel was in his last year of medical school; he didn't need her to say anything else to him about the disease. He already knew everything there was to know, the most important being that there was no cure.

"It's gotten a lot worse over the past few months while you were gone." Her tone soured at that part.

When Angel's head rose so that they were making eye contact, he could see the hate she had for him in her eyes. It was burning wild and bright. He wanted so badly to be angry with her for feeling that way, but he couldn't. She had every right to feel the way she felt.

He had been gone with people who couldn't care less about him, when he should have been there with his father.

"Had I been here, I would have caught this."

Snow sucked her teeth. "Yeah, but you weren't, Dr. DeLuca."

Angel ignored her comment. "How bad is it?"

Snow looked away from him for a moment, and blinked a few times. For the first time since he'd seen her that day, he noticed she was in just as much pain as Empress. Her poker face had been disguising the hurt that she was harboring for Vinny as well.

"He's a little angrier these days as you can see, but that's about it." She sniffed. "He left the grocery store one day while Empress was shopping, and we couldn't find him for hours."

"Where was he?"

She wiped her eyes quickly and shrugged. "We don't know. A detective from the police station who recognized him called Empress, and we went and got him from there."

Angel's head fell forward as he covered it with one of his hands. Snow's words were killing him softly, and though he wanted her to stop, she couldn't. He needed to know these things. Out of all the people in the house, he would know what to do more than any of them.

"You keep saying *we*. You've been here with them?" He raised his head and looked at her.

She narrowed her eyes at him. "Somebody had to be. Empress couldn't do this alone, and you and I both know that D'Angelo is nothing but an untrustworthy tyrant with no experience. So yes, I've been here for them, where you should have been."

Once again, Angel ignored the anger in her tone. "Why didn't your mom come?"

Snow stood from the counter and dropped her arms to her side. "Because Zulema doesn't run dope anymore, Angel, but I do."

Damn.

Angel's chest sank. That had been the last thing on his mind. "So, you've been working here?"

She nodded once, and her beautiful chocolate skin glistened beneath the light. "And fighting your stupid-ass brother the entire way." She rolled her eyes and sighed with annoyance.

"You good? He hasn't been fucking with you like that for real, has he?"

Snow looked all around the kitchen before she looked back at him and smirked. "I ain't thinking about D'Angelo's annoying ass. I can handle him." She gave Angel the once-over while touching her bottom lip. "But if I'm not good, are you going to help?"

When Angel didn't say anything, she rolled her eyes.

"I didn't think so." She leaned back against the counter and crossed her arms again. "Listen, Angel, I know this is a lot to handle at one time, but you have to get your shit together. This is your shit. That's your damn daddy in there. He can barely remember his own wife some days, so I would advise you to spend as much time with him as you can. Soak up what he might be able to teach, and make you some memories." Her voice broke. "It's getting really bad. He doesn't have long."

When her tears began to fall, it was instinctive for Angel to comfort her. He was off the counter and in front of her in no time. With his long arms wrapped around the top of her shoulders, he pulled her body against his and squeezed her tightly. Snow's shoulders relaxed, allowing him to really feel how soft her body was.

Her breasts were pressed into his chest, while her head lay snuggled beneath his chin. Every so often her body would jump from her sobs, and he'd hold her tighter. When the sound of her cries began to get the best of him, Angel even found himself kissing the top of her head and forehead in comfort.

It was natural the way his lips found various places on her head to render his sympathy. "It'll be okay, Emelia. Don't cry. Vinny will be all right."

She sniffed and nodded but didn't say anything, and Angel was glad that she didn't. What he'd just said was a lie, and he wanted to keep it that way. It felt better. Right then, that was one truth that he wasn't ready to acknowledge.

"You've been staying here?"

She nodded. "Whenever I have time to sleep or when your brother is not here, yes."

Angel's hand slid from her shoulders, down her back, and circled her waist. The way she came to him so willingly, wrapping her arms around him in return, gave him a sense of peace. A peace he hadn't experienced in so long, it almost felt foreign.

"You haven't been sleeping?" He stepped back some and looked down at her. "That's not good."

"Between work and watching your parents, I don't have much time." She looked at him, and apparently made herself angry all over again, because she pushed out of his embrace.

Angel wanted to object but chose not to. "Empress? How has she been?"

Snow shook her head. "Horrible."

Angel figured that. The way Empress and Vinny loved

one another was magical, so for her to have to watch the man she'd spent her entire life with vanish right before her eyes had to have been torture. Just thinking about it made Angel feel even worse. She'd needed him all this time, and he hadn't been there.

"Well, I'm here now. I'll take care of y'all," he stated with finality.

Snow's eyebrows knitted together as she gave him the once-over. "Y'all? Don't you mean them?"

Angel stared down at dominantly. "No. I said what I meant."

"I don't need you to take care of me. I can handle myself, just like I've been doing."

Angel's eyes traveled from her face down over her stomach and stopped at her hips. Angel had always been fond of thick women, and the way Snow was shaped was knee weakening. If the moment had been different, he probably would have grabbed him two handfuls of her and just held on until he felt better, but they weren't like that. Furthermore, she probably wouldn't even let him.

Angel ogled her a little longer while rubbing his bottom lip with the pad of his thumb. "I'm sure you can, but you don't have to. Like I said," he stepped closer to her again. "I'll take care of y'all."

Snow moved to the side, placing a safe distance back between them.

"That's cute, but I'm good on you. If you'd run out on your own family, you'd probably throw my ass to the wolves."

She and Angel stared at one another combatively until she turned and exited the kitchen, leaving him alone. Once she was gone, Angel took a seat on the barstool near the island and put his head down. He had no clue how he was about to get through this, he just knew he had to. As painful as it may have been, he had to. His family needed him.

D'Angelo had been standing in the hallway listening to Angel's soft-ass talk to Snow. Like he'd learned a long time ago, Angel was weak as hell and would do anything for a woman. Judging from the things he'd said to her, he was probably about to try and spark their old flame or some boring shit like that, but D'Angelo had other plans.

"Where you running to so fast?" D'Angelo side-stepped so that he blocked Emelia's path to the living room.

Without uttering a single word, her hand grazed her ponytail swiftly before coming down and slicing the skin on his forearm open. Bright red blood shot out instantly.

"You'd better get your ass away from me if you want to stay alive. I've told you one too many times already, I'm not here for your bullshit. I'm tired of saying the same shit over and over to your non-listening ass." Her bloodshot eyes were cold and dark as she stared at him with her blade still in her hand, clearly ready to slice him to pieces if he didn't back off.

"Fuck you, bitch." He held his arm as blood leaked between his fingers. "I know what to do for you." D'Angelo looked her up and down with a frown on his face.

"I dare you to try it so I can murder your conniving ass." Snow's murderous glare stayed on him until he was halfway up the stairs and out of her line of vision.

Once he was back in his room, D'Angelo hurried to

the sink to wash his arm. It was bleeding terribly, and the last thing he needed was to have Angel or Empress in his business about what happened. How in the hell would he explain to them that Snow was the one who had cut his arm without giving them a reason why?

It took him a little over ten minutes to get cleaned up and to cover his arm with bandages before throwing on a long-sleeved shirt and joining his family back downstairs. When he walked into the living room, his parents were sitting in their same spots with Snow seated on the floor in front of Vinny's chair.

D'Angelo dapped into the living room, took a seat on the sofa in front of them, and gave Snow his full attention. Her beautiful dark skin, thick wide hips, big full breasts, everything about her made him crave her in the worst way. Too bad she'd slit his throat if he got within two feet of her.

It had been so long since he'd seen her that when he finally did, it was hard for him to stop looking at her. She was such a beautiful sight to behold that even with her hating the ground that he walked on, she still held a special place in his heart.

"D'Angelo, are you staying in tonight, baby?" Empress looked at him lovingly.

"I have a quick run to make first, then I'll be in for the night," D'Angelo replied.

D'Angelo needed to hit the ER and get some stiches for the cut on his arm. It was burning like hell, and he needed to make sure he was good before going to bed. He hadn't intended on leaving the house again that night because he'd rather sit around and watch Snow switch her thick ass around, but she'd fucked him up.

Empress smiled. "Good. It's too late to be out anyway, so hurry back. All kinds of people be in the streets this time of night."

"Him being one of them." Snow's voice was like ice.

Empress giggled and tapped Snow's arm playfully. "Stop that, Emelia."

Snow rolled her eyes but said nothing.

D'Angelo, on the other hand, scooted to the edge of his seat and smiled at her. "Why you have to be so mean all the time? What have I ever done to you?" D'Angelo taunted her.

Snow grimaced before giving him her undivided attention. "You have some nerve, you ugly bastard." She moved her mouth and her blade slid to the front of it. "I hate you, now stop talking to me."

"Y'all stop that bickering." Empress interrupted them before it could get too out of hand. "Y'all have been doing this since you were kids. I thought you would have grown out of it by now."

"It's hard to grow out of something when you still haven't grown up." Snow's remark was humorous to D'Angelo.

After laughing, he smiled and winked at Snow just as Angel walked back into the living room with his face long. D'Angelo looked down at his phone to keep himself from frowning at Angel in disgust. He was so annoyed with the person Angel was. He was too kind-hearted to be a part of the drug game.

Why in the fuck their parents continued to try and pass everything off to that nigga was beyond him. He wasn't even ready for that kind of shit. He didn't have enough heart, but D'Angelo had long ago given up on trying to convince them of that. If they didn't want to give it to him, he'd take it. He'd given them more than enough opportunity to see that he was worthy of the job, and they refused to. So now it was time to take matters into his own hands.

D'Angelo sat with his family for a little while longer
before gathering his bearings and leaving the house. He
was headed down the sidewalk to his car when he felt
someone behind him. When he turned around he wasn't
shocked to see it was Snow. She wasn't even five feet
away, and in her hand, she held a small black gun.

"Why you out here fucking with me?" D'Angelo
opened his car door but didn't get in.

"You wish I was fucking with your snake ass,"
Snow told him once she was within a few inches of
him. "I came out here to give you a warning since I see
you think shit's sweet around here."

D'Angelo, looked down at her with a smirk on his
face. Her dark skin glowed in the moonlight as she
stood with her pistol gripped tight in her hand. Her perfect nose and mouth made him want to kiss all over
them, but he already knew how that would play out if
he tried it.

"Go ahead, then, warn me."

"I'm not the same little girl I was back then. If you
keep fucking with me," she stepped closer to him with
a deadly look in her eyes, "you will die. I don't give
a fuck about who you are, who your family is, none
of that shit. Empress will be burying your ass. Don't
test me."

"You know this tough shit makes my dick hard,"
D'Angelo whispered to her.

"I said what I said." She stared him down and turned
to walk away. "Live or die, bitch. It's your choice."

D'Angelo watched the way her ass jiggled with
every step she took. It was so big and bouncy, just like
some shit a black girl would have. Black women—
they were his weakness, and he couldn't stop thinking
about Snow. No matter how many threats she directed

at him, she still made his heart move and his dick hard. All he had to do was figure out a way for her to see he was the type of nigga she needed, and not Angel. If she ever gave him a chance, he and she could be the king and queen of the cartel. He just needed to find a way for her to see that.

D'Angelo watched Snow until she was back in the house before hopping into his car and pulling away. He hit the highway headed to the hospital, smoking a blunt along the way. When he finally got there, he pulled into the closest parking space he could find and got out. The waiting room was ridiculously packed and almost made him want to turn around. The only thing that stopped him was the little chick sitting behind the checkout desk. She looked like somebody he could finesse.

"Excuse me, beautiful. How long is the wait?" he asked.

With much attitude, the girl looked up while smacking on her gum. Upon laying eyes on D'Angelo, she lost the sassiness and smiled. "I'm not sure, but what do you need done?"

D'Angelo smiled at her. "I like your hair." The purple weave wouldn't have normally been to his liking, but the way she had it styled was nice, plus his compliment had her blushing. "But I need a few stitches."

She ran her hand over the back of her hair. "Thank you. Just have a seat right there." She pointed toward a chair. "And fill out that paperwork. I'll get you right on back."

D'Angelo winked at her and took the clipboard she was extending toward him. The seat she motioned for him to sit in was in the corner of the room right next to the check-in desk. D'Angelo took his seat and began filling out the paperwork. It didn't take long for the girl to come back into the waiting room, and when she did, she was calling him to the back.

"Your man paid for that purple hair?" D'Angelo asked as she put a little extra twist in her walk.

"Nah, I don't have a man."

"Well, come holla at me before you leave so we can do something about that." D'Angelo winked at her again as she showed him to his room.

"I'll be sure to do that." She smiled as she exited the room, pulling the door closed behind her.

He didn't know what kind of pull the little receptionist had, because not even five minutes later the doctor had come in and examined his wound. After acknowledging it wasn't deep and hadn't severed anything major, he sent the nurse in to stitch him up. His entire visit lasted almost thirty minutes, and then he was on his way.

D'Angelo strolled up the hallway casually looking for the receptionist when he heard his name being called. When he turned to see who it was, he saw Genesis. She was sitting in a wheelchair holding a baby. Though D'Angelo had heard all about the shit that had gone down with her and Angel, he hadn't reached out to check on her. He didn't care enough.

They hadn't had sex in a while either due to her being too big, so he really didn't see the need to be calling just to check on her. They weren't like that. D'Angelo didn't have a problem fucking her as long as her stomach didn't get in his way, but the moment it began to get too big and prevented her from performing in different positions, he had to let her cool off for a minute. On top of that, that pregnant shit had her looking weird, and he didn't love her enough to look past it.

Her nose and lips had gotten so big, she looked like an ogre. D'Angelo didn't even see how Angel was still laid up with her looking like that. It had to be love, because that baby had Genesis fucked all the way up.

"What's good, Genny?" D'Angelo walked toward her and kneeled down so that he could see the baby.

She pulled the blanket over just enough to show his face.

"Damn, this li'l baby black as hell." D'Angelo chuckled. "I guess I wasn't the only one dipping in Angel's honey pot, huh?"

Genesis rolled her eyes. "Shut up, D'Angelo. I'm not in the mood for your mouth today."

"I feel you, ma, but you know you need your ass beat. If you wanted to keep my brother, you could have at least let me splash off in you. The baby would have looked just like Angel's ass." D'Angelo chuckled at himself.

It may have sounded absurd to anyone who didn't know their history, but it would have been Genesis's best bet if she'd wanted to continue being with Angel. Too bad that was no longer an option. She'd hung herself by getting knocked up by another nigga. Now, Angel had Snow and wasn't giving her ass a second thought.

"I should have just never done this stupid shit in the first place."

D'Angelo could hear the remorse in Genesis' voice and actually felt bad for her. "Yeah, but we all make mistakes. Just take care of li'l man, and holla at me if you ever need some dick." He chuckled and stood up straight.

"How's Angel?" Genesis yelled out just as D'Angelo began to walk away.

"He's cool. Just fucking off with li'l mama from his party."

"Who, Emelia?"

D'Angelo smiled and nodded. "Yeah, her."

Genesis's eyes began to water as she nodded. "I should have already known."

"It's a dog-eat-dog world, boo. Chin up. It ain't like you were doing the nigga right anyway." D'Angelo shrugged and walked away.

He could hear her behind him mumbling something, but he continued on his way. D'Angelo may have not really cared for Angel on a social level, but he was still his blood. Genesis hadn't been right for him. He didn't necessarily think Snow was either, but at least D'Angelo knew without a second thought that she loved the nigga. That was a fact. Snow had been loving Angel since they'd been kids, and even after he'd left for school, she doted on that nigga.

For months, Snow walked around sad as fuck. She'd stopped going places and doing things with her friends, and it started showing. All she did was train and hang out with Mack and Vinny's old asses. One day he'd felt compelled to say something to her, just to make conversation. At first, she hadn't been hearing it, but she eventually let her guard down and conversed with him.

As time passed, they became good friends. At least good enough to hang out and grab food and shit. Somewhere along the way, D'Angelo ended up catching feelings for Snow that she didn't reciprocate, and that fucked him all the way up.

"I'm sorry, D'Angelo, but I love Angel."

D'Angelo sucked his teeth as he thought about what she'd told him the day he told her his truest feelings for her. He couldn't believe she'd been leading him on all that time. They had hung out together plenty of times just laughing and having fun. D'Angelo was sure she'd felt the same way about him but got his feelings crushed when she revealed that she didn't. From that moment to the current one, he hadn't fucked with her.

They'd been through some tough shit together, which only magnified the strain on their relationship, but D'Angelo wouldn't take it back even if he could. For a while, after she moved and he'd gone back to jail, he'd wondered what she was like as an adult, how she was living, and a lot of other stuff that boiled down to him missing her. The day he walked into Angel's party and she was there was the best day of his life. Whether she or anybody else knew it, she was going to be his, and that was the end of that.

"Mr. and Mrs. D'Angelo DeLuca. The muthafucking king and queen of the cartel." D'Angelo laughed to himself.

Soon, and very soon, that would be his reality.

Chapter Ten

I'm a boss

One month later

"What the fuck are y'all doing up in here?" The feminine bass in Snow's voice echoed off the walls of the cool room. "It's not social hour. Y'all hos better get back to fucking work."

She looked around at the empty stations where the women should have been cooking, cutting, and bagging dope, and got angry at how empty they all were.

All of the women clad in the white paper jumpsuits moved around getting back to their stoves. Some of them moving faster than others, but all of them moving. Snow watched in disgust as the ladies made it their business to walk at their own pace as if she was some type of joke. As calm as she was trying her hardest to be, she could still feel her temperature rising.

It had been a little over four months since she'd begun running the spots that Vinny had established in Columbia, and for some reason, the women he had working for him felt the need to test her patience. She'd given them the benefit of the doubt being that she was a fresh face and they never heard of her a day in their life, but her patience had just about run out.

"We get an hour every day for lunch," the mouthiest girl of the group sassed just as Snow walked past her.

Snow spun in her bright red Nike Shox with the speed of lightning. "Your point?"

"It's only been fifty-six minutes. We have four minutes left."

A few snickers could be heard throughout the room from the other childish workers Vinny had hired. One thing Snow hated was being disrespected. Especially by a bitch. The heat that she felt rising up her back wasn't a good sign for the little class clown in her face, but she was doing her best to calm herself down . . . even if theses bitches were trying to feed the beast inside her.

"You think you're funny, don't you?" Snow was surprised by the remark, but her voice remained stern.

The girl looked at the girl next to her before looking back at Snow with a smirk on her face. "Not at all. I was just stating facts."

Snow raised her eyebrow. "Facts, huh?"

She nodded.

"Bet." Snow's hand went to her hair quickly, then swiped across her bun before she swung swiftly at the girl's face.

Blood shot everywhere just as Snow stepped out of the way so that it wouldn't hit her. The long cut from the girl's eyebrow to her chin was leaking uncontrollably as she did her best to stop the bleeding with her glove-covered hands.

"The next time you feel like telling a joke, don't." Snow walked away from her before yelling over her shoulder, "You have the last four minutes of your lunch break to get yourself cleaned up and get back to work before I slit your fucking throat." Snow looked around at the rest of the women, who were looking like deer caught in headlights. "The rest of y'all ugly bitches get back to work."

The room was so quiet you could hear a pin drop, and that was how Snow liked it. They would learn sooner or later that she wasn't the one to be fucked with.

Once she was back in the small office located at the front of the room, she took a seat behind the desk and picked up her phone. She scanned through her messages and missed calls. There were only a few that she deemed important enough to return, Empress's being the first. Empress answered on the first ring.

"What's going on, love?" Snow asked as soon as she heard Empress's voice.

"Nothing, sweetheart. Are you busy?"

Snow looked out the large window of the office to make sure the women were all doing their jobs, and they were. Even Scar Face was at her stove whipping up that work like she'd been taught. Raggedy ass bandage and all.

Snow smirked at her little dumb ass before going back to the call with Empress. "Not really. You need something?"

When Empress paused, Snow knew what was coming next. There was only one subject that Empress held her tongue on, and that was her baby-ass son.

"Well . . ." She paused again. "Have you spoken with Angel today?"

"No, ma'am. Why would I have talked to him? You know your son doesn't like me anymore."

"Don't say that. He does like you."

Snow sucked her teeth as she held her hand up in front of her face so that she could admire her fresh set of nails.

"Well, he sure does have a funny way of showing it."

"He's just going through a lot right now with Vinny being sick and all." Empress said something to someone in the background before coming back over the line with Snow. "Plus, he's trying to get used to all of this right now. You know drugs have never been his thing."

"And clearly it still isn't. That nigga doesn't do anything but get in my way. He's been running around behind me switching up everything I've put into place, and it's really starting to get on my nerves." Snow rolled her eyes. "He'd better be lucky he's your kid and I love you, or else he'd already be dead. Excuse my language, Mrs. Empress, but I'm tired of his ass."

Empress chuckled. "Y'all just be cussing like y'all grown."

They both laughed a little before Empress went back to their conversation.

"Snow, be the bigger person for me, baby. Angel is stubborn like Vinny, and trying to talk to him is like talking to a brick wall. I really need for the two of you to at least get along for business purposes. He's never done any of this before, and you have."

"So, basically you need me to help him?"

Empress laughed quietly again. "Yes, Snow. Help

the boy. He's messing stuff up. You're not the only person calling me."

Snow sat up and palmed her forehead. That was news to her. She'd thought everyone else liked Angel.

"What is he messing up?" she asked eagerly.

"Well, that's the thing. He's not really messing things up, he's just . . . making enemies. He's so mean, no one likes him. They're complaining about him being hard to work with, and how they'd prefer to work with Vinny, and you and I both know that's not about to happen." Empress sighed. "I need the transition from Vinny to Angel to be as smooth as possible."

Snow frowned. That was ho shit. She didn't necessarily care for Angel at the moment, but she was on his side about being mean. The drug game didn't have room for niceness. Who the fuck needed to be friends just to do business? The drug game wasn't a tea party, and the people Vinny had working for him needed to learn that.

"Now, Mrs. Empress, that's crazy. Tell me who said that so I can get rid of them. That's weak."

"Oh Lord, you and Angel are going to be the death of the cartel." She tittered. "It was one of the distributor's wives. She handles all the cocaine intake, and she's complained two weeks in a row about his behavior."

Snow rolled her eyes. "I should have known it was a woman. Women are always doing too much." She stood from the chair. "Okay, I'll handle him."

"Thank you!" Empress exclaimed.

"No problem, but you owe me, because your son is a really big pain in my you-know-what."

"I know, but he's trying." She laughed before ending their conversation.

Snow stayed at the building a little longer before leaving to go find Angel. It had been a month since he'd come to help, and it had been hell on wheels for Snow ever since. From the time he'd decided to quit school and take over the cartel, she'd been having one bad day after the next. He was nothing like the old Angel. He was always so rude that it was hard to even have a casual conversation with him. They fought so much, she might as well have been working with D'Angelo's bitch ass.

Though Snow was extremely okay with not talking to that nigga, it was hard for business. It was bad enough he didn't really know what he was doing, but then he was doing it with an attitude. Snow wasn't the least bit friendly in the streets, but she was tolerable. Angel was downright mean. The only people he acted as if he had some sense with was his parents.

She'd tried to talk as nice to him as she could, being that she wasn't really feeling his disloyalty, but after having her head bitten off every time, Snow kept her distance. The only reason she was even driving to where he was right then was because of Empress. Other than that, she would have continued to move in her circles while he moved in his. He handled paperwork, she handled the streets. Never seeing each other was easy if that's how they chose to keep it.

"Lord, help me so I don't kill this fool," Snow said out loud to herself as she stood in the hallway of the insurance office building that all of the DeLuca Cartel's paperwork was run through.

From where she was standing, she could see Angel sitting at the desk that was farthest back with his head down shuffling through papers. There were three other

desks strategically placed in front of him, all occupied
by women. Anybody who worked there took care of
the technicalities, as well as the legal and illegal illu-
sions of the company. One of them was a real insurance
worker, while the rest of them simply played the role.

Snow stood back watching him for a little while
longer before taking a deep breath and going inside the
room. All three women greeted her as she walked in.
Angel looked up and looked right back down.

Bastard.

Snow rolled her eyes just as she stopped and took a
seat in one of the chairs facing his desk. She waited for
a moment, assuming he would look up and say something. When he didn't, she slammed her phone and
keys down in front of him.

"Good afternoon, Rudeness," she said.

Angel remained silent, reading over the papers in
front of him. With his head down, Snow was able to
take in the beauty of his silky black hair. It was so lus-
trous. Snow sat quietly, watching the thickness of his
eyebrows scrunch up across his face every so often.
The smell of his cologne traveled up her nose and
dampened her panties every time he moved one way or
the other.

"You make me so sick with your mean ass," Snow
spat.

This time he looked up. He stared at her through
dark, piercing eyes as he held the papers in his hand.
The frown on his face was so sexy, Snow wanted to
bite her lip or kiss his. Either one would do her no justice, but it would have been better than torturing herself just by looking at him.

The look on his face showed how disgusted he was
with her presence, and it was pretty comical to her. It

was as if just the sight of her had ruined his entire day, and she couldn't stop herself from laughing.

"What do you want?" His bluntness interrupted her giggles.

Snow held her hand up so that her open palm was flat in her face. "First of all, don't talk to me like that unless you want your throat slit. Secondly, I'm only here because your mama sent me."

His face frowned in concern. "My daddy all right?"

"Your daddy is fine. She just wanted me to come check on you to make sure you're not fucking up their shit."

"Man, get your ass out of here with that. My mama ain't said no mess like that."

Snow raised her eyebrow at him. "You think I'm here just because I wanted to look at your li'l ugly ass? I think not."

Angel's nose twitched on one side as he looked at her. "That makes two of us."

Again, his distaste for her had Snow snickering to herself. "I look better than your ass."

Before she could utter another word, Angel reached across the desk to grab her. With the same swiftness she'd used earlier, this time going to her head, she snatched a small blade out of her bun and cut the top of the hand he had on her. He let her go as soon as he felt his skin slice open.

"Don't put your fucking hands on me." She pulled a tissue from the box on his desk and wiped her blade before sticking it back into the ball of hair on her head.

"Why the fuck would you do that?" Angel glared at her as he stood from his desk, holding his bleeding hand.

Snow didn't flinch as she watched him walk back to

where the bathrooms were located. When he returned, his hand was wrapped in a hand towel. Snow rolled her eyes at his dramatics.

She hadn't even cut him deep enough for him to really bleed, let alone nurse his hand with a towel that dramatically. She had been using her blade since middle school; she knew what to do with it. If she'd really wanted to hurt him, he would have been dead. He was just doing the most right then.

"You better watch your fucking self. You keep doing all that stupid shit if you want to, and see what happens," he threatened her.

Snow smirked at him as she crossed one of her legs over the other. "What you gon' do?"

Angel glowered at her before checking his watch and snatching her from the chair she was sitting in. "Bring your ass on."

"What did I just tell you about putting your hands on me?"

"I don't give a fuck. You don't run me." He looked over his shoulder at her like she was some sort of disobedient child. "And I hope you clean them damn blades you're always whipping out."

Snow snickered at him. "Don't insult me. I don't use the same blade over and over. You think I'll cut people and stick the same blade back into my mouth?" She scoffed in disbelief. "I have bags and bags of blades. I get new ones as soon as I use one. Thank you very much."

"I don't give a fuck what you do, you just better watch yourself when it comes to me." He spoke to her just as nastily as he'd been doing all day while continuing to pull her behind him.

Instead of continuing to fight him, Snow allowed him to pull her from the building. When they got outside, there was a large, black SUV waiting near the curb. It was shiny, and the tint was so dark she couldn't see through the windows. The closer she got, the more she could feel her heartbeat speeding up again. She didn't know what Angel called himself about to do, but she hoped he knew she was going to fight his ass back if it was stupid.

She was prepping herself for battle when a short man dressed impeccably in a black suit with a white undershirt came around to open the door for them. His warm smile and familiar face eased her nerves just a tad as Angel released her hand and shoved her toward the open door. When she stumbled, reflexes made her turn around and swing toward Angel's face, but the man grabbed her hand and helped her into the back seat of the truck instead, while Angel's dumb ass stood there watching.

"You're lucky he grabbed me," she hissed before getting completely into the truck.

As soon as she was inside, every breath she took was filled with the intoxicating and familiar smell of some sort of male cologne. It was mouthwatering and had her breathing a little deeper with each breath. As she continued to inhale, she realized where she knew it from. It was Angel's.

This was his truck and Vinny's driver. She watched intently as Angel moved around the front of the truck to get in. When he and the driver were both inside, she tried her best not to look at him. His whole little "take charge" tantrum was turning her on, and she refused to let him know it. Once they were in, the driver pulled away. She looked around, anticipating something rude to come from Angel's mouth, but it didn't.

He hadn't spoken to her, nor had he looked her way since they'd been in the truck, so she would give him the same treatment. She kept her head straight, only looking out the window as they passed her truck to make sure she'd locked her doors. Once she'd stuck her key fob back into her small gold wristlet, she made herself comfortable.

As the ride grew more and more uncomfortable, she tried her best to be discreet as she looked over at Angel. Vinny, Mack, and all of the rest of the men she'd grown up around were nice and doted on their women. The love and adoration they showed their wives was out of this world. She didn't know what the fuck happened to Angel and D'Angelo.

Maybe it was that ho Genesis. She probably had his trust jacked up. Then again, maybe it was just that nigga's blood, because D'Angelo was even worse than his ass. Snow turned her nose up when she looked at him again sitting there looking all extra sexy in his expensive suit. Why couldn't he wear street clothes like everybody else?

The black-on-black suit he was wearing was tailored to fit his frame. She eyed the way his body poked out in certain spots; muscles across his chest and filling out his long arms. The way his legs were stretched out showed how tall he was even with him sitting down. Making him even sexier, the long curl of his eyelashes rested comfortably over his eyes, guarding the low pupils she could hardly see due to the scowl on his face.

The full reddish pink lips weren't too big, but they

stuck out in something similar to a puckered-up pout. As if he was waiting for someone to come along and kiss them. A small task she wouldn't be opposed to completing if he wasn't such a jackass.

Snow subconsciously licked her lips when she noticed the dark black hair that lay down around his face and down near his ears. How had she missed all of that sexiness before? She could bet it was his attitude. It had probably blocked her vision.

Snow rolled her eyes at herself, because even with her not being able to see his full face and take in his full appearance, she was weakening. Angel was such a panty wetter, and it was irritating, because he didn't need to be, for two reasons. The first one being she didn't want to crave him that way anymore, and the second was because he probably had hos coming out of the woodwork. Snow was possessive and didn't have time to be killing bitches every day for fucking off with Angel.

Even having been with Genesis, Snow could bet Angel had more women than he knew what to do with. She could tell by his appearance alone. He was so beautiful from the side, she could look at him forever, but she was sure his mouth wouldn't allow it.

"Nigga, don't be trying to kidnap me," Snow said to ease the sexual tension she felt building.

They had been driving for a good bit of time and still hadn't gotten anywhere. The abruptness of his departure from his office had been startling, but being tossed in the back seat of his vehicle with him was even worse, especially since he wasn't saying anything to her. It didn't make Snow nervous or anything, but she still wanted to know where she was being taken to.

"Shut up," he hissed.

Snow chuckled and was about to hit him with something else smart but changed her mind. He was clearly still pissed off, so she'd leave him be.

"Mr. DeLuca, would you like to stop by the house first?" the driver asked.

"No. Go ahead to the spot," Angel asked.

Snow wanted so badly to fan herself. She wasn't sure if it was being stuck in the back seat with him, or the fact that she hadn't had sex since the last time he'd touched her, but everything about Angel was killing her. It was as if she was seeing him for the first time again. When she thought about it, she realized she was.

Before his birthday party, she hadn't seen him in years, and he was still somewhat of a child back then. Totally different from now. He was now a delectable grown man, and she was tired of ignoring it. He had been nothing more than a friend, and even an enemy over the past few months, and that left no room for a lover. But in that moment, he was all of that. Snow couldn't understand how one person could ooze so much sex appeal without even trying.

He moved over a little in the seat and cleared his throat. Snow wanted to spin completely around and just stare at him. She wanted to watch him do absolutely nothing, just talk and be sexy. Even the way he cleared his throat made her body yearn.

Angel. His name surely was fitting. He was indeed an angelic fixture to gaze upon. Snow covered her face. She was getting carried away, and she was embarrassed for her own self. He obviously hadn't thought about her like that again, so she needed to stop.

"So, you're really not going to say anything?" she asked.

He kept his gaze forward but pressed the towel wrapped around his hand down a little more, and she smirked. Clearly, he wanted to remind her that he wasn't dealing with her right then. Snow tried her hardest but couldn't stop the laughter that vibrated from her chest. She laughed a little while before Angel cut his sexy eyes at her. She stopped that time.

They remained quiet until they got to their destination. When the truck stopped, Snow began to get anxious again. She cleared her throat and touched the top of her bun where her blade was resting before sliding her hand to the base of her back where her gun was and patting it to be sure it was secure.

A few seconds later, her door opened and the driver helped her from the back seat again. Once she was on her feet, she turned toward the truck and checked her appearance in the tint. She made sure her clothes were still fitting her right before looking around. They were at some expensive-looking hotel.

Snow smirked to herself as she instantly became a little more relaxed. Sex with Angel was something she could handle. Maybe it would even get them on the same page and they could stop fighting. She waited near her door but began to get impatient when it took Angel too long to come around the car.

"Angel, come on so I can get back to my day," she yelled through the glass as she tapped on it.

The driver standing behind her chuckled before wiping the smirk from his face when Angel rounded the car.

"One day, you're going to learn to respect the position that you're in." Angel looked down at her.

"Position I'm in? You have clearly lost your mind." She waved him off dismissively.

Before she could even utter another word, Angel walked up on her so that their chests were touching. He frowned a little, causing his thick, black eyebrows to connect, giving an illusion of a unibrow. Snow stood her ground, not budging an inch. Angel didn't intimidate her.

"Yeah, as a woman," he clarified.

For a moment, Snow was taken aback by his verbiage. "Excuse me?"

Irritation and annoyance leaked from every word he said. "You heard me." He was just as short as he had been with her lately.

Snow didn't appreciate his belittlement at all. He was always trying to pull rank on her for being a woman, and she despised it. True enough she was a woman, but she'd put in just as much, if not more, work than men. Him especially. His condescending remarks about her being a woman were two minutes from getting him cut from his throat to his forehead.

"Angel, this is my last time telling you to respect me and to stop treating me like I'm one of these other women." Snow's eyes pinched in the corners as she frowned at him. "I won't say it again." Snow meant that from the bottom of her heart. She looked at him only a few seconds longer before looking at the driver. "Are you coming along?"

"No, ma'am. I'll be in the car," the driver answered.

She nodded at him before looking back at Angel, who was wearing his same frown from a few moments ago. "Lead the way, rude ass."

"Learn to follow, and I will." His voice held the familiar sternness she'd been hearing all day.

Instead of arguing with him or saying anything that

might stir up any more ill feelings between the two of them, she gave a curt nod and motioned her hand in front of them for him to lead the way. He gave her the once-over before grabbing the bottom of her arm and pulling her up next to him.

Chapter Eleven

I don't want to
need you

Although she could think of a million things she'd
rather be doing, Snow stayed close to Angel. His attitude was annoying, and really irritating her, but she
needed to focus on the matter at hand. She hated he
was taking her somewhere she had no knowledge of.
She never allowed that. Snow prided herself on being
aware of her surroundings at all times, and thanks to
Angel, that wasn't happening today.

Angel was moving up the sidewalk with purpose,
leaving her a few steps behind. Though he wasn't going
too fast, she wasn't sure she wanted to catch completely
up to him, so she fell back and took in her surroundings.
When they got inside, he walked straight past the front
desk and over to the elevators. Once they were on it, he
pressed the button for the eighth floor.

"When we get inside, just be quiet and pay attention. I want you to give me your take on these characters," Angel said.

"Yes, sir, Daddy," Snow sassed sarcastically. He didn't have to tell her to pay attention, she was going to do that anyway.

Angel cleared his throat and crossed one of his ankles over the other but kept his gaze straight ahead. When the elevator dinged, Snow stood to the side to allow him off before her. Once he'd exited, she followed closely and stopped when he stopped.

There was no noise on the other end of the door he'd stopped in front of, but he knocked once anyway. A few seconds later, from behind the door, they heard a quick shout. Someone was telling them to come in.

Snow looked at him. "You familiar with these people?"

Angel nodded and opened the door. He stood to the side so that she could walk in first. Once Snow stepped seductively in front of him, he pushed the door closed behind them. There was a small table in the center of the floor with two men seated at it. Upon seeing Angel, they both smiled and extended their hands for a handshake. He walked to the table and shook both of their hands.

Before sitting down, Angel pulled the chair next to him out and turned toward Snow. Surprising her, he held his hand out toward her, and she took it. Giving a warm smile to both men, Snow took the seat that Angel had pulled out for her. She made herself comfortable as the three men took in her presence, clearly enjoying it, being that they hadn't taken their eyes off her since she'd come in. Angel shot Snow a smile that had to be the most beautiful thing she'd ever seen, and he grabbed her hand.

Holding it in his, he turned to face both of the men. "This is my business partner, Snow." He looked at her. "Snow, say hello."

Snow wasn't sure whether the last few months of his growing irritation for her had been all a figment of her imagination or if he was really that great an actor. The way he was talking to her right then, one would assume he had sugar dropping from his lips. Even the simplest thing sounded sweet.

"Nice to meet you." Snow greeted the men.

"Good to have you," both men said before returning their gazes back to Angel, while his lingered on Snow for a little while longer. Once he'd taken her in enough, he turned to handle business.

"Shall we get started?" Angel asked.

The larger of the two men nodded and jumped from the table to grab a briefcase. He fumbled with a few folders before pulling out two manila ones and laying them on the table for everyone to see. Angel, still holding Snow's hand, leaned forward and examined the papers that had just been placed in front of them.

Snow wanted so badly to look over the paperwork as well to see what the meeting was about, but she chose to stay upright in her chair. With Angel leaned over reading the documents, there was no one to watch the men except for her. Which she had no problem doing, especially since they were both still ogling her. Snow glared at them both for a moment, hoping to let them know that she wasn't there for their viewing pleasure, but obviously they completely missed that memo, because they continued to stare.

"Is there something I can do for you gentlemen?" Her eyebrow raised in question.

The larger one smiled and looked away while the smaller one shook his head. "No, ma'am. You're just very beautiful. Excuse me for not being able to look away."

A small chuckle left the other one's throat before he returned his gaze back upon her.

"Are you two here to do business or to lose your lives?" Snow scooted forward in her seat.

Both of their facial expressions changed. One looked angry while the other apparently thought she was a joke. A small smirk rested on his lips as he licked them at her. Angered by their lack of respect, Snow reached behind her back. If her words hadn't showed them how serious she was, she was more than positive her gun would.

Before she could remove it from her holster, Angel's hand that had just been holding hers now rested on the top of her hand. His grip tightened, stopping her from pulling her gun out. Snow's eyes went to his momentarily, only to find out that he wasn't looking at her, but at the men instead.

"We're here to set up distribution to the lower region of your country, correct?" Angel's voice was low and calm as always.

Both men looked to him before nodding once.

"Disrespect Snow again, and our meeting is over."

Snow wanted to kiss all over Angel's sexy face for defending her like that, but she had to remain professional. That would be all the three men needed to further disregard her presence as if she wasn't just as important as they were. "Along with any future hopes of connecting with the DeLuca Cartel," she added instead.

"Our apologies, ma'am," the larger one said. "We're not used to doing business with women. In our country, women aren't allowed to be involved in this type of thing."

"Well, Snow is the queen of the DeLuca Cartel. It'll do you both well to remember that from this day on," Angel warned.

The men nodded feverishly at Angel before darting their eyes back to the paperwork. Snow's chest relaxed some as she felt Angel's grip on her hand release. She assumed he was about to put it back in his lap but was surprised when he grabbed and held her other hand.

Although she'd never tell him, she liked holding his hand. It felt good. Safe, even. True enough she felt safe wherever she was, being that she could protect herself. Angel's grip on her was different. The type of different that she'd done her best to avoid for many years, but had no desire to right then. He could hold her hand until the sun set, and she'd be just fine with it.

"Will it be you two every time?" Angel sat back in the chair and rested his and Snow's hands on his thigh.

Oh Lord. Snow's chest sank. She wanted to snatch her hand away so badly, but remained calm. It was way too close to the bulge in his thin suit pants for her comfort, and she couldn't be sure that she wouldn't reach out and grab it. With her top lip tucked between her teeth, Snow concentrated on her breathing and not the warmth coming from Angel's lap.

"Yes, sir," the smaller dealer replied as he shuffled all their paperwork back into the black briefcase in his lap.

"Cool. See y'all next month." Angel went to stand up but was stopped by the man that had been smiling at Snow.

"Send our blessings to Vinny, will you?"

Angel nodded before rising to his feet.

"Didn't know he was retiring this soon. We just spoke a few months back and he didn't mention a thing."

"His retirement wasn't any of your concern. Business is business. His personal life is reserved for those that love him," Snow responded before Angel could say anything.

Both men expressed their understanding as Snow and Angel prepared to leave. He was still holding her hand, and she had no desire to pull it away. A few more things were spoken between Angel and the men before they were back on the other side of the door and headed for the elevator.

"You okay?" Snow asked Angel as soon as the door to the elevators closed.

His face was long with sadness, but he nodded anyway. Snow could tell that he was lying, so instead of continuing to interrogate him, she walked so that she was directly in front of him and grabbed his other hand in hers. With both of his smooth hands in hers, she leaned forward and kissed his cheek.

His eyes came to hers, and the sadness that accompanied them was enough to make her want to shed a few tears, but right then wasn't the time. She needed to be strong for him.

"You're going to be okay. Vinny has lived a full life, Angel." She gave him a sympathetic look when his eyes glossed over. "Oh, Angel." She sighed before grabbing his head and pulling it down onto her shoulder. "Don't be sad, baby. I know it's hard, but you have to be stronger than this. Everyone that depended on Vinny is going to need you."

He nodded against her shoulder, but didn't say anything. Snow could feel his chest rising and falling against
hers, and her heart went out to him. Angel wasn't like
her. She'd been in the streets so long that she was accustomed to taking losses, no matter how they came. Angel
was not. His life had been nothing of the sort, so having to watch his father circle the drain was taking a
major toll on him, and Snow was positive that he was
going to fall apart before it was all over with.

"I'll be here, okay?" Snow assured her once best
friend. She rubbed her hand up and down his back as
the elevator dinged.

He nodded again, but remained silent.

When the doors opened, Snow stepped out of his
grasp and held his face in her hands. His dark eyes appeared darker, and void of emotion.

"You're stronger than you think, Angel, and so am
I." She smiled at him. "I'll help you take care of everything until you can manage it on your own."

"Then what?"

Snow frowned, unsure of what he was asking.

Angel exited the elevator and she followed. They
were outside walking down the winding sidewalk to
his truck before he began talking again.

"You said you'll help me take care of things until I
can do it on my own," He looked back at her. "Then
what? Once I'm able to handle everything, what are
you going to do?" He stopped in front of his truck,
blocking her from getting in. "You're going to leave?"

Like it had been doing all day, his voice awakened
the softer side of her. Snow wanted to wrap her arms
around him and tell him that she would be there as long
as he needed her to be, but she couldn't. That would be

too weak and too girly for her image. Furthermore, Angel was just in his feelings right then. He normally hated the ground she walked on. There was no way in the world he actually wanted her to stay with him.

"You are, aren't you?" He squinted his eyes at her.

Snow looked away for a minute before giving him back her attention. "You want me to?"

His handsome brown face was sad, but still strong, and a tad bit intimidating as she stood there looking at him. Snow couldn't explain why she felt like she was in love with him at that moment, but the feeling was so strong, she almost belted out the words. As if maintaining her composure wasn't hard enough, when he shook his head that he didn't want her to leave, she nearly bowed out and gave him her heart.

"You want me to stay?" she asked in disbelief.

Angel closed his eyes momentarily before opening them and grabbing her by her waist and pulling her to him. With one of his long arms draped loosely around her waist, Snow stood chest to chest with him.

"I need you to stay," he whispered into her ear. "I don't think I can do any of this without you."

Take me now, Lord. Snow melted in his embrace. "You can, but I'll stay until you know that for yourself."

Angel released a deep sigh as if he'd been holding his breath, and kissed her forehead. "Thank you, beautiful."

"Angel." His name was a desperate plea on her lips.

"I know, baby girl. I know." He hugged her to him before resting his lips on her temple a few times and then finally allowing them to land on her mouth.

Whatever self-control Snow had left flew out of the

window at that moment. Her body weakened for his, and she opened herself up to the passion that he was relaying through his mouth. The softness of his pink lips meshed with the warmth of his thick tongue made her stomach float with butterflies.

Angel's mouth was intrusive and controlling as he dominated their kiss. With greedy hands resting on her back, pulling her closer to him, he kissed her with a ferocity that she welcomed wholeheartedly. The way his mouth on hers made her body feel was indescribable, and all Snow wanted was to feel it forever.

"I don't want to need you, Emelia." He pulled back only enough to whisper against her lips.

Snow wasn't sure what he wanted her to say to that, so she said nothing. She waited in anticipation of his lips finding hers once again, but when they didn't, she gathered herself and pulled out of his embrace. Before looking at him, she fixed her clothes and took a deep breath. She needed to make sure she had herself together before his gaze disarmed her, as it had been doing all day.

When she was finally ready, she looked up and he was staring at her.

"I'm sorry. I shouldn't have kissed you like that." He spoke remorsefully.

Snow giggled nervously. "You're right. You shouldn't have."

Angel's smile was soft, and barely there, but she saw it.

"You ready?"

Snow nodded before stepping around him and letting him help her into the car. Once she was in, she turned so that she was facing the window, and that was where she remained until they parked next to her car. Before getting out, she looked over her shoulder at him.

"Don't overthink this, Angel. You've got it."

He smiled and grabbed her hand. "As long as I have you too."

"Angel." She said his name with warning, and he smiled before raising his hands in surrender.

"Sorry. I can't help it."

"Well try to," she told him, and got out.

When she was in her car, his truck pulled away. Snow laid her head on her steering wheel and took a few deep breaths. Angel was seriously killing her. One minute he hated her, the next he was kissing her like she'd never been kissed. She wasn't sure which one she preferred, but judging by the way her stomach was flipping, she was going to have to go with him hating her. At least then she could trust herself. Trust herself not to like him, not to touch him, not to crave him, but most importantly, not to love him. She'd done it before and had vowed never to do it again.

"What do you mean you're leaving?" Emelia sat on the edge of Angel's bed with her heart in her throat.

Angel kneeled on the floor in front of her. "I got accepted into Clemson University, so I have to leave."

"Why can't you just stay here and go to school?"

"Clemson has a better program for my major." He grabbed both of Emelia's hands. *"Why don't you just come with me?"*

Emelia stood from the bed and walked near the window. "I can't. My family needs me here."

Angel stood to his full height and stared at her. "And I need you there . . . with me. Don't you want to be with me?"

"Yes, Angel, but you know I can't leave the cartel right now."

Angel's head dropped, and his room grew quiet. "So, you're going to choose the cartel over me?"

Emelia grabbed both sides of her head. She hated that this was happening. They'd only been together for a few months, but she was in love with him. So deeply that she could literally feel her heart breaking in her chest. Though they'd been doing their best to keep it a secret, their relationship was the best part of her young life.

Before getting involved with Angel, all she'd known was the love from her father, but after receiving real love from a man, she never wanted to be without it. Especially the kind of love Angel gave. It was like taking a breath of fresh air. Now it was all about to be taken away, and she could already tell she wasn't going to be able to handle it.

"There are schools here, Angel. Please stay with me." She walked to him and wrapped her arms around his waist, squeezing him tightly to her. "I don't want you to go."

"I have to. Just come with me."

Emelia's tears began to flow. She couldn't do that. The cartel may have meant nothing to Angel, but it was everything to her. She loved that life and wouldn't trade her family for anything or anybody. With regret in her heart, Emelia pulled away from him.

"Emelia." Angel called her name and tried to pull her back to him, but she wouldn't go. "Come with me."

"I can't."

He looked at her for a few minutes longer before nodding in defeat. "So, does that mean you can't be my girlfriend anymore either?"

"Yes," she whispered, trying to stop herself from crying.

"What? Why?"

Emelia leaned down to grab her backpack from the floor. "Because you'll find somebody else once you're there and break up with me. I don't want to do that." She sniffed and wiped her face with the back of her hand.

"No, I won't."

"Yes, you will. I know you. They're going to love you, and you'll forget all about me." Emelia shook her head. "I'm sorry. I have to go." She turned to leave, but Angel grabbed her from behind before she could walk out of his bedroom.

"I love you."

"I love you too. Have fun at school."

The pain that Snow felt in her chest had lingered on for months and resurfaced whenever she thought about him. It took her nearly a year to be able to hear his name without getting sad again, not to mention all of the heartache she experienced after that. Snow promised herself the day that Angel left for school that she'd never love again, and she'd kept the promise without a problem, until now. Being near him and around him was bringing it all back, and she didn't know if she could handle it.

A'zayler

Being friends and coworkers with Angel was one thing, but giving herself to him again was too much to handle. The way she'd loved him back then was stronger than anything she'd ever felt, and she had been a child, so she could only imagine what loving him as a grown woman would do to her.

Chapter Twelve

You're going to learn to listen

"That's not what I asked you. I know what's already been ordered. I asked you to add another." D'Angelo leaned back in the chair of Vinny's home office. "Very well. When should I expect it?" He paused and listened to the woman's voice. "Thank you. I'll be looking for it." D'Angelo placed the receiver back onto the hook, ending their call.

It was about time for him to get things rolling. He'd been sitting back on his thumbs for long enough. He couldn't possibly take over the streets waiting on his parents to dismiss their feelings for Angel long enough to appoint him the leader. He'd given them enough time to make some changes, and they still hadn't, so he would.

"What you doing in here, boy?" Empress walked in with her hands on her hips.

D'Angelo looked up at her with a smile on his face. "Nothing, just thinking about Daddy. What do you think is going to happen with him?"

Empress's face saddened as she walked farther into the room and sat down on the small sofa in the corner. "I wish I knew."

D'Angelo hated to make his mother sad, but he needed some sort of distraction. His mother was a very smart woman, and sneaky. If he didn't throw her mind away off to something else, she probably would have snooped all around behind him, asking a million and one questions along the way to make sure he wasn't lying. She'd been that way since he was a child. True enough, he was indeed a liar and a crafty person who needed extra supervision, but she didn't have to make it so blatant.

"Yeah, that's something we probably need to figure out sooner rather than later. There's stuff that needs to be handled."

Empress's facial expression changed immediately. "Things like what, D'Angelo? Your ass is always up to something." She began looking around the room. "You probably had your ass in here trying to find a way to come up." She stood and walked toward him.

D'Angelo had done exactly what he hadn't wanted to do, but he needed to begin mapping out his game plan. Time was passing too fast, and before long, the cartel would become comfortable with Angel becoming the new leader, and D'Angelo didn't want that.

"I ain't up to nothing, Ma. I'm just saying we can't sit around letting all Daddy's hard work go to waste. If we don't put the right people in place, that's exactly what's going to happen."

Empress stood next to Vinny's desk and leaned on it. "Right people?" She frowned. "I know you're not trying to talk about Angel."

D'Angelo's entire mood shifted. It was no secret that Angel was Empress's favorite. Anybody with eyes could see that, but it still irritated him that she didn't try to hide it from him. The least she could do was pretend to not have a favorite.

"You love taking up for that nigga."

"I'm not taking up for anybody, I'm just trying to gain clarification. You're just sitting here saying everything but what you really want to say. Open your mouth and tell me what's on your mind." She leaned against the desk and folded her arms across her chest.

"I'm just saying I can help out. Y'all have put Angel in charge, and that nigga doesn't know shit. I don't see how y'all would look right over me and go straight to him."

"Because he's more focused than you, D'Angelo. We can't entrust everything we've worked for to you, and then you wind up back in jail or doing some stuff that will get us busted." Empress shook her head. "You're just not right for that job, but that doesn't mean you can't help in other areas."

"Y'all love that nigga Angel. He's your favorite."

Before he could see what she was doing, Empress jumped up and grabbed the bottom of his face. "Listen to me, D'Angelo. You've been using that same excuse since you were a child. Stop it now. Just stop it. We don't favor Angel over you. We favor the things he does. All you do is buck against us and get into trouble, while Angel goes to school and does whatever we ask of him." Empress squinted her eyes at him. "I love you just as much as I love him. I don't favor one of my boys over the other. Maybe if you would stop worrying about the way we are with Angel, you could see how we are with you."

Empress let his face go and walked back toward the door. "All the money we've spent getting you lawyers and paying people off to keep you out of court is love. Continuing to keep you around even when we know you don't really care for us is love." She looked at him over her shoulder once more before leaving. "Get out of your feelings so you can see that your family is for you, not against you." After that, she left.

D'Angelo watched her retreat out of the office and held his head down on the desk. He'd heard what she was saying and had even thought about that on many days, but actions spoke louder than words. They could tell him all day how they felt, but the things they did for Angel showed him how they really felt.

"Fuck them. I'm all I got." D'Angelo rose to his feet. "I want it all, so that's what I'ma get." He stretched and exited the office.

He had places to go and people to see. He was done wasting his time at the DeLuca estate.

Angel sat in the back seat of the truck with his mind all over the place, from his father's health to Emelia being back in his life. He had been doing everything he could to stay away from her, but it was getting harder and harder. For months he'd been doing his best to avoid her, even going out of his way to be mean to her, but that was all starting to become impossible as well.

Had he known giving up medical school to take over the cartel would have put such a mental strain on him, he probably would have never done it, but it was too late to turn back now. After the night he found out about his father's health, he fell into a depression. One so strong that he'd even considered giving everything over to D'Angelo, even when he knew that would be equivalent to flushing it down the drain. D'Angelo was too hotheaded, with not an ounce of business savvy. Deep in his feelings, it took nearly two weeks for Angel to come to terms with what he had to do, and when he finally did, he was slapped in the face with yet another hardship.

Being in love with Snow was something he'd thought he'd gotten over. Apparently, he hadn't. The love he'd held for her had been so many years ago, he'd thought for sure it had blown away with the wind. How wrong had he been? Just the sight of her made his heart happy, so actually, tasting her lips and touching her body put him into an entirely different state of mind.

"Going home, sir?" his driver asked from the front seat.

"Yes, please," Angel said.

The driver nodded once before taking the route to Angel's condo. That was another thing he'd done to help rid his life of Snow. She had been staying down the hall from him at his parents' house, and it was killing him. He had to watch her walk around in her tight little pajamas every night or bump into her in her towel every morning when trying to get into the bathroom.

Her presence was consuming him, so he ran. Just like he'd done when they were kids. The way he loved Emelia had him second-guessing everything he'd planned for his life, so the moment he got his acceptance letter to college, he'd been on the first thing smoking out of California. It had hurt like all hell to leave her behind, but that only confirmed that it was the right decision. He was too young to be that deeply involved with anyone.

"Your friend, Miss Snow, she's a gem." His driver's voice brought him out of his thoughts.

Angel looked out of the window before nodding. "She's something."

His driver chuckled. "Why are you so hard on her? You seem to be really sweet on each other."

Angel ran his hand over his face. "That's the problem."

His driver nodded as he pulled into the parking space in front of Angel's condo. The truck was quiet as Angel got out and closed the door. His driver was standing to the side, waiting for Angel to retreat before getting back into the truck.

"Happiness is good for the soul, Mr. DeLuca. You're young, live a little." He tipped his hat at Angel before getting back into the driver seat.

Angel stood stuck as the truck pulled away from the curb. His heart agreed with his driver, but his mind wanted no part of a love with Snow. Love took too much out of a person. After Genesis, Angel wasn't even sure if he was capable of loving a woman the right way anymore.

He stood outside only a few moments longer before going inside. With nothing better to do, he turned his video game on and played that until he got hungry. After shutting it back off, he walked into the kitchen to find something to eat. Angel sifted through all of the cabinets and the refrigerator before growing angry.

"Fuck!" he groaned.

He was fresh out of groceries and had no interest in going to the store. It was going on eight o'clock at night, and he wanted nothing more than to just get into his bed and go to sleep. Too bad his body had other plans. His stomach was aching and growling at the same time, so he called his mother. She answered immediately.

"Hey, baby." She greeted him warmly.

"Hey, Ma. Did you cook?"

She snickered. "Not tonight. I took your father to his favorite Italian restaurant. It was a good day, so I wanted to make sure we enjoyed it."

Angel smiled upon hearing his father had been himself that day. It was rare that he had "good days," as Empress liked to call them, so when he did, they made sure to take full advantage of it.

"Okay, well I won't hold you. Tell Daddy I love him."

She snickered at someone in the background before coming back on the line. "Vinny says get your own woman to cook for you, and stop calling his."

Empress's happy laughter made Angel feel even better, at least for the moment.

"I'll be right back, Vinny. Give me one second," Empress told his father. A few seconds later she was back on the phone. "A detective came by the estate yesterday. They couldn't get in, but the fact that they were even here is what's worrying me."

Her words knocked the wind completely out of Angel. "Did they leave a card or any form of contact?"

"No, I just saw them snooping around the gates," she whispered. "I don't want to tell Vinny and upset him on such a good day."

Angel held his head down. "I understand, Ma. I'll take care of it."

"Okay, baby. I love you."

"Love you too, and give Daddy my best."

"You just do like your father told you and get your own woman." Empress's laughter carried through the receiver, pulling a small chuckle from Angel as well.

He laughed and joked with her for a little while longer before ending their call. His father was right.

Maybe he did need his own woman. Angel sat stretched out on his sofa for a little while longer before getting up and getting dressed. He threw on a hoodie and some flip-flops, and then grabbed his keys.

He was in his car and headed down the highway in no time. It felt so good to be in his car that he took the long way to his favorite restaurant. Being driven around in his father's truck was annoying, but a safety precaution that Empress felt the need to take, so he obliged. Now, with all of the sporadic police visits, he was starting to think she was right. With a deep sigh, Angel pulled into the parking lot of the restaurant with a heavy heart and full mind. He was doing everything he could for his family, and he was still being met with hardships.

Angel was still bothered by what his mother had shared with him when he pulled around to the window to get his food and saw a familiar face standing on the inside. He watched her and the way she laughed with the man standing behind her. Momentarily, he wondered if they were together, but quickly pushed that from his mind. That wasn't his business, at least he didn't want it to be.

He was so enthralled by the woman and the man that he didn't even hear the man trying to hand him his food.

"Sir!" the guy with the greasy brown bag yelled again.

Angel shot the man a menacing glare before snatching his food and driving to the parking space in front of him. He didn't know what had gotten into him, but he was out of his car within seconds. He walked with a purpose and snatched the door to the restaurant open.

She must have felt his presence because as soon as

he got inside, she turned to look at him. The smile that had just been on her face shrank some as she turned back around so that she was no longer facing him. That one action pushed Angel over the edge, because she had just been laughs and giggles with the dirty-shoe-wearing nigga that was next to her but had the nerve to frown at him.

Hell no. He wasn't having that. Without thinking, Angel walked to her and grabbed her arm. "What you doing out by yourself this time of night?" he asked her with his eyebrows knitted together.

She snatched away immediately, causing somewhat of a scene. "I have already told you too many times about grabbing on me like that."

Angel's temper shot through the roof as soon as he noticed people looking at them. "Snow, don't fuck with me," he gritted out.

"You started it, snatching on me and shit. What's wrong with you anyway?" She looked at him with her frown mirroring his.

Angel's eyes surveyed her smooth chocolate face as her words circled his brain. What was his problem? Why was he so concerned about her safety or so angry at the man's presence next to her? He was all fucked up and couldn't even think of what to say.

"How did you even know I was here?" she asked with an attitude.

Angel looked around at the people looking at them before speaking lower. "I saw you from the drive-thru."

"And you wanted to check on me?"

He nodded.

"Oh, okay. I'm good. Just hungry." Her tone softened some after his admission.

Angel was about to tell her he'd see her later and

just go home until the man she'd been talking to earlier touched her shoulder in an attempt to nudge her up in line. Angel's blood boiled over for a reason he couldn't explain, and he pushed the man before he could stop himself.

"Don't fucking touch her," he said, his voice low.

Snow frowned along with the rest of the people in line. "Angel, what the fuck are you doing?" she asked before looking from the man back to him.

"Bruh, you better keep your fucking hands to yourself." The man began walking up on Angel like he was going to do something but was stopped by Snow's hand.

She pressed it into the middle of his chest at the same time she grabbed Angel's arm. "Y'all stop it."

"Fuck this dude, li'l mama. He got the right nigga tonight," the man said as he swelled up like he wanted to fight.

Angel, on the other hand, stood tall and quiet. He wasn't the type to get hype during confrontation. He remained as cool and calm as he could until it was time to get forceful. Vinny had taught him on many occasions that cooler heads always prevailed, so in order to gain the upper hand on his opponent, he had to remain calm.

"What you gon' do?" Angel taunted with a smirk on his face.

He hadn't gone to the restaurant for a fight, but he wasn't running either.

"My nigga, you trying to get murdered tonight, ain't you?" The dude pushed toward Angel, pushing Snow's hand in the process.

Before Angel could say or do anything, Snow had snatched her gun out and had it pressed to the side of the man's neck. Gasps and screams could be heard around them as people scrambled to get out of the way.

"You gon' do what to him?" she gritted out with her eyes slanted into slits. "Don't make idle threats in front of me."

The man's eyes got big as saucers as he looked down at Snow and raised his hands in surrender. "My fault. I ain't mean no harm."

Angel chuckled as he watched the man cower. He was so busy trying to get bad with Angel, when all along he had been a pussy. How the fuck did he let a woman make him turn weak that fast? So what if she had a gun? If she hadn't used that shit as soon as it came out, then she wasn't going to use it. Another thing Vinny had taught him.

"Be cool, Snow." Angel pinched the corner of her butt.

Her hand flexed on her gun before she let the front of the man's shirt go. "Get the fuck out of here, bitch-ass nigga," she told him.

Angel didn't miss how cold her voice was as she spoke to him. Vinny had told him Snow wasn't to be fucked with, but actually seeing it for himself was still something that was taking him some time to get used to. He was used to the sweet Emelia, not the hard-core woman in front of him. Though it was sexy as hell to watch her strong-arm niggas, he was still going to need a minute to get adjusted to the street-made queen, Snow.

The man took off out of the restaurant so fast, he stumbled over a few chairs on his way out. Neither Snow nor Angel blinked until they watched him get into his car and drive out of the parking lot. Once they were sure he was gone, Snow turned back around so that she was looking at the people in the restaurant. They were all staring at her with terrified looks on their faces.

Snow sucked her teeth and rolled her eyes. "Get y'all scary asses up. I ain't gon' do nothing to y'all."

It took a moment for people to begin rising from the floor. Once they were all back to their feet, Snow turned to face Angel.

"I don't even want nothing to eat no more because of you." She frowned before stomping off past him and leaving the building. "Let's go before the police get here. I'm sure somebody probably called them."

Angel followed behind her and snatched her arm as soon as he got close to her. Her hand went to her mouth and came up near his neck, but he was faster that time. Angel squeezed her hand until she dropped her blade.

"You better stop that shit." He shook her lightly. "Try to cut me one more time, and see what I do to your ass."

Snow rolled her eyes and looked away. "Stop grabbing on me like that, and I will."

"You know I'm not going to do nothing to your ass, you just be doing that shit for no reason."

Snow sucked her teeth again and looked away but said nothing. Angel looked at the side of her face for a minute before letting her go. She headed toward the black truck in the corner. It wasn't until then that Angel noticed she was with Vinny's driver. He felt like a fool then. Had he known she wasn't out alone, he never would have even gotten out of the car. Then again, maybe he would have. Truth be told, it had been her giggling with another nigga that had taken him out of his element, but he wasn't going to tell her that.

"So, you ain't getting no food?" Angel yelled as he watched her switch toward the truck.

Her big, round ass was moving to a beat of its own while her thick thighs rubbed together slightly. Angel licked his lips and even had to stretch his legs to keep himself from getting too hard in public. Snow's body just had that effect on him. No matter how hard he tried to ignore her feminine presence, he failed every time.

"I ain't hungry no more," she sassed.

Angel laughed at her attitude. "Man, go get you some food."

"No thank you. You might show up there acting a fool too. I'll just starve and cook me something in the morning."

Angel jogged over to the truck where she was and reached for her hand, this time giving her a warning. "Don't cut me."

Snow spun around with a smirk on her face. "I can't. You made me drop my blade over there."

Angel looked over his shoulder briefly before looking back at her with a smile on his face. "My fault."

She rolled her eyes with a small smile tugging at her lips.

"I don't know why you're trying to act like you're so mad with me. You were just ready to blow that nigga's head off in my defense, but now you want to have an attitude."

Snow crossed her arms over her chest. "That's because I don't play about my food."

"Clearly, you don't play about me either." Angel stepped closer to her, invading her personal space.

His hand went to her waist and stayed there, gripping the soft flesh just above her hip. When she didn't make him move, he stepped closer.

"I got some food in the car that you can share with me if you want to."

Her nose turned up on one side. "No thanks. I'll get my own."

"Why you always got to be so hardheaded? You need to learn to listen," he joked.

The frown on her face showed him that she saw no humor in what he was saying. "Learn to listen? Nigga, I don't listen to nobody but myself."

Angel didn't like her tone at all, so he took a deep breath before speaking. "Watch your fucking mouth, Emelia."

"Watch my mouth? Boy, please." She moved around him, trying to get into the truck, but he stopped her.

With her arm gripped firmly in his hand, he snatched the back door open so that he could talk to his driver. "You can go ahead home, I'll bring her."

His driver nodded with a smile on his face. "Yes, sir."

"No! Don't leave me," she yelled back.

Angel looked down at her with a frown. "What the fuck I just say?"

Even though she showed her disapproval for the force he was using with her, she kept her mouth shut that time. That surprised Angel more than anything. He just knew she was about to buck back at him harder than that, but when she didn't, it made him feel good. At least he now knew that she was capable of listening to a man.

After closing the door, he pulled her across the parking lot and to his passenger side. As soon as the door was open, he shoved her toward the seat and she slid in roughly.

"Nigga, don't throw me."

"Shut up," Angel told her before slamming the door closed.

Once he was in, he buckled his seat belt before making sure she had hers on as well. When he noticed she did, he cranked up, but stopped when he noticed she was stepping on his food.

"Damn, Emelia. You got your feet all over my food and shit." He reached down and grabbed the crumpled bag of chili cheese fries.

"So? Fuck your fries, nigga."

"Nah, Snow, fuck your stupid ass," he yelled out of anger.

Before Angel saw it coming, Snow's hand had landed across the side of his face. The sound of her open palm slamming against the soft flesh of his cheek sounded throughout the car like the snap of a snare drum.

Angel's nostrils flared as he stared in her direction, trying to calm himself down. "Don't put your fucking hands on me again, Emelia."

"Nigga, if you don't stop talking to me like you're my fucking daddy, I will continue beating your ass." She went to slap him again, but this time her hand was caught in his.

Angel's grip around her wrist had her unable to move. She tried to pull away, but he hadn't even left enough room for her to wiggle her wrist. The long breaths he was taking as he stared at her through the darkness were strong enough to send chills down her spine. Though he was sure Snow hadn't been, and still wasn't, the least bit scared of him, her sweaty palms let him know she was nervous.

The silence following her abuse was eerie and was clearly causing her to rethink putting her hand on him. Her breaths became softer and a lot shorter as she maintained eye contact with a very angry Angel. He was frowning, probably giving him the same unibrow illusion that always happened when he was upset.

With a swift yank of her arm, Angel snatched Snow clean across the seat so she was now leaning directly next to him, her face only inches from his. His dark eyes roamed over her face as his jaw jumped.

"Emelia, if you ever put these pretty little hands on me again, I will personally cut them the fuck off. Don't fuck with me or your life like that again." Before throwing her back across the seat with the same arm he'd pulled her with, Angel leaned forward and took a whiff of her scent.

When he'd had enough of the way she smelled and felt in his presence, she was back in his passenger seat.

"You're such an asshole," she said.

Angel's head whipped around rapidly with his face balled into a scowl. "You're really pushing my fucking buttons tonight."

She turned in her seat. "So, Angel. You're pushing my damn buttons too. I don't know who you think you are, trying to be all forceful with me, but you are not my man, so you can kill that shit." She smacked her teeth and sat back in her seat.

Angel grabbed the bottom of her face and turned her head back to face him. Snow pushed at his hand, but he held her face tighter.

"I'm not trying to be your fucking man, I'm just trying to look out for your ass," he fumed before letting her face go and backing out of the parking spot. "You could never be my fucking woman anyway, you don't damn listen," he yelled at her.

Hearing her tell him he wasn't her man had him mad as hell. Not that he was trying to be her man or no shit like that, but that didn't mean he wanted to hear her downplaying the option either. Angel expected to hear her say something else, but when he didn't, he flipped the music on instead and hit the highway. He was so angry that he pushed his car to maximum speed. He zipped between cars, switched lanes, and burned up the highway with speed as she sat quietly unfazed in the passenger seat.

When he finally pulled into his parking lot, he kept the car running before tossing her the set of house keys he had in his armrest.

"Go inside and sit your ass still. Don't go no fucking where until I get back."

"You ain't about to leave me here."

Angel looked at her with the same frown he'd been wearing since she told him he wasn't her man. "Emelia, just do what the fuck I told you to do."

She snatched the keys from her lap and her purse from the floor, and pushed his door open roughly before letting herself out and slamming it behind her. Angel wanted to cuss her out for slamming his door, but gritted his teeth instead. He waited for her to go inside before pulling away. He needed a minute to calm himself down, so versus joining her inside, he drove around the block to the store.

Though she'd been fighting against him and everything he'd been saying for months, something deep inside him knew she was going to listen to him and stay at his house until he got back. All he hoped was that she was obedient enough to make them some food as well. He was in the checkout line with an array of breakfast foods for her to cook once he got back.

Snow, the queen of the streets, may have been used to bucking back against everything people told her, but Emelia, the woman, was going to learn today. Angel wasn't the rest of the men she was used to—he could and would tame her ass. He was confident enough in himself to be the dominant man she needed. It was clear running dope in California had her thinking she could run whatever man she came in contact with, but that stopped at Angel. He was the perfect one for her hardheaded ass.

Chapter Thirteen

Second time,
shame on me

The red tips of her long nails held Angel's blinds open as she checked to see if that was him pulling back into his yard. When she noticed it wasn't, she walked away and retreated to his room and undressed. If she had to be there, then she would at least be comfortable.

She rummaged through his drawers, looking for a nightshirt. When she found nothing but a tank top, she grabbed that along with the small makeup bag she kept in her purse for times like this. In it were panties, soap, a toothbrush, and a host of other feminine products she might need if kept from her home for too long.

Next, she showered and got relaxed in the pair of low-cut blue panties and the worn-out tank top she'd

found. Her hair was pushed back with a thin headband
as she padded up the hallway to his kitchen. She was
hungry, and since that nigga had her trapped, she was
about to eat his food. He had her fucked up if he
thought she was just about to do whatever he said. He
was lucky she was already tired and could feel that his
patience was wearing thin with her, or she would have
never walked into his house in the first place.

When she couldn't find anything that matched
enough to make a complete meal, she grew even angrier. Not only had that fool practically kidnapped her,
but he was obviously going to starve her to death as
well. With an attitude out of the world, Snow walked
into his living room and plopped down on the sofa
with her arms crossed over her chest.

Snow sat on his sofa fussing to herself for only a little while longer before she heard the engine of his car
outside. Unable to help herself, she jumped up and
marched toward the window. When she saw him un-
loading a handful of bags, she rolled her eyes. That
nigga had some nerve. Past irritated and ready to confront him, Snow stormed to his front door and snatched
it open.

His tall, lean body moved smoothly up the sidewalk
to his front door as he held his head down, shuffling
with his keys. Snow watched him intently and her
heart rate began to speed up. From his wavy hair to the
sexy scowl on his face, Angel's presence was having
such an unnatural effect on her.

For some reason, she felt a tad bit nervous. His
rudeness and continuous mean streak toward her made
it so hard for Snow to understand why, in that moment,
her mind was telling her to kiss him, and her heart to
love him. Whatever it was about Angel, she had to get

herself together quickly before he took notice to her vulnerability.

"It took you long enough." She spoke sarcastically.

Obviously just becoming aware of her presence, Angel looked up at her while simultaneously dropping his keys on the ground. His mouth parted a little as his eyes trailed over her body shamelessly. He observed her face for only a minute before tucking his bottom lip into his mouth and clearing his throat. Angel looked at her for an awkward moment longer before bending down to retrieve his keys. Once he had them secured in his hand, he continued up the sidewalk and took the two stairs to his porch before stopping directly in front of her. Snow's face was level with his chest as he looked down at her.

"What you doing out here with no clothes on?" he asked her.

Totally forgetting that she was barely dressed, Snow looked down at herself and pulled at the bottom of the shirt. It was already barely covering her ass, so she was sure pulling at the bottom of it was pointless.

"I forgot." Her voice was low as she backed away from him and into his house.

Angel stood in the same spot watching her until she'd backed completely into the condo. The way his eyes roamed from her bare face down to her breasts before stopping at the panties hardly covering her bottom, only to continue down the length of her thick legs again, made her immediately uncomfortable in her attire. She hadn't actually considered the possibility of him gawking at her like that when she'd put it on, though now she wished that she had. Snow shifted some, crossing one ankle over the other before holding her hand out for the bags.

"I can help you," she offered.

Angel shook his head and walked into the house. "I got it. Just close the door."

Snow hurried to close the door and lock it before following him into the kitchen. Gone was her attitude. It had been quickly replaced with apprehensiveness the moment Angel laid eyes on her. Now all she felt was a stomach full of butterflies, and she needed to do anything that might help her get rid of them. The way he looked at her made her think of all the good times they'd shared in California, when he would stare at her for what seemed like forever only to eventually relay his love for her.

Get yourself together, Snow!

"You could have called me. I would have come and helped you get the bags." She spoke nervously.

Angel's small eyes surveyed her clothing once she rounded the corner. "Like that?"

Snow wasn't sure whether he was disgusted or if he was really asking. His tone was unreadable, so instead of copping an attitude like she normally would have, she remained cordial. "I could have put my jacket back on or something."

He nodded. "That wasn't necessary, I had it. Plus, I like looking at you in that." Angel looked at her once more before removing the food from the bags. "You feel like cooking? I bought food."

Snow blushed and nodded. "I'm glad you did. I was about to cook when I first got here until I realized you're living like a poor man."

Angel smirked. "Cut it out." He chuckled and headed for the kitchen door before stopping and turning back around to face her. "Can you cook?"

"Can you fucking eat?" she asked with a frown on her face.

Angel's face didn't frown. Instead, it curved into a small smile. "I'll let you have that one, but yeah, I know how to eat."

"Well then."

Snow didn't waste any more time playing around with Angel. Instead, she moved past him and into the kitchen to prepare them a late meal. When she noticed he'd gotten all breakfast foods, she wasn't surprised. He'd been hooked on cheese grits since they'd been young. He loved them so much, Empress would make him a small pot with almost every meal that she prepared. Snow loved grits as well, but not as much as Angel.

Thirty minutes passed before Snow finished making their late-night breakfast. Angel had long ago left her to go watch TV and hadn't returned since, which was fine by her. She wasn't sure how much cooking she would have gotten done with him staring at her like she was the last woman on earth. Though it made her feel good, she also felt uncomfortable. His eyes disarmed her in a way she couldn't withstand.

After fixing their plates, she walked into the living room, carrying only Angel's food. She had his plate in one hand and his bowl of grits in the other. She'd go back for her plate once she'd served him.

Snow placed his plate on the end table next to where he was seated on the sofa. His eyes went to the plate of steaming hot eggs, bacon, and biscuits and the large bowl of cheese grits. The way his eyes lit up at the bowl of grits had Snow smiling.

"I know you ain't that happy about some grits." She chuckled.

When he smiled up at her, Snow felt her insides melt. He was so handsome. "You know I love grits." He picked his plate up and stirred his food around before looking back at her. "They better be good, or I'ma talk about your ass."

Snow giggled. "Boy, please. They're probably the best grits you've ever tasted."

"That's a lie. Ain't nobody's grits better than my mama's."

"Taste mine and see. I bet I gave Empress a run for her money," Snow yelled to him as she returned to the kitchen to grab her food.

Versus sitting on the sofa next to him, she made herself comfortable on the love seat across from where he was seated. She shifted around, getting situated before looking up. When she did, she looked dead into his face. He was watching her with a calm expression on his face.

"What?" she asked.

He shook his head. "Nothing. I'm just trying to figure out why you would put something like that on around me."

There was that uncomfortable feeling again. Snow shrugged and stuffed some eggs into her mouth.

"It's not like I had much of a choice. You kidnapped me, remember?"

"Man, ain't nobody kidnapped your ass." He chuckled.

"So, throwing me in your car and telling me to bring my ass in your house and be still was what exactly?" She looked at him with a confused look on her face. "I mean, if it's not kidnapping."

Angel stretched his long legs out so that they were

resting beneath the coffee table and gave her a smile sexy enough to melt her panties off. "That wasn't kidnapping, that was me teaching you how to obey authority."

Snow raised her eyebrows with a smirk on her face. "Obey authority? Angel, you are not my daddy."

Angel stuck a fork full of grits in his mouth before shooting her a lazy grin. "Good, because obviously Mack ain't taught you shit. All you do is fight the power."

A fit of laughter took over Snow as she covered her mouth to keep her food from falling out. She laughed so hard she almost started choking.

"A'ight now, girl. Don't sit over there and kill yourself being silly." Angel laughed with her.

When Snow was finally able to calm down, she set her plate to the side and looked back at Angel. He was stretched out on the sofa in nothing but a pair of sweatpants and a tank top. He scarfed down the food on his plate with a smile.

"You make me so sick. I don't fight no damn power. I just be myself."

"Well, yourself is hardheaded as fuck and be about to have me putting my foot in your ass."

Snow waved him off and stuck her feet beneath her body. "You're all talk, Angel. I watched how you used to act with Genesis. You let that ho get away with anything but be ready to hop down on me for nothing." Snow made eye contact with him and rolled her eyes playfully. "That's whose daddy you should have been trying to be."

Angel was quiet for a minute. So quiet that Snow almost thought she'd gone too far with her comments, until he sat his plate down and leaned over so that his forearms were resting on his knees.

"I wasn't trying to be her daddy, I was trying to be her man. She just didn't have enough sense to know that."

"Well, I'm sure you're not trying to be my daddy or my man, so why must you come for my neck the way you do?"

"How do you know what I'm trying to do?" He licked his lips as he waited for her to answer.

"I don't."

"Exactly. I could be trying to be your man and your daddy, but you're so busy being a little tyrant, you can't see that shit no more than Genesis could."

Snow snickered at him calling her a tyrant. She needed something to ease the tension she felt building in her core from him referring to himself as her daddy and her man. Those were two things that she wasn't sure she wanted to bring to the forefront right then.

"Emelia." Angel paused until she looked at him. "You need a daddy?" His face was straight and penetrating as he owned everything he'd just said.

Yes, Angel! Be my daddy, baby, she screamed on the inside, but kept her poker face on the outside as she watched him watch her. "I don't know about a daddy, but I do need a man," she forced herself to say.

The living room was quiet as they sat gazing at one another. Snow wasn't sure what was going to happen next, but she knew one thing for sure, she wasn't making another move until he did. The last thing she wanted to do was be too forward and he leave her again.

"You need a man, huh?" He sat back on the sofa and stretched his legs out again.

She nodded.

"If you had one, would you know how to be submissive?"

Snow shrugged, because she truly didn't know if she could. She didn't necessarily try to fight against everything people said, she just couldn't help it. It was like second nature to her. She'd been taught to fight in every aspect of her life, so it was hard not to in certain situations.

"I could try . . . I mean, I could try if the man was worth submitting to. If not, I'm bucking on his ass."

Both of them burst out laughing. Angel laughing a little longer than Snow. When he finally calmed down, he stood and grabbed his plate and hers before walking into the kitchen to put them away. Snow sat in her same spot feeling awkward because of how their conversation had turned from serious to joking in a matter of seconds. She almost hated that she'd made a joke, because she'd actually wanted to explore the topic of Angel being her man. She kicked herself for being too immature to keep up a real conversation.

"You staying here with me tonight, or you going back to my people's house?" He stopped in front of her.

"You taking me back?"

He smiled and shook his head. "Hell nah."

"Well, why would you even ask that?" Snow asked with a hint of attitude.

Angel picked up on it immediately and lost the smile on his face. "You can lose that li'l shit. You ain't about to cut the fool at my house," he told her as he proceeded down the hallway.

Snow rolled her eyes and smacked her teeth. Angel got on her nerves. He was the only person in her entire life who had the ability to make her happy and mad at the same time. She hated it, and him. If he thought he was about to just tell her what to do, then he had the wrong idea. Nobody controlled her . . . well, almost nobody.

The more she sat there fuming to herself about him, the angrier she got. Before she could stop herself, she was up and marching down the hallway to tell him about himself. When she got to his room, he wasn't there, so she looked around the hallway. When she saw the bathroom light on, she pushed the door open and walked right in without considering his privacy.

"Ang—" She stopped herself. "Damn, my fault," Snow said when she bumped into him wrapping his towel around his waist.

He had been standing in front of the door with the towel halfway around his waist when she walked in. The moment the back of the door hit him, a corner of the towel dropped from his hand, exposing the mouth-watering male part that Snow had been secretly dreaming about for years.

Thanks to the mirror he was in front of, Snow had caught a glimpse of it from where she was standing, and now she couldn't take her eyes off it. The silky black hair that lay against his stomach and leading down to it made Snow weak in the knees. It was crazy how just the sight of the thick caramel-colored collection of throbbing veins and blood weighed so heavy on her mind that she suddenly couldn't feel her legs.

It was as if the perfectly shaped tip of it had touched her brain and erased every coherent thought that had been there before. No matter how hard she tried, she couldn't move her eyes or her feet. It wasn't until it was taken out of her view that she regained all of her senses.

Dazed and looking just as guilty as she felt, Snow made eye contact with Angel through the mirror. He was staring at her while securing his towel around his waist. The way his muscles bulged with every movement he made was making her just as weak as she had been moments prior. His chest and arms were covered in tattoos and oh so sexy. She'd always known they were there, but seeing them glistening beneath the droplets of water while being encompassed in the heat from his shower made them appeal to her even more.

"Don't even do yourself like that. You ain't ready for me." Angel spoke coolly, but sexy enough to drive Snow crazy.

He was torturing her something terrible right then, and he knew it.

"You don't know what I'm ready for," Snow shot back.

Angel stared at her in the mirror for a few more seconds before he reached behind him and grabbed her wrist. He pulled her until she was standing in front of him in the mirror. The moment she was steady on her feet again, Angel's hands went to her breasts. With one in each hand, he massaged her nipples while maintaining eye contact through the mirror.

If Snow thought she had been barely hanging on before, she was damn near on her deathbed when his lips found her neck. The way his tongue moved around in circles, wetting and warming up every spot that he touched, had her near combustion.

"I can tell you you're not ready for me, because I know you're not," he whispered in her ear before dipping his tongue inside it and sliding his hand down the front of her body and into her panties.

Snow's back arched when his long fingers dipped into her sticky, wet tunnel. "Angel, yes, I am," she moaned, her eyes on the verge of closing.

"I like to be in charge, Emelia." He licked up the side of her neck before biting it softly. "That means you have to let me be in charge of you too."

She shook her head slowly. He couldn't be in charge of her, she needed to control herself.

"No!" she yelped when he removed his fingers from her panties. "Don't stop."

Her face held a small pout as she stared at him with sad eyes. Angel stood behind her looking like some sort of warrior.

"Tell me you'll listen," he growled to her before releasing her breast and grabbing the front of her neck. "Tell me right now that I'm in charge of you."

Snow wanted so badly to tell him what he wanted to hear, but she didn't want to lie. She could tell him he was the boss of her, but she didn't know if she'd actually let him be. It sounded good, and would probably feel even better, but she wasn't sure.

She was still battling herself mentally when he turned her around and picked her up. Snow's thick thighs circled his waist just as quick as her arms went around his neck. Without another word to her, Angel carried her into his room and sat her on his dresser. His large hands rubbed up and down her thighs, squeezing here and there as he leaned into her neck, inhaling her scent.

"What do you want from me, Emelia?" He lifted his head just enough to make eye contact with her again. "You want my love, or do you just want my dick?"

Oh shit!

Snow's eyes closed as his words vibrated her whole

body. In that moment, every wall she'd been trying to build around her heart began to tumble down. He sounded so sexy, she could hardly take it.

"I won't force you." He pecked her lips. "I know what I want you to have, but I'll give you whatever you want."

"Which one do you want me to have?" she asked before grabbing his bottom lip with her mouth and holding it between her teeth.

She sucked and pulled at it before sliding her tongue into his mouth. He took it with no problem, allowing his to glide expertly with hers. They exchanged their passion for one another through their mouths for a little longer before he pulled away again.

"First, you have to tell me you gon' be a good girl and listen to me." Angel's eyes were low as his voice came out raspier than before. "Say, 'Angel, you're my daddy, and I'm going to listen to you.'"

His smile was so sexy that Snow wouldn't have been able to fight against him even if she wanted to, and for the first time in her entire life, she didn't want to.

"Angel," she sighed in his ear when she felt his fingers exploring the depths of her body again. "Baby, you're my daddy, and I'll do whatever you say." Her eyes fluttered when his mouth took hers aggressively.

"Yeah," he boasted with a lazy grin on his face. "That's my girl." He pecked her mouth once more before picking her up and walking her to his bed. "I'm about to give you this dick. You ain't gon' have no other choice but to listen after that."

Snow lay on her back staring at him with not an ounce of fight left in her. If he was going to give her his dick, she just hoped his love came along with it.

Maybe if he did it right this time, he wouldn't hurt her as much as he had last time. She hadn't thought she'd ever have him like that again, but now that she did, she wanted to keep him. Her first heartbreak had been inevitable, but this time, it would be voluntary.

Chapter Fourteen

Daddy's girl

The darkness of his room had nothing on the darkness of his eyes as he stared down at the love of his life. He had been doing everything in his power to keep his feelings for her at bay, but after touching and tasting her the way he'd been dreaming of, he could no longer deny it.

Snow's gorgeous face held a look of apprehension and fear as she lay with her hair spread out on his pillow. The whites of her eyeballs appeared to be glowing as she stared at him through the darkness. Angel wasn't sure if it was the water he saw glossed over them, or if it was the hidden love she'd been holding back from him for so long.

"You wanna cry?" Angel asked as he lowered himself onto the bed with her.

She nodded before swiping at one of her eyes with the back of her hand.

Angel sat back on his haunches and grabbed both of her chocolate thighs in his hands before draping them over his legs.

"What you wanna cry for, baby?" His tone was soft as he rubbed his hand up her stomach while gripping her waist with the other. "Tell Daddy what's wrong."

When his hand found her dripping wet love again, he closed his eyes momentarily. When he opened them back up, her eyes were still wet, but she was smiling.

"Now you smiling? You must know you're about to fuck my life up with this good pussy."

She nodded and smiled wider.

"Fuck me up then, baby." Angel leaned over and circled her nipples with his wet mouth. He alternated between licking and sucking both of them before leaning back up so that she could see his face. "I want it so bad," he growled. "I haven't stopped thinking about it since the last time I got it."

"I don't believe you." She finally spoke.

"You should. I've been driving myself crazy thinking about who you been letting get up in my spot since I've been away." Angel grabbed his fully erect dick and placed it at her opening.

His head fell back, and his eyes closed as he felt her juices soaking the tip. The tingly feeling that shot through his body took him over completely. It felt so good. "I'm about to erase all them other niggas. Your body belongs to me now, a'ight?"

Snow said nothing, instead she reached out and covered the rest of his dick with her hand and pulled it so that it was dipping deeper into her body. She even rocked her hips forward a little more to make it slide deeper. Angel's body shivered in anticipation as her pussy swallowed the head of his dick. In an effort to calm himself down, he bit his bottom lip while simultaneously squeezing the base of his dick.

"Don't talk, just love me." Snow reached up and grabbed him.

Angel went willingly, pushing himself into her body. The scream that Snow belted out in his ear rocked his entire body. The pain that it conveyed almost made him feel bad, but he couldn't focus on that right then. Instead, his mind was on how tight she was. The way her body was squeezing him right then was mind boggling.

"Damn, Emelia. What you doing with pussy this tight?" he questioned while kissing her face.

"I've been saving it for you," she managed to get out between her moans of pain.

Angel lifted himself up and looked down at her. "Say what?"

"You heard me."

It took him a minute, because Angel just knew she couldn't have been saying what he thought she was. Though he didn't want to ask, because he really didn't want to think about her and other niggas, he needed to be sure.

"You ain't gave it to nobody else?"

She shook her head.

"Just you. Now give me what I've been waiting for." Her smile was the most beautiful thing on Angel's earth.

With his heart weighing heavy on his dick, Angel made love to his girl. With her soft thighs resting against his back, Angel delivered stroke after stroke to her body, each time drawing a moan louder than the last. Snow's body was clearing every ache and pain that Angel had been feeling since leaving Genesis.

All of the built-up hurt and anger he'd felt, he pushed into Snow. Her open mouth let out a gasp every time he pulled out and pushed back in. Never in all of the years he'd been separated from her had he known that the moment he was back inside her, the feelings he'd been harboring would come rushing back.

It was as if they were taking over his every thought, and without thinking, he let her know that. "I love you, Snow."

She opened her eyes and shook her head. "I don't want to be Snow with you, just Emelia."

Angel felt her words in his soul. With him and only him, she would be different. She could be Snow to the world, but with Angel, she would forever be Emelia.

"I'm sorry, baby." He grabbed her mouth with his at the same time he pushed himself deep inside her. "You're my Emelia."

The tears that had been resting in her eyes slid down the side of her face.

"I love you, okay?" Angel said again.

She sniffed while holding his face. "I love you too."

"I love you so much." Angel could feel his throat get tight as he stared at her perfect face. "You can listen to me. I'd never lead you wrong. I'm here to protect and love you. So don't fight me."

"I'll stop." She kissed the center of his throat.

Angel could feel his orgasm taking over him as he continuously massaged the warmest spot of her. When her legs clamped tightly around his back, he knew she was just as close as he was.

"Wet me up, baby girl."

Snow's eyes were squeezed shut tightly as she arched her back so high off the bed, she pushed Angel with her chest. Seconds later, her legs were stiffening, and her moans sounded throughout the room. All control Angel had after that dissipated and he released as well with a few grunts of his own. He was tired and worn out, but sex with Emelia had been better than he'd dreamed it would be.

Together, they lay sprawled out in his bed until they fell asleep. Hours passed, and before they knew it, the sun was peeking through his blinds. Angel scooted down some so that Snow's back was shielding his face from the bright rays that managed to seep past his curtains.

With his arm circled tightly around her waist, Angel pulled Snow closer to his body and kissed the back of her neck. Finally having her in his arms where she belonged would never get old.

"Don't be trying to go back to sleep. Wake your butt up." Her voice made him smile.

Angel slid up just enough to place his hardening wood on her butt before biting her shoulder playfully. "Give me something to wake up to," he grumbled sleepily.

Snow flipped over quickly so that she was facing him. She pecked his forehead and ran her hands through his hair. Angel closed his eyes, enjoying the feeling of her hands on his scalp while nuzzling his face closer into the warmth of her breasts. They were directly in his face, and he couldn't think of any other place he'd rather be.

"Wake up, Angel. I'm not sleepy anymore."

He chuckled before kissing her just below her collarbone. "What does you not being sleepy have to do with me?"

"You have to entertain me." She snickered. "Let's get up and go grab some food or something."

"All you think about is food."

She was laughing again. "Where you thought all this ass came from?"

Angel grabbed two handfuls of her butt and rubbed his body against hers playfully. "Well, if that's the case, then come on, let me feed you. I need your ass to stay fat."

Snow giggled and pushed his head away from her as she slid out of bed. Angel flipped over on his back so that he could watch her walk from his room. His eyes were glued to the sway of her hips until his cell phone began to ring. When he sat up to grab it, he saw his mother's face on the screen. Before saying anything, Angel hit the speakerphone button and set his phone on the pillow next to him.

"What's going on, Ma?"

"I know you're not still in the bed." She sounded wide awake.

"Why wouldn't I be?"

"You never sleep this late."

Angel checked the clock sitting on his dresser. "Ma, it ain't even eight o'clock yet."

"Boy, I know what time it is." She coughed and cleared her throat a little before coming back over the line. "Anyways, that's not what I called for. I was calling to see had you talked to Snow. She wasn't in her room when I checked on her this morning, and she's not answering her phone."

Before Angel could tell Empress anything, Snow came running back into the room waving her hands and shaking her head. "Don't tell her I'm here," she mouthed.

Angel raised his eyebrows at her before mouthing back to her, "Why?"

"Angel!" His mother yelled his name a little louder this time, Angel having not responded the first time. "I know you hear me talking to you."

"My fault, Ma. What you say?" Angel stammered.

"I said have you talked to Snow? I know you and her aren't really the best of friends right now, but we need to find her. I asked D'Angelo had he seen her, but he said no."

Angel looked back at Snow, who was standing at the door in his tank top biting her nails. It was crazy how nervous she was about Empress finding out about them. Unfortunately for her, he didn't feel the same way.

"I ain't got to go find her, I already know where she at." He smiled broadly when Snow's eyes shot to him.

"I will kill you," Snow mouthed to him with her eyes bucked in warning. "You better not tell her."

Angel was so tickled at Snow that he couldn't stop his laughter.

"Angel, I said, where is she?" Empress's voice regained his attention.

"She right here with m—" He was cut off by Snow's hand being pressed over his mouth.

Before he could stop her, she'd grabbed his phone and hung up in Empress's face. "I'ma kill your ass." She hopped on top of him. "I just told you not to tell her I was here," she told him with a smile on her face.

Angel laughed hard as he grabbed onto the side of her hip. She was straddling him with her arms folded across her chest as his phone lay on the floor ringing. They both knew it was Empress calling back, but refused to answer it. Snow watched it until it stopped ringing before looking back at Angel.

"You be talking about me, but you don't listen either," Snow said.

"Why you don't want her to know you over here?" Angel asked through his laughter.

"Because, Empress ain't no fool. As soon as you tell her I'm over here, she gon' know we've been fucking."

Snow shook her head. "You need to learn to listen too, Angel."

Angel smiled as he calmed down from his laughter. "Let's get one thing straight." He sat up on his elbows. "What I did to you last night wasn't fucking. That was lovemaking." He gave her a large smile before lying back down on the bed and placing both of his hands behind his head. "Now that I checked your ass on that, you can go ahead and discipline me for not listening."

His smile matched the one on Snow's face. He could tell she liked the way he was handling her by the way she kept blushing.

"What you mean discipline you?" she asked.

"You see how I dicked you down when I got tired of you not listening to me." He shrugged. "You better put this pussy on me and show me who's in charge."

Snow covered her mouth as she allowed her head to fall forward in the midst of her laughter. "I thought you told me you're in charge?"

Angel thrust his hips upward, and she blushed again. "I am, but I'll share the power with you when it's time for us to make love."

Snow's face grew serious as her body shivered as if she was cold. "Hearing you say make love makes me so weak for you."

Angel reached up and grabbed the side of Snow's neck. He pulled her mouth to his and slid her his tongue. He kissed her with as much passion as he could muster before releasing her again.

"Well, actually making love to you makes me weak, so I feel you, baby girl." He slapped the side of her ass hard before his smile returned. "Now ride this dick like I know you can."

Snow covered her face quickly. "I don't know how."

Angel frowned again. "So, you mean to tell me you've seriously been saving your pussy for me?"

"Well, sort of." She looked away. "I didn't necessarily know that I was saving it for you when I turned all of the men in my past down, I just knew you were the only person I wanted to have it." She shrugged her shoulders. "I saved it on accident." Her smile widened, as did his.

"Accidentally ride my dick, then."

She snickered. "I told you I don't know how."

"Well, do your best, I'll teach you the rest."

Her hands fell from her face slowly before resting back on his abs. "Don't laugh at me." She pulled his tank top over her head, exposing her body again.

Angel's eyes followed and got lost in her curves. "There ain't no way in hell I'd ever laugh at you. Ain't nothing about the desires we share for each other funny to me." His face was as relaxed as it always was, but solemn enough for her to know he was serious.

She nodded slowly as she maintained eye contact with him. Angel watched her until she raised from his lap a little and grabbed his dick. She held it steady enough to slide down on before frowning her face up in anguish.

"It hurts, Angel."

"It needs to. Maybe it'll remind your hardheaded ass that Daddy ain't nothing to play with." He gripped both sides of her hips and pushed upward.

Snow's scream was so sexy he had to hear it again. Angel thrust into her a few more times before allowing her to take control of their sex again. Although she hadn't had much faith in herself, she ended up riding his dick so good that she made his toes curl. At one point, it had even gotten so good, Angel was moaning out loud, and that was something he never did. The duo went at it a few moments longer before their love-making came to a pleasurable end, and they moved to the shower.

"Empress about to be on your ass today," Angel told her as he stepped into the shower behind her.

Snow looked over her shoulder at him with a smile on her face and stepped beneath the water. "You better help me. Don't let her corner me."

Angel chuckled. "I know big bad Snow ain't scared of Empress's old bourgeois ass?"

"Man, you already know how Empress is. I can bet she done called my mama already." Snow shook her head and Angel laughed again. "I got missed calls from both of them. I didn't even bother to answer."

His laughter took over the shower as he pulled her body to his before kissing the top of her head. "You ain't got to be scared of Empress or Zulema. I'll protect you. The next time they call, I'll answer. I dare them to ask me what you're doing with me."

Snow smirked at him with her body full of soap bubbles. "What you gon' say?"

"I'ma tell them I did everything except ate your pussy last night, which I plan to do the next free minute I get, so they need to stop calling you because you're about to be too tired to talk." The water rushed over Angel's face as he smiled down at Snow.

She was so busy laughing that she couldn't even rinse her body properly, which was something Angel had no problem helping her do. With no type of fight being put up from her, Angel pulled Snow into his arms and beneath the water with him.

They remained at his condo for a few more hours before leaving to get to work. They both had a full day ahead of them and needed to get to it.

Being that Snow was in need of clothes but refused to go to Empress's house to get any, Angel had to run to the nearest mall to grab her something. The little pink and silver shirt and jeans he'd gotten her fit her perfectly. Almost too perfectly, making Angel think twice about letting her check the traps without him. After promising that he'd be back to get her for lunch, he dropped her off and went about his day.

Chapter Fifteen

I don't hide my love

"Empress, you're so beautiful." Vinny's voice could be heard before Angel rounded the corner.

"Thank you, my love."

"Move away with me and be my wife."

Empress gasped. "Of course I will, Vinny."

Angel stopped in his tracks before hearing his mother break out into a fit of giggles. Being around his father on the days he couldn't remember his life wounded Angel deeply, but there was nothing he could do. He'd bent over backward trying his best to be there with them whenever he had a free minute, and though that didn't help much, it still gave him time with Vinny.

He didn't know how Empress was holding up as well as she was, but she was making it happen, and for that he was grateful.

"All of my cousins are going to be jealous. I'll have the prettiest wife in all of California."

Angel walked around the corner just as he heard his father's voice again. When he walked into the kitchen, D'Angelo was at the table scarfing down a plate of fruit. Vinny was also seated at the table with a large plate of food in front of him, while Empress leaned against the counter with her arms folded. Her face lit up when she saw Angel.

"Well, well, well, look who decided to show up."

Angel smiled before walking to her and circling one of his arms around her neck. "Stop that. I told you I was coming."

Empress looked at her watch. "Yeah, hours ago."

"I had to make a few stops first." Angel walked over to his father and held his hand out.

Vinny shook it and nodded at him. "I keep telling her you're a busy man. Being a doctor isn't easy." He smiled at Angel before looking at Empress.

"Right. Everybody can't practice medicine and run an entire drug corporation." The bitterness in D'Angelo's voice couldn't be missed, but versus correcting him, Angel smiled and addressed his father instead.

"It's okay, Daddy. You know she doesn't listen."

Both men laughed together before Empress joined in and took a seat at the table with them. The three of them talked for a little while while D'Angelo scrolled on his phone completely out of their family conversation. Since it was somewhat the norm, Angel disregarded his brother's jealousy for the day and continued to converse with his parents.

He needed to do everything he could to make sure the conversation kept going. He already knew that the moment it stopped, Empress would be asking about

Snow. Unfortunately for him, Snow hadn't gotten that memo and came walking into the kitchen.

Her hair was pulled back into a bun with a few strands falling around her ears and neck, while her face frowned slightly. The shirt he'd purchased her from the mall earlier was covered by a black jacket, while the jeans hugged her curves just as sinfully as they had that morning.

The way the large gold earrings meshed with her dark skin had stars in Angel's eyes. She moved with so much grace and authority at the same time that her presence commanded the room without her even having to say anything.

She looked around the large kitchen until she saw them. She looked completely over D'Angelo, but stopped and smiled at Vinny and Empress giddily as she waved, before her eyes landed on Angel. He could feel the energy between them shifting as she tried to suppress the urge to smile even larger at him. Instead of giving in to her happiness, she wiped her face clean of the smile she'd been sporting and nodded once at him. Angel smirked but kept his mouth shut.

"Little girl, I've been looking all over the place for you this morning." Empress didn't even give her time to sit down.

Snow smiled. "I was out, Mrs. Empress. I'm good." She giggled.

Angel watched his mother look her up and down. "Uh-huh," she mumbled before looking over at Angel. "I just bet you are good."

Snow's soft giggles made the pit of Angel's gut jump with excitement. It was becoming such a task to stay in his seat and not shower her with kisses right there in front of his parents, but he was managing the best he could.

"You were so good you couldn't answer your phone too, huh?"

"You know I don't answer my phone when I'm working," Snow answered, finally able to stop smiling.

"Ma, leave that girl alone." Angel rose to his feet. "She's a grown woman. If she wants to be out here in these streets laying up, that's her business."

Snow narrowed her eyes at him. "Nigga, don't try me. I wasn't out laying up."

"Better not have been," Empress scolded playfully.

Angel smirked at Snow as he stopped next to the counter she was leaning over. When he was only a few feet away from her, she looked over her shoulder at him, pleading with her eyes for him not to say anything. One thing she was going to have to learn when dealing with Angel was that he was a lover, and he loved on his woman whenever he felt like it. Even if it was in front of his parents.

Before she could stop him, Angel pressed the front of his body against her butt and leaned over the counter with her. Snow did her best to move, but Angel wasn't having it. Now, practically lying on top of her, Angel ran his nose along the back of her neck.

"So, you weren't laying up last night, Emelia?" he asked her with his nose continuing to roam around her neck.

"Oh Lord," Empress gasped. "I knew I heard you tell me she was with you this morning. Well, I'll be." Empress stood up from the table while grabbing Vinny's plate along the way. "I knew something in the milk wasn't clean when she didn't come back over here last night."

D'Angelo got up from where he was sitting and walked toward the sink. "Well, ain't this some shit?"

"It sure the fuck is," Snow fired off at D'Angelo.

Angel licked Snow's neck as she pushed at him with her elbow. "Calm down, and ignore him." He licked her neck again.

"Stop, Angel." She fought her smile. "Get off me."

Angel enjoyed being in her personal space a little longer before standing completely back up and pulling her with him. "Her ass ain't little, Ma. Believe me."

Empress covered her face playfully. "Oh, my goodness. Y'all are too much." When she moved her hands, she looked at Snow with a large smile. "I thought more of you, Snow. Y'all just wait until I tell Zulema about this mess." She eyed the way Angel was holding on to Snow's waist before smiling again. "And look at Angel, holding on to you like I'ma take you from him or something."

Snow held her head down and giggled when Angel kissed the side of her face.

"You in love with Mack's daughter, Angel?" Vinny's voice came from behind them.

All of their heads turned in his direction, and they were pleased to see that he was smiling. "Yeah, Daddy. I am." Angel hugged her to him tighter. "Have been for a long time. You okay with that?"

"It's a little too late for that, ain't it?" D'Angelo chuckled before walking out of the kitchen.

Angel and Snow both decided to ignore that comment.

Vinny threw his hands up in surrender and nodded. "Mack is going to kick your ass, but hey, love is love." He stood from the table. "Just don't go having any babies. You two are still babies yourselves."

They all laughed together as they watched Vinny retreat from the kitchen and into the living room. When he was gone, Angel turned his attention back to Empress. She was still standing in front of him and Snow with a large smile on her face.

"What, Ma?" Angel asked her.

"I'm just surprised is all. Y'all have been getting around here like you hate each other, when all along you've been together."

Snow tried to walk out of Angel's embrace, but he wouldn't let her. "It just started last night. I did hate this nigga."

Angel and Empress both laughed at her, but just like he'd been doing all day, Angel called Snow on her lies.

"Last night? Emelia, come on now, baby girl. You know we've been doing this since we were kids." Angel twisted his mouth to the side while raising his eyebrows.

Empress's eyes bucked. "For real?"

Angel nodded while still grinning. "Yep. I used to be busting li'l Emelia down in that basement at our house in Cali."

Empress covered her ears dramatically while Snow covered her face. "Angel!" They both screamed his name.

Angel found the entire situation to be quite comical, while the women stood in front of him acting as if he and Snow were children. He'd never been the type of man to hide his relationships, and he didn't plan on starting with Snow. Not that he could if he tried. The way his body drew to hers, there was no way he would have been able to keep Empress out of their business.

"Y'all really need to cut it out." Angel finally let Snow go. "Ma, Emelia is my baby. Emelia, tell Empress we're together so we can stop all this mess."

Angel didn't even bother to wait on them to say anything else before he left the kitchen. He didn't have time to be playing with them. There were street affairs that needed to be handled, and he and Snow needed to be on their way.

To give the women some time to do whatever they felt the need to do, Angel took a seat in the living room with his father and watched TV. When Snow finally came into the living room, she was smiling. He raised his eyebrows at her in question and she gave him the thumbs-up. That was all he needed. Angel was back on his feet and leaning over Vinny's recliner to hug him.

"See you later, Ma." Angel hugged Empress as well when she met him at the front door.

"I love her for you," she whispered to him. "Treat her good."

Angel pecked Empress's forehead. "Always."

When he pulled away from his mother, she hugged Snow before closing the door behind them. Once they were outside and headed to his car, Angel grabbed Snow's hand.

"You good?"

She squinted her eyes at him. "I would have preferred you hadn't done it that way, but I'm straight."

"Emelia, when I'm in love, I don't keep it a secret. I did that with you once before, and I've regretted it every day since then, so I'll never do it again. You're either with me or you're not."

She stood quietly with her hands in the small pockets of her jacket. "I'm with you."

Angel rounded the corner so that he was standing in front of her before wrapping his arms around her waist and pulling her to him. Her arms circled his neck immediately.

"It's some people Mack needs me to meet out of state next weekend. I wasn't going to take you with me, but now I don't think I can leave you."

"Take me." Snow's face was serious as she spoke. "You need somebody that's going to watch your back. Let me help you."

Angel observed her fearless face as he considered what she was saying.

"I'm only Emelia with you. I'm Snow with everybody else. You need me there with you. Meeting new people can be tricky, Angel. I'm going," she told him with finality. "Don't let our sex cloud your judgment. You know I'm the best to ever do this shit."

Angel nodded slowly. "That's the same thing your father said."

"So, he told you to take me with you?"

Angel nodded once.

"Well, why are you second-guessing it? If us being together is going to have you trying to shield me from this life, Angel, I don't know if we're going to last. You know this is me, and I don't know if I'll be able to stop being who I am."

"I'm not asking you to do that. I just wasn't sure, because the men we're meeting, you . . ." Angel paused for a moment.

"What about them?" Snow asked eagerly.

"Mack said you have history with one of them."

Snow frowned in confusion as she looked past his head. "Did he give you names?"

Angel nodded. "Juan and Julio Alsados." Snow's face relaxed in understanding while Angel watched her to gauge her reaction.

He needed to make sure she was good to do this job. The last thing he needed was to end up getting hurt, physically or emotionally. From what Mack had told him that morning on their phone call, Juan had been the man Snow had dated for most of her adult life, only breaking up after she'd found out about him cheating with her best friend.

"My father told you about Juan's and my relationship?" Snow asked.

A small nod from Angel answered her question.

Snow stood quietly for such an extensive amount of time, that she began to make Angel nervous. He'd been heartbroken enough for one year, he wasn't really trying to feel it again. Genesis had scarred him enough for ten women, so if Emelia was still stuck on her old nigga, he wasn't taking her, and it was that simple.

"Where are they requesting to meet?" Snow questioned.

"A club in North Carolina."

Snow looked down at her hands as she fidgeted with her fingers. "What day do we leave?"

"Next Friday." Angel raised Snow's head so that he could see her face. "You with it?"

"Work is work. Fuck him. I'm over that."

Angel wanted to believe her, but he wasn't too sure. Her face was just as serious as it always was, so he had no other choice but to take her at her word. He would have to watch her to make sure he wasn't setting himself up by opening his heart to her if she was still in love with another man. Something in him wanted to believe that she wouldn't let him down, but only time would tell.

"Cool, get in. I have a few things I need to get in order before we meet them," Angel said.

Once they were both in the car, Angel pulled away from his parents' house and sped toward the interstate. Snow was his business partner and lover; maybe she'd remain both, maybe she wouldn't. Either way it went, by the end of the meeting next week, Angel would have his answer.

One week later . . .

The dark club was cool and packed from wall to wall with people as the different colored lights flickered across the building. The subtle breeze of air brushed against Angel's face every so often as he sat in the velvet VIP booth with a table full of liquor in front of him.

An expensive glass bottle of pink liquor was in one hand, while he held a thick blunt between his fingers in the other. The bass from the music was vibrating his back as he nodded slowly, with his eyes drooping lazily from the potent weed he'd been puffing on for the past few minutes.

Clouds of smoke lingered in the air as the smells of weed, cologne, and perfume mixed with heat wafted up his nose. Angel's long legs were stretched out in front of him while his arms draped loosely over the back of the black bench he was seated in. Women and men surrounded his booth, careful not to cross the velvet rope that separated him from the rest of the party-goers.

Sounds of the latest songs blasted through the speakers as Angel slouched down some and took another pull from his blunt. His head bobbed to the beat of the song as he pushed the circular clouds out of his mouth and into the rowdy atmosphere around him.

"You sure you don't want any company?" the cute little bartender with the large breasts asked him for the thousandth time that night.

Angel smiled up at her lazily from where he was seated before shaking his head. "I'm just chilling, beautiful. Appreciate the offer."

"You just look so lonely. I'm sure there's plenty of pretty women that's dying to keep you company."

Angel took the bucket of ice and cups from her hand. "I got a few people on their way already. I'll be cool until they arrive."

She gave him a flirtatious smile once more before telling him to let her know if he needed something. Once Angel told her he was good, she left and mixed back in with the thickening crowd. It was going on two o'clock in the morning, and he had been in the same spot for the past two hours just relaxing and surveying the scene.

Mack and Empress had instructed him to arrive early to make sure everything was good before proceeding to do business, so that's what he'd done. Being that he was still relatively new to the whole drug scene, he had to double-check everything with his predecessors before acting out his plans.

Snow had done everything but get on her knees and beg for him to let her come early with him, but he'd instructed her to wait until he called her. He had another twenty minutes before Juan and his brother Julio were due to arrive, so he'd shot her a text and let her know that she could make her way to the club.

He'd initially been hesitant about leaving her alone in a city to travel alone so late at night, until she reminded him who she was. Angel chuckled as he thought about her and the things she'd said to him earlier.

"These niggas know not to fuck with me, Angel. It's you that might need the escort."

Angel smirked again. Snow loved to make jokes

about him being such a fresh face in the cartel, but what she didn't know was that he was more than what met the eye. He'd chosen to be less involved in the cartel, but that hadn't stopped Vinny from schooling him throughout the years.

Angel might not have had as much hands-on experience as Snow, but he was smart, and always five steps ahead of the next man. Vinny had taught him to use his brain instead of his hands, and due to his father's current state, Angel was more than grateful for it.

Emelia Snow: Just parked. Your car is fast as shit.

Angel chuckled before responding to her.

Angel: You better not tear my car up.

Emelia Snow: You need to be worrying about me tearing your dick up. It's the only thing I don't know how to ride

Angel covered his face as a smile a mile wide crossed it.

Angel: Your fast ass. Probably just as fast as my car. Get in this club

Emelia Snow: lol!! I'm coming, so look for me. I look really sexy too, so don't be trying to feel on me

Angel responded, telling her to hurry up and get to him before shoving his phone down into the pocket on his suit pants. The black dress pants and black dress shirt were tailored for him and had him looking like money. The black suede shoes and expensive gold jewelry he rocked aided in his bossed-up appearance.

"Sir, your visitors are here," the same bartender that had been serving him all night told him.

Angel took another pull from his blunt before waving his hand to signal it was okay for them to come in. The two men standing behind her were accompanied by two more men who were much larger than all of them. They were decked out in black suits and shades, so Angel assumed they were bodyguards. His assumptions were proven to be correct when they came into the section, looking around before taking their place back outside his booth.

Juan and Julio walked in wearing silk shirts that were covered in an array of colors. Julio, the younger of the two, wore the shirt that was mostly covered in red, while Juan wore one with blue. They were both in black dress pants with some colorful-ass shoes on their feet. The heavy gold jewelry was too flashy, and nothing that Angel would ever wear, but everyone had their own style.

Since Juan was the one that he was there to do business with, Julio not so much, Angel gave Juan his attention. He'd already taken in his entire appearance as well as the frown on his face but had totally missed the large tattoo going down the side of his face. It was *SNOW* written in bold letters. That shit threw Angel for a loop, but he remained cool. After all, his calmness was what he was known for.

"Juan." He introduced himself, extending his hand toward Angel. "This is Julio." Juan nodded toward his brother.

Angel stood, towering over both men, and shook Juan's extended hand. He could tell the brothers were sizing him up, but they took their seats when he took his. The black briefcase that Juan had been carrying was next to his feet as he leaned forward with his hands crossed on his knees as if they were at some sort of social visit.

Instead of getting right down to business, as Angel would have liked, the brothers began pouring themselves drinks and bobbing their heads to the music.

"I was told it would be two of you," Juan said over the music.

Angel nodded once. "There is. My partner should be here in a second."

"You new? I've never seen you before." Juan gave him the once-over.

Angel leaned back in his seat and stretched one of his long legs out in front of him. "I'm sure you've heard of me. Angel DeLuca."

Juan's eyebrows raised before he stretched his hand out again. "Pardon me. I had no idea. The streets never really see you. How's Vinny?"

"Well. Thanks for asking." Angel kept it brief.

Though no one really saw him much, they were all aware of who Vinny's son was. After all, he was next in line to become their boss. Why wouldn't they know him?

"Your partner in the club?" Julio asked.

Angel looked in his direction but didn't answer. For some reason, Julio struck him as the pesky little brother type, so he couldn't really respect him. From the way he'd been dancing nonstop since getting in the booth, to the spiked-up way he was wearing his hair, he wasn't anybody Vinny would have ever done business with; therefore, neither would Angel.

Clearly, Julio had gotten the hint when Angel didn't answer, because he whispered something to Juan before turning back toward the dance floor and continuing to dance in his seat. Angel had just turned away from him when he noticed one of the large guards leaning down speaking to someone.

He didn't have to see Snow's face to know that was her; he could see her legs. He wouldn't miss those sexily toned calf muscles and big soft thighs anywhere. He'd fallen too deeply in love with them already to let them pass him by without noticing. The burly guards were blocking the rest of her body, but he'd seen enough to recognize that was his baby.

Angel tapped Juan's arm. "Let your boy know she's with me."

Juan looked up and yelled to the man in Spanish to let the girl past. When the man moved and Snow came into view, Angel's world stopped. The short black dress that was wrapped temptingly around her curves stopped mid-thigh, with a long gold zipper down the middle.

It was zipped up just enough to allow her breasts to spill out of the top. A small gold necklace wrapped around the center of her neck, while his favorite gold earrings of hers dangled from her ears. Her normally curly hair was straight and parted on one side so that some of it fell in her face.

On her wrists were an array of gold bracelets and a large diamond-studded gold watch. Her chocolate skin was shining and looked to be speckled with gold glitter. Angel could hardly breathe in the fitted pants he was wearing due to the rising hardness he could feel building.

Snow's face was calm, yet so serious. No traces of a smile anywhere as she stood like a stallion in the middle of the floor. Her dark slanted eyes looked even smaller due to her observing her surroundings in the dark.

"Got damn," Angel mumbled as he sat up in his seat.

"Shit," he heard Juan mumble as well.

Angel cut his eyes at that nigga quick as hell, but it didn't matter since his attention was trained on Snow. His mouth was open and everything. If he had stared any harder, Angel was sure Snow's clothes might have fallen off.

"Welcome to the meeting, gorgeous." Angel's raspy voice got her attention.

Snow's eyes zoomed in on him, and the once hard look that had been placed there turned into a smile. As soon as she began moving in their direction, Angel stood and reached for her hand. He held it until she was next to him taking her seat. When he was sure she was comfortable, he took his seat and looked across the small table at the brothers.

"Let's get down to business, shall we?"

Chapter Sixteen

She's been mine

The tension in the booth was so thick it could have been cut with a knife. All eyes were on Snow as the brothers struggled to find the words they wanted to say. Angel could tell from the look on their faces that Snow was not who they'd expected to see.

"Snow, how are you, my love? I thought you were still in California." Juan found his voice first.

Angel didn't care for him calling her his love, but he wouldn't say anything that might turn their business meeting into a personal one. However, he did look at Snow to see what was coming next. When he noticed she was looking at Juan but hadn't parted her lips yet, he turned back to face the men. It was obvious she wasn't there for the pleasantries.

"Snow, it's going to be like that?" Juan reached out

and looked at the paper. "You thought Mack would be sending flunkies that you could get over on." Snow rose to her feet. "You were wrong, playboy. Excuse me, I need to use the restroom."

All eyes were on her as she exited the booth. The moment she was gone, Angel ended their meeting. "No deal. Take this shit back to California."

"She with you now?" Juan asked, further letting Angel know he wasn't anyone they'd ever do business with.

Juan had just been turned down in a major financial way, and all he could think about was Snow. He was weak and definitely somebody the cartel needed to stay away from. Since he clearly had no issue showing Angel just how weak he was, Angel saw no reason to respect him.

Without uttering a word in response to Juan's question, Angel grabbed the things he'd brought with him into the booth and prepared to leave.

"Angel?" Juan rose to his feet when Angel stood. "Is Snow your girl?"

Angel stretched his long limbs before standing to his full height in front of Juan. He looked down at him with a smug look on his face. "Is she yours?"

Juan frowned. "Not anymore."

"That means she's not your concern, then." Angel moved to the side so that he could walk out of the booth but was stopped by Juan's words.

"She'll never love you like she loves me." He chuckled deviously.

Angel looked at him and smirked. "So, that's why she's been popping her pussy for me every time I look up, huh?" Angel stepped closer to Juan when he noticed Juan's chest puffing out as if he wanted an issue. Angel made sure to get close enough to him that their chests were touching. He needed Juan to know he didn't intimidate him. "I'm not the nigga that competes for a woman. I brought her here knowing who the fuck you were, so don't end up at the bottom of a river about some ass that don't even belong to you. She's been mine."

Juan's breathing grew rough, but Angel wasn't scared. Juan could try him if he wanted to, and Julio would be his mother's only living son.

"Angel." Snow interrupted the men's minor confrontation. "We're leaving?" She stopped next to him and looked between the two men.

"Yeah. We ain't doing no business with these niggas." Angel looked Juan up and down before shooting Julio's wimpy ass the same mug.

Unlike Juan, Julio retreated immediately. Juan, on the other hand, either loved Snow more than he loved himself, or he had too much pride, because he reached out to touch Snow's face, and Angel lost it. He'd seen Snow's hand moving toward her mouth out of his peripheral, but he was faster. His right hand caught the front of Juan's shirt while his left hand simultaneously went to his face.

Angel used his pointer finger swiftly just like Vinny had taught him. Juan's eye was gauged out and hanging from the socket before anyone had a chance to stop what was going on. Unable to do any more damage due to being snatched by the large security guard, Angel wiped his finger on the bottom of his shirt.

"Let him go, now." Snow's words were low and deadly as she held her gun pressed against the side of the man's head.

His hands released Angel's arms immediately and went up in surrender. "I'm sorry, Miss Mack."

"Whatever, get the fuck out my way," she told him with her gun still drawn.

able to help himself, he grabbed the side of her neck, raising her head so that they were making eye contact.

"I'm trying to make some good love tonight," Angel said.

Her head fell forward once more as she blushed. "Business, Angel. Let's do business," she whispered before pushing his arm softly.

Angel gave her the once-over once more before licking his lips and winking at her. When he turned back around, Juan's eyes were blazing with fire. He was angry, Angel could plainly see that, but what he wasn't seeing was another nigga grilling him like he wanted to make a move.

"You good?" Angel's question was laced with a warning that Juan caught.

After fluffing his shirt out some and twisting his neck from side to side, Juan nodded and picked up the briefcase that he'd brought into the booth with him. Angel made sure to watch his every move, more than positive that Snow was probably doing the same thing. When he did nothing that stood out, Angel scooted to the edge of the table to look over the contracts that they'd drawn up to do business with the cartel.

With Snow behind him, he was free to read everything thoroughly. Had he been alone, he would have never bowed his head and taken his eyes off the men.

"So, you want to move to the South? You didn't mention that to Mack," Angel sat up and told Juan.

"I thought that was something we could discuss in person," Juan said.

"You didn't think shit. You know that's not how the cartel does business." Snow's soft voice carried over Angel's shoulder. "Lay all your shit on the table. No surprises. You've been dealing long enough to know that shit, Juan." Snow leaned over Angel's shoulder to grab her hand but was stopped by the blade that she'd whipped out of her mouth.

Apparently, he was more accustomed to her rapid reactions with her blades, because he drew his hand back before she had the chance to cut it.

A subtle chuckle left his mouth. "Still carrying that blade, I see."

"Don't you put your hands on me, Juan," Snow fired off quickly.

Angel stopped moving and looked over his shoulder at her once again. The only time he'd ever heard her voice sound that cold was when she'd pulled the gun on the man at the restaurant for threatening his life. Her expression was a deep but very sexy scowl as she twisted what he assumed to be her blade around on the tip of her tongue. The rapid rising and falling of her chest was also an obvious sign of her anger.

Angel's hand went to her knee and rested there. Her eyes shifted from Juan to Angel, and her facial expression changed almost instantly. Gone was the anger, and replacing it was love. Her eyes softened at the same time her mouth curved on one side. She wasn't completely smiling, but she wasn't as tense as she had been before.

"You okay?" Angel spoke so only she could hear him.

She nodded.

Angel gave her knee a light squeeze. "You look so fucking sexy. I had to stop looking at you before my dick got hard."

Snow's half smile turned into one much larger, and infectious. Angel even thought he saw her eyes twinkle when she held her head down to stop the blushing. Un-

Angel watched her with a smile on his face and a hard dick in his pants. Snow running niggas would never get old to him. He loved that shit. After all the years of trying to see why Mack and Vinny allowed Empress and Zulema to run the streets with them, he finally saw it. That shit was like foreplay to a street nigga. Angel didn't know where she'd hidden the gun in her little dress, but he didn't care either. All he cared about was that she knew when and how to use it.

"Angel, let's slide," Snow said.

"Say no more." Angel grabbed her elbow and ushered her out of the club.

Pushing through the throngs of people was a little harder due to the number of people on the lower level of the club. Where Angel and Snow had been conducting their business meeting had been a tad bit more secluded, so they hadn't known just how many people they were surrounded by until descending the stairs.

Large crowds were something that Angel despised, especially in an area he was unfamiliar with, so with his hand at the small of Snow's back, he pushed her briskly toward the exit. When they were finally outside, he grabbed her hand and pulled her along with him.

"Where'd you park?" he questioned her as he looked over his shoulder.

"Right there, across the street." She pointed.

Angel looked toward where she had her finger pointing and spotted his car. "Why didn't you valet?"

Snow sucked her teeth. "So they could put something in our car, or hold it so that we could be ambushed?" Snow switched past him and grabbed the handle to the driver side door. "I think not. You've got to be quicker on your feet, Angel."

Angel stood at the front of his car watching her as

she fumbled around in her purse for what he assumed to be his keys. He wanted so badly to tell her that all she had to do was key in the code on his keypad, but since she thought she knew it all, he would let her be. Plus, he enjoyed watching the beautiful scowl that crossed her face every so often.

"You need some help?" Angel asked with a smirk.

"Hell no."

"You sure?" Angel probed mockingly.

Snow finally stopped fumbling with her purse and looked up at him with her hand on her hip. "Do you want to help me or do you want to stand there getting on my nerves?"

A casual smirk crossed Angel's face as he walked to the passenger side of his own car and leaned over the hood.

"You might want to hurry up. I'm sure your little boyfriend is on his way out of the club." Angel looked over his shoulder toward the club entrance before looking back at Snow. "He's probably going to want to retaliate. I fucked his eye up pretty bad."

Snow's face was calm when she looked across the hood of the car at him. "Don't fucking play with me right now, Angel."

With subtle laughter, Angel said the code lowly to her, and seconds later they were in the car. As soon as the warmth of his interior encompassed them, they made themselves comfortable before she pushed the start button and the car purred to life.

"Is this what took you so long to get here? You couldn't get the door open?"

Snow's eyes rolled. "No, I was getting dressed." Her head moved left to right, checking for any oncoming cars before merging into traffic. "It wasn't that I couldn't get the damn door open with the key, Angel. I couldn't do the shit with you standing there staring at me like that."

"What did I have to do with anything?"

Snow looked out of her window and continued driving as if she hadn't heard him.

"Snow?" Angel's hand slid between her thighs and rested there.

She jumped from his contact but remained quiet as she drove. Angel watched the way her eyes shifted as he rubbed and squeezed the inside of one of her trembling thighs.

"Baby, you good?" He leaned forward some so that he could see her face better.

"I'm fine."

"You don't look fine." Angel turned in his seat some so that he could see her better. "You were cool a minute ago. What happened that fast?"

Snow's chest sank a little as she exhaled and ran her hand though her hair. Angel was mesmerized by the way it fell into her face. It looked so soft and smelled even better. Every so often she would move her head and he'd catch a whiff of whatever it was she used on it.

"So, you're really not going to tell me what's wrong?"

"You are what's wrong, Angel." She sounded exasperated.

Angel's brows knitted together. "What the fuck I do?"

"Nothing," she sighed. "It's just I'm not used to having you around. I wasn't fumbling with the keys or my purse. I was getting ready to pull my gun out. I saw Julio running out of the club looking around. I didn't know if he was looking for us or not, so I was going to shoot him." Snow turned her head only long enough to make eye contact before looking back to the road. "Angel, you just . . ." Snow scratched her head again.

"You make things harder for me. I'm used to working by myself. When I'm alone, I don't have to care about anything or anybody, I can do whatever I want without any worries. But your ass"—she pointed at him dramatically—"you make shit hard."

Angel snickered, as did she. They laughed the seriousness of their situation off for only a moment before the mood was right back solemn. Angel wasn't sure what she wanted him to say, because he wasn't going anywhere anytime soon.

"What can I do about that?" Angel asked.

She shrugged. "Nothing. It'll probably just take me some time."

"Time for what?" Angel squeezed her thigh. "You do realize I'm grown as fuck, right? I don't need you trying to protect me, nor do I need you worrying about shit you should already know. You're way more into this shit than I am. If you feel like there's something that needs to be done, then handle your business. I'm good."

Snow nodded, but the silence remained. Angel wasn't really fond of the quiet, so he spoke again. "What is it about me that has you off your square? Because we don't have to work together if it's that bad for you."

"I don't know. It's like when you're there, I'm so busy trying not to step on your toes or looking too rowdy that I hold back, and that's not good. Holding back could get one of us hurt."

"Well, stop doing that. When you show out, my dick gets hard." Angel's mouth curved into a smile when Snow covered her face and blushed. "If you really want to get rowdy, sit on my dick and do it."

"You make me so sick." She giggled just as she pulled into the parking lot of their hotel.

Angel released her thigh long enough for her to get

herself together and out of the car. By the time she was out and at the hood of the car, so was Angel. Before walking away, he grabbed her hand and led her through the doors. The hotel lobby was empty and quiet as they headed for the elevators.

With no words having been spoken until they reached their hotel room, Angel was shocked when he walked into the bathroom to Snow seated on the counter with her legs open. His eyes went from her face to the strapless bra she wore, before traveling down to the lace panties resting snugly around her bottom.

"Me not stepping on your toes or getting rowdy is me showing you how loyal I am to you. I value your position in my life, and contrary to what you may believe, it doesn't bother me to submit to you." Snow's eyes batted, giving Angel a chance to admire the extralong eyelashes she was sporting. "In fact, I find myself wanting to more and more these days, but when it comes to being Snow and Emelia," she held her head down momentarily as she battled with what to say next, "I'm not that good at separating the two."

Angel leaned against the frame of the door with his hands stuck deep into his pockets. Her words sat heavy at the forefront of his brain as he did his best to understand where she was coming from.

"You're the only person on this entire planet that makes me Emelia. Everyone else but you knows Snow and that's it." She shook her head and smiled again before hopping from the bathroom counter.

Though he was doing his best to keep his mind on their conversation, seeing her ass bounce back as she steadied herself on her feet was too distracting. Angel's hands were on her and pulling her panties down before he could stop himself.

His face only inches from hers, Angel pecked her

nose. Snow's mouth found his immediately. Their tongues danced to a lover's tune, entangling them into a moment much deeper than they'd anticipated. Heavy breathing and aggressive touching quickly filled the small bathroom.

Snow's hands had just reached his belt loop when Angel stopped her. Reluctantly, he pulled away and took a step back. He could feel his erection pressing hard through the fabric, doing its best to break free, but he needed a moment.

With Snow standing a few feet away from him bottomless and breathing hard, Angel closed his eyes momentarily.

"Emelia, you don't have to compromise who you are just to be with me." His eyes opened and found hers. "As a matter of fact, don't do that. Be yourself, or don't be with me."

She stood staring at him with an unreadable expression.

Angel raised his eyebrows. "Got it?"

"Got it."

"Good." Angel rushed back to her with an unexplainable amount of urgency and picked her up.

With her legs and arms circling his body, Angel carried her to the bed and laid her down. He hovered over her while doing his best to remove her bra. It took him a moment, but once he finally got it, he was rewarded instantly. Her breasts sprang to life, stretching the erection in his pants further.

"I love having you," Angel confessed.

Snow's smile lit up the room. "I love being had."

Angel was sure his smile mirrored hers as they got lost in their own thoughts admiring each other. One day when he was free with nothing but time on his hands, he was going to have to seriously think about how he'd gone so many years without her. With the way he was feeling right then, he had no clue. Just the thought of being away from Emelia too long gave him a sick feeling in his gut. Hopefully that wasn't something he'd ever have to experience again.

Chapter Seventeen

Because you broke my
heart before

The noisy pots and pans clinked together as Snow
made her way through the narrow aisles of her drug lab.
With droopy eyes, she covered her mouth and yawned.
Normally, she would have never come to work as fa-
tigued as she was, but she had no other choice.

Although she was beyond tired, family and the cartel
came first, and since they both needed her right then,
she was there. It was a little after eight o'clock in the
morning, and she'd been up since five with Angel driving back to Columbia. Had she known last night that
she was coming right back to work the next morning,
she would have taken her ass to bed, but she hadn't.

She and Angel had just come in from a night of partying and eating when he received a call from one of their

workers letting them know that another shipment of cocaine had come in. Being that their dope deliveries were scheduled, the call caught them both off guard. They'd stayed up half the night trying to figure out what had gone on, only to find out the order had come from Vinny's home office.

Snow sighed just thinking about it. Poor Vinny. Since they'd agreed not to let anyone in on his sickness, the call had seemed completely normal, therefore bringing about a large and very unnecessary shipment of dope. She and Angel had been working tirelessly to get everything back in order, and now she was paying for it. Her lids were barely open, but she had to get through the day.

"Looks like somebody had a late night with the boss." The young girl with the bright pink weave spoke as Snow passed her station.

Snow spun around quickly. "Say what?"

Pink weave smiled and showed the mouth full of gold. Snow frowned. "I said, it looks like you had fun last night." She giggled again as if what she was saying was actually funny to Snow. "Who can blame you, though? Mr. DeLuca is fine as fuck."

A few snickers and agreements sounded out around Snow. Her insides grew warm immediately as she listened to the women speak on Angel.

"If y'all worried about this dope, how y'all worried about me? We'd be done in here by now." Snow rolled her eyes and began walking away. "And stay the fuck out of my business," she grumbled.

When she got into her office, she slammed the door behind her and flopped down into her seat. She was already tired, so the last thing she wanted to do was entertain a bunch of gossiping bitches. Normally she might not have gone off on the women so bad, but right then wasn't the time. She was dealing with enough from Angel's ass. She didn't need theirs too.

Angel had been acting annoyingly moody since finding out Vinny had been the one behind the order. Though she could understand how his father's illness was affecting him, she still didn't see a point in reverting back to the angry butthole he'd grown to be, every time something went wrong. Why couldn't he just be like normal people and talk about his feelings?

Snow rolled her eyes at the thought of Angel's attitude.

She'd been doing her best to not think about how distant he'd been with her all last night and that morning, but it was hard. Now, thanks to the dummies she had working for her, he was back on the brain, and Snow hated it. To rid herself of Angel and his shenanigans, she immersed herself in her work.

The day moved in slow motion as Snow serviced one distributor after another. By the time it came time for her to take lunch, she was more than ready. A large hot coffee from the coffee shop had been on her mind for hours, and she was going to make sure she got it. Still not in the mood to talk to her mouthy workers about her personal life, she hurried and left the building.

Snow was walking out the door when her phone rang. It was Angel, so she didn't bother to answer it. She was in no mood to talk to him. After ignoring his call, she walked down the sidewalk in search of her car. It didn't take long for her to realize she was stranded. Angel had dropped her off that morning.

Her arms were still folded over her chest when her phone began ringing again. It was Angel. This time she answered because she needed a ride, and she wanted to make sure nothing was wrong.

"Hello," she answered with an attitude.

"Stop all that cutting up and come get in this truck."

Snow looked all around the parking lot until she noticed the black SUV parked in the back of the parking lot. She tried to hide the smile on her face but failed miserably. It spread from one ear to the other. Even when she was mad at him, he made her happy.

"What are you doing here?" She talked to him as she walked to the truck.

"Taking you to get some food. Come on."

Snow hung up and made her way to the truck. When she was next to it, Angel's driver, Hector, hopped out and helped her inside. The strong smell of Angel DeLuca wafted up her nose as soon as her butt hit the seat. As she'd done every other time she'd ever ridden with him, she breathed a little deeper and savored his scent.

Unsure if she wanted to still be angry with him or not, Snow sat straight in her seat without looking at him. She was going to wait for him to speak first. When he didn't, she glanced in his direction quickly. The tailored gray suit, red vest, and slim-cut tie looked magnificent on him.

Snow had always known the importance of a man having his suits tailored, thanks to Juan. But Angel was killing it. Juan had long ago made her appreciate the beauty of a man in a suit, and Angel's long, toned body was taking her up a notch.

The way the material lay closely against his chest, arms, and thighs made him appear delectable and rich. Like her favorite chocolate. Only Angel wasn't chocolate, more of a coffee brown with a teaspoon of milk and sugar.

With one of his hands resting on his thigh as he looked out the window, he sat relaxed. The curl of his

long lashes took her breath away every time he blinked.
His full lips pouted out just as they had since they were
kids, only now they were different. Now, they held a
trickle of her on them. The puckered red kiss that had
hung from them so many years was now gone, having
been placed between her thighs during the weekend's
sexual explorations. Snow's mouth dropped open when
he stretched one of his legs and the print of his manhood
strained through the fabric of his pants. Though she
could tell it wasn't hard, it was so thick and full, the
way it was stuffed down in his pants made her want
reach out and touch it, but she wouldn't because she
was mad. She must remember that.

"How are you feeling today, Emelia?" Angel grabbed
her hand and held it in his.

"Fine, now that you're back to normal. How are
you?"

He smiled and held the back of her hand up to his
mouth and kissed it. "Back to normal?"

"Yes. You are killing me with this back and forth.
One minute you're a spawn from Satan, the next you're
the sweetest thing I've ever known. I just don't understand. Your ass is giving me whiplash with all these
damn mood swings."

The driver's laughter gathered both their attention.
He was trying his hardest not to laugh but had completely failed. His light brown cheeks were turning red
as he focused on the road. When he noticed they were
both looking at him, he covered his mouth.

"My apologies, Mr. DeLuca."

"Call him Angel," Snow spoke up.

Angel looked over at her with a raised brow.

"Mr. DeLuca sounds so formal. I like Angel better,"
she tried to reason.

"Well, Angel it is then, Hector," Angel told him.

Hector shook his head casually. "Mr. DeLuca is fine. Thank you, Snow." He smiled at her.

"So, I'm Snow and he's Mr. DeLuca. I must not be as important as him?" Snow crossed her arms over her chest, playing like she had an attitude.

Angel rubbed her hand and kissed it again. "What would you prefer?"

Snow tapped her chin playfully as if she was thinking. "Mrs. DeLuca." She was smiling at Angel as his cheeks turned red.

Snow didn't think she would ever grow tired of the way she made him blush. It was the cutest thing. To have a grown man blushing on her account made her feel warm on the inside. Especially one as sexy and powerful as Angel.

"You'd have to marry me first."

"You think I'd make you a good wife? Hard-core, rowdy, drug dealer, mean, I could go on." She smiled playfully as she rattled off some of her most unfavorable characteristics.

Angel gave her the once-over before rubbing his chin. "As long as you make me cheese grits every morning, then hell yeah, you would. I don't care about all the rest of that shit."

Angel and Snow both fell over laughing. Her a little louder than him.

"Speaking of cheese grits, you should make me some tonight," Angel said.

The both of them held on to their serious faces for as long as they could before they were laughing again. Snow was so thankful that he'd lost his attitude and was back to being the Angel that she loved.

The truck pulled to a stop. "I hope you don't mind me picking lunch, but I wanted some ribs bad as hell." Angel rubbed his stomach for emphasis.

Snow looked out the window and noticed they were at a place called Sticky Fingers. It was a popular rib shack that had some of the best burgers and ribs in town. She had eaten there on a few occasions with Empress since being in town, and they were pretty good. She'd tried many different dishes, and they'd all been delicious. She was sure today would be no different.

"I love it here." She clapped her hands softly as she thought about the ribs.

"Me too." Angel handed Vinny's driver some money, and he hopped out of the truck. "I hope you didn't want anything in particular, because I already ordered. I didn't know how long you were going to take for lunch, and I didn't want you to get back to the spot too late. You know them hos in there don't know how to act."

"You ain't lying! I had to check one of them smart-mouth bitches today. Talking about the boss got me tired and shit." Snow rolled her eyes. "That ho had me fucked up thinking my personal life was open for discussion."

Angel's beautiful smile had her smiling right back at him. "You don't want them to know you're with me?"

"It ain't that. I just don't want them thinking we're friends or no shit like that. That's how people lose respect for you. The moment they start thinking we're friends, they're going to slack off and I'ma have to fire their asses up."

Angel's smile was still there, taking her breath away. It was sinful for a man to be as fine as Angel. Every time she looked at him, nasty thoughts took off through her brain.

"Leave them girls alone."

"Nope. Then they gon' say some shit about you being fine." Snow sucked her teeth loudly. "I almost cut all of their damn hands off."

His deep laughter made her chest vibrate as his hand covered hers. "You don't have to do that."

"Why I don't?"

"Because I only want you. Hard-core, mean-ass Snow." He rubbed up and down her arm. "Even if I don't know you that well."

"Why would you say that? You do know me."

"We've been apart for a long time, Emelia. There's things I've missed."

"Like what?"

When Angel's shoulders shrugged subtly, the truck got quiet again. Neither of them saying anything else, just waiting for their driver to return. It was torture for Snow because there was so much she wanted to say but didn't know where to start.

She'd observed over the past few weeks that Angel still wasn't much of a talker, which was the total opposite of her. It had been that way since they'd been kids, so she wasn't surprised, but it was still hard for her to contain herself sometimes.

"Tell me about it." The pad of his thumb rubbed the skin on the back of her hand.

Wide-eyed, Snow looked at him. "Tell you about what?"

"What's on your mind? I can tell you're thinking about something. Your eyebrows are frowned a little, and you have your eyes squinted."

"I wasn't thinking about anything in particular. I just want to talk to you. Tell you whatever it is you feel like you don't know about me."

"Well, tell me."

"I don't know what you want to know. You never say very much, so I'm always left to figure things out."

"That's a lie. I talk to you all the time."

Snow turned in her seat and tucked one of her legs beneath the other. "Lies. Tell me something now then, I don't care what it is."

Angel stretched some in his seat, showcasing the hard ripples in his chest. The thin shirt hugged his body upon his movement and captured Snow's eyes immediately.

"I need more than that, baby. You got to tell me what you want to know." He ran his hand over his wavy hair. "I could say some random shit that might not mean nothing to you."

"Well, you can start by telling me how you're mad with me one minute and super sweet the next. You're like a Sour Patch Kid. I get Vinny is sick, but every time he has a bad day, you treat me like I'm the one that gave him dementia or something."

Angel's dimples deepened as he smiled at her before ducking his head momentarily. "I can't help it. I'm like this with everybody. You just happen to be around me the most. So it seems like it's just you, but it's not. I'm sorry about that."

Snow waved him off. "You ain't sorry. You do it too much to be sorry. Sorry people apologize and never do it again. You just continue to turn up on me. I be ready to knock all your teeth down your throat." She rolled her eyes at him playfully. "You're lucky I think you'll be ugly with no teeth, or else I would have hit you in your damn mouth." Snow shook her head dramatically. "And it's so crazy, because you always look so handsome when you have an attitude, but then you open your fucking mouth. I don't be knowing whether to slap you or make love to you."

"You ever slap me again, and I promise I will break your wrists."

"See what I mean?" Snow frowned. "You're holding my hand while telling me you'll break my wrists. What kind of mess is that, Angel? Why are you so mean to me?"

He shrugged.

"There has to be a reason. Tell me. Is it because of Genesis? Because I would never do no shit like what she did to you."

"I'm not mean to you, and no, it's not because of Genesis. I just told you what I was. Vinny being sick just takes me out of my element whenever I think about it. I don't mean to take it out on you, but I really can't help it."

"Well, you better start helping it before I stop being your friend."

Angel smirked at her. "So? I don't want to be your friend anyway."

Snow raised her eyebrows at him. "Oh, you don't want to be my friend? Dang, that hurt."

For a reason she couldn't quite grasp herself, his words hurt her feelings. Even with her knowing he was probably joking, she could feel herself getting down. Although she was doing her best to remain calm and collected, her thoughts were getting the best of her. Before long, she felt her throat getting tight. She hurried to clear it before it got too far out of control.

The truck was quiet, and she was more than certain Angel had become privy to every ounce of emotion that was weighing in her silence. He gave himself away when he turned in his seat so that he was facing her. The hand that had been holding her hand was now touching her scalp as he massaged his hands through her hair.

"Of course I want to be your friend. I just don't think it'll work out for us in the end because I love you too much. I just want to be your man, not your friend."

"Why not? We should be friends too."

Snow hated how vulnerable she sounded, but she had to get this out before it was too late. She'd replayed her and Juan's relationship a million times in her mind, trying to make sense of where they'd gone wrong, and she always ended back up at the fact that they weren't friends.

They had been a couple, and occasional business partners, but never friends. When she'd asked why he'd slept with her best friend, the only answer that stood out was the fact that he considered her his friend. Whereas Snow was too busy to be "fun," her friend had been. It had taken Snow forever to see the foundation in that, but now she did. Thanks to Angel.

He ran his other hand over his face as he released a sigh. "Because I think you're pretty. You make me laugh. You make me angry. You make me feel . . . good, for lack of a better word. Everything that a lover should evoke. Trying to be friends has the potential to fuck up our intimacy."

He grabbed the back of his neck and rubbed it before scratching his jaw. He then rubbed his face once more before touching her hand again. His fidgeting was a clear sign of his discomfort. Seeing how nervous he was let Snow in on his vulnerability when it came to her. He too was scarred from the past, whether he admitted it or not.

"I don't like any of this." He waved his hand around the car, referencing his life. "It's too fancy. I'm a laid-back dude. I like to drive fast cars, fuck the city up with my girl, shop, take trips, and just do me. You know? But

all of that changed in the blink of an eye. I had go⟨⟩
tentions before, even thought I had the relatio⟨⟩
thing figured out, but then Genesis's ass showe⟨⟩
how wrong I'd been."

"I thought you said it wasn't because of her?" Snow
interrupted.

"It's not, it's you. I know how I am when it comes to
women I love, and as I mentioned a moment ago, I
think we'd do better to remain lovers. Friendliness
causes boundaries to be crossed, and plainly putting it,
I don't have time for that shit. Be my girl, and let me
love you without all the complications."

Snow sat at a loss for words as she stared at his
strong jawline and chiseled lips. The thick eyebrows
with the heavy crease in them. The deep dimple in his
cheek. Such a beautiful man.

"So, you seriously think we can't be lovers and
friends?" she asked as she noticed his driver walking
to the car.

Though her stomach was growling ferociously, she
almost hated to see him coming. Angel didn't have to
tell her that he was going to end their deep conversation once Hector got back inside; she already knew.

"Angel, tell me. Why wouldn't it?" Snow asked
hurriedly, trying to get as much out of Angel as she
could before the conversation came to an end.

He looked at her with a sad and lost look in his eyes.
It was nothing like the self-assured man she had been
around for the past few months. This one was worried
about something. But what? She hoped it wasn't her,
because she was simple. He didn't have to worry about
anything when it came to her, him, or them together.

"Angel?"

With his unmoving eyes on her, he answered. "Be-

...use I was your friend before, and you broke my heart."

The front door opened, and his driver climbed in with the food. He handed the bag back to Snow before buckling his seat belt and pulling away. The thick silence surrounding Angel and Snow as they sat in the back seat was driving her crazy. It was on the tip of her tongue to ask how she had broken his heart when he was the one who left her, but she couldn't. His driver would probably hear her, and she was sure that wasn't what Angel wanted.

The sounds of their chewing slowly became louder than the music as they feasted on the savory barbecued ribs and French fries. Snow was trying her best to eat like a lady without messing up her face or her clothes, but the raging animal next to her practiced no such thing. His hands and face were speckled with barbecue sauce as he nearly devoured the bone in his hand.

"You are such a messy date." She smiled at him to lighten the mood.

Angel stopped mid-bite and looked at her, the rib bone still dangling between his fingertips.

"You fucking barbarian." She tossed a napkin at him.

When he couldn't do anything else, he laughed at her. He laughed so heartily that she joined in. Before long, his driver was also laughing.

After his laughter subsided, Angel tried his best to clean his hands and mouth before continuing.

By the time they'd gotten back to her lab, Snow had finished eating and was cleaning her hands with the wet wipes that had come with her meal. She then pulled her compact mirror out and checked her face. When she was sure she looked okay, she put it away and fixed her clothing. She loaded all of their trash back into the bag.

"Thank you for lunch, Mr. DeLuca," Snow said.

Angel looked at her and winked. "No problem. What time do you think you'll be finished here?"

"Maybe around five."

"I'll be here twenty minutes before."

"Will we finish talking?"

He looked a little smug. "Probably not tonight. I want to do something a little different."

Different didn't sound good to Snow, but she didn't want to speak on it right then. Instead, she nodded as the driver got out to open the door for her. She leaned over toward Angel as Hector rounded the back of the truck.

"I'll forget how rough you made love to me last night if you'll just be my friend," she offered in attempt to lighten his mood again.

He shook his head. "Nope. I'm not that kind of man."

"What kind are you?"

"The kind that wants you to remember."

"Why?" she probed as her door opened.

"I want you to always remember the good things. The way I make you feel . . . if it's good. I want to be remembered for it."

There were still a few things that Snow wanted to say, but they would probably take too long, and she had to go. "You headed back to your office?"

He nodded.

"Okay. Well, text me so I won't miss you too much."

Angel smiled as Snow slid out of the truck and to her feet.

238

A'zayler

Before closing her door, Snow blew him a kiss and watched as he caught it and placed it on his lips. She then headed back inside. As she took the stairs two at a time, she inwardly wished she was still in the back seat of the SUV with Angel. She wasn't sure how she'd broken his heart when he'd been the one to leave her, but hopefully he wouldn't leave her unknowing for too long.

Chapter Eighteen

Was it easy for you to leave me?

What the hell is wrong with that nigga? Angel wondered as he watched D'Angelo storm into the house and up the stairs without even acknowledging his or his father's presence. Rude was an understatement when it came to that fool. He was always on some other shit. Versus bringing attention to him, Angel ignored him just like he did all of the rest of the time and turned back to his father.

"What you say, Daddy?"

"Mack is going to have your head, son." Vinny's voice held a hint of humor as he rocked back and forth in his favorite recliner.

"I'm not scared of Mack." Angel sat on the floor next to his father's chair, looking over the pile of paperwork in his lap.

Since he was extremely tired and only had paperwork to complete, he'd decided to spend some time
with Vinny. Though today wasn't a "good day," Angel
was still enjoying his father's company. From the moment he'd walked into the living room, Vinny had been
excited to see him.

His face lit up as it always did whenever Angel was
around. Even with him turning down the cartel at
every turn, Vinny had still been very proud of Angel
and all of his accomplishments. Much like he was right
then. He'd been going on and on about how happy
Mack should be to have him as his son-in-law. Angel
had considered telling Vinny that he wasn't married to
Snow yet, but changed his mind. Him being fake married seemed to bring Vinny joy, so he'd leave it like
that.

"Damn right you aren't. No son of mine will ever be
afraid of another man." Vinny sipped from the large
cup of water in the armrest of his chair. "So, when will
the grandbabies start coming?"

Angel smiled brightly as he stopped reading the
paper in front of him. "Soon, I hope," he told Vinny as
he entertained the thought of what his and Snow's
baby might look like.

"Babies? Whose having babies?" Empress walked
in and sat on Vinny's lap.

Angel scooted over some to give them some room
before turning his attention back to the paperwork in
his lap. He didn't bother to answer Empress because
she got carried away too fast. All he'd have to do was
say he and Vinny were talking about him and Snow,
and she'd be planning the baby shower.

"Angel. He's married to Mack's daughter," Vinny
told his wife.

Empress hit Angel's shoulder. "Say what now?"

Versus saying it aloud and disrupting Vinny's thoughts, Angel shook his head subtly.

"Oh, so that's where all of this baby talk is coming from?" Empress said.

"Yeah, Daddy wants grandkids," Angel said.

"Well, so do I. When you do you plan on giving us some?"

Angel looked over his shoulder at his smiling mother. "After the honeymoon."

The two of them exchanged smiles just as he heard the front door slam closed. He momentarily wondered who it could have been until he checked the time. It was a little after five, so he was sure it was Snow. She'd sent him a text earlier telling him she had a ride. He'd asked her a few times who was picking her up, but she hadn't responded.

He hadn't talked to her since, so his eyes were glued to the door, waiting for her to appear. When she finally did, he could tell something was off with her. She looked stressed, worried, or something. Her eyes were lazy, and her mouth was flat.

"There's my daughter-in-law." Vinny welcomed her warmly.

Snow's face perked up instantly. "Vinny, how are you today?"

"Good, but I'd be even better with a few grandkids running around here."

Snow frowned. "Sorry, but I'm not having any kids with your son. He's selfish."

The room was quiet as they all looked at her. Angel couldn't see the look on his parents' faces, but he was sure theirs probably looked like his.

"Damn, Angel. What in the hell have you done to this girl?" Empress snickered.

"That's the same thing I want to know." Angel stared at Snow.

Angel didn't take too kindly to being called names, but he would let her slide right then. It was clear she had something going on, so he'd grant her that temporary pass.

"Excuse me, y'all, I need to shower and get some sleep," Snow told them before walking out of the living room.

Angel sat in place, watching her exit. It was silent for a moment after she left until Vinny spoke. "You'd better go check on her. Never let your woman stay mad with you." He nudged Angel's shoulder, urging him from the floor.

As bad as Angel wanted to stay seated, he pushed his work to the side and left the living room. He took the stairs to the bedroom Snow occupied and went in. He could hear the shower running as soon as he opened the door. He looked around the bedroom before going into the bathroom.

When he walked inside, she was bending over removing her pants from her ankle. Her round ass was barely covered by her small boy short panties, which almost made him forget why he was there.

"The fuck is your problem?" Angel asked.

Snow jumped upon hearing his voice. With her hand over her chest, she looked at him through the mirror.

"Get out."

"Not until you tell me what the hell has gotten into you."

Snow went back to removing her clothes and ignoring him. Angel watched her get almost naked before snatching her arm and pulling her to him. His face was close to hers when he squinted his eyes.

"Tell me what's wrong with you, Snow."

Her facial expression changed momentarily before she looked away. "Don't call me that."

Angel didn't miss the fact that she didn't want him calling her Snow, so clearly whatever she was mad about wasn't going to make her leave him. That was a plus.

"Emelia." He grabbed both sides of her face and softened his voice, hoping to gain some answers. "Tell me what's bothering you."

"Nothing." She shook her head out of his grasp and leaned back against the sink.

Angel closed the distance between them again. "Tell me, so I can fix it."

Snow's head tilted to the side as she swiped at her eye quickly. When she raised her head, he noticed her wet eyes.

"All day I've been trying to figure out how I broke your heart, when you're the one that left me." She finally made eye contact with him. "You're penalizing me for something that you did. That's not fair, and I won't let you do it."

Damn. Angel hated that he'd even said anything about that earlier. The moment it left his mouth, he'd known she wasn't going to let it go. Now there he was, caught up in bringing up old shit that he had no interest in talking about anymore.

With one hand, Angel rubbed across his face before making eye contact with her again. She was still staring at him, apparently waiting for an answer. When it became obvious that he wasn't getting out of this one, he figured he might as well get it over with.

"You broke my heart because instead of holding me down, you chose to dip."

Snow stood from the counter. "What? Are you serious right now? You left me, Angel." She poked the center of his chest for emphasis.

"Yeah, I'm serious. I told you I didn't want to break up, and you still ended it."

"Because you were leaving me, Angel!" she yelled.

"So the fuck what, Emelia? I was leaving California, not you. That was you that chose to be on that *let's separate* bullshit. Not me. I would have loved your ass just the same." Angel's body grew warm as his emotions began to take over him. "I blew up your phone for months, and you ignored me like I ain't mean shit." He fumed as he leaned down so that he was in her face. "Why did you shut me out, Emelia? Huh? Why the fuck did you leave me?" Angel was full out yelling at her.

He hadn't meant for his emotions to get the best of him like that, but it was too late. Her shutting him out of her life had been one of the hardest things he'd ever had to go through, and he almost hated her for it. He'd known how strongly he felt about this topic, which was the main reason he'd been planning to avoid it for as long as he could.

Angel was so angry that he wanted to ignore the tears streaming down her cheeks right then, but it was too hard. Everything in him wanted to be so angry that her hurt feelings wouldn't bother him, but that wasn't happening. Her tears and his heart didn't mix. He loved her too much.

"Chill out, Emelia. It's over with now, baby. We don't have to talk about this anymore." He pulled her to him and hugged her.

She cried for a few more minutes, but stopped long enough to drop a bomb on him. "I left you because I was pregnant, Angel."

Wait a minute. Did he hear what he thought he'd heard? To be sure, Angel pushed her away from him so that he could see her face. "Come again?"

Snow's lashes were wet and stuck together as she batted them slowly. "I was pregnant." Her voice was just as low as it had been before.

"What? Why didn't you tell me?" Angel questioned before taking a few steps back.

He could feel himself getting angry and didn't want to accidentally hurt her.

"I didn't want to ruin your life, Angel."

Angel's head turned to her quickly. "Ruin my life? A baby with you would have been the best thing that could have ever happened to me, to us, to our family! Why would you hide something like that from me?"

Snow shook her head and wiped at her face again. "You're saying that now, but we were kids then. You wanted to be a doctor more than anything in the world. Had I told you I was pregnant, you would have stayed in California, and I didn't want that for you. I wanted you to follow your dreams and be happy." She sniffed back the fresh set of tears resting in her eyes. "I left you for you. It was the best decision."

Angel's world felt like it was spinning as he slid to the floor in front of her. With his knees up and his elbows resting on them, Angel held his head in his hands. His mind was all over the place trying to make sense of her admission.

"What happened to my baby?" he heard himself whisper.

"Some stuff went on, and I ended up having a miscarriage."

Angel breathed a sigh of relief. His chest had been tight up until that moment. The last thing he'd wanted to do was hate her for aborting his child.

Snow slid onto the floor in front of him and grabbed his hands from his head. "When I had the miscarriage and went through everything that I went through, I figured that was the world's way of telling me that we weren't meant to be."

"Did your parents know?"

"My mom did. I made her promise not to tell anyone." Snow sat comfortably on the floor. "After I lost the baby, I threw myself headfirst into the cartel. At first it was a coping mechanism for losing the both of you, but then it became my life." She shrugged. "In the world of drugs, I don't have to care or feel anything."

"But with me, you care and feel everything?"

She nodded, and oddly, Angel understood.

"I'm sorry, baby girl." He opened his legs and pulled her to him.

Snow went willingly. With her arms circled around his neck, she held him to her. "Angel?"

"Mmm?" he mumbled.

"Was it easy for you to leave me?"

Angel squeezed her tighter. "Hell fucking no. I don't think I ever got over it."

"Me either. I always thought that was weird being that we were so young and didn't even know what real love was."

Angel pulled his face away from her body. "I don't care how old we were, what I felt for you was real." Slow and softly, Angel's hands slid up and down her bare back. "I ain't never loved nobody like that, not even Genesis."

"Juan and I were never like you and me. What we had was more of a business relationship with fun times. We never did the lovers thing for real. That was actually one of the main reasons why I allowed him to live after catching him with my best friend." Snow pushed backward some so that she was seated on the floor. "He didn't know about the way I loved you, but she did. She should have never done that."

Angel watched the way Snow's facial expression changed as she spoke of her friend's betrayal. She'd gone from having tears in her eyes to having them squinted tightly in a scowl.

"Forgive me for not understanding why you're still so mad at her, and not at that nigga." Angel spoke as evenly as possible, being careful not to make her angry with him.

Unfortunately, the softness of his voice meant nothing to her. She proved that by hopping from the floor and removing the rest of her clothing and getting into the shower. Angel sat in place, trying to decide whether he felt like patting her up or allowing her to continue throwing her very unnecessary tantrum.

After removing his clothes, he joined her in the shower. Though in the back of his mind all he wanted to do was go back down the stairs and sit with his parents, he didn't. If he brushed off her attitude and acted as if it was no big deal, he was more than positive that the problem she had with Juan would turn into the problem she had with him, and Angel didn't want that.

"You've been cutting up bad today. I don't know what's wrong with you, but you need to check that shit. You were good earlier, then you came home acting like the damn Wicked Witch of the West," Angel said.

Snow's chocolate face was hard before, but curved into a small smile as Angel stood in front of her vocalizing her antics. "Shut up. You just don't understand."

Angel grabbed her waist and pecked her head. "Make me."

Snow looked away and played with the streaming water before reaching up to grab his shoulders. "I killed her because I felt like she took advantage of me. I'd told her all of my deepest feelings, including the ones I had for you, and she took them and used them against me."

"You're talking in circles, Emelia."

"I told her that I would never have sex with someone that I didn't love, and that included Juan. She pretended to understand, but I found her in my bed with him the very next day." Snow scoffed. "That little bitch. She knew that I'd tried having sex with Juan on multiple occasions but could never go through with it because I loved you, and she used it as her way to get him. Conniving li'l trick."

"So, you killed her for betraying you, not because she slept with your nigga?"

Snow nodded before moving around him and stepping beneath the stream of water.

"I'll kill anyone that betrays me." Her voice was cold as it flowed over her shoulder.

Angel stood stuck, unsure of how he wanted to respond. It was obvious that she was warning him not to follow in Juan's footsteps, but she didn't have to do that. He would never willingly betray her, and she needed to know that.

With his chest to her back, Angel wrapped one of his arms around her chest and held her close. "You think I'd betray you?"

Snow said nothing, but shrugged her shoulders instead.

"Answer me."

"You never know what a person might do, so it's better to just stay prepared." She turned in his embrace. "Do I think you'd betray me? Probably. Do I want you to? Of course not."

"Damn." Angel was flabbergasted at how little she thought of him. "That's fucked up."

Snow maintained eye contact with him as she raised one of her eyebrows. "You chose a woman over your family, you can't blame me for feeling the way I feel."

It just got worse and worse with that girl. Angel was so offended that he couldn't even think of one thing that he wanted to say to her. Versus continuing to take her offensive remarks, he showered and left her in the shower alone. Once he had her towel secured around his waist, he left her room and went to his.

Being that they were practically next door to one another, he hadn't run into anyone in the hallway. Too tired to do anything other than lie down, Angel released the towel from his waist and fell face first onto the bed. Clearly, he was a lot sleepier than he'd known, because as soon as his eyes closed, he was out.

Chapter Nineteen

Love makes
people crazy

"I can't believe you actually think you're better than me. I handle my gun way better than you handle yours." Emelia laughed.

"Man, please. Your daddy has you thinking that, but I'm really better." D'Angelo smiled down at her as they took the long path to their houses.

Emelia pushed through the trees as they made their way through the trees and tall flowers. She and D'Angelo had just left from grabbing some milkshakes and were on their way back home.

"Well, we're going to have to go to the range together one day so I can show you my skills," Emelia joked.

"Why we can't go right now?"

Emelia held her stomach with a small frown on her face. "That milkshake got my stomach hurting."

D'Angelo walked closer to her and wrapped his arm around her shoulder. Emelia's first instinct was to pull away, but he held her closer.

"Chill out, girl. I'm just trying to comfort you since you're feeling bad."

Emelia wasn't really feeling their contact because it felt too intimate, but she didn't push the issue. D'Angelo was always trying to be too touchy when they were together anyway, so she was somewhat used to it. Still didn't care for his advances, but since they were almost home, she'd let it slide. They were both quiet for a good minute as they walked, but D'Angelo interrupted the silence.

"Emelia, you know I like you, right?"

Emelia's stomach flipped. "I know, that's why we're friends."

"I don't like you like a friend, though." He stopped and stepped in front of her. "I like you as more than that."

"More?" Emelia asked to be sure she was hearing him right.

D'Angelo nodded. "I was thinking maybe you could be my girlfriend. Since we've been hanging out, I think I've fallen in love with you."

Emelia looked away and held her head down so that she was looking at the dirt beneath her feet. When she didn't speak fast enough, he got a little more aggressive and grabbed both of her arms.

"Nobody has to know. It can just be between us. I just want you all to myself."

Emelia's young mind was all over the place, but one thing she knew for sure was that she loved Angel. D'Angelo was cool to be around, but that was it. She'd never looked at him as anything more than a friend.

"I'm sorry, D'Angelo, but I love Angel." She looked up at him slowly.

When she finally met his eyes, she could see the anger behind them. It was so strong that she momentarily felt afraid.

"Just because you love him doesn't mean you can't love me too. He's not even here. He left you!" D'Angelo began yelling. "Why would you even still love him after he did some shit like that to you?"

Emelia shrugged while still holding her stomach. "I don't know, I just do."

"You're so stupid for still loving a nigga that doesn't give a fuck about you." D'Angelo brushed past her, bumping into her hard enough to make her fall.

Emelia hopped off the ground, dusting the dirt off her hands. "You can't get mad at me because I don't want your ass," she screamed at his back.

"I'm not mad about that shit, you were just in my way."

"I wasn't in your way, you just have an attitude because I love your brother and not your pathetic ass." Emelia was so busy dusting the dirt from her hands that she didn't see him coming toward her, and by the time she did, it was too late.

Her small body was rolling and slamming into all kinds of things as she tumbled down the hill. She hit trees and a host of logs and other things along the way. She was moving with so much force that she even accidentally kneed herself in the stomach. She screamed and cried for it to be over, until she slammed forcefully into a large tree trunk.

"D'Angelo," she cried to herself. "Why would you do that?" She continued to cry as she tried to pull herself from the ground.

She was in so much pain that she couldn't figure out what was hurting the most. Everything on her body ached the entire time she walked home. By the time she'd finally pulled herself from the ground and got back to the top of the hill, D'Angelo was gone. Her clothes and face were such a mess, it made her glad that the path was directly behind her house, and no one would see her. The dried-up tears on Emelia's face were covered by dirt and a little bit of blood by the time she stood in the foyer of her home.

Since it was late in the evening, she'd known that her father wouldn't be there. Her mother was a different story. When she went into the house, Zulema was sitting on the sofa talking on the phone. The second she laid eyes on Emelia, she dropped the phone and came to her.

"Oh, my baby, what happened to you?" She touched all over Emelia's face.

Emelia winced in pain before bursting out in tears again. "Come on, let's go upstairs before Daddy comes."

Zulema looked like she wanted to protest but
followed Emelia anyway. Once Emelia's bedroom door was closed, her mother was right back
on her.

"What happened to you?"

"I was coming through the path and fell down
the hill," Emelia lied.

On the rest of the way over, she had analyzed
every scenario that she could possibly tell without
causing a rift between the families, and couldn't
think of one. Though her parents and D'Angelo's
parents were friends, they were also business partners. Naturally, parents would take up for their
children, and the last thing she wanted to do was
cause trouble, so she'd decided to keep what
D'Angelo had done to her to herself.

"Lord, come on. We have to get you to a doctor." Zulema stepped back to examine Emelia's
injuries, but stopped and looked back at her face.
"Emelia, there's blood on your pants . . . why?"

Emelia looked down, and just like her mother
had said, there was blood soaked through the
crotch and down both legs of her jeans. Tears
gathered in her eyes because she already knew
what was wrong. Overtaken with grief, she fell to
the floor and bawled her eyes out.

Zulema kneeled in front of her. "Emelia, were
you raped? Tell me right now. Did somebody do
something to you?"

Emelia cried even harder as she listened to
her mother go off about calling the police and
finding out who'd hurt her. When it got too overwhelming, she blurted out a truth that would rock

her mother's soul but give her understanding at the same time.

"I'm pregnant, Mommy," she whispered.

Zulema grabbed both sides of Emelia's face and held it up so that she could see her. "What? Since when? By who? Why didn't you tell me?" She, too, was now crying.

Emelia fell over into her mother's arms and told her all about her secret pregnancy with Angel's baby.

Snow wiped the lone tear that had just slid down her cheek as she lay in bed thinking about the day she miscarried her and Angel's baby. That had been one of the worst days of her life, and it hurt just the same, no matter when she thought about it. She'd made her mother promise not to tell Empress about the baby, too afraid for Angel to find out.

Some days she wished he had found out, but she didn't dwell on it. She was young and couldn't change what happened. In her heart, she still wanted to kill D'Angelo, but she'd even hold that down until the time was right. She'd had plans to keep her child and maybe even become a family with Angel one day, and D'Angelo ruined all of that for her.

Another tear fell, and Snow wiped it away. No need to cry over the past. God had blessed her again, and for that she was grateful. Only a few days pregnant with her and Angel's second child, Snow cradled her stomach and said a quick prayer for a healthy baby. She'd found out the day before and was waiting on the right time to tell Angel. She'd thought about telling him right after telling about the miscarriage but had changed her mind.

"We'll tell Daddy when the time is right." Snow rubbed her flat stomach. "Ain't that right, Angel baby?" She smiled to herself before reaching for her beeping phone.

She'd just gotten a text about a money drop-off that she needed to handle the next morning. She replied with the necessary specifics before placing her phone back onto the charger and closing her eyes.

It had been almost two hours since Angel had left her in the shower alone, and though she wanted to run to his room and check on him, she hadn't. At no point did she want Angel to get the wrong idea about any of the things she'd said, because she'd meant them. They may have come out a lot harsher than she'd intended, but that was still the way she felt. If only he could understand.

Snow sighed loudly as she kicked the covers from her body. She wanted Angel. It was torture to know that he was so close and she couldn't get to him. The fire that burned deep inside her for him was so strong that she found herself outside his door within minutes.

She'd held out long enough. It was time for her to go get her man. Snow had been completely sure of herself up until she was inside his room and standing at the door watching him sleep. She wanted to kick herself for staying up worrying herself about him, when he'd been in his room asleep the entire time. Apparently, not thinking about her.

"Bastard." She rolled her eyes.

"Call me another bastard, and see what I do for you."

Snow gasped and covered her mouth with her hand. "I didn't know you were awake."

Angel shifted some in the bed, but kept his eyes shut. "I wasn't until you walked in."

"How? I was quiet as hell creeping in here, and I know I was because I didn't want your mama to catch me."

A small smile curved his lips. "My mama ain't thinking about your ass. She knows I'm fucking the shit out of you. She ain't coming up here." Angel rolled over and finally opened his eyes. "Empress ain't trying to see this dick. Trust me."

Snow was giggling as she stood unmoving in front of his door. "You really need to stop talking like that."

"Why? It's the truth. Empress is a lot of shit, but crazy ain't one."

"Well, at least that makes one of us." Snow scratched at her head nervously. "I'm batshit crazy sometimes." Her eyes wandered to his face again.

He rested his head in the palm of his hand. "Why you say that?"

"I just am."

Angel extended his hand to her. "It's all right. Love makes people crazy. You'll be fine."

"You think so?"

"I know so. Come here." Angel's fingers moved, gesturing her over.

Snow walked to Angel and slid into bed with him. Immediately afterward, he was all hands. They were everywhere, groping and squeezing all over her. Though Snow wanted to continue pouting, she couldn't. She wanted sex just as bad as he did.

With shaky hands, Snow pulled at his arms until he got the hint and climbed on top of her. Angel's mouth found hers and took over. His tongue slid in and out while his lips devoured hers. Snow was in such bliss that she couldn't do anything but moan into his ear. That was all she wanted to do. He needed to know how good he made her feel.

"Your parents are downstairs," Snow whispered to him when he pulled her nightgown over her head.

"So what?"

"So, they might hear us."

Angel's mouth found her neck and circled it with his tongue. Snow felt like she was on the verge of falling apart as she lay there allowing his tongue to take her to new heights. With his hands and mouth on her, Snow felt like the luckiest girl in the world. Angel's advances were always so gentle and loving that they pulled out even the deepest emotions she harbored for him.

"I wouldn't be able to kill you." Snow looked up into his face.

Angel stopped kissing her leg long enough to make eye contact. "Yes, you would. But it's okay, because I wouldn't do anything to betray you." Angel removed her leg from his mouth and wrapped it around his waist. "You wouldn't compromise who you are for love, you've proven that before. I don't expect anything different."

Snow wanted so badly to yell to the rooftops that she really wouldn't kill him, but she didn't. Maybe him thinking that she'd do it would keep him on the straight and narrow. For her to kill Angel she'd have to be on her deathbed. There was no way she would ever be able to kill him and live with herself afterward. Having him all to herself was a joy that she couldn't fathom living without.

"You ready?" Angel's voice brought her back to their current situation.

Snow nodded and reached to grab his waist with both hands, but he stopped her. Angel winked at her before sliding off the bed and standing next to it. Naked and sexy as hell, Angel stood next to the bed reaching for her hand. Once she'd given it to him, he pulled her to the edge so that she was sitting up on the corner.

"I want you to do something different tonight." He looked down at her. "And don't worry about not being good at it. I'll teach you."

Snow stared at his very erect penis that was damn near poking her in the eye. One of his large hands held it at the base while the other rested on the side of her neck. She knew what he wanted her to do, but she just wasn't sure if she could or not. She'd never done it before, and though he was telling her he'd teach her, she still didn't want to embarrass herself.

"You straight?" he asked her with raised brows.

Snow cleared her throat and licked her lips. "Yeah, just don't laugh at me."

Angel's face hardened some as he pulled her head toward him. "I would never do no shit like that."

Snow nodded slowly before scooting closer to the edge of the bed. Once she was comfortable, she grabbed his dick with one hand and pulled it to her mouth. Even with just the head touching her lips, Snow could feel the heat from his body. The thick tip was soft as it rested against her mouth. That feeling alone had Snow ready to put in work.

Oddly, she was excited for what was to come. Without any effort, Angel was the kind of man that women desired to please. He was so handsome and so perfect that the only thing that came to mind upon looking at him was sex. Any woman who thought otherwise had to be gay. Angel DeLuca was an orgasm waiting to happen, and Snow was about to take full advantage of that.

"Go ahead and get it wet for me." His voice was a lot huskier than it had been, and it turned her on.

Snow's mouth dropped open, and as soon as it did, his dick slid inside. It flowed so easily, it was as if it had already known the way. Being that she welcomed it with wet and waiting jaws, her lips clamped shut immediately. The first taste of him felt like heaven on earth.

The weight of his tool resting on her tongue, meshed with the way his head had just fallen back, had Snow on the edge. As soon as she saw his eyes close in pleasure, and his head fall back, she wanted to go harder. She had to. Her mouth slid up and down his length at a slow, steady pace, while her hand stroked the areas her mouth left wet.

"Fuck, fuck, fuck." Angel squeezed his eyes shut.

Snow's stomach leapt in joy as she suctioned her cheeks tighter, pulling him deeper with each slurp. With determination and his moans fueling her, Snow did her best to suck the life out of Angel's dick.

"Go slower, Emelia. I don't want to bust yet." Angel grabbed a handful of her hair and pulled her head back some.

Versus letting her hair go like she thought he would, Angel continued using it to guide her mouth. The slower she sucked, the more his body jumped. Clearly, he was fighting the urge to combust, and she was loving it. So, instead of following his directions, Snow alternated between going slow and fast, and before she knew it, Angel snatched himself from her mouth.

"Your ass don't listen," he growled at her as he lowered them back onto the bed. "I told you to go slow, but you just do what you want to do, huh?" His hand went to her throat and squeezed lightly. "Do what the fuck I say." With a loud sloppy kiss placed to the side of her face, Angel pulled away so that he could enter her. "Get up and bend over."

His tone was much harsher than it normally was, and even though she probably shouldn't have been, Snow was turned on. She was used to being in charge and handling niggas, but the way Angel was bossing her around right then had her on the brink of an orgasm all by itself.

Snow was bent over the bed with her ass in the air when the loud sound of his hand slamming against her butt sounded throughout the room.

"The next time I tell you to do something, that's what you do. You hear me?" Angel asked.

Snow nodded.

The sound came again, this time twice. Angel had slapped both sides of her butt and grabbed a handful of her hair before she could say anything in objection. He was leaned over with his mouth to her ear when she felt his dick at her opening.

"Answer me."

The tingling sensation in Snow's body had her so riled up, she wanted to turn around and just take the dick. Not even caring if he gave it to her or not. She was so hot from the rough foreplay that he was delivering, she could ride his dick into the sunset without any help from him at all.

"I hear you, Daddy," she moaned over her shoulder.

Her eyes were slanted as she took in all of his naked glory. Angel was hers, and she was never letting him go.

"Love me harder this time, baby." Her voice was soft as he inched his dick inside her slowly. "I want it so hard."

"I got you, my baby." Angel pushed deep inside, and Snow had to bite down on the covers to keep from screaming.

His deep thrusts were so hard and powerful, she could hardly feel her legs anymore. The pit of her stomach was full, and the walls of her vagina quivered. He was pushing in and out of her with so much force and expertise that she already felt herself about to climax.

"I see you like this rough shit. Your pussy so muthafucking wet right now." Angel thrust in and out of her with each word he spoke.

"It's you . . . you make me wet like that," she barely got out before her legs began to shake and she creamed all over his dick.

"Oh fuck, baby." Angel's deep growl set her body on fire. "Look at all this sweet stuff you got dripping on my dick." Angel leaned over and placed kisses up the center of her back. "I'm about to be calling you Snow for a totally different reason." He pushed harder into her and Snow fell face first onto the bed.

Her body was weak from her orgasm, but listening to Angel talk to her so nastily had her praying their sex would never end. She'd lie there and enjoy the feeling of him beating her walls down until her entire body went numb if she could.

"Turn around and let me see that pretty face," Angel told her as he slid out and pulled her from the bed.

Snow was standing in front of him about to lie back down on the bed when he grabbed her by her neck and kissed her mouth. His tongue was so hot as he gave it to her to suck on. With Snow wanting any part of him that she could get, she ravished his mouth as he lowered them back onto the bed.

With neither of their assistance, his dick found its way right back to her opening and Angel pushed in. Their moans sounded in unison.

"I love your ass," he whispered in her ear, "so fucking much."

Snow's limbs circled his body as she held him to her. "Fuck me like you love me."

That gorgeous smile that melted her heart every time it surfaced curved his face and warmed her soul. "Come on and make me nut," he gritted out.

His dark, piercing eyes bored into her as his hips pushed his passion deeper inside her body. Snow clamped her legs around his waist while simultaneously squeezing her lower muscles. When Angel's eyes closed and his mouth fell open, she knew she had him.

"Stop holding back," she whispered against his lips.

Angel nodded and continued stroking until he released a loud groan and fell on top of her. The weight of his body was immense, but she could handle it until he moved. Being that close to him was a feeling she wasn't ready to let go of. Breathless and worn out, Angel lay on her for a few more seconds, trying to catch his breath, before he was rolling over onto his back and pulling her with him.

"I should have known your little thug ass would like it rough."

Snow covered her face in embarrassment.

Angel chuckled before pulling her hands from her face. "Don't hide. I like it rough too."

"I see," she whispered as she played with the silky black hair on his stomach.

The room fell quiet as they lay lost in their thoughts. Snow's eyes were on the spinning ceiling fan as she enjoyed being encompassed in the warmth from Angel's body.

"You want to know something?"

"Sure."

"Dominating the woman that dominates everybody else made my dick hard." He chuckled, as did she. "I know it sounds crazy, but so many people are scared of you, and I'm not. I be dogging the shit out that pussy, and you can't do nothing but let me."

Snow's core was awakening as her heart was expanding. She could feel the slick juices seeping down her thighs in anticipation of what was to come.

"I don't think that'll ever get old," Angel added.

"Good." Snow sat up and slid on top of him. "Do it some more."

Angel's eyes trekked over her body lazily as he began to harden beneath her again. "Nah, baby. You get it this time."

Snow smiled and nodded. She was about to show Angel just how dominating she really was. They spent the rest of the night making love to one another until they were both too tired to move. After receiving a night full of passion, Snow found her way back to her room.

After taking her shower and handling her hygiene, she dressed in some athletic gear and grabbed her phone and keys. She had a run to make, and she couldn't allow the obvious limp in her walk, or the pain in her body, to stop her. Angel had beat her body down so good, she'd barely made it out of bed that morning, but the cartel came first.

"Where you headed?" Empress's voice caught Snow's attention as she walked past the kitchen.

"I got a message last night about picking up some money this morning, so I'ma go do that then get my nails done." Snow walked into the kitchen. "You need something?"

Empress took a sip from the large, mint-green coffee mug she was holding before shaking her head. "A grandbaby or two would be nice, but I'm sure that can wait."

Snow smiled at her. "You and Vinny and this grandbaby talk. I haven't even been with y'all little raggedy son that long, and y'all already applying pressure."

Snow and Empress shared in laughter as Snow walked to the cabinet to grab a to-go coffee cup. She poured herself some and fixed it how she liked it before turning back around to face Empress. When she did, Empress was frowning slightly with her eyebrows raised.

"What? Why are you looking at me like that?"

"Honey." Empress shook her head. "I ain't know my baby had it like that."

Snow could feel herself getting warm from embarrassment. "What you talking about?"

"I could be wrong, but you weren't limping like that when you came in yesterday, were you?" Empress stared at her, waiting for an answer. When one didn't come, she just smiled. "I didn't think so."

Empress walked around the counter and over to Snow. She was smiling when she touched the side of Snow's face. "Just wait until I tell Zulema about this." She couldn't even hold her laughter in after that, and neither could Snow.

"Mrs. Empress, don't do that. Zulema gon' be all in my business."

"Baby, everybody you walk past today is going to be

in your business, so there's no need to worry about your mama." She laughed again. "You're telling on your own self walking with that big-ass gap between your legs like that."

Snow held her head down in shame as she snickered at herself. "See, you play too much. Let me get out of here and get to work." Snow walked toward the kitchen door but bumped right into Angel's bare chest.

He was shirtless in a pair of pajama bottoms. His eyes went directly to her, as did his hands.

"You were gon' dip without telling me?" He pulled her to him by her waist.

"You were still asleep."

He pecked her forehead at the same time that he grabbed a handful of her butt. "I would have woken up for you."

"Uh-huh," Empress mumbled behind them.

Snow's face fell into Angel's chest again as she shook her head. "Your mama needs help."

Angel chuckled before squeezing Snow's butt again. "Don't worry about her, worry about me," he whispered in her ear at the same time he pushed himself against her.

Snow could feel the hardness in his pants, and it made her want to climb on top of him right then. She was sure Empress would have a field day with that.

"Can y'all take that shit back upstairs?" D'Angelo's voice came from behind Angel as he pushed his way past him and Snow.

He pushed past them so hard that he bumped into Angel and made him lose his footing. That boiled Snow's anger right over the top.

"Watch yourself, D'Angelo. I won't say it again." Her eyes cut at him.

D'Angelo turned his nose up at her. "Girl, you better watch who the fuck you're talking to." He stepped forward like he wanted to do something, but Angel stepping in front of him stopped it.

"Ay, go head on with that shit," Angel warned his big brother.

D'Angelo looked Angel up and down with the same scowl. "Nigga, you better get up out my face. Your little ass don't want these problems." His tone got cocky in the midst of his anger.

"Both of y'all better calm the fuck down, because don't neither one of y'all want no problems with me." Empress stepped between her sons and pushed them away from each other. "D'Angelo, carry your grouchy behind on up out of here messing with people, and, Angel, take your ass on and put on some damn clothes. You and little Ms. Fast Behind over here ain't grown enough to be fucking in my house."

Angel smiled when Snow turned her head in embarrassment. Instead of continuing to bicker with D'Angelo, he walked back over to Snow and grabbed on to her waist, pulling her back to him. She was grateful for his affection in that moment. Empress had thoroughly embarrassed her. D'Angelo stormed out of the kitchen as fast as he'd come in. Nobody watched him leave.

"Ma, why you keep bothering my baby?" Angel asked.

"You're worried about me when you're the one that needs to stop bothering her. Got her walking around here limping and shit." Empress laughed again. "I see why she was making all that damn noise last night."

Snow died a thousand times as she realized Empress had heard them having sex. "Oh my God," she mumbled into Angel's chest.

Angel, on the other hand, couldn't stop laughing. "Ma, stop for real." He spoke through chuckles.

"I'll stop, but don't y'all do that shit no more. Take it right on back to your house where you've been doing it." Empress walked past them. "Me and Vinny ain't running no ho house." She walked out of the kitchen still laughing.

Since Snow's face was still covered by Angel's chest, he had to push her away from him so he could see her. "You straight?"

She nodded. "Yeah. Empress just be fucking around. She's cool."

Angel sucked his teeth. "I ain't talking about my mama's talking ass. I know she's just clowning. I'm talking about your body. How's it feeling?"

Why did every word he spoke to her have to sound so sexual? Or was it just her? Either way, his statement made her want more sex.

"My body wants you." Snow's arms circled his waist and she pulled him to her.

Angel's eyes darkened. "That's why you fucked up now." He pecked her lips. "Stop that shit, girl."

Snow blushed before releasing him. "I know, I just can't help it. But I'm good."

"You sure?"

Snow nodded and prepared herself to leave.

"Where you about to go?"

"I have some money to pick up, then I'll be at the lab."

"Cool. I'll swing through there later and we can go grab some food."

Snow nodded before standing on her tiptoes to get a kiss. Angel obliged and took it too far like she'd known he would. By the time they were pulling their mouths free of each other's, Snow's panties were damn near soaked with her sweetness.

"You should feel my panties right now." She smiled up at him. "They're so wet."

Angel closed his eyes and groaned as if he was in pain. "Come back upstairs real quick. I just want to taste it."

"I can't, babe. I have to get to work."

"Fuck work." He held on to her by her butt.

"Nah, fuck me . . . later." Snow smiled when Angel smiled. "I love you."

"Love you too, beautiful. Call me when you get a free minute."

Snow told him she would before walking out of the kitchen and continuing on her way. As bad as she wanted to stay with Angel and lie in bed all day, they both had work to do, and sexing until their bodies were sore wasn't going to get it done.

Angel and Snow had him fucked up if they thought they were about to pull that happily-ever-after bullshit and take what should have been rightfully his. He could see it happening already. They were about to link up and make the business look sweet. Maybe if Snow hadn't had a hand in it, he wouldn't be so mad, but she hated his ass. There was no way she would ever allow him to work with or for her.

At first, he'd dreamt it would be him and her, but after hearing them up fucking all night and all over each other again in the kitchen, that shit was long gone. Fuck Snow, fuck Angel, and fuck his parents. D'Angelo was fire hot as he sped down the highway in his car.

"I see everybody thinks I'm somebody to play with. I'll show them." D'Angelo reached for his phone and dialed his partner in crime.

He too wasn't very fond of the knockoff Bonnie and Clyde. He answered on the first ring. "What's good?"

"Ay, we got to speed this shit up. I'm tired of fucking around," D'Angelo said.

A low chuckle came over the phone. "Say no more. I have one of my people about to meet up with Snow now. He can take her with him or leave her. The choice is yours."

D'Angelo rubbed his chin. He didn't want her gone just yet. He only wanted her gone when she was running around town playing house with his brother. If Angel was out of the picture, then maybe she would act better. As long as she was lonely, he could move in on the pussy, like he'd tried to do last time. Only this time he would be successful.

"Nah, let her stay. If you get a clean shot on my punk-ass brother, though, you can take his ass out of there."

Heavy laughter came from the other end of the phone. "Okay. I'll put somebody on that. Did you get the shipment?"

D'Angelo's anger flared again. "Hell nah. They found out and sent that shit back."

"What!" he yelled.

"It's cool, though. We're about to have more than we can deal if we just play our cards right. Once Angel is gone, that only leaves my sick-ass daddy and my mama. Neither of them will be able to stop me, so just be patient."

The phone went silent for a little too long for D'Angelo's liking. Just when he was about to get nervous, his partner came back over the line.

"Don't fuck this up," he told D'Angelo sternly.

Although D'Angelo didn't really care for his tone, he bit the bullet because he needed the nigga. "Just do your part, and I'll handle the rest."

"I'm on it."

They ended the call after that. D'Angelo's mind traveled from one place to the other as he put what he was doing into perspective. He'd been doing a lot of shit, and hopefully it wouldn't be in vain.

Chapter Twenty

What went wrong?

Snow had just pulled up to her normal meeting point to get the money when her phone rang. It was her father. Since she was still seated in her car, she hit the Answer button and it picked up on her Bluetooth. "Hey, Papa."

"Hello, darling. How are you today?"

"Fine. What about you?"

"Could be better. When will you be back home?"

Snow leaned her head to the side and thought about it a little. It was the same thing she'd been wondering for a while now. Being in South Carolina had been planned to be temporary, but since being with Angel, it felt more permanent.

"Not sure yet, Papa. Do you need me for something? You know I'll be there if you do."

"No, my darling. I just miss you."

She could hear the smile in his voice, and it made her happy. On top of that, he was right. When she was home, she visited her parents at least once a month. It was nothing for her to travel to them at any given minute. But being in South Carolina was different.

"Well, I'll try to be back there soon. I just need to finish helping out here first."

"Sure, you do, darling. Family first. How's business? Angel informed me that you two chose not to do the deal with Juan."

Snow's eyes rolled at the mention of her ex's name. "He's a liar, Papa. I'd never do business with a person I can't trust."

Mack was quiet for a moment before speaking again. "I trust your judgment. Just be safe, my darling. You know he's a real prideful one."

"I'll kill him." She spoke with no hesitation.

Laughter resonated through the phone. "I know you will. That's the careful part I was speaking of."

Snow laughed and talked business with her father until she saw the black pickup truck pulling up. After ending the call, she made sure her gun was secured in the holster at the small of her back and got out. The man in the black coat was the same man she'd met on many occasions since doing business for Vinny.

He was a trustee of one of their largest distributors and had never tried anything funny with her before, but for some reason, she wasn't too sure of his presence today. Something about the way he kept switching the bag from one hand to the other was off with her, so she moved a little slower toward him.

Snow's eyes shifted around quickly, surveying her surroundings, and though she saw nothing out of place, she trusted her gut feeling. When he noticed her approaching, he smiled and nodded.

"Good morning, Ms. East, how are you today?"
Ms. East?

Snow noted that he was calling her something different. No one in the streets of South Carolina knew her by anything other than Snow. That was all she'd ever given and all she ever would give. So for him to be using her government, something was definitely off.

"Excuse me, who?" she asked for clarification. "What did you just call me?"

His eyes shifted from right to left quickly before he ran his hand over his bald head. "I'm sorry, Snow. I just thought a woman of your caliber deserved some respect."

Snow squinted her eyes at him. "Is that so?"

He nodded quickly while extending the bag out toward her. "Your cash."

"Did you count it?"

"I didn't have any time."

Snow raised her eyebrow at him. "Since when do you not have time to do your job?"

The sweat beads on his eyebrow proved her suspicions. He and she had exchanged money numerous times, and he'd always been calm and collected. Today, he looked like he could barely stand still.

"I, uh, I just had to stop and check . . . check on my, um, daughter." He stammered over his words while Snow stood patiently watching.

"Since you normally do good business, I'm going to go sit back in my car and give you time to get your shit together. Twenty minutes, that's all you have." Snow turned on her heels and walked as calmly as she could.

She could hear him behind her fumbling with the bag as she counted to ten in her head. Once back in the safety of her own car, she locked the doors and cranked up the engine. A heavy sigh of relief came seconds later. She'd been so nervous about what the man had going on that she could hardly think straight.

Fully aware of what she wanted to do but unsure if it was the right thing to do, Snow called Angel. She needed him to make this decision for her. She had many connections on the West Coast, but South Carolina was a totally different ball game, and she didn't want to do anything that would cause the DeLucas more trouble than they were able to get out of.

Snow sat impatiently in her car watching the man kneel on the ground to count the money. The loud ringing in her car stopped the moment Angel answered the phone.

"Hey, gorgeous, what's going on?"

"It's some weird shit going on with the nigga I just met. He's real shifty today."

"What nigga? Where you at? Leave right now." Angel's voice changed drastically as he fired off one question after the other.

"It's the same guy I always meet from the Santorini family, but today he just seems off. He called me by my last name, and nobody even knows me like that here."

"Snow, get out of there right now."

"I want to kill him."

"No!" Angel yelled. "Don't kill him. He could be wearing a camera for the feds or anything. You don't want to get yourself into that kind of trouble."

Snow sighed and held her forehead in her head. "I know. That's why I called you. I didn't know if Vinny had pull that could get me off for murder."

"I'm sure he does, but you and I both know he's in no position to make that happen right now."

Snow watched the man rise back to his feet and wave at her.

"Are you still there?" Angel asked her.

"Yeah."

"Why? Leave now."

Even with her trigger finger itching something crazy, Snow put her car in reverse and pulled out of her parking spot. She could see the man waving her down in her rearview mirror, but she kept her pace anyway. There was no need to go back and end up getting herself into something that would take forever to get out of.

"I just left," she advised Angel.

"Bet. Meet me at the bank."

Snow told him she would before ending their call and heading to their bank downtown. She'd been there plenty of times before with Angel and Empress since being in South Carolina. It was where they kept their safe and all of their important assets. She had no idea why Angel would want to meet there right then, but she was going.

It was a good distance away from where she'd just been, so it took her a little while to get there. When she pulled into the parking space along the street, she saw Angel's truck pulling in behind her. Snow checked her face and hair before getting out and meeting him at the trunk of her car.

He was dressed immaculately in another tailored suit, with his hair waved to the back. His face looked fresh and he smelled just as good as he always did.

"I don't think I'll ever get tired of you and these suits," she told him with hearts in her eyes.

Angel smiled at her before kissing her mouth sensually. "I don't think I'll ever get tired of you, period." His hand laced with hers as he led them to the door.

Once they walked in, a few of the tellers greeted them enthusiastically. They were valued customers and it showed every time they went there. Along their walk upstairs to where Vinny's personal banker was, they were offered water, muffins, and a host of other things to make their visit comfortable.

They both turned it all down, and continued on their way. The office of their family's banker was located at the far end of the long hallway. They were approaching it when his secretary stopped them.

"Hello, Mr. DeLuca, Ms. Snow." She smiled brightly. "He's with some people right now. Can you two wait for him out here until he's ready?"

Snow and Angel both looked at her as if she was speaking a foreign language. One thing they never did anywhere was wait. They were treated like royalty because that was who they were. So for his secretary to be standing there treating them as if they were ordinary didn't sit well with either of them. Snow was about to say something, but Angel beat her to it.

"You want us to wait?" He paused and pointed at the chairs placed along the wall. "Out here?"

She smiled nervously. "Yes, sir. If you don't mind."

"We mind," Snow informed her.

Her lips twitched a little as she tried to maintain her smile. "I'm really sorry for the inconvenience, but he's with a few others at the moment."

Angel stepped forward and the lady jumped. "With who?"

It was clear she was just the pawn. Her fear was loud and clear. "Please don't hurt me, Mr. DeLuca, sir."

Snow frowned at her comment, as did Angel. When he turned and looked at Snow over his shoulder, he raised his eyebrow at her in question. Clearly, he was just as shocked by the secretary's comment as Snow was.

"Why would you assume I'm going to hurt you?" Angel interrogated her.

Her hands went up in mock surrender. "I didn't, I just . . ." She sighed and held her head down.

"Angel, let me holla at you really quick," Snow called him to him.

She was getting tired of the secretary's foolishness. There was something going on, and for it to all be coming out of nowhere was what alarmed Snow the most. She could continue sitting back and waiting for things to unfold, or she and Angel could take matters into their own hands.

Snow took a few steps away from the nerve-wracked secretary and pulled Angel along with her. When he was standing in front of her and leaning down so that he could hear her, she whispered her thoughts.

"This is some bullshit. Something is up, and I think we need to get out of here until we figure out what it is."

Angel nodded. "I was thinking the same thing." He rubbed his chin as his eyes wandered off into the distance.

He was thinking, and Snow envied how calm he was right then, because she was all over the place. His calming aura was helping her keep it together, but the itching in her trigger finger was getting out of control. She didn't normally take the kind of ignorant behavior they'd been encountering all day without dropping bodies behind it.

"After hearing that shit about that nigga you met earlier, it made me think. There's no telling who he's working with, and I really need to check on the cartel's money and shit. I would hate for him to have been the feds for real and they start seizing all of our shit before we've had a chance to move it." The muscle in his jaw jumped as he continued rubbing his chin.

Snow wanted to stand still and allow him time to think, but her street instincts were kicking in. They needed to do that shit another time. Somewhere safe from the outside world.

"Angel, let's go. We'll think it through at home." She grabbed his hand and pulled him toward the stairway they'd used to get up there.

He followed willingly. They were at the top of the stairs when the door to his banker's office opened. Out walked two men in black suits. Not the sexy tailored kind that men with money, like Angel, wore but the basic kind they'd probably gotten for church on Sundays. His banker followed close behind wearing a nervous expression.

Snow and Angel both were halted by the men's presence, but Snow was the only one who saw the danger and acted quickly. Before she could stop herself, she had her gun out and pointed at the men.

"Angel, get down!" she yelled as she posted up to shoot.

Angel was in the middle of turning around to face her but reversed his actions the moment he saw the large black guns being aimed at them. Had they been anywhere else, Snow would have had to commend him on his quick thinking.

The two massive long slide guns that she'd seen him shoot at the range too many times to count were out and being fired immediately. To say things went from bad to worse within seconds was an understatement. The loud booming and heavy clouds of gun smoke took over everything around them.

BOOM! BOOM!

The sounds of the various guns ripped through the

air like cannons. Shattering glass and bullets were flying everywhere as Snow, Angel, and the two men fired
at one another. The backfire from Snow's gun shook
her arms, but she continued pulling her trigger like the
professional that she was.

The vibrations from the guns shook not only her
body but the floor as well. With a rapidly beating heart
and sweaty palms, Snow took steps forward so that she
could get closer to the men. Though the bullets were
still flying, she was doing her best to dodge them and
the shattered pieces of furniture and Sheetrock.

"Snow!" Angel looked over his shoulder at her
while backpedaling toward the staircase. "Let's go!"
he yelled to her.

"Don't run now!" Snow heard one of the men say
just as a few bullets came ripping past her head.

She could hear the air and feel the heat from each
bullet sent her way. Screams and the sounds of alarms
were sounding off in the distance, but all that mattered
to her was Angel yelling for her to get out of there.

"Shit!" She ducked behind the secretary's desk to
take cover.

More bullets were being fired toward Angel, but he
was sending them back just as fast as they were coming. Then out of nowhere, the gunfire stopped.

"Teno! Get up!" The second voice caught Snow's
attention.

It was thick and filled with a native tongue that she
could recognize. When she looked over at Angel, who
was hiding behind the bullet-riddled wall, he didn't
look fazed at all. Instead, he was looking at her, mo-
tioning for her to come to him.

Snow knew that the moment she stood from behind
the desk, the shooting would probably start right back
up, but Angel was just going to have to cover for her.

They needed to get out of there and fast. They'd been shooting for a few minutes. There was no telling how many police were on their way.

"Fuck it." Snow jumped up and immediately aimed her gun.

She and Angel both resumed their fire, as did the other man. Snow was almost to Angel when she felt the hot metal collide with the bone in her leg.

"Ahhhh!" she belted out as she tried to hurry to Angel.

The bullet had wounded her leg terribly, so she was falling to the ground before she had the chance to take another step.

"SNOW!" Angel's deep voice sounded strained as he rushed to her.

"No, Angel! Keep shooting," she yelled.

He'd completely dropped both of his guns and was about to head her way until she reminded him that they were still being targeted. His guns went right back to blazing. Snow was writhing in pain as her leg burned unbearably from the gunshot.

Although she was in more physical pain than she'd ever been in before, she couldn't give up. Angel needed her. She ducked and crawled to him the best she could as he continued to fire at the man who was now ducking behind the other side of the secretary's desk.

Just as Snow got near Angel, he stopped firing and picked her up. With her gun in hand, she picked up his slack. She was firing over Angel's shoulder when the top half of her body jerked backward. Another bullet had ripped through her shoulder, causing her to drop her gun.

The shriek of pain that left her mouth must have put some fire under Angel's feet, because he ran so fast down the stairs and through the main lobby that everything they passed looked blurry. Snow didn't know if it was due to her gunshot or if Angel was really moving that fast.

People were everywhere scattering to get out of their way as Snow hung over Angel's shoulder, bleeding profusely.

"Oh my God, she's shot!"

"Why aren't the police here yet?"

"I knew I should have stayed at home today."

Snow listened to an array of things as Angel moved through the lobby, still ducking from the bullets being fired behind them. When the fresh air finally hit Snow's face, she felt relieved, but that was short-lived. Before she could even lift her head long enough to look around, everything went black.

Chapter Twenty-one

I'll take care of you

The silence in the living room of his house was eerie and more than he could handle at the moment, but there was nothing he could do about it. Angel was seated in the middle of the floor with an array of packed bags next to him.

He scanned over the floor in front of him before looking toward the sofa. Snow was lying on it wrapped in nothing but a sheet. She was still sleeping and had been since receiving the pain meds he'd given her a few hours prior.

Angel's mind was doing numbers as he watched her lie there peacefully. How could something so beautiful be surrounded by so much chaos? That alone should have been a sin. Snow was too beautiful and too awesome a woman to have people trying to kill her just because.

A deep sigh left Angel as he held his head in his hands and closed his eyes. Flashbacks of the shootout in the bank clouded his mind. No matter how hard he thought about it, he couldn't think of one logical reason why things were being flipped upside down so rapidly and unexpectedly.

True enough, the sporadic police appearances when he'd been pulled over and again at his parents' house had been out of the blue as well, but what happened at the bank had to be something totally different. There was no way the feds would have done something that reckless. Angel was stressed to the max. Not only did he have some unknown people coming for his and his girl's heads, but he was sure it had something to do with the cartel.

That alone was enough to drive him crazy. His family was everything to him. There was no way that he wanted things to get so bad that they went sour for his loved ones as well.

"Going somewhere?" Snow's voice startled him.

Angel moved quickly from where he was sitting and went to her. She looked tired as she gazed at him through weary eyes. Angel rubbed his hand though her hair and kissed her forehead before kissing her mouth.

"How are you feeling, beautiful?"

Snow tried to move but winced in pain and went back still. "Horrible. What happened after I blacked out?"

Angel released a frustrated breath. "I put you in the car and drove away just as the police were pulling up. Thankfully they didn't catch up to me before I was able to get you here. I had one of my old buddies from school come over and help me patch you back up.

Your wounds aren't life-threatening, thank God."
Angel turned so that his back was pressed against the
sofa she lay on. "After that, we gave you a few fluids
and some pain meds."

"What kind of pain meds?" she questioned.

"Morphine."

"You didn't give me too much, did you?" she asked
with a sense of urgency.

"No. Why?"

"Because I can still feel some pain," she answered
hesitantly before giving the bags her attention. "The
bags?"

"We're leaving." Angel's voice was even and void
of any emotion.

"We, as in you and me?"

Angel nodded.

The room was quiet as Angel tried to give Snow
time to sort her thoughts out. When it took her too long
to say anything, he turned back around to face her. She
was lying still and looking up at the ceiling. Her face
was blank as she blinked every so often. The large bandage across her shoulder was neatly wrapped and securing her wound from infection.

"What's on your mind?"

"Too much." She turned her head and looked at him.
"Where are we going?"

"California."

"Your parents know about this?"

"My mom does. She doesn't want to worry Vinny."

Snow nodded and touched his face with her other
hand. "You're stressed out, aren't you?"

"You have no idea how much."

"Yes, I do. I feel the same way."

Angel stared at her for a few moments longer before rising to his feet. He looked at her once more before grabbing all of the bags at once. He then took them out of the house. Being that his house was brand new and in his mother's maiden name, no one would know where he lived for a while.

After leaving the bank, Angel had driven straight to his place to keep the heat from his parents. He was no fool to think the people after them wouldn't find him, but he was sure he had enough time to get him and Snow out of town before they came.

When he was sure all of their things were in the rental SUV his mother had delivered to him, he went back upstairs to retrieve Snow. The private plane to California was scheduled to leave within the hour, and he needed to get them there.

She was in the same spot on the sofa as he'd left her in, only this time her eyes were closed. He went to her in a hurry to make sure she was okay, and her eyes popped open immediately. Her hand went to her chest in fear before she breathed a little deeper.

"Calm down, baby. It's just me. You ready?" Angel raised his eyebrows at her.

"As ready as I'ma be." She scooted some, trying to sit up, but was halted by the pain. "Owww, Angel!" she moaned in agony.

Angel grabbed her quickly and carefully, lifting her from the sofa. After taking a seat, he placed her in his lap, holding her close without putting too much pressure on her wounds.

Snow's head went to his chest immediately as she began to cry. "This is too much for me, Angel."

Angel's face frowned up. He'd never heard Snow

talk down on herself like that. She was one of the strongest people he knew. Though he never told her, her strength gave him the courage he needed to keep going on most days.

He pecked the top of her head a few times before kissing her forehead. "Don't talk like that, Emelia."

"It's the truth." She circled her abdomen with her arms and tried to snuggle closer to him. "I can't handle all of this right now." She sniffed.

Angel held her tighter. "You're one of the strongest people I know, Emelia. You can't get down on yourself like this."

Snow shook her head and wiped her nose. "I'm not down on myself. I just know what I can and can't deal with, and getting shot up like this is too much for me."

Angel gave her a sympathetic look as he rubbed his hands up and down her back. "You'll get better soon, and your body will be back to normal before you know it."

Her head tilted to the side as she looked at him through wet lids. Her mouth was pushed out in a pout as her ponytail hung sloppily off the side of her head. "No, it won't." She sniffed. "My body won't be back to normal for another few months."

Angel chuckled. "It's not going to take that long, girl. You had flesh wounds. Those only take a few weeks to fully heal." He tittered a little more at her dramatics.

"I'm pregnant, Angel."

All traces of humor left his face as his eyes searched hers for some sign of sincerity. Outside of the fact that right then wasn't the time to be playing games, her face showed no signs of playfulness.

"You pregnant for real?" he asked in disbelief.

Snow nodded. "Have been for days now."

Angel's mouth fell open as his eyes dropped down to her stomach. There were no signs of a baby being in there, but he still believed her.

"Damn, no wonder you were asking me questions about the pain meds." He hugged her to him. "Don't worry about any of this. Let me worry for the both of us. Okay?"

Snow nodded, but didn't say anything. Angel kept her in his lap until she'd stopped crying, then carried her from the house and placed her in the car. Once he'd secured his house, he was back in the car with her. Hand in hand, he drove them to the airstrip to catch their flight to safety. He had a family to protect, and he would do whatever was necessary to ensure their safety.

The plane ride to California was relaxing and allowed them to get some much-needed rest. Midway through their trip, Angel noticed Snow had tears in her eyes. He was out of his seat in no time and squatting in front of her. On one knee next to her chair, Angel grabbed her hand.

"Emelia, what's wrong?"

She kept her eyes closed and allowed the tears to roll down her cheeks. "I don't feel good."

"You need me to get you something?"

She shook her head slowly. "Can you just help me clean up a little?"

Angel wasted no time helping her out of her chair and taking her into the small bathroom. Before getting the shower water ready, he sat her down on the small bench attached to the wall. After flipping the shower on, he was back in front of her helping her get undressed.

She made a series of whimpers as he removed her

pants and the jacket she was wearing. Both areas were still bandaged up securely, which made him reconsider her bath just a tad. He'd left all of his medical materials at home, so if her bandages were to get wet, they'd be that way until they landed in California.

"I don't know how we're about to do this without getting your bandages wet," Angel said.

Snow looked all around the small bathroom before her body sank a little in dejection. "We can just hit the hot spots, and that'll be fine until we get there."

Angel smirked at her. "The hot spots?"

For the first time in a long time, she smiled. "Yep. The parts that matter, and that's it."

Angel nodded at her before going to the shower and soaping up the washcloth for her. When he came back, he washed her good arm and leg before moving to the damaged ones. He was careful not to touch the bandages before moving on to the next spot.

He slid the washcloth all over her body, cleaning her the best he could before it was time for him to remove her panties. His hand stilled as his eyes found hers.

"I don't know why you're stopping like you ain't never cleaned it before."

Angel's skin grew warm from embarrassment as he thought back on the few times he'd cleaned her after sex. Though it was the same thing, it felt different then. It was steamy back then, now he was afraid he might hurt her.

"The only thing I'm scared of is sticking my hand down there and my dick getting hard." Angel shook his head dramatically. "The last thing I need is to give you this dick and have your pussy and your back hurting too."

Snow's laughter made him smile harder than he'd smiled all day.

"You make me so sick." She giggled as she lifted up so that he could pull her panties down.

Once they were down and off her hurt leg, Angel used the soapy washcloth to glide his fingers between her thighs and into her slippery wet folds. He could tell by the way her breathing grew heavier that he wasn't the only one struggling with their current task.

Angel slid his fingers slowly up to her sensitive love button and circled it with the pad of his thumb. "You wanna give me this pussy, don't you?"

His eyes were on hers as she nodded slowly.

"Well, that's too bad with your hot ass."

Snow's smile crept back as she grabbed his wrist and held it still. He tried to pull it away, but she clamped her legs shut and held it there. Angel looked to her to see what she wanted to do so that he could follow her lead. The lust-filled way she watched him had him reconsidering not sexing her down in the little bathroom.

"I'll just rub it for you, how about that?" Angel suggested.

"Please," Snow begged.

Angel moved his hand back just enough to drop the washcloth. When he went back with just his fingers, he massaged around in her love, touching all the right places for her. Her subtle moans and closed eyes let him know she was enjoying it.

"Little Angel got you hot like this?"

Snow's eyes smiled. "I call it Angel baby, but I believe so." She whimpered and grabbed his wrist to slow down his movements. "I be wanting you all the time. I swear I do." She moaned again when his long fingers dipped into her body. "I want it so bad right now, but I'm afraid I'ma hurt myself."

Angel chuckled and leaned over so that he could kiss her lips. "You might, so just let me feel on it until you cum. I think that'll be better for the baby."

Snow rolled her eyes and bit her bottom lip. Angel's mouth was on hers moments later, trying to aid in her orgasm. He kissed and sucked from her lips down to her neck. He thought about giving her breasts some attention as well, but with the way her bandage was wrapped, there was no way he could.

"Oh, Angel," she gasped. "You're the best baby daddy ever."

Not even a whole second after the words left her mouth, her juices coated his fingers. Snow's body vibrated delicately as the small orgasm took over her body.

Angel was all smiles as he picked up the washcloth, rinsed it off, and went back to washing her. Once he was done, he grabbed the lotion to rub on her body.

"What do you plan on doing here in California?" she asked as he held her foot in his hand.

"Making a game plan. So much was happening around us in South Carolina, we had nowhere safe to think without getting busted in on."

Snow nodded her understanding. "I concur. My parents can help us too. How long do you want to stay here? I know you don't want to leave Vinny and Empress alone too long with all that crazy shit happening."

"I don't, but they'll be fine until I get back. That estate is locked down tight, and I sent some more niggas up there too. I just need to keep shit straight until I can get back."

"Who do you think is doing this?"

That was the one question Angel had been trying to find the answer to. "My first thought was the feds, but after that bank shit, I think it's some outside people. Maybe somebody that's jealous of me or some shit. I don't really know right now."

"Do y'all have any enemies?" Snow asked, referring to him and his parents.

"Not any that's bad enough to speak on it."

"We're hitting the ground running as soon as we touch down in California. I'll have my people look into the bank attack and see if there's something they can get their hands on." She shifted some in her seat.

"Already on it, but you can still reach out to your people as well. I alerted mine the moment we were safely away from the bank."

Snow and Angel sat bouncing ideas off one another for the rest of the flight. They had gotten so involved in their conversation that they lost track of time. It felt so good to Angel to be able to talk and hang out with her. It reminded him of the old days when they were kids. Since being adults, they'd had so much other stuff surrounding their conversations, he hadn't given himself time to just enjoy her friendship.

"Emelia, I owe you an apology."

She frowned in confusion. "Apology for what?"

"You remember that day when we were at the rib joint and you were pressing me for friendship? I kept telling you that we needed to focus on the lovers part, and not so much on being friends?"

Snow's pretty face was stoic as she nodded.

"I was wrong."

She smiled.

"It feels so good sitting here talking to you right

now, and the best part of it all is because it's on some friend shit. We ain't kissing, touching, and none of that other boyfriend and girlfriend shit. Just Emelia and Angel chilling."

"I told your mean ass that I was a good friend to have."

Angel leaned back against the shower door and stretched his legs. "It's even better because I can kick it with you like this whenever I want to, and still lay up and make love to you all night when I feel like doing that too." Angel crossed his legs at the ankle. "I'm living the life." A broad smile stretched from one side of his face to the other.

"I tried to tell your hardheaded behind." Snow was all smiles as well.

Angel basked in the happiness she exemplified.

The rest of their flight went smoothly. They even found time to get a few minutes of sleep before the plane landed. Angel wasn't sure what was to come, but he was sure that as long as he had Snow, and she had his back, they would be fine.

When they finally landed and the warm air at the airstrip greeted them, Angel closed his eyes and enjoyed being back at home. He'd gotten so caught up with school and Genesis that his visits to California had stopped. He couldn't remember that last time he'd been there just to visit with family, and that was a shame.

"You miss it, don't you?" Snow's voice next to him pulled his eyes away from the trees and buildings in front of them.

He looked down at her and nodded. "I didn't know how much until now."

"Now you see why I don't miss the South?"

Angel nodded with a lazy grin resting on his face. He was looking around, surveying the people walking around them. So many of them had already greeted him and Snow respectfully, and for that he was grateful. That meant whatever was going on back in South Carolina hadn't reached there yet.

"Ms. East, Mr. DeLuca." The short man in front of them nodded before pushing the wheelchair toward Snow. "Compliments of your father." He smiled before walking away.

Angel maneuvered around their things and helped her into the chair before standing behind her. Being that a few other men had already come and grabbed their bags, he was free to push her. They moved through the people and out toward the car that Mack and Zulema had sent for them.

They spotted it as soon as they got into the parking lot. The driver was out and trying to help him with Snow, but he didn't need that.

"I got her. You can go ahead." Angel ushered the man away.

On the ride over to Snow's parents' house, she could hardly sit still. Angel enjoyed watching her get so excited, but he was ready to get with Mack so they could handle business. He'd already informed him of everything that had transpired, and Mack had been making arrangements to get them there to him ever since. Though Angel had expected nothing less, he was still grateful.

"Did you tell your parents we're together?" Angel asked Snow.

"I didn't tell my papa. My mama knows."

"Well, that means he knows as well."

They smiled at each other but said nothing else. Angel watched her as his mind drifted. He was so tired, but he knew he wouldn't rest until he'd gotten everything figured out and his family was safe. That was a promise.

Chapter Twenty-two

He makes you unfocused

The winding road to the East estate was nothing short of amazing. From the tall water fountains to the various statues placed around the yard, it was a delight. The black iron fence circling the property was tall with the letter *E* engraved in every other bar. The grass was neatly trimmed with multicolored flower beds on both sides of the door.

Snow's eyes danced as she eyed one of her most favorite places. It felt like it had been forever since she'd been home, and she was glad to finally be there. She was sure her father was happier than she was. He'd been worrying her about coming back every time they spoke on the phone. Now he'd finally gotten his wish.

"Baby, you good?" Snow asked Angel.

His face was just as calm as it always was, only this time it was accompanied by heavy bags beneath his eyes and stress lines across his forehead. She could tell he'd been trying to hold it together all day, but everything happening around them was weighing heavily on him.

"As long as I have you, I'll forever be good."

Snow's heart warmed, prompting her to reach for his hand. "How can you be as tired as you are but still find the strength to make me feel good?"

"Because you make me whole and right. I don't know any other way to be when you're near me."

He looked so comfortable and casual that Snow almost forgot he was a part-time doctor, part-time drug lord. Everything about his appearance screamed that he was just a normal young hustler living life. From the way he wore his Jordan sneakers halfway laced up, to the subtle sag of his pants. On his wrist was a large gold watch, while a thin gold chain and bracelet decorated the rest of his body.

"Stop staring at me." Angel's baritone voice drew Snow's eyes back to his face. "I'm not going nowhere. I'm all yours."

"Leave me alone, Angel. Ain't nobody staring at your ass."

Angel smiled and rubbed his hand down the sides of his face playfully. "I know a nigga sexy and shit, but you ain't got to be all in my grill like you are."

Snow giggled uncontrollably. "You better be glad my body all jacked up, or I would be all in more than just your grill."

"Swear?"

"I swear." She winked.

"Bet. I can probably handle you a little bit later. Let me get some sleep and some food, and I'm tearing your ass up."

"I'll be waiting." She smiled at him before looking out the window.

The car had just come to a stop at the top of their driveway. She looked around as she waited for the driver to come around and open the door. Once he did, Angel got out first. He grabbed all of their bags and set them near the door before going back for her.

"Slide this way so I can grab you."

Snow did as she was told, and he pulled her the rest of the way to take the pressure off her shoulder. When she was fully out of the car, he helped her into the wheelchair and headed for the entrance of the home. In true best friend style, Zulema was out of the door greeting them in the driveway before they could even get to the door.

With open arms, Zulema hugged Angel first before bending down and nearly snatching Snow out of her wheelchair. "Look at y'all! I've been waiting in that window all morning."

Angel laughed at her. "You and Empress need to find y'all something else to do."

"Don't talk about me and my friend. Y'all just better be glad we love y'all's asses." Zulema beamed at Angel, then Snow. "Look at my baby. I'm so glad you're here, mama."

"Me too, Mommy. I missed y'all."

"Good. Y'all hungry? I cooked." She grabbed Snow's purse from her. "Push her on in here, Angel, so that y'all can sit down and eat."

Angel pushed Snow inside the house and toward the

kitchen. Old memories hit Snow all at once as they passed through the foyer, then into the great room. She and Angel had spent many days and nights in there playing games and training. It was crazy how fast time went by, because it seemed like it was just yesterday when they'd hit her house for some sort of snack before heading to the gun range or to a training meeting.

"Damn, it's been a long time," Angel said from behind her.

"I swear I was just thinking the same thing," Snow replied.

"We had some good times up in here."

"Too many good times, from my understanding," Zulema said over her shoulder.

Snow's hand went straight to her face as she palmed her forehead. Zulema was always talking and never caring about anything she said. "Mommy, stop."

"Ain't no point in being ashamed now. Y'all wasn't ashamed when y'all had y'all young asses up in here fucking around."

Angel's laughter made Snow feel better about her mother's mouth. He was chuckling so hard behind her that she ended up joining him. "I swear her and Empress should be sisters and not best friends. She be saying all that out-of-line shit just like my mama."

"I'ma pop you in your mouth just like Empress too, if you cuss like I'm not standing here again," Zulema said.

"My fault, Mrs. Z."

As they rounded the corner to the kitchen, Zulema turned to face them again. "From what Empress tells me, you might as well call me your mother-in-law now, right?"

Once again, Snow was hiding behind her hand while her mother embarrassed her further. Angel, on the other hand, was the total opposite. He was eating Zulema's nonsense up whole.

"She told you right." Angel moved the chairs around and parked Snow at the table. "I'ma marry my baby as soon as I figure out what's up with all of this mess going on around us."

Zulema's eyes bulged dramatically as she covered her mouth giddily. "Oh, Emelia, he said he's going to marry you, girl. You heard that?"

Snow was just about to tell her mother she'd heard Angel loud and clear, but her father interrupted her before she could.

"Marry who? Who's getting married?" Mack walked into the kitchen slowly.

His long gray hair was in the same braid he'd worn at the back of his neck for as far back as Snow could remember. His reddish-brown skin was wrinkled and rough from the many years of hard work he'd put in. He was dressed in all black with a pair of black and gold loafers on.

"Don't everybody speak at once. What's with this marriage talk that I heard?"

Snow wasn't sure about Angel, but she wasn't about to respond to Mack. He was known for going a little off the deep end when it came to her, and she had no plans to open that can of worms tonight.

"Mack, ain't nobody scared of your old ass." Zulema's voice took away the seriousness of the room, but Angel's brought it right back.

"I said as soon as I can figure out what's going on, I'm marrying Emelia." Angel took a few steps toward Mack and extended his hand.

Mack's thick eyebrows scrunched up together as he studied Angel's hand for a little longer than necessary, in Snow's opinion.

"Mack." Angel's voice was a lot sterner than what Snow was accustomed to, but she was happy that he was standing his ground. "You're going to act like you don't know me?"

That last statement was most definitely something Snow could agree on. Her father was seriously standing there as if he hadn't known Angel his entire life. Furthermore, as if he hadn't invited him to his house. Angel had told Snow all about his and Mack's conversation while they were on the plane. Snow had been elated to hear that her father had ushered them out to California without a second thought.

"Daddy." Snow called his name, he looked at her.

For the first time since he'd walked into the kitchen, his eyes softened. He didn't smile, but he did bypass Angel to hug his daughter. Snow didn't appreciate his dismissal of Angel, but she was happy to be in his arms again. It had been many months since she'd felt his embrace, and she welcomed it. Her father was the love of her life, just as Zulema was, but she was a daddy's girl.

"How are you, darling?" Mack smiled at her.

Snow's eyes darted to Angel as soon as her father released her, before going back to Mack's face. She could tell from his expression that he didn't appreciate her checking for Angel before answering him, but he didn't speak on it. She knew her father, and she knew when he was angry.

"I'm fine, Papa. I missed you."

He patted her hand before looking at the bandaged leg that Angel had propped up. "He taking care of you?" Mack nodded in Angel's direction but didn't look at him.

"Papa, yes. He's the only thing that's been making my time in the South bearable. Angel is truly heaven sent."

Mack grumbled before rising back to his feet and walking over to Angel. Though Angel's hand was no longer stuck out for a handshake, Mack grabbed it anyway. He shook it firmly before releasing it again. "I'm glad to see you again, son."

Angel's face told that he wasn't sure what to think, but he just went with it anyway. "Likewise. It's been a long time."

"That is has. It's terrible that it had to be on these terms for me to see the both of you again."

"Agreed, but life in South Carolina has been pretty hectic."

Mack nodded. "It's not easy being the boss."

Angel nodded but didn't say anything else, and Snow couldn't blame him. Her father was being downright rude, and she couldn't understand why. Mack had always loved Angel, but he'd treated him terribly for the short time they'd been there. Snow didn't know what it was but chose to believe maybe it was because he now knew Angel as her man, and not her friend.

"Angel, go sit next to Snow so you can eat, baby," Zulema instructed.

Angel nodded obediently. "Yes, ma'am."

Snow watched him walk toward her and wanted to cry. He was so sweet and worthy of way more respect and hospitality than what her father was giving him right then. She loved Angel so deeply in her soul that if he grabbed her wheelchair right then and rolled her from her house, she'd go with no reservations.

"I love you," Snow whispered to Angel as soon as he was close enough.

Angel stopped in mid-stride and leaned down to kiss the top of her head. "I love you too. Don't worry about me." He kissed her hair again before taking his seat.

When Snow looked toward her parents, her mother's smile was out of this world, while her father had his own frown thing going on. Snow turned her head and totally disregarded him. He was acting nasty for nothing, and she wouldn't entertain it.

For the rest of the time they ate lunch, Zulema and Angel did most of the talking. Mack barely said anything, while Snow matched his mood. Just like he didn't care for Angel's presence, she didn't care for his. After the continuous failed attempts at talking to Mack, Angel focused solely on Zulema. That pissed Snow off to no end, and that was most definitely not what her father wanted.

"Snow, are you not feeling well, darling?" Mack asked her from across the table.

"I'm fine, actually. How are you?"

"Could be better."

"And what is it that's ailing you?" She leaned forward a little in her chair but shuddered in pain.

Angel, Zulema, and her father all jumped to her rescue, but being that Angel was sitting right next to her, he was able to tend to her first.

Angel's voice was low as he stood to check on her arm. "You okay?"

Snow nodded, but her shoulder was on fire.

"Don't lie. Let me know so I can make it better."

Snow tried to suppress her smile. There he was again,

making everything sound so sexual. She was positive it was her fault and not his, but she couldn't help it.

"How you gon' make it better?" She smiled at him over her shoulder.

"I'ma kiss it," he whispered.

"Well in that case, it was my—"

"Listen, little fast ass, remember your parents are sitting here before you say something inappropriate," Zulema warned her. "Empress told me about y'all touchy-feely asses."

Neither Snow nor Angel could hold their laughter after that. Angel had even leaned partially over her shoulder as they laughed.

Zulema snickered along with them as well. "I just had to go ahead and throw that out there, because you sounded like you were about to take it there."

Snow covered her mouth as she blushed. "I was not. I was about to tell him it was my shoulder."

Angel wasted no time going to her shoulder and probing it in certain areas. He was so gentle with her as he moved it around, checking the bandage for bleeding. Snow thought it was the cutest thing how he was so attentive to her wounds. The skillful way he moved his hands was so comforting, she could see why he wanted to be a doctor so badly. And for the first time since being back with him, she wanted that for him as well.

His compassion toward her might have been a little extra due to their relationship, but she was sure he would show his patients no less.

"How does that feel?" Angel asked Snow.

"Too much touching. All you two do is touch, touch, touch." Mack threw his hands up in the air. "You're not focused, Emelia. He makes you unfocused." Mack's tone was harsh, emphasizing how angry he was. "This is why this happened to you." He motioned his hands toward her shoulder and leg. "You're not focused, Emelia! I taught you better than this." Mack rose from his chair. "Better than to be some foolish girl chasing after love," he grumbled to himself as he headed for the exit.

"Mack, watch the way you're speaking to her," Angel stood tall and voiced firmly.

Mack waved Angel off and gave his attention to Snow only. "Love loves no one, Emelia! No one!" he yelled before leaving the kitchen.

Snow's eyes watered continuously. Every time she wiped them, more tears came. She was so wounded by her father's outburst that she couldn't even calm herself down.

"Emelia, stop crying, baby." Her mother grabbed her hand. "Ignore your father. He's just not used to sharing you with anyone. He's afraid that your love for Angel will get in the way of the bond you and he share. He doesn't mean anything he's saying."

Snow continued to cry. "Yes, he does, he does mean it. Daddy always means what he says." She broke down crying again.

"Not this time, sweetie. He's just afraid that you'll fall in love and forget to be your own woman."

"I would never do anything to change her." Angel leaned down and kissed the side of her wet face. "Stop crying, Emelia. What he said doesn't matter. You and I both know that the way we love each other will only make us grow. That bullshit he's yelling about means nothing. You can love me and be focused at the same time. This didn't happen because you're unfocused." He used her chin to turn her head toward him. "Look at me."

Snow sniffed hard and wiped at her face feverishly.

"He wasn't in that bank with you, I was. He didn't see the way you were busting your guns. He didn't see how you took those bullets like a soldier, he doesn't see how you run shit in South Carolina. I know that's your daddy, but fuck him. You're focused as fuck and I see you." Angel grabbed both sides of her face. "You hear me? I see you."

Snow was trying her hardest to keep from crying as she listened to Angel. He was right. He was so right, but it still felt wrong to have her father disappointed in her. She'd spent her entire life doing things to make him proud, and the one time she did something for herself, he made her feel like a piece of dirt.

"Stop all that damn crying." Angel grabbed her face and placed several kisses on her mouth before looking at Zulema. "I'm sorry for cursing like that, Mrs. Z, but she needs to know that she doesn't have to accept that shit. Not even from Mack. After all of the work that Snow has put in, he should have never come at her sideways like that." Angel took his seat but pulled it closer to Snow's chair so that he could wrap his arm around her. "He may be her father, but I'm not going to let him or anyone else hurt her."

Zulema's eyes were wet with a sheen of tears as she nodded in agreement. "I just love you, Angel." She wiped her eyes as her smile returned. "I just love you, baby. You are just the type of man that every mother wants for her daughter." She sniffed. "All I've ever wanted for my baby was for her to find a man to love her the way she deserves to be loved."

"Mommy," Snow cried to her. "I don't know what Daddy wants me to do. I'm not leaving Angel."

"And I don't expect you to, baby. Don't you dare ruin your happiness for your father. I've been with him and loving his old stubborn ass for years. Who is he to think he can stop you from having the same thing?" Zulema waved her hand toward the door Mack had just left through. "I know how much you love Angel, so love your man. I'll worry about your father."

"Why would he bring us out here just to do this?" Snow questioned.

"Girl, your father has been missing you so much, he'd do anything to get you here. I'm not surprised at all. This was the perfect reason to get and keep you here. Mack's old ass ain't slick." Zulema chuckled, but neither Snow nor Angel found anything funny about that.

"He could have kept his invitation if we were coming to be mistreated," Angel responded, and Snow agreed.

"I agree, but like I said, don't worry about him. Y'all just get all the rest y'all need. Make plans, arrangements, whatever you both came here to do, get it done. And you"—she pointed at Snow—"you must be pregnant again?"

Snow's crying stopped then. She probably looked like a deer caught in headlights as she stared at her mother in shock. "What? Why you say that?"

"The look on your face just answered my question, but I asked because you're crying. I can count on one hand how many times you've cried since you've been an adult." She was smiling. "Does my best friend know we're about to be grandmas?"

Angel smiled and shook his head. "No, ma'am. She just told me on the way over here, or you know I already would have told her."

Zulema stood from her chair. "Well, consider it done. I'm about to go call her right now."

"Please don't say it in front of Daddy," Snow begged.

"Oh, damn. You're right. I guess I'll have to wait until tomorrow when he leaves for the distribution center. This is something I have to call and tell her. I can't send this tea through a text message."

Snow sniggled. "My business should not be classified as tea, Mommy."

"As old as me and Empress are, anything that we don't do ourselves is tea."

Angel's laughter brought about Zulema's as well. They laughed with her mother for a little while longer, giving her details on the pregnancy before Angel wheeled her down the hallway toward her old room. When they got there, it was clean and decorated with new linen. Other than that, everything else was still the same.

Angel closed the door behind them and looked around. "I remember when I used to have to sneak in here just to see you."

Snow sat in her wheelchair staring at him with a large smile on her face. "You ain't lying. We used to be pulling out all of the stops to sneak you up in here. Just to fall asleep for an hour and be right back out before it was time to get up for school."

"Those were the good old days." He laughed. "Couldn't nobody tell me I wasn't sexing you like a grown man back then."

Snow's giggles turned into full-blown gales as she laughed hardily. "Man, what! Just like I thought I was getting dicked down. Little did I know that dick down would have my ass running around here trying to hide a baby from my parents."

Angel's eyes stopped roaming the room and landed back on her. "I'm sorry you had to go through that alone."

She twisted her mouth to the side while scratching her head. "It was my own fault. I should have told you. I just didn't want to ruin your dreams, ya know?"

He nodded but didn't say anything.

"You know something? I want you to be a doctor."

Angel's eyebrows raised in question. "Where did that come from?"

"I can just tell by the way you take care of me that you have a passion for it, and I want you to do something that makes you happy." She looked around her room. "Running this show makes me happy, but not you."

"Well, if I'm a doctor and you're my wife, don't you think it would be kind of wrong for you to still be out here slanging dope? On top of that, where would your happiness come from?"

"You make me happy, Angel. I don't ever have to sell another ounce of cocaine in my life as long as I have you with me every day."

"You're serious?" Angel asked her.

Snow nodded, because she was. She had never been more serious in her life. Drugs and the cartel had been her entire life. She was actually ready for something new. Angel made her feel like she could have more than just a swift blade and an aggressive trigger finger. Lately, all of the things she'd grown up thinking made her happy really didn't anymore.

"I think my father was right," Snow said.

Angel was standing in front of her with his hands tucked in his pockets. "About?"

Snow's eyes felt heavy as she looked at him. "Being unfocused."

Angel sucked his teeth and walked over to her. "Don't you do this. Do not let him get inside your head, Emelia."

"I'm not. He really was right. I'm not focused." She shifted some in her seat. "I haven't been focused in weeks. It's like I'm good at the stuff I do because I've been doing it for so long, but my heart isn't in it like it used to be."

Angel's arms rested around his kneecaps as he watched her intently. "Where is it?"

Snow licked her lips while her eyes searched his for the safety she needed to divulge her deepest feelings. "With you."

"With me?" Angel questioned, in shock from her revelation.

She nodded. "Yep, and with you is where I want it to stay." She looked down at her feet. "With you I feel free. I don't have to watch my back, I don't have to worry about money, drugs, shipments, none of that. I can drop my toughness and be Emelia. Being Emelia brings me more joy than being Snow."

"But you love Snow."

"I do, but I love Emelia even more. Since I was a child, I've been trained and molded so much to become Snow that I had no idea who Emelia really was. My father has been grooming me to become a miniature him. Though I've accomplished a lot because of it, I'm happier without it." She gave Angel a weak smile. "Any time you're around, you bring out the best in me, and I don't think my father understands that. But you know what? I don't even care. All I kept thinking in the kitchen when he was being rude to you was that if you rolled me out of this house and took me back to the airport, I'd go willingly."

Snow wasn't sure at first, but once the lone teardrop

rolled down Angel's cheek, she was positive. He was crying.

"Why are you crying, baby?" she asked him.

"Because the amount of love I have for you is immeasurable. Every woman that I've dealt with always wanted something in return. Whether it was money, cars, the places I took them, even just the sex, it was always something. With you, it's not like that." He scooted closer to her and touched her good foot. "You actually make me a better person, and I'll beat anybody's ass that thinks they're going to change that. Including your old-ass daddy."

Feminine laughter sounded throughout her room as she released her expressions of happiness. Angel was truly a character.

"So, what now? Where do we go from here?" Snow asked.

Angel shrugged. "To take a shower, I assume. I feel dirty for some reason."

Snow kicked him with her good leg. "Stop it."

His sexy smile made her night brighter as he sat cheesing at her. "I say we make our own story. If that means we stay in the cartel, then we'll stay. If it means I become a doctor and you're my gorgeous ass housewife, then that's fine too."

Snow tapped her bottom lip as if she was thinking. "I think I'll take the latter."

"Barefoot and pregnant?"

She nodded with a large smile on her face. "Barefoot and pregnant, baby."

"Now, don't get me happy and then change your mind on me." Angel stood up and pushed her chair toward the large bathroom.

"I'm not. We just have to find a way to make this work."

Angel pecked the side of her face. "We will. I promise."

Snow didn't know whether Angel made a lot of promises or not, but what she did know was that she didn't think he'd break one. So, with a fresh outlook on life, Snow would follow him into their new world. Only time would tell whether or not it was worth it.

Chapter Twenty-three

Blood is thicker than water, but water tastes better

"I can't wait to meet you, whoever you are. I've waited a long time to be someone's father, so you're going to have to be patient with me and all of the love I'm ready to give you." Angel rubbed Snow's flat stomach as she slept.

It was going on three o'clock in the morning, and he still hadn't been to sleep yet. After the shower he'd taken with Snow, they rebandaged her wounds with the dressings he'd gotten from the family doctor Zulema had called for her, and climbed into bed. After Angel propped pillows and a few blankets under Snow, she'd fallen right off to sleep.

He couldn't blame her. They'd had a long day and

an even longer weekend. On top of that, he was sure her body was tired. It had been through more than enough for a woman that early in pregnancy.

Angel, too, was ecstatic that his baby was still in there baking, even after all of the trouble Snow had been through.

"You're tough like your mother, I see." Angel spoke again. "That's a good thing. Stay that way, she's the best person you'll ever meet."

Angel kissed the back of Snow's head as she stirred in her sleep. He lay still, rubbing her arms and back until she stilled again. Once he was sure she was back asleep, he got out of bed. His mouth was dry as all hell, and he needed to grab something to drink from the kitchen.

In his pajamas, Angel padded up the hall. Not wanting to bump into Mack or anyone else at that hour, he hurried to grab his bottled water and headed back down the hall. On his way, he decided to hit his blunt before going back to bed. The small balcony at the back of the house overlooked the pool and would be the perfect place to sort some things out.

After darting back into the room quickly and grabbing his blunt, he headed back down the hall. Thanks to Snow, he knew there was no alarm on that door, so he eased out with no problem. Once seated in the plush lawn chair, Angel lit his blunt and inhaled deeply.

His eyes closed as he exhaled the potent weed. He took a few more puffs before he was able to relax enough to think about what was going on around him, and who could possibly be behind it. Angel looked at his and Snow's life from every angle and still couldn't make up one scenario that made sense.

One puff after the other, he ended up getting himself riled back up versus calmed down. When he couldn't make sense of any of it, he began to get frustrated. When he got so overwhelmed that he could no longer even think straight, he began to pray.

Praying always eased his mind. He asked the Lord for a number of things, but the main one was to reveal to him who was behind it all, and to grant him the strength to handle whoever it was.

"Amen." He opened his eyes and sat up some so that he could look over the balcony.

The East estate was almost as big as the DeLucas'. The only thing that separated them was the flowers. Empress didn't like flowers. She was more of a bricks-and-stones kind of person. Nor did she like sneaky muthafuckas that had to sit outside to talk on the phone.

Angel's eyes had just landed on Mack. He was at the bottom deck walking alongside the pool with the phone to his ear. Angel couldn't really hear what he was saying at first and was straining to hear, but God must have felt like answering his prayers right then, because out of nowhere, Mack began yelling.

"You said you had this shit under control. You almost killed my fucking daughter, you idiot."

Angel's entire face frowned up, because he knew like hell that he hadn't just heard Mack involve himself in the shooting.

"No! No, D'Angelo! You're a fucking fool. If I could get my hands on you, I'd kill your ass myself."

Angel's body might as well have been a blazing fire right then, as hot as he was. He could literally feel his blood boiling and rushing through his veins as he sat putting two and two together in his head. He knew he'd prayed for the Lord to reveal the truth to him, but he didn't think it would come that fast, and he most definitely didn't know it would be his family.

They were some of the main muthafuckas that screamed loyalty day in and day out, but were plotting on him and Snow behind their backs. That was seriously some fucked-up shit.

"I wouldn't go in business with your sloppy ass for nothing!" Mack fired off before continuing his abuse in Spanish.

Angel wanted so badly to sit there and listen for more information, but he'd had enough. Furthermore, he didn't want to get caught snooping, so he got up and left. He walked forcefully down the hallway until he reached Snow's room again.

She was still in bed sleeping peacefully. Too riled up to join her, Angel paced the floor. He needed to talk to someone, somebody who would be able to help him figure shit out. The only person who could do that was Vinny. Just thinking about his father and how he no longer had the luxury of having simple conversations with him anymore brought Angel to tears.

Before he knew it, Angel was kneeling on the floor, overcome by emotion. This was all too much, and he wasn't sure if he could find a way out. He'd always known his brother was jealous of him and wanted the cartel for himself, but he never thought he would stoop to trying to kill him to get it.

More tears fell as he realized just how blind he'd been all this time. He should have known that something was up. The way D'Angelo acted sometimes was downright ridiculous, but Angel had dismissed it, assuming it was just something siblings went through.

"Fuck!" he screamed and punched the floor.

"Angel?" Snow stirred in the bed, trying to sit up. "Baby, where are you? What's wrong?" she asked as she lay on her back in the middle of the bed, still propped up on pillows.

Angel cleared his throat the best he could. "I'm fine, sweet girl. Just go back to sleep."

"No, you're not. Tell me what's wrong."

Angel's tears resurfaced as he tried his hardest to get himself together. It was so hard trying to hold it all in that he ended up wailing a little louder than he'd wanted to. The anger, the pain, the fear, the uncertainty, the stress—everything that had been weighing him down for months—poured out onto the floor.

"Angel, baby, please come here and let me see you. I need to know that you're all right," she begged, now in tears herself.

When Angel noticed that she too was crying, he got up from the floor and went to her. In no way, shape, or form did he think he was ready to tell her what he'd just heard, but he didn't want to leave her up there scared either.

"I'm cool, Emelia. I just got a little overwhelmed thinking about my father. I wanted to call him so bad just now but couldn't because I don't know whether he's having a good day or a bad one." Angel sniffed again. "Vinny was my best fucking friend. I don't know what to do without him."

Snow used her good arm to pull his head to her and rub it in comfort. Angel lay with his face cradled in her neck, crying his eyes out.

"It'll be okay, baby. If it makes you feel better, I'm here for you," Snow said.

Angel wrapped his arm around her stomach. "It does make me feel better." He closed his eyes and sniffed away the snot threatening to drip out of his nose. "I'm ready to go home, Emelia."

"We can go tomorrow."

He nodded but didn't respond verbally. Angel was

so exhausted with everything going on with him right then he couldn't fathom having to figure out what needed to be done on his own. In the back of his mind, he knew what he was about to do wasn't the right thing to do at the moment, but she'd find out eventually.

"Snow?" Her name reluctantly fell from his lips.

"Yes, baby?"

"D'Angelo was behind the shooting."

Her hand stopped stroking his back. "What?" Her voice grew so cold he could feel the ice dripping from her words. "How do you know?"

Angel sat up and took a deep breath, because here was the hard part. He touched the side of her face while softening his eyes at her.

"How do you know?" she asked again, this time much colder than she'd asked the first time. "And stop rubbing me." She swatted his hand from the side of her face.

"I went outside to smoke my blunt and heard your daddy fussing at him about almost getting you killed."

If at all possible, Angel could see the fire burning in her eyes. The dark irises were blazing with an intensity Angel had never seen before.

"Calm down." He went back to touching her face.

She swatted his hand. "Stop touching me." She looked off into the distance. "Are you sure that's what you heard?"

Angel nodded.

"Okay." She nodded.

"Okay?" Angel questioned.

"Yes. Okay." She lay back and closed her eyes.

"Okay what, Emelia? What are you thinking?"

She turned to him. "What do you mean what am I thinking? I'm thinking about what has to be done."

Angel looked at her in confusion. How did she know

what had to be done that fast, and he didn't? "What needs to be done?"

She looked at him with a coolness that sounded so deadly it made him shiver. "They have to die."

"Die?" Angel clarified in confusion.

"Yes. I'm going to kill them."

Angel didn't know what to say, so he said nothing. He could understand her thought process, because that's what they'd been taught. Any signs of disloyalty resulted in death. Although Angel had never seen the actual retribution, he'd heard about it enough times to believe that Snow wasn't joking around.

The early morning air in the room grew cooler as the two of them lay in complete silence, lost in their own thoughts. Angel looked at Snow every so often, but every time he did, her face was expressionless and void of any emotion. He wasn't quite sure what she was thinking, but he was sure he had an idea.

The whole situation was pure torture, and he couldn't wait for it to all be over. The following hours ticked by a lot slower than what he'd hoped for, but when daylight finally hit and it was time to get out of bed, he did. Snow, on the other hand, was still lying perfectly still, staring at the ceiling.

"Emelia, you ready to get out of bed?"

"No," she answered sourly without moving.

"You can't stay in there all day."

She turned her head toward him slowly. "I know that." Her words sounded a lot harsher than what Angel was used to, and he didn't like it.

"Yo, I get that you're feeling some kind of way right now, but don't take that shit out on me. I'm just as fucked up as you."

"Sure, you are," she told him sarcastically. "I'm ready to get up."

"If you think I'm about to help you after you just got done talking to me like I ain't shit, you'll be laying your ass right there all day." Angel walked off and went to shower again.

Afterward, he brushed his hair, threw on the jeans and T-shirt that he'd brought with him, and went back to where Snow was. She was in the same spot, except this time her face was a little more relaxed.

"You ready to act like you got some sense?"

He watched her nose twitch before she nodded. Since she was more compliant that time around, he helped her get dressed and ready for the day. It took them a little longer to get her hair together, but once they did, they made sure all of their things were packed before going to look for her parents. When they found them they were both in the kitchen eating.

It took everything in Angel not to break Mack's neck right then, but he composed himself. There was a time and place for everything. He didn't want to go off, exposing his hand without a plan in place.

"I thought the two of you were going to sleep the day away." Zulema was all smiles when they walked in.

"Just a little tired," Angel said.

"Got you some rest, darling?" Mack asked Snow as Angel placed her in the kitchen chair next to him.

Snow glared at him across the table. "No."

"Why not?"

"I don't want to talk about it," she responded.

Mack's eyes shot to Angel. "Did you do something to her?"

Angel turned his nose up at him and said nothing.

"You know what? I can't hold my tongue." Snow spoke up.

Angel looked at her in alarm. He already knew what

she was about to do, because he knew her. All he hoped was that it went smoother than he'd imagined it would all night.

"Papa, did you have me shot at?"

Mack stopped chewing for a moment, but resumed upon laying eyes on Snow. "No," he grumbled out. "I had Angel shot at."

"What?" Zulema asked, stunned.

His honesty shocked Angel. He'd known Mack was a tough old bastard, but he hadn't known he was that open and shut.

"Why would you do that?" Snow asked, just as even toned as Mack had been when he answered.

"Because you're not focused with him. You're throwing your life away." Mack threw his fork down onto the plate. "He's not meant for the top. I don't know why the hell Vinny would ever think so. I'd been telling him for years that Angel doesn't have the heart for it." His voice raised at the end. "He refused to listen, so the moment I learned he was sick, I decided to take matters into my own hands."

"That was not your choice," Snow spat.

"How could you do that, Mack? Emelia could have been killed. I can't believe you'd do something like that," Zulema fussed as she stood and left the room.

"She wasn't supposed to be there with him. That's the shit I'm talking about now. She's never doing what she should be doing as long as she's with him."

Angel's mind was blown as he sat listening to Mack speak about him like he was a nobody, and not the son of his best friend. If he had to be cold like Mack, then they were right, Angel didn't have the heart to be the king. Never in his life would he have crossed his family, no matter what the case was. Loyalty was one of the main reasons he'd continued dealing with D'Angelo after all of the envious run-ins they'd had over the years.

"What happened to the loyalty, Papa?" Snow asked.

Mack picked his knife up and pointed it at Snow. "My loyalty lies with you, not him." He pointed the knife at Angel. "If it weren't for him, the whole cartel would be ours."

"Ours?" Snow asked incredulously. "I don't want this shit, Papa. Especially not with people that would do the shit you and D'Angelo just did."

"Vinny would have never done no shit like this," Angel told him.

Mack's devilish laughter filled the room. "Well, we'll never see that, now will we?"

Angel lunged across the table, quickly snatching Mack from his chair and throwing him to the floor. He had his foot raised to kick him but stopped when Snow called his name.

"Don't. Let's just go," Snow said.

Angel looked down at Mack and lowered his foot. "You're going to get what's coming to you."

Mack struggled to get to his feet. When he was finally back upright, he smiled at Angel. "And who's going to give it to me?"

"Me," Snow stated with finality.

His eyes darted to hers. "Really?"

She nodded.

"Good. I'd rather it be at the hands of someone that I respect anyway."

"What's blood to people these days?" She shook her head in disgust.

"My dear darling, blood may be thicker than water, but water tastes better." He chuckled deviously.

Angel could feel his anger getting out of hand, so before he did something to Mack and hurt Snow forever, he grabbed her from the table and left the kitchen. When they got back to her room, he placed her in her wheelchair and grabbed their things. They needed to get out of there before Mack tried some more sick shit. It was obvious he had no limits.

"I can't believe he would do something like this," Snow whispered as Angel pushed her out the front door of her home. "How am I going to kill my own father?" She looked to him for an answer.

"Don't." Angel wanted Mack just as dead as Mack had wanted him, but he didn't want Snow to be the one to do it. That would be too much for her to carry.

"I have to."

"No, you don't. Just leave his lonely ass in California, and don't fuck with him no more."

"That's not how the game goes."

Angel looked down at her as their car pulled up. "You don't have to stick to the way things are supposed to be. You can make your own rules."

Snow's head shook subtly. "I know my father. I have to do it, or else I'll have to watch my back forever, and I'm not going to do that anymore. That's not the life I want as Emelia. He has to go."

Angel didn't know what else to say, so he said nothing. Her mind was made up. If that was how she wanted to handle things, then that was what they'd do. After all, that was how the game went.

Chapter Twenty-four

I'll leave and never come back

"Shit!" D'Angelo cursed as he hit his knee on the bottom of the bed.

He was so busy running around his room trying to gather all of his things that he was being clumsy. He already had pretty much everything he would need packed up, but he had a few more things to get before getting out of town. Mack had already called and warned him that Angel and Snow knew what had happened and to be aware, because Snow would be after him. D'Angelo had been running around wildly ever since.

"Where you going to all fast?" Empress asked from his bedroom doorway.

D'Angelo stilled and looked at her. "On a vacation with one of my li'l women."

Empress walked completely into his room and took a seat on the corner of the bed. "Oh, really? To where?"

D'Angelo tried to think of something but couldn't. "It's a cruise. We're going to a bunch of places."

"Uh-huh." She crossed her legs and arms at the same time. "You see what you're doing now? This is why we could never trust you to run the cartel. You don't have what it takes."

That statement pissed D'Angelo off. "I don't have what it takes? Let me guess, Angel does?"

Empress nodded. "Yes, he does." She sat up on the edge of the bed so that she could give him her undivided attention. "You see, Angel would have never crossed you the way you tried to do him. To him, family actually means something."

D'Angelo stilled. How did she know? Too embarrassed to even ask, he continued packing his things to leave.

"It's sad that your own greediness wouldn't allow you to prosper. You could have worked alongside your brother and had just as much as he did, but no. You just had to have it all for yourself." Empress's voice broke. "Your disloyalty hurts me to my soul, D'Angelo." She stood and walked to him. Before he could object, she wrapped him up in a one-sided hug. "I love you, son. I pray you never reap what you've sown." She kissed his cheek once more before leaving just as quietly as she'd come in.

D'Angelo stood in place for a minute, letting his mother's words marinate. "Too late now," he said aloud before grabbing his things and leaving the house.

He hurried to get into the waiting car before Angel and Snow could catch sight of him. After throwing all of his things in the trunk, he hopped in the back seat. "To the airport, please," he told the driver.

"Yes, sir." The driver pulled away and merged into traffic.

"Thank God." D'Angelo exhaled roughly while wiping his hands over his face.

D'Angelo had done a lot of fucked-up things in his past, but he wasn't quite ready for them to all come catching up to him just yet. He still had a life to live.

"Don't thank him just yet." The malevolent feminine bass of Snow's voice raised the goose bumps on his arms. "Save that, you're about to see him in person."

D'Angelo sat with his eyes straight ahead and sweat suddenly pouring down his forehead. Snow was sitting shotgun, but he couldn't see her because of the seat's large headrest.

"Hector, pull over right here, please," she instructed the driver.

"Keep driving," D'Angelo requested, but was ignored.

Hector pulled the car over to the side of the small dirt road. "The other car is on the way, Ms. Snow."

"Thank you. Wait for me in there."

Hector nodded, hopped out, and hit the locks. As soon as the door was closed, D'Angelo began snatching on his door handle trying to get out, but couldn't.

"You might as well be still. I child-locked all of these doors for your childish ass." She turned around in her seat, pinning him with her intense gaze. "I told you when I first got here I wasn't that same little girl anymore, and not to fuck with me. I guess you thought I was fucking around."

The sound of a gun cocking sent D'Angelo over the edge. "I'm sorry, Snow. It was your daddy's idea. I just went along with it."

"Shut the fuck up. I don't want to hear that shit."

She did something else, making the gun click loudly again. "Any last words?"

"Please don't do this. I promise I'll leave and never come back."

Snow chuckled. "You're about to do that anyway."

D'Angelo nearly died when he saw the gun in her hand.

"Now you get to see how my baby felt when you kicked me down that hill."

"What bab—"

His words were cut short by the bullet that ripped through his forehead, splattering his brains everywhere. And just like that, life was over. All of the low-down things D'Angelo had ever done meant nothing to him in that moment. His life was over.

The smoke floated from the end of Mack's cigar as it sat in the clear ashtray next to his chair. The half of cup of brown liquor next to it held small beads of sweat from the melting ice, while the ring of moisture fogged up the table beneath it.

Angel could see his hand hanging over the chair as he sat facing the large window in his office. The lights were low, while music played in the background. Like Snow had relayed, Mack was home alone and in his office.

"Snow sends her warmest regards," Angel said as he walked around the chair with the gun in his hand.

Mack's eyes were cast down to the floor, and his mouth hung slightly open with foam running out the side of it and down his chin.

"I know this muthafucka didn't," Angel said to himself as he reached out and touched the side of Mack's neck. "You coward." Angel frowned at Mack's dead body in disgust.

The empty pill bottle in his lap was now in plain view, and so was the folded piece of paper. Angel had completely overlooked both of them before but grabbed them that time. He dropped the pill bottle onto the floor and opened the note.

> *Emelia, my darling,*
> *I knew you were coming today. I could feel it. I knew when you left here that day that you would be back. I love you so much that I wanted to save you the burden of killing me. You're my girl, and I couldn't have you holding on to that for the rest of your life. I taught you to be tough, so don't mourn me. I deserved this and so much more. Go on, live your life, and maybe I'll see you again someday in the afterlife. I love you.*
> *Papa*
> *P.S. Don't worry about your mother, I talked to her about this, she knows. She has a note of her own. Make me proud, my dear sweet Snow.*

Angel wanted to crumple the paper up and throw it away, but just like Mack had known, Snow would need it, so he kept it. Snow was a tough girl, but at the end of the day, Mack was still her father, and she loved him. The note would probably bring enough peace to get her through his death.

Somewhat grateful he didn't have to use his pistol, Angel lowered it and exited the house and the East estate. Though the place held many fond memories for him, it was now a part of his past, and that was one place he planned to never revisit.

Epilogue

"Angel, get them down from there," Emelia yelled as she watched her sons climb across the top of the monkey bars.

"Emelia, get your behind over here and sit down. Let them babies be boys," Empress yelled after her.

"I'm telling you, those poor boys can't catch a break," Zulema chimed in.

Emelia rolled her eyes at both of the women without turning around to face them. She got so tired of them always telling her what to do with her kids. They'd had their chance to raise kids and hadn't done very well, in her opinion, but she'd keep that to herself.

"I'ma tell them you're over here rolling your eyes." Angel walked up to her in his long white doctor's coat, smiling.

"They get on my nerves." She stopped frowning and laughed at herself.

Angel wrapped his arm around Emelia's shoulder and pecked the side of her face. "They mean well."

"I know, but still."

"Try to take it a little easier on them. They're two lonely old widows that are used to a life of crime. Our kids are the most excitement they get all day." Angel looked across the park at their mothers. "I don't see how you let them get to you anyway. They did horrible raising their own kids."

"I just thought the same thing." Emelia giggled giddily as she grabbed onto his waist. "But I think it was just Zulema that did horrible. Empress did a hell of a job. I don't know where I would be right now if she hadn't popped that pussy for Vinny."

Angel's head fell back in laughter. "I swear your ass will say anything."

Emelia shrugged her shoulders. "Only anything that'll make you smile." She pecked his chin. "You think we could sneak away for a quickie?"

Angel looked around the park once more. "Didn't I just tell your ass we're their excitement? They'll be all up in our business. You know since Vinny passed, my mama be watching all of us extra close now. I think she's scared we're going to leave her or something."

"It's a lot to get used to. She loved Vinny more than life itself."

Angel wrapped both of his arms around Emelia and kissed all over her face. "Kind of like I love you, huh?"

Emelia blushed and nodded at the same time. "Just like you love me."

Angel's head dipped, and their tongues entangled in a passionate kiss that involved a lot of touching and moaning. When they finally pulled away, Angel was smiling down at her with bright red cheeks.

"When I left you all of those years ago, I never would have thought that you would be my wife and the mother of my kids. I knew I loved you, but I didn't know that I couldn't live without you."

"I knew it. You were always ambitious, so I knew you would come back, you just had to follow your hustle. I understood that."

"But my hustle was different back then. It was for all of the wrong shit." Angel looked around at their three kids as they played on the playground. "Now you and my kids are my heart. I hustle for y'all on a totally different level."

"That's even better. Now we're the heart of your hustle?"

Angel's handsome face made her heart skip a beat when he nodded. "If I could marry you a million times, I would."

Emelia pecked his mouth once more and held up her ring finger. "You don't have to. Once was enough, Dr. DeLuca."

"One lifetime with you isn't enough for me."

"Me either, so let's die together and live and love again." Emelia winked at him.

He winked back. "Let's."

Emelia smiled up at her husband with hearts in her eyes. He was the best thing to ever happen to her. He'd been there for her through every hardship she'd ever had. Angel had helped her get through things she thought would kill her but that ended up only making her stronger. They'd lost family, lost money, lost respect, and a host of other things together, but remained the same.

Angel was her best friend and did whatever he could to put a smile on her face. He was definitely a blessing that she'd never take for granted. His love was out of this world, and the fact that he was sexy with his own medical practice, making more legal money than they knew what to do with, wasn't too bad either. He was truly her Angel on earth.

Want more A'zayler? Get your copy of

In Love with My Enemy

Beautiful and educated, with just enough Atlanta street smarts to give her a sexy edge, hood princess Danna Mendoza has a dream life. Her temporary bodyguard-turned-undercover lover Don makes it complete. As her father's best friend and longtime drug partner, Don's devoted to keeping her safe. But Don's underlying vendetta against her father is one danger Danna never saw coming . . .

Cannon Collier has finally found her way in the world—as the newfound love interest of handsome basketball superstar on the rise, Ezra Mendoza. But Ezra doesn't plan on falling for her. And he doesn't plan on her becoming a casualty of his father's game. But things don't always go as planned . . .

Available wherever books and ebooks are sold.

DON'T MISS

I Do Love You Still by Mary B. Morrison

From *New York Times* bestselling author
Mary B. Morrison comes the seductive,
no-holds-barred novel of a dazzling power
couple who play their scandalous love-hate
affair one game too far . . .

The Vows We Break by Briana Cole

Kimera Davis had a plan to jump start her life and
land on easy street. But someone's playing a desperate, dangerous game with her life . . . and she'll have
to win if she wants to survive.

ON SALE NOW!

Turn the page for an excerpt from these
thrilling novels . . .

Chapter 1

Xena

Silence gave sound to the voice inside my mind.

Rolling onto my side, I lay in bed facing the open window. Curtains flapped, whipping a summer breeze that brushed my naked body as though I was its canvas. I inhaled the warm air. I didn't want to be here.

Why was I living with one man, knowing I was still in love with my ex? Exhaling, I turned onto my back, bent my knees, placed my feet flat on the mattress, then stared into the darkness of the bedroom.

Remember why you left him, Xena. I know. But I don't want to be here.

In the beginning, I was happy with my new guy. Doubling back to a former boyfriend, I'd never done that. After all the shit my ex had put me through, I should hate him. I really wanted to, but . . . what had I proven by trying to hurt him the way he'd done me?

I touched my stomach. God knew my aching heart was filled with love for my ex and repentance for what I'd done. Couldn't stop thinking about it or missing him. Doubted he'd take me back if I told him the truth of why I'd left him.

4:50 a.m.

A familiar hand caressed my breast. I scooted, hips first, to the edge of the queen-size mattress. Closing the gap between us, he hugged my waist, pulled me toward him. I resumed my previous position. Stared toward the ceiling fan that clicked each time it rotated.

Leaning in, he sucked my nipple. Didn't deny it felt good. My breaths became shallow, wishing it was my ex.

"Not now," I said, facing him, trying to assume a fetal position to create space between him and my parts I knew he wanted to access.

Dragging me closer to the middle of the bed, he crawled on top of me, began licking my areolas. His hand massaged my B-cups, then he twisted my nipple with his fingertips. I didn't want to enjoy his touch right now, but my body could not deny the percolating energy circulating throughout my chakras.

Pop. Crackle. Pop. Noises emanated from the settling of his old colonial home, recently renovated on the inside.

He used his knee to spread my thighs, then penetrated me. Our morning ritual had begun. *Squeak.* Headboard. *Squeak.* Frame. His hips thrust back and forth. No side to side, figure eight, or round and round clockwise followed by counterclockwise the way my last boyfriend used to do.

Our music was the chorus of a love ballad. I liked

my current. I had done a good job of separating the sexual act from my feelings for him.

Closing my eyes, I squeezed my vaginal muscles supertight, pretending he was my ex. Shallow breaths deepened into a soft "haaa," as I exhaled into orgasm number one.

"That's my girl. Let it out," he said. Bracing himself on his forearms, he paused, then he sexed me in slower motion. "Give me another one."

The stimulation inside my pussy intensified. I released a bigger climax. For me. Not him.

"Don't hold back, baby. Give me all of my sweet juices," he moaned, shifting his mouth toward mine.

Quickly I pivoted in the opposite direction as he kept stroking. In and out.

"Kiss me, baby." This time he slid his tongue from my cheek to my lips—trailing saliva—then forced it inside . . . lizard-style.

Lust transitioned into frustration with each probe. He was never a good kisser. I cleared my mind. Focused on my task list for the day to calm myself.

Meditate. Go to the market. Meet my contract deadline for our client.

5:05 a.m.

His dick moved back and forth, all five inches in, then all the way out. Lightly he circled the tip of his penis at my opening, glided back in, pulled out. Entering me again, he poked my G-spot. Couldn't lie. Our sex was never wild, but he always made me wet.

Imagining he was my ex, I pulled my boyfriend's ass to me, hugged his shoulders, started groaning loud. "Ah, yes." I told him, "Go deeper inside me, baby." With my ex, I wouldn't have to ask.

"Um-hmm. I love you so." Abruptly his words ended midsentence, then he asked, "I'm not hurting you, am I?"

Nice of him to ask, but he didn't have the proper equipment to inflict vaginal pain. The lump in my abdomen hadn't gotten larger, but it'd been there for almost a year. I shook my head in response to his question. The doctor said it was a fibroid tumor, and that it didn't need to be removed. Nor would the lump prevent me from conceiving.

Escaping into a fantasy of one of the best lovemaking sessions with my ex, I visualized his long girthy shaft snaking up the walls of my vagina. The opening of his penis moved about the depth of my pussy as though it were a searchlight looking for my soul. I'd pretend to hide my pleasure point, and he wouldn't stop fucking the shit out of me until he made me scream soprano . . . I missed him so much. Instantly my pussy became hot and my juices flowed like a waterfall for my current boyfriend. I tilted my pelvis up, granting him total access to Niagara.

5:12 a.m.

"You're making me cum early," he said, then added, "You ready?" Delving to his max, inches shy of reaching my cul-de-sac, my new boyfriend froze.

Suddenly his ass jerked backward. *Squeak.* He paused. Thrusting forward, he paused again. *Squeak.* One. Two. Back. Forth. His rhythm grew closer, becoming one continuous motion until he and the squeaking came to a stop. I felt his throbbing shaft, then he collapsed on top of me. His accelerated heartbeat pounded against my breasts.

5:16 a.m.

After rolling him onto his side of the bed, I pulled the spread up to my neck, stared toward the ceiling. Lying next to my current, not a day went by where I didn't miss my ex.

Was Memphis in a relationship? Had he forgotten about me? Did he crave spooning me the way I longed to cuddle with him? Trying to convince myself I'd made the right decision to break up with him, I told Adonis, "I love you, baby." My head understood what my man needed to hear. My heart knew the truth.

Lifting the plush yellow comforter away from my naked body, I scooted away from Adonis, sat on the edge of the bed, gazed over my shoulder.

I didn't choose him. On our first date at Paula Deen's Creek House, he'd told me he wasn't looking for a girlfriend; he wanted a wife. I wasn't in search of a husband. Desperate, I had to get out of my mom's house. Didn't want to move in with my best friend, Tina-Love. Her pussy had a revolving door. Men came and went. None of them stayed.

Adonis was considerate, generous, and in love with me. From day one I allowed things to be his way. Sighing, I pivoted in his direction, touched his face, traced the front of his neatly trimmed hairline. The dark hairs of his crown had started to thin. The softness of his beard against my fingertips flowed to a mustache that arched over supple red lips, which had greeted mine each day since we'd met a year ago.

Every day I told myself to stop reliving my past, each time I replayed the reel of my walking out of Memphis's house into my mother's. In less than a week I was out of my parents' place, and into Adonis's apartment building. Planting a kiss on Adonis's forehead as he snored deeper and louder, *Please, don't leave me, Z, I'll be back in Savannah twelve months tops* echoed in my mind.

Not wanting to ruin the biggest opportunity of his lifetime, I'd made a unilateral decision. Aborting my ex's baby without telling him we were pregnant was wrong. I knew that.

Chapter 2

Memphis

"**I** know you have to leave, baby, but I wish you could stay with me a little longer," she professed, trailing kisses along my spine.

She was a sexy motherfucker. First time I saw her I knew straight up I was going to fuck the shit out her. Thin lips. Deep throat. Long wavy blond hair. Ice-blue irises. Tall. Six feet. Perfect size ten. Former high school volleyball Hall of Famer, she'd broken the record for the most game-winning spikes during her four years on the team.

Time was almost up for me here on the West Coast. All I wanted was to get back to the South and confront Xena regarding our unfinished business. I had to know the real reason why she broke it off. Tina-Love pretended Xena hadn't told her.

Yeah, right.

I lay facedown across the massage table Natalie had bought me, fixated on my ex. I'd been nothing but good to her for five years. A brotha had recently turned legal when I'd met Z but the fact that Z—my nickname for Xena—was five years older and salivating ova me kept my dick pointing north every day we were together. An athlete like me could have my choice female. But I wasn't average in any department. Also, I wasn't perfect.

Telling Natalie the same thing Z had told me the day Z walked out of my life, I replied, "You'll be all right." Not certain about my future, not caring about hers.

Natalie dug deeper into my quads. I felt her frustrations. She wouldn't understand, I had a lot riding on Z's love for me.

Olympic Training Camp was coming to an end. I didn't want to return to my hometown a failure in search of a nine-to-five, listening to fans reassure me I could beat Usain Bolt, having my IG followers DMing me not to give up. Sports flowed through the blood in my veins. I would become the world's champion; if Z hadn't abandoned me, I would've gotten an acceptance letter by now to represent the United States in track and field. I know I would've.

Venting to Natalie, I lamented, "I can't comprehend why she ended our relationship. I mean, I-I wasn't going to be gone forever, you feel me? Didn't want any other woman securing her spot. Gave her my all. But it's cool."

The hell it was. Blindsided, I hadn't sensed she was unhappy with my performance in or out of the sheets. A few hiccups here and there were the norm for guys, especially a track star like me. Z had issues, but I wasn't the one who'd fucked her up in the head.

Breaking her silence, I had to ask Natalie, "What do

women want? I-I mean her mother was the one who abused her. I'd never mistreat her. You. Any female. Most of y'all have man issues. Can't find, keep, or please one. That's not my fault."

Wanted to add, Why do females do everything for a man thinking that's going to make him love y'all, then when he steps to the next woman y'all feel betrayed when what really had happened was . . . you played yourself. But I wasn't that stupid.

Heard from our mutual friend Tina-Love Z had found my replacement shortly after I'd left Savannah. "I took her off the market first date. Something wifey about her that other women can't compete with. She's better than a Willy Wonka golden ticket. She's more like a gold medal only one man can win, keep, and treasure until he dies. I thought I'd won her for life. I—"

Slap! "Shut upppp! Memphis!" Natalie screamed, commanding my attention. "I'm sick and tired of hearing about your precious Z! You don't call *her* name when I'm sucking your dick!"

Actually, I do. You just don't hear me.

Naked and accessible, I was not arguing with Natalie while I was facedown. Xena Trinity was in a unique category. Passion for me was in her voice, her eyes, her touch, her pussy when I tasted my baby. Penetrating her . . . damn. My dick hardened. She'd never disrespect me the way Natalie had done. Yelling out of control. Z had that silent cry that would break my heart when I saw the sad look on her face. I stared at the twenty-pound barbells on the black carpet of my living room as I listened to Natalie sniffle. Teardrops plopped on my legs, trickled down to my shins.

"I told you when we started this was temporary. Please don't cry." I didn't want to hear it.

"I thought you were over her. Now that you're leaving me you're bringing her up again. Are you planning on getting back with her?" Natalie's fingers firmly glided from my ankles up to my glutes. She squeezed my butt hard with both hands.

Verbally. Mentally. Spiritually. I'd never terminated things with Z. I couldn't, even if I wanted to. Circumstances were beyond my capability. Real love secured home plate. No matter how many pussies I hit, Z had my heart on lock. We had history. Z was forever my girl. All the other females were on first, second, third, the mound. I'd never told her, but Natalie was somewhere in the outfield. Spoiled, rich, privileged white female wanted this middle-class black man's dick to continue making her feel good.

If I never saw her again, that'd be okay.

"What are we?" she questioned. "What's our relationship status?"

You don't wait almost a year to solidify your place in a man's life.

Repeating the same motion, foot to cheek, Natalie had gotten better at releasing my tension, not hers. She'd also grown bitter over the year, wanting what I wouldn't agree to: a commitment. I couldn't take a white woman home to my Jamaican mother. I was going to miss all the generous things Natalie had done for me on a daily. Laundry. Cooking. Stroking my ego and sucking my dick at the same time.

Natalie was upgraded from her tryout spot. She was a free agent. If she traded me the way Z had done, I'd miss the perks. Not Natalie. I hadn't asked her for anything she didn't want to give me. Lifting my head, I readjusted the pillow, lowered my face into the doughnut hole cushion. "What we have is and always will be special."

"Special? And what exactly is my place? Huh?" She stopped touching me.

Sitting up on the table, I placed my hand on her hip, cupped the nape of her neck, pulled her close. "Kiss me." I couldn't lie, she made me feel amazing. "Don't cry. We'll work this out when I get back," I lied.

Slowly she shook her head, then said, "You're not coming back."

"I have to," I lied again. "My things are here."

I'd received an e-mail that boxes were being delivered to my unit. Upon receipt, I was to pack up my personals, print and adhere the shipping labels. Someone would call me to arrange a pickup time and tracking information would be e-mailed to me.

"To get your clothes, Memphis. Really?" Gazing into my eyes, she continued, "I love you. What am I supposed to do without you?"

Natalie sounded like Z, except Z walked out on me. "I've got to get ready for practice. I'll hit you up when I'm done."

Natalie wrapped her arms around my neck. Smashed her clit against my flaccid dick. "I've invested a lot of time into you. I want to go with you to Savannah."

That was not happening. I glanced around my furnished apartment. "Nah. You need to go on your mission trip to Havana. People in Cuba need you."

"And you don't?" she cried.

"That's not what I'm saying. I have to focus on qualifying for the Olympics. When you get back, we'll see where I am and take it from there."

Natalie was a twenty-three-years-young female who grew up in Beverly Hills. Didn't know what a W-2 with her social security number on it looked like. Post–high school she traveled the world on missions to help people. Most women needed something or someone to care for. I'd become her stateside philanthropic recipient.

"You love me?" she asked, lowering her hands to my thighs.

One bedroom, bathroom, living, dining, and kitchen. I resided in eight hundred square feet. Natalie owned, free and clear, a two-bed, two-and-a-half-bath town house here in Chula Vista. Her parents didn't believe in her renting real estate. If I were the type of man to dog a female, I would've had her have me on payroll making weekly deposits into my bank account.

Puckering my lips tight, I shifted my mouth and eyes far to the left, then nodded, thinking . . . I loved her in an appreciative kind of way, for all she'd done. Yeah, that was it. "I do."

Natalie stepped back from the table, then demanded, "Say it, Memphis."

I stood. "For real. I've got to get ready for practice in a few hours." I accompanied her to my door and opened it. "We'll talk things over tonight. I promise."

Standing in the hallway, she said, "A radio producer named Rick in Savannah contacted me about you. He's trying to get me to—"

Natalie was trying too hard to solidify her spot. Closing the door, I turned the lock, got my cell. Scrolling through photos of Z and me, I bit my bottom lip. Tears clouded my eyes, splattered on my screen. I wasn't a bad dude.

I didn't know if I could ever forgive Z for breaking my heart.

Prologue

"We should just kill her."

Those words broke through my subconscious and sent a startling chill up my spine.

The pain, at first excruciating, had long since subsided into a dull ache and whether it was the handcuffs binding my wrists or the minimal rations of stale food and lukewarm water I'd been having to live on for the past few days, my body was now numb. Like a shell. But despite my snatches of blurred vision as I toggled in and out of consciousness, this man's face was crystal clear. What I didn't understand was why was he here? Why wasn't he helping me?

I struggled to lift my lids and through tears that blurred my vision, I stared into the eyes of a dead man.

"My love." His accent was deepened by the emotion clogging his voice. Pity. Apologetic. But he didn't move any closer, even though I'm sure I looked like the death I was slowly succumbing to.

I tried to replay everything that had happened in the past few months. Clues I had missed. Then, footsteps brought the other person into view and I remembered. My mind suddenly settled on the missing pieces that had been hidden in plain sight. How could I not have known? More importantly, what were they going to do with me now that I did?

Chapter 1

I knew I was wrong, even as I hiked up the bustle of chiffon and tulle that adorned my dress and quickened my pace toward the bathroom, my retreat causing the muffled noises of the wedding reception to fade against my back. At this point, I would just have to apologize later. For now, I needed peace. If only for a moment.

I swung into the restroom and quickly stooped to peer underneath the three stall doors. Empty. Grateful, I locked the door and walked to the porcelain countertop.

I almost didn't recognize myself. Sure, I was still Kimmy; same dramatic pixie cut, sharp cheekbones, and almond-shaped eyes. Physically, for sure, not much had changed. But what *had* changed, those mental and emotional scars sure as hell couldn't be hidden under makeup or a distracting smile. Those still waters ran deep.

I shut my eyes against my reflection, inhaling sharply through my nose before letting a heavy sigh escape my parted lips. For the first time all day, hell, weeks if I wanted to be honest with myself, I felt like I could breathe.

Of course I should have been happy. It was a wedding that I had long since given up hope would ever happen. But from the time I woke up that morning, it felt like both my brain and body were stuck on a déjà vu repeat. Everything was perfect, just like we had planned it. From the coral décor to the arrival of the vendors, right down to the gorgeous weather that hung appreciatively at seventy-four degrees despite the forecast of rain. Decorations had adorned the sanctuary, a collection of neosoul ballads had wafted through the speakers, and guests had arrived and arranged themselves in the pews with bottles of bubbles (because Daddy wasn't having rice thrown in his church) and tissues ready for the tears that were sure to come. Pictures were snapped, both from smart phones as well as by the professional photographer who crouched and maneuvered around to capture moments from every angle possible.

And I knew, even as I clutched my bouquet with sweaty palms and started my own descent down the sheer aisle runner, I knew exactly why it was taking all of my strength to feign the same excitement that was clearly evident among everyone else. And for that, I felt terrible.

Tears stung the corners of my eyes, and now that the ceremony was over, I finally let them spill over, trailing makeup streaks down my cheeks. I hadn't meant to spend the entire time comparing everything. They were two entirely different circumstances.

Last year, I had signed a contract to be a "love partner" or wife to the rich Leo Owusu. I would be just another along with the two women he already had. It had been nothing more than a business arrangement in my eyes, and I had treated it as such. But for Leo, I was his wife number three in every sense of the word. I couldn't help but shake my head at the memory of the lavish wedding from months ago, a wedding I neither wanted nor cared for. Nothing but an elaborate showcase of the extent of his money. So I stood at the altar with his other wives right up there by my side, like they too weren't wearing wedding rings vowing their lives and hearts to the same man. The entire event was fit for a queen, with all its bells and whistles and fake glory.

I grimaced at the thought, then turned my memories to the ceremony that had just taken place only moments before. I could not have foreseen I would be here again so soon. But sure enough, I was, listening to my dad's proud voice as he officiated. *Genuine.* That was the main word that came to mind as I reflected on the emotions that hung thick in the air. Vows and rings were exchanged, tears were shed, and every moment that ticked past I wanted to hold longer in my heart because it was so damn strong and authentic. This was how it was supposed to be. A constant reminder that was enough to heighten my own regret for selling myself so short before.

The door pushed against its lock as someone apparently tried to come in. I sniffed and wiped my hand against my face, smearing my makeup even more. *Pathetic*, I scolded myself as I snatched paper towels from the dispenser and blotted my cheeks. Turning, I flipped the lock and pulled open the door.

"Girl, I was looking for you." Adria breezed in with a laugh. She glanced at my face and immediately engulfed me in a hug. "Aw, I love you so much, sis. I can finally say that now."

I returned the hug with a small smile, swallowing my own pangs of jealousy. I was sure I was officially kicked out of the best friends club for being so damn selfish. While I was wallowing in my own self-pity and regret, I couldn't even be happy for my own best friend at her wedding.

Adria released me and turned to eye herself in the mirror. She had lost a few pounds, just enough to really accentuate her curves in the bead-embellished corset of her halter gown. A jewel-encrusted tiara fit neatly around her high bun and clasped an ivory veil to the back of her head, allowing it to cascade down to her mid-back. Despite the tears she had shed and the sweat that now peppered her forehead, my girl's makeup was still flawless from when I had spent two hours that morning brushing, contouring, blending, and getting it perfect. But more than anything, the pure joy that was emitted from her gaze and wide smile really made her glow with another level of beauty I hadn't seen before. Not in her, nor myself.

"I am hot as hell," Adria breathed, pulling paper towels from the dispenser and stuffing wads underneath her armpits. "Would I be too ghetto if I go back out there like this? They'll understand, right?"

I grinned, welcoming the humor. "Please don't," I said. "I don't think my brother could handle that."

Adria's lips turned up into a devious smirk as she winked. "Trust me," she said. "He can handle all of this and very, very well." She rolled her hips to exaggerate her statement, and I pursed my lips to keep from laughing out loud.

"Yeah, keep all that shit for the honeymoon."

"Honey, this honeymoon started four months ago when he proposed." Her eyes dropped to the three-carat diamond engagement ring and wedding band that glittered from her finger. I turned back to the mirror.

Her innocent gesture had tugged on another heart-string. Through the entire ceremony, I had wondered if Jahmad had been thinking about me. The man was still the love of my life, so I wondered if his imagination had taken over like mine, picturing me, instead of Adria, walking toward him in our own wedding ceremony of happily ever after. But, frankly, after everything that had happened between us, maybe that was too much wishful thinking.

"I actually came in here to talk to you about the store," Adria stated, pulling my attention back to her.

I frowned at her mention of our cosmetic store, Melanin Mystique. Thanks to the little seed money I had received from my husband's will, Adria and I had been able to rent a building and get the products for our dream business. "Girl, we are not about to talk business right now."

"I know, but I'm about to be off for a bit for the honey-moon—"

"And I can handle everything until you get back," I assured her, tossing a comforting smile in her direction. "Between me and the new guy. What's his name?"

"Tyree."

"Yeah. He started last week, and so far, he seems to be catching on quick."

"So you'll be able to make sure everything is ready for the grand opening?"

I nodded. Come hell or high water, we were opening that store. I had made too many sacrifices not to. "I'm not saying you can't," Adria went on, circling her arm through mine. She rested her head on my shoulder. "It's just that I would feel comfortable doing this last little bit of stuff with you. I don't want you to think I'm not doing my part. And with my nephew coming home next week too, you're going to have your hands full."

The mention of my son brought an unconscious smile to my lips. I couldn't wait to bring Jamaal home from the hospital. The overwhelming joy I had for that child made me wonder why I had even considered an abortion in the first place. No way could I have lived without him. But initially, the uncertainty about my child's father, whether it was my husband, Leo, or my boyfriend, Jahmad, was enough to scare me into making an appointment and even going as far as taking the first of two medicines that would cause the abortion. But by the grace of God, I had forgotten all about my pregnancy when I got a call about Leo's car accident. Now, my son's paternity didn't even matter. As far as I and Jahmad were concerned, he was the biological father. End of story. At least I hoped.

"It's all going to work out," I said, meeting her eyes in the mirror. "I don't want you worrying about the store, the baby, nothing. Just worry about enjoying my brother and being a newlywed. Can you do that?"

Adria's expression relaxed into an appreciative smile, and I didn't feel quite as bad anymore about my little selfish jealousy. At the end of the day, this girl was my best friend, now sister-in-law, and I loved her to pieces. Anything I was feeling was personal, and I would just have to deal with it myself. No way could I let it affect our relationship. Adria certainly didn't deserve that.

I let myself be steered back into the hallway and toward the reception hall. A collection of old-school mixes had everyone on the dance floor, moving in sync with the electric slide. I groaned, knowing no one but my dad had initiated the line dance that was a staple at every black wedding reception, family/class reunion, or cookout from coast to coast.

The venue was minimally decorated, to appeal more to comfort, with its beautiful assortment of coral flowers and floating candle centerpieces adorning each round table. Chiffon sashes draped from a stage where the wedding party sat, the remnants of the catered soul food dinner and white chocolate cake now being cleared by the waitstaff.

We hadn't even stepped all the way in the room before I was blinded by yet another flash from the photographer, and obediently I plastered another smile on my face. Adria would surely kill me if I messed up her wedding pictures.

Talking about cost efficient, Adria had certainly managed to save her coins when it came to planning this thing. Of course, my dad offered the couple his church and services free of charge, and the reception was now being held in the refurbished church basement, the sole location for numerous church events and family functions. Her aunt Pam was good friends with a caterer, and her small wedding party consisted of me and another young lady who worked at the bank with Adria. It had all worked out like it was supposed to, because Adria was set on putting as much money as possible toward their honeymoon and a house they were looking to close on in a few weeks. My sigh was wistful as her boisterous laugh rang throughout the room. Of course Adria had done everything right. Me, on the other hand, well, I was still picking up the pieces.

Speaking of pieces, my eyes scanned the crowd for Jahmad. Between this morning's argument and the chaos of the wedding operations as soon as we arrived

to the church, we hadn't said much of anything to each
other. Even as I had taken hold of his arm and allowed
him to escort me down the aisle at the ceremony, the
tension had been so thick I could taste it, and I prayed
the discomfort hadn't been obvious to Adria nor to
Keon. Or the photographer. Wanting to break the ice, I
had given his forearm a gentle squeeze. I even tossed a
smile his way, but both gestures had gone ignored.

I sighed again as I noticed him on the dance floor, his
arms around one of the guests, Adria's cousin Chantel.
Her face was split with a flirtatious grin and Jahmad,
well, he looked more relaxed than he had in months.
And that shit pissed me off.

I was weighing how to get in between them and put
hands on this chick in the most discreet way when an
arm draped over my shoulder. Glancing up, I met my
dad's eyes and allowed my anger to subside. For now.

"Beautiful ceremony, huh," he said, and I nodded.

"It really was, Daddy."

"I'm so happy your brother finally grew up," he
went on with a chuckle. "I thought I was going to have
to take him to the mountain for sacrifice like Abraham
and Isaac."

I laughed. "You would've sacrificed my brother?"

"I was telling God to just say the word." He winked.
The humor instantly faded from his smirk as he turned
somber eyes on me. "What about you, baby girl?"

"What about me?"

"You know I wanted to officiate for *both* of my
kids. And, well . . ." He trailed off, and I shrugged,
trying to keep from looking back over at Jahmad and
failing miserably. I knew what he meant. Of course he
hadn't been able to do that with me when I decided to
up and tie the knot with Leo. I hadn't given him that
honor. And I knew he was still hurt by that.

A slow song now had Jahmad and Chantel swaying closer, his hand on the small of her back. If I wanted to be logical, the two didn't look all that intimate. Quite platonic, actually. But I didn't give a damn about logic at that point.

My dad could obviously sense the heightened fury in my demeanor, because he took my hand and gently guided me to the dance floor, in the opposite direction.

"When are you going back to the hospital to see Jamaal?" he asked as we started to dance.

I sighed. Obviously everyone had some secret mission to keep me from wallowing in my own self-pity. Dammit.

"I went up there yesterday," I said. "He's doing really good."

"You sure you don't want him to stay with us for a few weeks? Just until you get situated in your place with the move?"

I tightened my lips. If I played my cards right, I wasn't planning on going anywhere but to Jahmad's house. In fact that's what we had been arguing about this morning when I had come over so we could ride to the church together.

The thing was, my heart still completely belonged to that man. But somewhere in these past few months, he was becoming distant. One minute it was as if we were on the same page, trying to focus on us, or so I thought. But then I would feel like I was struggling to breathe under this suffocating tension that hung between us. And I really wasn't sure how to get us back on track.

So when I suggested we move in together now that our son was coming home, I certainly hadn't expected the frown nor the subsequent questions about my motive for asking like I was up to some shit.

"What is the big deal, Jahmad?" I had asked as I paced his bedroom. "I mean I thought we agreed we would try to work on this? Us?" I pointed a wild finger first at him, then myself.

"What does that have to do with us moving in to-gether?"

The tone of his question had a twinge of hurt pierc-ing my heart. Here I was thinking we were taking steps forward only to realize we were actually moving back-ward. Why else would the idea of living together come as such a shock to him? I mean after the whole ordeal with Leo, I had moved back in with my folks because I wanted to focus on the business, which was already stressful enough. And I honestly knew, however false the hope, that it would be temporary, because Jahmad's stubborn ass would finally realize exactly where I be-longed. With him. Apparently I was still in Neverland.

"Kimmy, that's doing too much." Jahmad sighed in frustration as he shrugged into his suit jacket. "The way I see it, we don't even know if there is an 'us.' And we damn sure don't need any more complications."

I sucked in a sharp breath. "Complications? Since when is being with me a complication?"

"Since when? Since I found out you were married."

And there he went again. Throwing the shit up in my face. As if I hadn't berated myself enough. As if I hadn't been laying on apology after apology so much that I was sick of hearing the words my damn self. I masked the embarrassment with anger.

"You know what my situation was about," I snapped, jabbing a finger in his direction. "And you know it wasn't real."

"That doesn't make it any better," he yelled back. "Hell, if anything that shines a negative light on you, because all the conniving and sneaky shit was for money. My love didn't mean anything to you."

"How can you stand here and say that? You know that's not true."

"Do I?" He narrowed his eyes. "How can I even trust you or anything you say?"

"Jahmad, we've had this same conversation every week for months." I threw up my arms to express my frustration. "I can't change the past. What else can I do? Or say to move past this?"

This time he was quiet so I used the opportunity to keep pushing. "There is no more marriage. No more Leo. No more lies and secrets, Jahmad. I promised you that before. Now it's just us. And our son. That is what's important to me."

I had to mentally repent even as the words left my lips. There were still a few lies between us. Among other things, whether he knew there was a question of paternity with my son. I sure as hell had to take that to my grave. And the money: Leo had given me plenty of it and since technically he had staged his death, that money was still tucked safely in my accounts. Like hell I would give that up. That would mean the whole arrangement would have been in vain.

Silence had ridden with us to the church, and we soon became so engrossed in the pre-wedding preparations we hadn't bothered, nor had time, to resume the conversation.

I tried to bring my attention back to my father as he swayed with me on the dance floor, but thoughts continued to consume me.

I glanced around, my eyes eager to catch Jahmad once more, but he had long since disappeared. I stopped my scan when I noticed a certain face appear in the crowd. I squinted through the dimness and distance, struggling to blink clarity into my vision. The face I couldn't make out but the dress, I knew that dress. And the hair was the same, too much to be a coincidence.

My dad spun me around, and I quickly angled my neck to catch another glimpse of the woman I thought I recognized. But by then, the Tina look-alike was gone.

Connect with U s